ETHEL'S LOVE-LIFE

and Other Writings

Q19: The Queer American Nineteenth Century
Christopher Looby, Series Editor

Queer is a good nineteenth-century American word, appearing almost everywhere in the literature of the time. And, as often as not, the nineteenth-century use of the word seems to anticipate the sexually specific meanings it would later accrue. Sometimes *queer* could mean simply odd or strange or droll. But at other times it carried within itself a hint of its semantic future, as when Artemus Ward, ostensibly visiting a settlement of "Free Lovers" in Ohio, calls them "some queer people," or when the narrator of Constance Fenimore Woolson's "Felipa" refers to the eponymous child, who wears masculine clothing, as "a queer little thing," or when Herman Melville, writing of the master-at-arms Claggart in *Billy Budd*, tells us that young Billy, sensitive to Claggart's attentively yearning yet malicious behavior toward him, "thought the master-at-arms acted in a manner rather queer at times." *Q19: The Queer American Nineteenth Century* makes available again a set of literary texts from the long American nineteenth century in which queer appears in all its complex range of meanings. From George Lippard's *The Midnight Queen*: "'Strange!' cried one. 'Odd!' another. 'Queer!' a third."

ETHEL'S LOVE-LIFE
and Other Writings

Margaret J. M. Sweat

Edited and with an introduction by
Christopher Looby

PENN

University of Pennsylvania Press
Philadelphia

Publication of this volume was aided by gifts from the University of California, Los Angeles Department of English and the UCLA Dean of Humanities.

Published by
University of Pennsylvania Press
Philadelphia, Pennsylvania 19104-4112
www.upenn.edu/pennpress

Printed in the United States of America on acid-free paper
10 9 8 7 6 5 4 3 2 1

Library of Congress Cataloging-in-Publication Data

Names: Sweat, Margaret J. M. (Margaret Jane Mussey), 1823–1908, author. | Looby, Christopher, editor, writer of introduction. | Sweat, Margaret J. M. (Margaret Jane Mussey), 1823–1908. Ethel's love-life.
Title: Ethel's love-life and other writings / Margaret J.M. Sweat ; edited and with an introduction by Christopher Looby.
Other titles: Q19: the queer American nineteenth century.
Description: 1st edition. | Philadelphia : University of Pennsylvania Press, [2020] | Series: Q19: the queer American nineteenth century | Includes bibliographical references.
Identifiers: LCCN 2020028102 | ISBN 978-0-8122-5249-1 (hardcover)
Subjects: LCSH: Brontë, Charlotte, 1816–1855—Criticism and interpretation. | Sand, George, 1804–1876—Criticism and interpretation. | English fiction—19th century—History and criticism.
Classification: LCC PS2964.S749 E84 2020 | DDC 813/.3—dc23
LC record available at https://lccn.loc.gov/2020028102

Contents

MARGARET SWEAT

INTRODUCTION

Sweat, Sand, Sex

Christopher Looby

A dah Isaacs Menken, the celebrated actress and well-known bohemian, wrote a fan letter and mash note on July 21, 1861, to the popular poet Hattie Tyng. Menken was famous for touring the play *Mazeppa*, in which at the climax she scandalously appeared to be nude as she rode a horse onstage. She was visiting Wisconsin at the time, writing from the city of Racine on the shore of Lake Michigan, and she expected to be in Milwaukee the following week. Tyng lived with her family in Columbus, Wisconsin, some sixty or seventy miles away; perhaps, Menken hoped, they could meet in person. She had apparently read some of Tyng's poems and felt as a result "an uncontrollable magnetism of affinity" between herself and Tyng, with whom she had apparently had no relationship in the past. The highly wrought letter read in part:

> Do you believe in the deepest and tenderest love between women? Do you believe that women often love each other with as much fervor and excitement as they do men? . . . We find the rarest and most perfect beauty in the affections of one woman for another. There is a delicacy in its manifestations, generosity in its intuitions, an unveiling of inner life in its intercourse,

marked by charming undulations of feeling and expression, not to be met with in the opposite sex. Freed from all the grosser elements of passion, it retains its energy, its abandonment, its flush, its eagerness, its palpitation, and its rapture—but all so refined, so glorified, and made delicious and continuous by an ever-recurring giving and receiving from each to each. The electricity of the one flashes and gleams through the other, to be returned not only in *degree* as between man and woman, but in *kind* as between precisely similar organizations. And these passions are of the more frequent occurrence than the world is aware of—generally they are unknown to all but the hearts concerned, and are jealously guarded by them from intrusive comment. "There is a gloom in deep love as in deep water," and silence and mystery help to guard the sacred spot where we meet alone our best beloved.

I have had my passionate attachments among women, which swept like whirlwinds over me, sometimes, alas! scorching me with a furnace-blast, but generally only changing and renewing my capabilities for love. (231–32)

Apparently Tyng did not respond to this rather ripe missive, nor to another letter from Menken the following year.

What Tyng may not have known was that the florid language of this letter was borrowed wholesale (with a few minor elisions and emendations) from the novel *Ethel's Love-Life*, by Margaret J. M. Sweat (the passage in question can be found in the present volume on pages 64–65), which Menken must have been carrying with her on her travels and evidently had open beside her as she wrote the letter to Tyng into which she copied this passage. Certainly this is one of the stranger episodes in the history of this novel's reception, but it is a compelling testament to the novel's power. As Menken's biographer Renée Sentilles has written, borrowing Sweat's language almost verbatim, the actress Menken "essentially turned Sweat's character into a part she could perform in her own private life" (157). Menken's performance of a passionate role borrowed from Sweat is a good example of what I have elsewhere called "the literariness of sexuality" (Looby 841), by which I mean, among other things, the role literature plays in inventing, circulating, and depositing in readers' consciousnesses various styles of sexual being and different models of sexual worlds.

Two years before Menken's appropriation of the role of Ethel, Margaret Jane Mussey Sweat, a writer from Portland, Maine, had published what would be her only novel, *Ethel's Love-Life*. It gained some notice—the poet Henry Wadsworth Longfellow wrote excitedly to his sister Annie, "Have you read Mrs. Sweat's novel? I hear it *very* highly spoken of" (119). But it soon fell into obscurity, only occasionally given brief notice on account of its perceived queer content. The editor of Longfellow's collected letters explains in a note that it "treats of lesbianism" (120), a rather clinical turn of phrase.[1] Wikipedia describes it as "the first American lesbian novel," echoing Lee Agger in *Women of Maine* (100), while one literary critic remarked upon its participation—however complex and ambivalent—in the historical emergence of an idea of "lesbian pathology" (Diggs 317). *Ethel's Love-Life* went missing from the second edition of Barbara Grier's 1975 *The Lesbian in Literature: A Bibliography* (Damon, Watson and Jordan) but showed up in the third edition in 1981 (Grier 149), where it was identified with the code "A*," the "A" indicating "major Lesbian characters and/or action" (xix) and the asterisk signifying "some interest beyond the ordinary" (xx). Two historians of American sexual history cite the novel as capturing the "intensely emotional and even physical relationships" that sometimes formed within what the historian Carroll Smith—Rosenberg famously called "the female world of love and ritual," the sphere of intimate same-sex relations that were "normative within Victorian culture" (Smith-Rosenberg, D'Emilio, and Freedman 125, 126). Another scholar has elected to characterize Ethel as having a "bisexual orientation" (Eiselein 230). In the wake of queer theory and its complication of sexual taxonomies and its challenge to the normative, these may now seem like debatable annotations for a novel whose protagonist professes to love (and to have been loved by) both women and men, a novel devoted to the description of the unusual and sometimes torrid erotic history of its narrator. In this novel Ethel Sutherland details multiple passionate relationships with persons of both sexes, but she doesn't claim anything like a modern lesbian (or bisexual or any other) identity, and the married Mrs. Sweat did not do so either, apparently. Ethel relates these tales of her erotic history in a series of letters to someone who is only belatedly revealed (midway through the third letter) to be a man named Ernest, who is her fiancé, and from whom she is temporarily separated while he is on a diplomatic mission in Europe. So while she is planning what may seem from one perspective to be a normative marriage, she also intends (as we shall see) to continue her same-sex erotic career.

Ethel's Love-Life is an epistolary novel, albeit entirely one-sided— all eleven letters are from Ethel to Ernest. Epistolarity has several essential qualities that suit Sweat's purposes. As Janet Gurkin Altman has written, epistolarity characteristically involves certain paradoxes or polarities: letters serve as a bridge between persons but also call to mind their separation from one another; letters attempt to inspire trust or confidence but also stage an opportunity for performance or even dissimulation; the epistolary situation evokes the acts of writing and reading, with the correspondent(s) shifting between these positions (even the implied other correspondent in a monologic epistolary novel such as *Ethel's Love-Life*); epistolary narrative invokes the present con- sciousness of the writer in a specific now and in a particular place, even as it tracks a serial trajectory in time; it fluctuates between closure and open-endedness, alternating between the temporary closure of a given letter's sign-off and the continuity of a segmented chain of letters that is potentially limitless; the letter's duality as a self-contained unit and at the same time a segment in a larger configuration marks an episto- lary novel's suspension between narrative coherence and continuity, on the one hand, and fragmentation and interruption on the other (Altman 186–87). In the case of *Ethel's Love-Life*, epistolarity creates an effect of deep intimacy; but, as readers will see, it also dramatizes Ethel's unsettled and indeed turbulent interiority. These formal tensions are very well suited to the novel's unprecedented exploration of elusive, fundamentally innovative, forms of erotic personhood.

Readers get a few reflected hints about Ernest's side of the cor- respondence by virtue of Ethel's responses to Ernest's letters. Ernest, we can infer, is evidently undisturbed by Ethel's accounts of strong erotic attractions to other women and passionate relationships with them—one of these relationships quite happy (with "Claudia," an ongoing attachment) and another deeply troubled (with "Leonora"). Nor, we are led to infer, is Ernest worried by Ethel's strong justifica- tion of female same-sex eroticism: "Women often love each other," she patiently explains to him, using language that would be borrowed by Menken, "with as much fervor and excitement as they do men. When this is the case, there is generally rare beauty both in feeling and in its manifestations, great generosity in its intuitions, and the mutual intercourse is marked by charming undulations of feeling and expression. The emotions awakened heave and swell through the whole being as the tides swell the ocean" (64). Although Ethel carefully stipulates that this kind of same-sex relationship is "freed from the grosser elements of passion, as it exists between the sexes," she also insists that "it retains its energy, its abandonment, its flush, its eagerness, its palpitation, and its rapture" (64). As Dorri Beam has written, even though the novel presents female same-sex eroticism as devoid of "grosser elements," "we can't assume we know what Sweat would exclude or include among those 'grosser elements.' In the meantime, *something* in this passage is swelling and heaving, flushing and palpitating" (329). A key argument Beam makes about reading *Ethel's Love-Life* is that our modern homo/hetero binary is inapplicable to this novel, and equally important, our modern "desire to taxonomize relationships as sexual or nonsexual" is anachronistic with respect to Sweat's purposes (327). This is because, Beam writes, "for many Americans of the nineteenth century the carnal was a surprisingly narrow category, while the spiritual was a supple and capacious realm permeated with pleasure and sensation and bearing its own relationship to embodiment" (327–28). *Ethel's Love-Life* challenges us to try to understand erotic feelings and bodily practices that were understood and socially organized in ways that are now quite alien to us.

Ethel further explains to Ernest that "these passions are of much more frequent occurrence than the world is aware of" because they are "jealously guarded . . . from intrusive comment" (64). A few pioneering scholars have analyzed this novel with subtlety and contextualized it with care in ways that move beyond received binaries of homo/hetero and carnal/spiritual, binaries that this novel alone would inform us did not in fact obtain in any simple way in the mid-nineteenth-century American sex/gender system. Beam has already been mentioned, but Jennifer Putzi's work must also be consulted for the crucial biographical context of an important same-sex relationship that Margaret Sweat herself participated in from 1851 to 1854 with her fellow novelist Elizabeth Stoddard. The two women met in person on several occasions, but they also carried on an extensive correspondence when apart; only forty-five of Stoddard's letters have been found, however (it is clear that there were even more, but these were evidently destroyed), and none of Sweat's, so inferences must be made about Sweat's role in their relationship. It is clear from even this partial archive, however, that their romantic friendship was deeply important to both of them, and that it corresponded closely to the intense same-sex bonds that Smith-Rosenberg and other historians have described and analyzed.

Elizabeth Stoddard was famously a difficult personality: she reported that her own father had said that "he never saw any human being with such talent for the disagreeable" (Stoddard, *The Morgesons*, 340). One of her other friends labeled her "the Pythoness" (qtd. Putzi 131), and in one of her letters to Sweat she makes candid reference to her "exacting affection" (qtd. Putzi 119). As often happened with Stoddard and other women, her friendship with Sweat came to a bitter and angry end; years later she referred to Sweat as "a pedantic vain prig" and said acidly that "she wrote a still born novel" (qtd. Putzi 131), viciously merging Sweat's childlessness with her singular novel's eventual obscurity. Putzi speculates that "Stoddard could very well have been the inspiration for at least one if not both of the women with whom Ethel is romantically involved" (129). I agree, but it seems to me likelier that Stoddard was the model for the intense and dangerous Leonora—with whom Ethel had a relationship that, like Sweat's with Stoddard, came to a traumatic end—than for Ethel's happy ongoing relationship with Claudia. It is tempting to speculate that her delicious acerbity about *Ethel's Love-Life* stems in good part from her recognition of herself in her former friend Sweat's portrait of Leonora.

The brilliant *Ethel's Love-Life* remains to be brought to wider attention, and the work of its critical examination must continue, too, by expanding the literary and historical contexts that have been brought to bear upon it and by refining the critical terms that we employ to address its ambitious artistic project. *Ethel's Love-Life* is a great novel, an extraordinary and compelling literary performance that deserves a new life. Other published writings by Sweat are even less well known. The present volume reprints *Ethel's Love-Life* for the first time since it appeared in 1859; and it also reprints her collection of poems, *Verses* (1890), as well as a robust selection of her most important literary-critical writings, which have largely to do with the

genre of the novel and with her two most admired literary predecessors (Charlotte Brontë and George Sand). The critical writings by
Sweat on the novel as a form and on these particular female writers
give us many hints as to her agenda in writing *Ethel's Love-Life*; her
collection in *Verses* both continues her novel's project of dramatizing a
queer way of being in the world and may, in some ways, retreat from
that vision. The different texts collected here, that is, comment upon
each other in many acute ways.

One important approach to Sweat is to investigate her long-standing
fascination with the person and writings of George Sand, whose novels she championed in the face of widespread American suspicion of
them (Jones, Lombard, Lubin). Sweat kept a large scrapbook dedi-
cated to Sand, in which she pasted relevant clippings as she came
upon them, for example, an essay by Henry James (the scrapbook
survives in the Maine Women Writers Collection in Portland, along
with other Sweat archival materials), and she wrote an afterword to
an American translation of Sand's *Antonia* (orig. 1862; trans. Boston,
1870), as well as an obituary for Sand in 1876 (this afterword and
obituary are both included in the present collection). At first glance
Sweat and Sand seem to have had little in common. Sand was enor-
mously prolific, something Sweat admired and perhaps envied; Sweat,
on the other hand, wrote just this one novel. Sand's personal life
was notoriously complicated and scandalous; Sweat by contrast had
a long and outwardly contented marriage to a Portland nabob and
one-time Democratic congressman, Lorenzo de Medici Sweat, and
she dutifully fulfilled the duties that belonged to her elevated social
position in Portland and in Washington, D.C. Her diaries and personal
papers are, for the most part, quite unrevealing of the details of her
emotional and erotic life. Nevertheless, it is clear that she was infat-
uated with George Sand, and that Sand's literary example was of the
utmost importance to her. Charlotte Brontë was the other precursor
with whom Sweat was most passionately engaged (and who often used
the spelling Bronte or Brontê): in 1857 Sweat published a long essay
in the *North American Review* under the title "Charlotte Brontê and
the Brontê Novels" (also included in the present collection), and in the
aforementioned afterword to *Antonia* she explicitly linked Sand and
Brontë ("The Novels of George Sand").

Sweat gave careful thought both to the novel form and to the specific conditions of women novelists and novels about women (another review essay in the *North American Review*, from 1856, was called "A Chapter on Novels"—this too is reprinted in the present volume). Note that two of these essays—"A Chapter on Novels" and "Charlotte Bronté"—appeared in the years 1856 and 1857, respectively, immediately prior to the publication of *Ethel's Love-Life* in 1859. Thus when Sweat was very likely at work on her own novel she was also reflecting at length upon novels as such and upon women's relationship to them. In "A Chapter on Novels" she notes with dismay the recent vast proliferation of novels and wishes that one of the popular and prolific novelists she was reviewing, Julia Kavanagh, would "follow the example of Miss Bronte, one of the few authors who have had the good sense to refrain from writing until, as she so forcibly expressed it, [enough good material] had 'accumulated'" (245). "Quantity is no test of power," Sweat contends.

The earliest of the essays reprinted here, "A Chapter on Novels" (1856) was an omnibus review of three recently published novels by Margaret Oliphant, Edmond Abbot, and Julia Kavanagh. Sweat's fundamental contention was that it had by then been conclusively "proved that a novel may, without losing its hold on the imagination, be something far higher than a sentimental love-tale" (243). By this standard Sweat judged the three novels before her to be decidedly inferior—and she was severe enough on one, Kavanagh's *Rachel Gray*, to merit a rebuke from the *North American Review*'s editor himself in the form of a demurring footnote. Sweat criticized Kavanagh, as stated above, for her over-prolific publication record, advising her to "follow the example of Miss Bronte" (245), who took her time with her novels instead of rushing them out. (As we shall see in a moment, Sweat did not hold voluminous productivity against her other main literary idol, George Sand.) But it is tempting to infer from her rebuke of Kavanagh's excess that Sweat was preemptively justifying the prospective publication of what would turn out to be her own only novel, *Ethel's Love-Life*: "There are still some who know it to be better to write one book, the concentration of ten years of thought and life, than to fill the shelves with undigested and unworthy matter" (245–46). Perhaps *Ethel's Love-Life* was in fact the work of ten years of Sweat's life. If so, this would mean—let's do the math—that Sweat began it around 1849, which was the year of her marriage to Lorenzo de Medici Sweat, and that, when published in 1859, it was truly the product of ten years of "thought *and* life," both critical contemplation of the novel as a form and a decade's experience of marriage, female friendship, and reflection on the life choices she had made for herself.

Having dispensed in short order with the three unsatisfying novels under review, Sweat proceeded to discuss the long history of the novel as such, and hers was a decidedly Whiggish version of literary history: novels had been getting better and better since the genre's eighteenth-century emergence, until in recent years there had been such remarkable accomplishments in the genre as "the glowing, passionate life of Currer Bell's [Charlotte Brontë's] creations, the wonderful world-knowledge of Thackeray, the intense psychological insight of Hawthorne, or the healthful moral energy of Dickens" (246). Chief among the "mature" aspects of the historically developed novel, Sweat insisted, was its dispensing with certain tired romantic conventions, such as "a faultless heroine" who chooses, from among "a crowd of besieging admirers," one man "to play the part of the hero" (248). In fact, Sweat disparaged the tedious "machinery of plots and counter-plots, assaults and accidents, showers of misfortune followed by equally heavy showers of fortune,—all busily and visibly at work to bring about the simple *dénouement* of a marriage" (249). Sweat didn't leave this disparagement of marriage as telos stated just once: a bit later she archly sneered at the complacent reader who, "having finally moored [the hero and heroine] safely in the wide harbor of matrimony, may lay down the volumes with the pleasant conviction that no after-experience can disturb the placid current of their united lives" (00). And yet again she scoffed at "those who consider marriage as the *summum bonum* of happy fortune" (250). We might recall here the dry way in which, in her matter-of-fact diary, Sweat reported her own marriage, at the age of twenty-six, to the improbably named Lorenzo de Medici Sweat (1818–1898):

> Tuesday, October 30th 1849—at 11 o'clock this morning I was married to Mr. Sweat by the Rev. Dr. Nichols—in the presence of about 50 friends. The ceremony was the Episcopal form varied by an extemporaneous prayer & one or two minor alterations. Bridesmaid Mary Neal, groomsman John Sweat,

bridesmen Putnam Richardson & Crosby Whitman. No tears were shed & there was of course less stiffness than usual, as no one felt called upon to look melancholy. The levee lasted till one—then a dinner to the bridegroom's father & mother & the assistants, in all about a dozen people. It was stormy till just before the appointed hour, then commenced clearing & by noon was delightful. (Diary, 1)

The arch tone of this passage is telling: there is no sentimental gush about this wedding. "No tears were shed & there was of course less stiffness than usual, as no one felt called upon to look melancholy." It is difficult to divine the meanings embedded here. "No tears were shed": no visible displays of emotional excess. "Less stiffness than usual": it was a relatively relaxed affair, no high drama. "No one felt called upon to look melancholy": perhaps there were no disappointed suitors for either the bride or the groom, or perhaps everyone present recognized this as a perfectly suitable rational pairing, not driven by love or sustained by passion but dictated by reasonable companionability and exemplary social propriety. One doesn't feel authorized to go so far as to describe the Sweat marriage as merely transactional; but it doesn't appear to have been entered into with anything like romantic fervor, either. "Mr. Sweat" or just "Sweat" (as his wife always called him in her diary) was an attorney in Portland who would later go on to a career in public service, as Portland City Solicitor, a member of the Maine State Senate (1861–1862), and a one-term Democratic U.S. Congressman (1863–1865), defeated for reelection in 1864 and failing to win back his seat in 1866. On the evidence of his wife's diary, she was a reliably active helpmeet with respect to her husband's political career while pursuing her own literary interests and conducting a social life that decidedly centered on various women's social, philanthropic, and cultural organizations and clubs.

But then again, there is something curious about the fact that Sweat disparaged marriage in novels and then wrote one in which the entire narrative trajectory is aimed toward its narrator Ethel's intensely longed-for wedding. It is no doubt significant that, while the marriage of Ethel and Ernest is ostensibly imminent at the end of the novel, it never actually transpires within the diegesis. If it is the novel's telos, it is nevertheless a permanently deferred one. Sweat crafted a careful compromise between acceding to the conventional novelistic "*dénoue-ment* of a marriage" and the eternal narratological deferral of it, as if to stake a measured claim against its being "the *summum bonum* of happy fortune" while still giving her novel a truncated nuptial trajectory.

In her subsequent essay, "Charlotte Bronté and the Bronté Novels" (1857), Sweat proved entirely ready to interpret novels by the several Bronté sisters in relation to the biographies of their authors, even to describe them as "what we may term autobiographic novels" (259). This may incline us to speculate, with some justification, about the "autobiographic" elements of Sweat's own novel, *Ethel's Love-Life*, although finally it seems that such speculation will have to remain richly suggestive but empirically inconclusive. Still, it is worth noting that the *North American Review*—the journal to which Sweat was herself a contributor, and to which she was therefore well known—alerted its readers, when in turn it reviewed *Ethel's Love-Life*, to the probable autobiographical elements in her novel: "The work is intro-spective in its whole character; and, while we by no means suppose that the incidents are recorded from experience, in a still profounder sense Mrs. Sweat must have given us an autobiography, for there is much in her narrative which is beyond the reach of fiction, and for which remembered or persistent consciousness alone could have fur-nished the material" (Anon. 276).

In her 1868 review of *The Friendships of Women*, by William Roun-seville Alger, Sweat drew special attention to his "chapter on Friend-ship in Marriage," calling it "perhaps the most impressive from its simple concentration and the pure height to which it ascends" (292). We might ask: Was Sweat's own marriage rather more of a "friend-ship" than anything else? It is noteworthy that after this affirmative remark about "Friendship in Marriage" she turned immediately to Alger's discussion of "friendships between women," then swiftly to the classical male same-sex pair "Damon and Pythias," and soon after to the female couple "Eleanor Butler and Sarah Ponsonby," the famous "Ladies of Llangollen," whose "simple dignity of an unflawed relation-ship for sixty years" she celebrated fulsomely (292).[2]

Sweat's 1870 afterword to the translation of Sand's *Antonia* is a carefully wrought rhetorical balancing act. On the one hand, Sweat extols Sand, claiming that she "has no rival but Balzac" among modern novelists (295). At the same time, she stipulates that "it is useless for the warmest admirers of French novels to deny that there is very generally prevalent in them an atmosphere of immorality, a disregard of many restraints dear to most English hearts" (295). Here Sweat is recognizing that to many Americans Sand was extremely disreputable, both as a scandalous person and as a controversial writer (Jones, Lombard, Lubin). At the same time, Sand was an immensely important and intellectually liberating figure for certain American readers, among them Julia Ward Howe and Margaret Fuller in addition to Sweat. Gary Williams describes, for example, how radically enabling it was for Howe to gain access to the novels of Sand, probably through her cosmopolitan brother Sam Ward, who, when asked by Longfellow for an introduction to Sand, had assured him with witty pronominal fluctuation that "nothing will be easier than for you to know him, should your travels lead you her way. . . . Should it be your fortune to fall in with him do not fall in love with her. He will enchant you more in an evening, if the fit of Psychic inspiration be upon her, than any being you ever knew, & is a kind of moral hermaphrodite" (qtd. Williams xvii–xviii). As Sand's person and work were an inspiration for Howe's revolutionary novel *The Hermaphrodite*, they were equally so for Sweat's novel. More on this in a moment, but let me continue with Sweat's two published essays about Sand.

The first, as mentioned above, was an afterword to a translation of Sand's *Antonia*. Here Sweat argued that "among the works of George Sand may be found some which certainly lie open to condemnation, if we judge them summarily and without regard to the circumstances under which they were written, which in our own opinion, by furnishing ample explanation of their origin, demand from the critic, at least, a modified verdict" (296). Later in this afterword, "We need not shrink from admitting that she [Sand] has sometimes erred, both as the woman and the author" (301). One burden of Sweat's is therefore to contend that the evident immorality of *some* of Sand's writings is mitigated by the biographical facts of Sand's painful suffering under the "social yoke" (298) Sand eventually threw off (that is, her marriage) as well as by the corrupt condition of French society depicted in her novels. Another of Sweat's burdens was to discriminate between various of Sand's writings, some of which she conceded to be morally dubious and others of which said were not; generally, Sweat claimed that as Sand's career progressed over time the moral tone of Sand's works improved.

Tellingly, she throws one early novel of Sand's, *Leone Leoni* (1834), under the bus: "'Leone Leoni,' written in 1833, while the author was residing at Venice, is in our opinion the most objectionable of George Sand's romances. . . . George Sand has produced a masterpiece of psychological analysis, but one from which the heart and taste alike revolt" (305). Simply stated, this short novel—Henry James with comparable ambivalence called it "a masterpiece" (719) but also held it up as proof that "the author had morally no taste" (730)—describes the hopeless infatuation of its young female inset narrator, Juliette, with a monstrously depraved, faithless, unscrupulous, and abusive man, the eponymous Leone Leoni, who also happens to be irresistibly beautiful, charming, clever, and sexually magnetic. The moral dubiety of the tale would seem to lie in the fact that Juliette, who confides that she was "as submissive to him as a slave to his master" (58), nevertheless was framed with rueful sympathy by Sand, her slavish devotion held to be heroic and almost saintly. "In spite of everything I loved him still," Juliette says even toward the end of her ordeal (158), when she has no remaining illusions about Leone's corruption. Leone's gorgeous depravity and Juliette's abysmal submission are treated in the novel as a kind of magnificently evil beauty. The plot is a particularly extreme version of a situation common to many of Sand's novels, which specialized in miserable marriages or attachments between sensitive, superior women and the tyrannical, crude, ignorant, unfeeling, or treacherous men to whom they were subjugated.

It is probable that Sweat didn't really object to this novel as much as she made out to do. Or, to put it another way, she may have felt as mixed about it as Henry James did but decided to condemn it on the theory that sacrificing one of Sand's novels would help her to redeem the rest. On the one hand, *Leone Leoni* is unapologetic about Juliette's entitlement to erotic pleasure and is insistent upon the value of passionate exploration, even at the cost of social respectability. At the same time, it is utterly brutal in its condemnation of the heavy "social yoke" that prevented women at that time from obtaining erotic and emotional satisfaction. When Sweat again wrote about Sand in 1876, she apparently felt less need to discriminate invidiously between different Sand works on moral grounds. This latter essay was the obituary Sweat published in the New York *World* on June 9, 1876, the very day after news of Sand's death arrived by cable. Quoting again— as she had done in her afterword to *Antonia*—from Elizabeth Barrett Browning's poem "To George Sand, A Desire," she described Sand as "the 'large-brained woman and large-hearted man'" (303) and asked, in a brilliant phrase, "How could such a one be content to dwell in decencies forever . . . ?" (310). With that derogation of mere social "decencies" as beneath the contempt of a heroic figure like George Sand, Sweat effectively disowned the pieties toward which she had felt compelled to genuflect in her afterword of six years prior.

Sand's *Leone Leoni* had found its subtle way into Sweat's queer imagination earlier, too. Sand's novel is framed by the narration of Don Aleo, the present lover of Juliette, who observes her unfathomable sorrow and asks her to explain it; she complies by taking over the narrative for most of its length and telling the tale of her exalting, wretched attachment to Leone Leoni. Sweat's novel, likewise, is a narrative of past romantic experience provided to Ethel's present lover, her fiancé Ernest. Remember that Ethel's letters tell Ernest about her past loves, both of men and of women; and that among the women, there are two who are most important. One is with a friend named Claudia, which is represented as a healthy romantic attachment, and an ongoing one, too. The other is with someone called Leonora (whose name must be taken as a direct allusion to Sand's *Leone Leoni*), which is characterized as morbidly consuming. The unhealthy romance with Leonora is understood to be over and done with. And yet, as Ethel explains to Ernest, it will always be a part of her; it cannot be disowned completely. "If a friendship is once formed, once incorporated into our being, we can never utterly destroy it, nor be as if it had never been" (58).

Ethel's Love-Life may thus be understood as a complex response to George Sand generally and to *Leone Leoni* specifically. In this novel of Sand's, supreme erotic enchantment is incompatible with social conventions. In this novel of Sweat's, Ethel imagines the possibility of passionate ecstatic devotion *combined* with social respectability and genuine friendship. *Ethel's Love-Life*, that is, may be understood as something of an antidote to *Leone Leoni*. In Sweat's queer imagination, erotic passion for women need not be at odds with what late in the novel she calls the "formalities of social etiquette" (102); Ethel's eleven long letters to Ernest comprise a careful anticipatory negotiation in preparation for a marriage in which erotic fulfillment and variety will be cultivated, not banished. In saying this, it is nevertheless important not to make Sweat sound too didactic, as if she were simply an avatar of today's bromide that "good communication" is the key to a happy marriage. And yet she did absolutely reject the "charge frequently urged against [Sand's] works . . . their depreciation of marriage; . . . It is, [Sand] says, because of her high ideal of what marriage ought to be that she has painted the horror of it as it too often is" ("George Sand," 315). Sweat's own high ideal of marriage evidently included erotic happiness, but—again—it's also important to remember that when *Ethel's Love-Life* ends, Ernest's return is supposed to be imminent but has not yet occurred; readers never get to witness the marriage itself. And we are left with the tiniest of hints that Ernest may have his own stake in crafting a marriage that leaves room for erotic variety: he is bringing home with him "one 'slight, pale student,'" as he has evidently written to Ethel (129). She is apparently more than ready to make this young friend of Ernest's welcome in their married life together.

Sweat's collection entitled *Verses* (1890) belongs, evidently, to a genre we may term "autobiographic poems." Although it is a somewhat heterogeneous gathering, containing, for example, some occasional poems, such as two written for sanitary fairs during the Civil War ("The Children's Table" and "Our Country's Cause"), or one written in response to Emerson's poem "Brahma," or another in praise of Leonardo da Vinci's fresco "The Last Supper," the themes are predominantly centered on intense friendship and painful emotional longing. Some poems are addressed to "my lady" (144, 150), "my love" (163), "my ladye love" (222), or "a lady fair" (216), and even to "the lady of my dreams" (205). This evocation of the archaic conventions of medieval courtly love—a sort of neo-medievalism—is one of the interesting ways Sweat here tries to articulate a style of erotic attachment that simply doesn't correspond to the later hetero/homo binary: she imaginatively displaces the nineteenth-century sex-gender system with a fondly resurrected alternative from the past. Sweat's poems often invoke some form of the "secret" (139, 182, 199, 221), the unspoken (141, 149, 203), silence (69, 216), or the unnamable (155). They are pervaded by the intense pain of absence from a beloved object—this recalls the separation between Ethel and Ernest—and occasionally they engage in gender masquerade, the speaker repeatedly posing as a knight or vassal worshiping his lady (for example, 205), or calculated pronominal ambiguity (177, 185, 206–207, 216–18). The poems constitute, alongside *Ethel's Love-Life*, Sweat's other major effort to imagine new queer possibilities for love.

A good way to begin to approach Sweat's little-studied poetry is in terms of what Michael C. Cohen has called "the social lives of poems in nineteenth-century America." That is, rather than abstracting the poems from their social contexts and interpreting them as precious works of art, or evaluating them as aesthetic objects, we should understand them as having had a variety of actual social uses, a variety of functions in the construction and maintenance of real social relations and networks. Whether they circulated in manuscript, were printed in periodicals, or both, and then eventually collected in the volume *Verses*, they reached readers and cemented human attachments of one kind and another. A good many of her poems had indeed been printed in newspapers and magazines before Sweat collected them in her privately printed volume in 1890. To give just one example, "My Friend—My Friend," one of her many plaintive poems expressive of yearning for a lost or absent presumptively female friend, appeared in the *Galaxy, a Magazine of Entertaining Reading*, in November 1872; there, in public print, it gave subtle expression to what we recall the historian Carroll Smith-Rosenberg termed "the female world of love and ritual," the normative nineteenth-century same-sex culture of intense female intimacy and attachment. When Sweat reprinted this poem nearly two decades later in *Verses*, she revised it in many small but telling ways and rewrote one line extensively: the third and fourth lines in the fifth stanza originally read in 1872, "Ah me! Such tears as these should ne'er be starting / To eyes that once have looked into thine own," a formulation that conveyed a gentle self-reproach with respect to the speaker's weeping loss of emotional control. But by 1890 Sweat had emended this to "Why should such bitter tears as these be starting / To eyes that once have looked into thine own?" which quite in another way expressed a questioning puzzlement about the sudden and unexpected appearance of tears that were qualified now as "bitter." Was it that Sweat, by 1890, felt the need to disclaim familiarity with or understanding of such an eruption of intense passion, whereas nearly two decades earlier she had been unselfconsciously prepared to avow familiarity with "such tears as these," only to chastise herself—and apologize to her beloved—for their impropriety?

An extensive, never mind exhaustive, account of the publication histories of Sweat's poems and a study of her process of revision are certainly beyond the scope of this introduction, but even this one example tells us that Sweat took painstaking care in conveying the subtleties (the "energy," "abandonment," "flush," "eagerness," "palpitation," and "rapture," to quote from *Ethel's Love-Life* [64]) of female same-sex passion, and tells us as well that her various accounts of it may have shifted in interesting ways over time. Indeed, Connie Burns, in her pioneering study of Sweat's life and writings, observed quite acutely that although "the vast majority of the love poems are written in the sensual passionate language of courtship, heard also in the romantic relationships revealed in *Ethel's Love-Life* as well as in the letters from Elizabeth Stoddard to Sweat," there is nevertheless a "secrecy shrouding" some of the poems and a careful ambiguity as to "the gender of the persona of these poems" (67). In other words, Burns claimed, while such "ambiguity and secrecy [were] missing from Sweat's earlier [1859] novel, [they] may well have become a social necessity by 1890" (67). Later in the nineteenth century, that is, as the homo/hetero binary and the emergent social type of the lesbian were coming to be formed (and the figure of the lesbian soon to be pathologized), earlier female same-sex practices of intimacy and same-sex protocols of loving behavior needed to be more carefully guarded from suspicious eyes. It is thus noteworthy that Sweat in many poems invokes *secrecy* in one manner or another: in the "Proem," she finds the "strength to utter / What my heart in secret owns" (139); in "The Voice of the Sea" each wave dying upon the shore bears a "secret" (182); in "Night and Morning" the speaker tosses upon her couch restlessly because in a dream she fears that "goblin phantoms . . . knew [her] secret," but she nevertheless vows to "bear [her] secret boldly" (199, 200); and in "Separation," one of many poems lamenting a painful separation from a beloved, the speaker addresses that distant person and imagines that they are together, whereupon "deep within a secret pulse is stirred," and magically there come "your sweet kisses to my waiting lips" (221).

Consonantly with the theme of secrecy there is another thread invoking various things *unnameable, unspoken, unwritten,* or *whispered*: in the "Dedication," "I name thee not . . . I do not name thee to the crowd" (138); in "My Friend—My Friend," there are "thoughts unwritten and unspoken" (141); "Midnight Visitants" features "eloquence unspoken" (149); "Silence" advises that a certain "deep and sacred feeling" should not seek for "utterance in speech" but should "let silence make [it] still deeper" (180); the beautiful "A Greeting" insists that "without spoken words" the speaker and a friend have formed an inseparable bond (203); and in "The Timid Lover," one of several poems that use a neo-medievalist frame—referring to "a lady fair / Who holds my spirit fast"—the beloved lady "bars my utterance the while" (216). Perhaps most poignantly, in "You and I," the speaker addresses a beloved other and cannot find the right label for their relationship: "How shall we name the tie / By which both you and I / Are bound together?" (155). "Friendship's too cold a word," she avers, and then a cascading alliterative sequence of soft fricatives ensues—"For . . . feeling . . . full . . . fire . . . fond . . . full . . . free . . . Friends . . . Friends . . . fairer . . . friendship" (155)—perhaps conjuring those very "loving kisses" the poem recalls, before the poem at its close boldly announces: "Let us,—and what's the harm? / Let us be lovers!" (155). *Kisses* reappear again and again, too: in "Renaissance" a lover is implored to "cover me with kisses sweet" (166); in "A Greeting" the speaker can "still feel that kiss you gave" (202); "Separation" imagines a faraway lover's "sweet kisses" (221); and the melancholy "Song" warns that the lover must "Give me no kiss at meeting / When our meeting is by day," must also "Give me no kiss at parting, / When the same rude world is by," but must save "your welcome kisses" for nonpublic occasions, for example, when "safe in some home seclusion, / Where feeling and thought are free," for those kisses "are too precious / . . . / For other eyes to see them" (229).

To return for a moment to the distinct thread of what I earlier called "neo-medievalism" in these poems, it seems possible that if, to follow Connie Burns, Sweat's collection of these poems in 1890 registers a newly felt need for ambiguity and for the protective veiling of same-sex desire, another kind of indirection may involve a temporal displacement. "True Blue" references "my lady" (144); so too does "Out in the Cold" (150), while "The Lady of My Dreams" casts the speaker as a "vassal" adoring a "Queen" (205), and "The Timid Lover," as mentioned earlier, claims "There is a lady fair / Who holds my spirit fast"

(216). This neo-medievalism reaches its culmination in "My Ladye Love," where the archaic spelling combines with yet another invocation of secrecy and unnameability—"I have a little ladye love,— / I shall not tell her name" (222)—to summon something like the archaic form of "sexuality" that James P. Schultz, in an important contribution to the recovery of earlier social systems for organizing bodies, pleasures, and attachments, has dubbed "courtly love" or "the love of courtliness" (xxii): the organization of desire and attachment not around the gender binary but around a different set of "courtly" qualities or characteristics that could be possessed by men and women alike.

It is easy to imagine that many of Sweat's poems may have circulated in manuscript before publication. Some of them may in fact have initially been specifically addressed to particular friends and may have functioned as part of a courtship ritual carried on by epistolary means. (Again, Jennifer Putzi's investigation of Sweat's epistolary relationship with Elizabeth Stoddard is relevant here. Unfortunately, Sweat's letters to Stoddard are lost, so we are in a position not unlike that of the reader of *Ethel's Love-Life*, needing to imagine the other half of the correspondence on the basis of a few hints.) Later, when *Verses* was printed for private circulation by the Lakeside Press in Portland, Maine, Sweat evidently gave or sent copies to her women friends, with dedicatory inscriptions. One of the first gifts, at the time of "Christmas 1890," was inscribed to her friend "Lily S. Macalester Laughton with the love of M. J. M. S." This was Eliza Lytle "Lily" Macalester Laughton (1832–1891) of Philadelphia, who had been a fellow vice-regent (in her case for Pennsylvania) of the Mount Vernon Ladies Association and later became regent. She was one with whom Sweat was closely allied during some difficult internal disputes within that female organization.[3] When this particular copy of *Verses* came on the antiquarian book market, it was sold with a shelf tag still inserted, with "Vice-Regents Shelf" written on it by hand and a typed notice below: "Not catalogued. Of interest only because it belonged to Lily Scott Laughton, V. R. for Pennsylvania, elected Regent in 1874." There is something very touching about that dismissive "only," and about the fact of the volume having been deaccessioned by the Mount Vernon Ladies Association. We might rather say that this copy is of interest especially *because* it belonged to Laughton, and because it is an embodiment of the avowed "love" Sweat offered to Laughton, as well

as being a material artifact of their mutual participation in an extensive array of female philanthropic, cultural, and personal networks.
Another copy of *Verses*, in a different binding (perhaps Sweat had
the Lakeside Press produce a number of book blocks, then had them
covered periodically as she ran out of copies ready to be gifted), has
a much simpler inscription: "Mrs. Farmer from M. J. M. S. 1894." We
need to imagine that these poems, some of them written to individual
women and perhaps given or sent to them in manuscript, then later
published in periodicals, and finally collected in *Verses*, often revised
at any of these steps along the way, "occupied a complex position in
the history of social life and sociality," as Cohen says, and had roles
in "creating lived and imagined relations among people" (9–10)—in
Sweat's case the history of female same-sex sociality as its various
forms metamorphosed over the course of the late nineteenth century.

One other way to approach this collection of poems would be to
acknowledge its internal variety and the arc of progression of the
poems as they are arranged in sequence. Although it is fair to empha-
size that many, and perhaps most, of the poems express erotic longing
or attachment (or lament the absence of a lover—see "My Friend—My
Friend," "From the German of Heinrich Heine," "To ———," "So Near
and Yet So Far," "Sweet Words," "The Pilgrim's Plaint," "Stanzas,"
"Sweet Heart," and "Separation"), there are also a few occasional
poems, some poems of landscape or seascape description, and,
especially clustered toward the end of the collection, multiple poems
expressive of Christian piety. This trajectory from human erotic
attachments toward devout religious attachment, characterizing the
sequence of poems in *Verses* as a whole, is captured also within one
poem: "The Christ." One of the longest poems in the book, it narrates
the quest of a sculptor who, having in his possession a block of white
Carrara marble of great purity, must decide what figure to portray
in it. He is stymied in his effort to find exactly the right subject. First
he imagines carving "a maiden young," a poet who cannot sing (her
"harp unstrung"), indeed, the ancient poet Sappho, often taken to be
a premonitory figure of lesbian anguish. "But Sappho's sorrow cannot be / The thought imprisoned there" in the marble, the sculptor
decides (209). He entertains other possible subjects: Aphrodite, other
"gods and goddesses of old," "heroes," "martyr, poet, saint, and sage"
(210), "Fantastic figures . . . / From legends old and strange," and

so on (210). Dissatisfied with all of these options, in frustration he leaves the city and walks out upon a sandy shore, where only the "sad moan the ocean makes" breaks the "Sabbath stillness" (211). The fact that it is the Sabbath day hints of what is to come: the sculptor falls asleep upon the sand and dreams that he glides up through the sky and has a vision of ranks of "angels clothed in shining white" (211), whose forms then part to allow him the astonishing vision of "a form more dazzling bright" (212), indeed, "the Master" (212). Upon waking from his dream the sculptor knows now to what he must dedicate his artistic skill and his exquisite block of marble: "A Christ from stone unsealed / . . . / The Master's self revealed" (213). It seems unavoidable that we should interpret the trajectory of this poem by Sweat in autobiographical terms: she is an artist who, like the sculptor, has crafted a collection, *Verses*, that in architectonic terms moves from something like secret Sapphic love to avowed Christian devotion, ending with such poems as "The Heavenly Guest," with its epigraph from the Gospel of Paul (230); "The Invalid," whose speaker's painful illness will be assuaged by the "heavenly Father" (231); "Be Strong," with its epigraph from Jeremiah (234); "Fear Not for I Am with Thee," advising Christian faith as the antidote to earthly despair (235); "Heavenly Voices" (236); and, finally, "Waiting on the Lord" (238).

It is possible, as I have suggested, to trace an arc in Sweat's career, a trajectory from what looks like, in retrospect, the comparative freedom of her depiction of same-sex love and queer existence in *Ethel's Love-Life* (1859) to the "language of concealment" (64), as Connie Burns puts it, that permeates her *Verses* (1890). It is possible, I have argued, to see this trajectory even within the latter collection of poems itself. This trajectory coincides more or less with a familiar narrative of the history of sexuality in the nineteenth and early twentieth centuries, an era that saw the emergence and development of heterosexual and homosexual categories of being, categories that had not yet been invented in Sweat's youth and may have been alien to her even throughout her adulthood—categories that were used to denigrate people and thus forced them into concealment. Sweat's writing thus contributes important evidence to the history of sexuality even as it is made at least partially intelligible in those sexual-historical terms. Nevertheless, Sweat remains in certain ways fundamentally enigmatic, both biographically and literarily—an anomaly in literary history who seems to resist explanation and who evidently felt no need to explain herself.

This may be what is most queer about Sweat in the end. The best known photograph of Sweat (reproduced herein) seems to capture this enigmatic dimension: she is expensively dressed like a proper matron, a stylish hat on her head and her hands mostly hidden in a muff, performing for the camera her gentility and respectability. But the sly smile on her face hints at something quite other—a willful illegibility, a reserved capacity for irreverence and mischief, a defiant refusal to be plainly known, a devious pleasure taken in eluding categorization. I would therefore affiliate Sweat to some degree with the writers discussed by Scott Herring in *Queering the Underworld*, who worked to undermine the cultural forces that tried, in the late nineteenth and early twentieth centuries, to expose, label, and police deviant sexualities. As Herring writes, these writers sought to replace a "hermeneutics of sexual suspicion" with a "suspicion of sexual hermeneutics" (14). But Sweat is paradoxical: as we have seen, she articulated and celebrated female same-sex passion ("we find the rarest and most perfect beauty in the affections of one woman for another") in a way that made it possible for at least one reader, Adah Isaacs Menken—and probably more—to adopt and inhabit a sort of erotic identity. At the same time, she showed no interest in essentializing that identity. The present collection of her brilliant writings aims to bring this elusive, mystifying Margaret Sweat to the attention of new generations of readers.

WORKS CITED

Agger, Lee. *Women of Maine*. Portland: Guy Gannett, 1982.

Altman, Janet Gurkin. *Epistolarity: Approaches to a Form*. Columbus: Ohio State University Press, 1982.

Anon. "Ethel's Love-Life: A Novel by Margaret J. M. Sweat." *North American Review* 89, no.184 (July 1859): 276.

Beam, Dorri. "Transcendental Erotics, Same-Sex Desire, and *Ethel's Love-Life*." In *Toward a Female Genealogy of Transcendentalism*, ed. Jana L. Argersinger and Phyllis Cole, 327–47. Athens: University of Georgia Press, 2014. A previous version of this essay appeared in *ESQ* 57:1, no. 2 (2011): 1–27.

Casper, Scott E. *Sarah Johnson's Mount Vernon: The Forgotten History of an American Shrine*. New York: Hill and Wang, 2008.

Cohen, Michael C. *The Social Lives of Poems in Nineteenth-Century America*. Philadelphia: University of Pennsylvania Press, 2015.

Damon, Gene [Barbara Grier], Jan Watson, and Robin Jordan. *The Lesbian in Literature: A Bibliography.* 2nd ed. Reno, Nev.: The Ladder, 1975.

D'Emilio, John, and Estelle B. Freedman. *Intimate Matters: A History of Sexuality in America.* New York: Harper and Row, 1988.

Diggs, Marylynne. "Romantic Friends or a 'Different Race of Creatures'? The Representation of Lesbian Pathology in Nineteenth-Century America." *Feminist Studies* 21, no. 2 (1995): 317–40.

Eiselein, Gregory. *See* Menken, Adah Isaacs.

Grier, Barbara. *The Lesbian in Literature: A Bibliography.* 3rd ed. Naiad Press, 1981.

Herring, Scott. *Queering the Underworld: Slumming, Literature, and the Undoing of Lesbian and Gay History.* Chicago: University of Chicago Press, 2007.

James, Henry. "George Sand." In *Literary Criticism: French Writers, Other European Writers, The Prefaces to the New York Edition,* ed. Leon Edel, 708–34. New York: Library of America, 1984.

Jones, Howard Mumford. "American Commentary on George Sand, 1837–1848." *American Literature* 3, no. 4 (Jan. 1932): 389–407.

Lombard, C. M. "George Sand's Image in America (1837–1876)." *Revue de littérature comparée* 40, no. 2 (1 April 1966): 177–86.

Longfellow, Henry Wadsworth. *The Letters of Henry Wadsworth Longfellow.* Vol. 4, *1857–1865.* Ed. Andrew Hilen. Cambridge, Mass.: Belknap Press of Harvard University Press, 1972.

Looby, Christopher. "The Literariness of Sexuality: Or, How to Do the History of (American) Sexuality." *American Literary History* 25, no. 4 (Winter 2013): 841–54.

Lubin, Georges. "George Sand and America." In *West Virginia George Sand Conference Papers,* ed. Armand E. Singer, Mary W. Singer, Janice S. Speth, and Dennis O'Brien, 11–17. Morgantown: Department of Foreign Languages, West Virginia University, 1981.

Mavor, Elizabeth. *The Ladies of Llangollen: A Study in Romantic Friendship.* Harmondsworth: Penguin Books, 1973.

Menken, Adah Isaacs. *Infelicia and Other Writings.* Ed. Gregory Eiselein. Peterborough, Ont.: Broadview Press, 2002.

Putzi, Jennifer. "'Two Single Married Women': The Correspondence of Elizabeth Stoddard and Margaret Sweat, 1851–1854." In *Letters and Cultural Transformations in the United States, 1760–1860,* ed. Theresa Strouth Gaul and Sharon M. Harris, 117–35. Farnham, U.K.: Ashgate, 2009

Schultz, James A. *Courtly Love, the Love of Courtliness, and the History of Sexuality.* Chicago: University of Chicago Press, 2006.

Sentilles, Renée M. *Performing Menken: Adah Isaacs Menken and the Birth of American Celebrity.* New York: Cambridge University Press, 2003.

Smith-Rosenberg, Carroll. "The Female World of Love and Ritual: Relations Between Women in Nineteenth-Century America." In Smith-Rosenberg, *Disorderly Conduct: Visions of Gender in Victorian America,* 53–76. New York: Alfred A. Knopf, 1985.

Stoddard, Elizabeth. *The Morgesons and Other Writings, Published and Unpublished.* Ed. Lawrence Buell and Sandra A. Zagarell. Philadelphia: University of Pennsylvania Press, 1984.

Sweat, Margaret J. M. "A Chapter on Novels." *North American Review* 83, no. 173 (October 1856): 337–51.

———. "Charlotte Brontë and the Brontë Novels." *North American Review* 85, no. 177 (October 1857): 293–329.

———. *Ethel's Love-Life: A Novel.* New York: Rudd and Carleton, 1859.

———. "The Friendships of Women." *Boston Courier,* date unknown [presumably 1868]. Folder 028, Book Notices, 1867–1871. Margaret Jane Mussey Sweat Collection, Maine Women Writers Collection, University of New England, Portland, Maine. My thanks to Cathleen Miller, curator, Maine Women Writers Collection, for providing scans of this clipping.

———. "George Sand." *World* (New York), XVI, no. 5407 (9 June 1876): 4–5.

———. Folder 031, George Sand [Scrapbook of clippings about GS in English and French; also contains MJMS handwritten notes; 1872 photo of GS], circa 1870s. Margaret Jane Mussey Sweat Collection, Maine Women Writers Collection, University of New England, Portland, Maine.

———. Diary, 1849–1880. Book 1. Margaret Jane Mussey Sweat Diary, 1849–1880 (2016). At http://dune.une.edu/mjms_diary/1. Margaret Jane Mussey Sweat Collection, Maine Women Writers Collection, University of New England, Portland, Maine.

———. "The Novels of George Sand." In George Sand, *Antonia: A Novel,* trans. Virginia Vaughan. Separately paginated afterword, 1–23. Boston: Roberts Brothers, 1870.

"Sweat, Margaret Jane Mussey." https://en.wikipedia.org/wiki/Margaret_Jane _Mussey_Sweat.

Williams, Gary. "Speaking with the Voices of Others: Julia Ward Howe's Laurence." In Julia Ward Howe, *The Hermaphrodite,* ed. Gary Williams, ix–xlvi. Lincoln: University of Nebraska Press, 2004.

Wright, Lyle. *American Fiction, 1851–1875: A Contribution Toward a Bibliography.* San Marino, Calif.: Huntington Library, 1957.

ETHEL'S LOVE-LIFE

A Novel

To the Reader

IF there is aught of truth within these pages, it will assert itself without assistance and without explanation.

If there is any power of expression in these words, it will speak to the hearts which recognise it; and if there is any charm of sentiment beneath the imperfect utterance, it lays itself at the feet of those who give it welcome.

"I am a part of all which I have met;
Yet all experience is an arch wherethrough
Gleams that untravelled world whose margin fades
For ever and for ever when I move."

TENNYSON

ETHEL'S LOVE-LIFE

LETTER FIRST

DEAREST AND TRUEST OF FRIENDS,

You ask me to tell you something of my childhood and my home, with which, though knowing me so well, you are still unfamiliar. Though the retrospect of vanished years must cause me pain, though the past has in it an eternal regret, which sits like the skeleton at an Egyptian feast, in the midst of the present joy that fills my heart, though tears rise to my eyes as I recall my sufferings, and self-reproach utters its mournful words as I recount my errors and my ignorances,—still I will not shrink from the revelation of my whole self to you. You who know my heart with all its strength and all its weakness, all its intensity of feeling and all its impetuosity of action, should know also the history of my past influences, the external environments and inner springs which have combined to make me what I now am. I will look back steadily upon my old self, and faithfully repeat to you what the past reveals to me. Two years ago you had never seen me; we who are now all in all to each other, whose pulses beat in magnetic sympathy, had never met. Two years ago my inner self was changed, old things passed away, all things became new,—old deadness gave place to new vitality, old passions were extinguished, old loves and hatreds were outgrown and thrown aside in one fresh, vigorous, new-born impulse of my whole nature. Never since then have I disturbed their repose, but now, at the magic power of your word, I reanimate them to a galvanic existence. I will call up at your bidding, the forms of the past, which, though now but weird-like phantoms in the sunshine

which surrounds me, and with its healthy glow shows them to be
unsubstantial and harmless, were once the giants of my battle-field,
and strode fiercely and relentlessly upon their mighty errands to
my soul. Once more they shall assume their grand proportions, and
play their parts before your eyes. I shall no longer fear them, for the
enchanter is near me to lay them again at rest. You shall know all
that I had suffered when I met you, the master of my heart—all that
made me the poor and prostrate thing I was when your love and your
strength raised me again to life. For this I must recall my childhood
and its externalities; I must paint the portrait of the little child, that
you may better comprehend the woman; and show you the bud in
which so many embryo leaves lay folded and almost invisible, that you
may recognise the flower when it blooms into the fulness of glowing,
panting, luxuriant life. The environments of our first years color our
whole future, and, whatever that future may be, we never wholly
forget or leave off the tone which we then acquired. The restraint
of some of our growing powers, and undue forcing of others, distort
the mature, when that which first bent the child-plant is forgotten;
the crushing of sweet and tender feelings in a young and impressible
heart will render the most susceptible nature callous, or force it to
keep silence when it would gladly speak. Too much restraint and too
rigid discipline distress and injure the eager nature of the child, break
the natural impulsiveness, and produce disastrous results in later life;
while the absence of all direction and control, the lack of judicious
suggestion and loving vigilant aid, allow the young impulses to run
riot; the weeds grow as fast as the flowers, and a wilderness instead
of a garden is the result. All the influences which act upon the child,
possess an enormous accumulative power for good or evil in the time
to come. The mould, still plastic, may receive distortion, which will be
always visible in the finished statue.

My childhood was peculiarly calm in its external environments; all
that made it individual and phenomenal was hidden in the recesses of
the little struggling consciousness within. Nursed in the lap of luxury,
I was almost undisturbed by ungratified wishes, and rarely thwarted
in my attempts to obtain anything that my childish tastes craved. Seldom required by circumstances or urged by temperament to go out of
myself, without companions of my own age with whom to compare my
experiences, I accepted without wonder and without thought the daily

pleasures of my life. Not inclined to the usual sports of children, and finding in my rare association with them neither sympathy nor satisfaction, I lost the frolic carelessness of childhood long before my cheek had parted with its infant roundness, or my form attained to any but the most tiny proportions. My mind was filled with vague questionings upon all mysterious subjects; I moved through an enchanted land, seeing and pondering over many wonders full of strange fascination for me. I did not, however, feel inclined to say anything of these fancies to those about me, for an instinct told me that they were sacred to me alone, so I kept them in my own heart with simple and loving reverence. My precocity of imagination was accompanied by a grave and quiet demeanor and a reserve of manner which protected me from notice, and my peculiarities of thought remained almost unsuspected. I kept nearly all my questionings safe within my own breast, seeking their answer only in my books and in unremitting observation of those older than myself. My eyes alone told the story of my eager quest, and I sometimes saw those I was watching grow uneasy beneath my strange glances; sometimes too I met, from those far older than myself, an answering look of sympathy, which, though I could not understand its full import, thrilled my child-heart with mysterious power.

As I grew older, and intellectual cravings awoke within me, I found close at hand all that could occupy and satisfy my mind. My studies were active but desultory, continued but undirected, kept up only by my own eagerness, and devoid of all stimulus from outward difficulties. I felt no sharp mental needs which only my own hard-working ingenuity might hope to supply, but had merely to stretch forth my hand and grasp whatever seemed worth having. A too luxurious and easily obtained intellectual nourishment, enervates even while it cultivates the mind; it weakens the creative power, destroys originality, and substitutes an exotic fastidiousness for the strong, natural growth of intellectual acuteness. This becomes doubly dangerous when the passions are growing up in their own strength, fed by the charms of dreamland fancies, and beneath the tropical influences of highly-wrought romances and the passionate utterances of poetry. I grew to womanhood under a hot-house cultivation, intense, unceasing, but also undirected and undisciplined. Mine was naturally a hungry, grasping mind; it would have grown strong by labor and have taken care of itself, had there been nothing near to pamper it. The rough weather of deprivation would have made it rugged and vigorous; in anything less than the absolute lavishness of intellectual wealth which surrounded me, it would, I think, have followed some decided bias and have wrought out some positive result. It would have saved me much effort at self-discipline in later years, had I been trained in a more self-denying school, and been thrown more upon the native strength of my own mind. As it was, I revelled in utter freedom, and whiled away the precious hours in day-dreams over the hoarded labors of other minds, lazily following in paths made smooth and easy for me. My health was delicate, and though I was not often seriously ill, I was always fragile in appearance and requiring careful watching, so that I was shut out from all those invigorating physical influences which ordinarily keep the balance between the child's growing body and expanding mind.

For the same reason all plan of formal scholarship, all routine of education, was for a long time impracticable. Had not my own insatiate love of knowledge led me to study, my first years would have been passed in quiet ignorance; as it was, my own instinct prompted me to sufficient intellectual industry. An occasional examination into my attainments by my mother more than satisfied her maternal ambition, and though she often wondered how I obtained my knowledge, and was really desirous that I should invigorate my bodily health by exercise, and leave my books for amusement out of doors, yet I was, on the whole, left to follow my own inclination. Indeed, the smile of pleasure which rose to her lips at any indication of quickness on my part, was a far more powerful stimulant to acquisition for me, than she was aware of, and completely destroyed the effect of her gentle suggestions of recreation. Not yet old enough to comprehend the difference between knowledge and wisdom, I fancied that in books alone I could find all I needed, and many an hour when I was supposed to be in the playground, I was hidden behind the heavy window curtains of the library, studying some volume that had captivated my imagination. My father's library was a very extensive one, the accumulation of many years and various tastes;—among the volumes were numerous old romances and histories, rare and quaint collections of voyages and travels, with all of which I made acquaintance, and over which I bent for hours, sometimes with sagacious interest, sometimes only with puzzled fascination. I reasoned with Mentor and Telemachus in the island of Calypso, or travelled confidingly with Gulliver; I pondered upon the mysteries of the Church Catechism, or grew faint over the Book of Martyrs. The narratives of the Bible had a peculiar charm to me, and I was familiar with them all, long before I knew what relation in time or space they bore to my own life. I wept bitterly when I discovered that I was a Gentile and lived a long way from Jerusalem. But my sorrows as well as my questionings I kept within my own breast, and no one knew how busy my young mind was, or felt the quick beating of my heart when the conversation of those around me turned upon any of the subjects which filled me with eager interest. I had not that inborn genius which creates spontaneously, and as a necessity unto itself, but I possessed a good deal of that active talent which makes constant use of the materials laid in its way, and builds them up into a thousand various forms.

Yet I was, in the ordinary sense, extremely indolent. I lay wrapt for hours in dreams—sweet, but very vague and apparently unprofitable. As I grew older, this habit of aimless reverie took from me more and more my mental vigor, my imagination subdued my reason, my fancy enchained my intellect. Creating for myself a charmed atmosphere of romance, I breathed it till I was thoroughly imbued with its spirit, and hardly knew which of my thoughts were really representative of my original self.

My home was luxurious in the extreme, the abode of wealth, not suddenly acquired, but of long hereditary descent, sitting easily and gracefully upon its possessors, and showing itself in the perfection of the general effect, and the refined harmony of the whole domestic movement, never obtruding itself coarsely and repulsively in vain and unmeaning ostentation. Every adornment, which a refined taste could suggest, was present; lavishness of expenditure showed itself in every direction, the only restraint upon luxury being that which the fastidiousness of carefully and highly cultivated taste itself imposed. There was no over-loading of expensive upholstery and gaudy display of unnecessary finery, but a completeness of finish, an elegance of detail, a solidity of comfort, a reality of splendor. It was in this extreme of luxury that my pleasant childhood passed—for it was pleasant in spite of the sad hours which the sensitiveness of my temperament caused me, but which were independent of my environments, and often chased away by the buoyancy of my disposition, which made my moods vary in most capricious fashion, and gave me the appearance of being strangely contrastive in my manifestations. But for the reserve of my nature, which always more or less restrained my expression, the extremes to which my inner movement vibrated must have often excited astonishment; as it was, a veil hung ever between me and my companions, and I walked on my own path without molestation, fulfilling the general courtesies of the child-life without difficulty, because I knew of nothing else within the serene atmosphere of my home. Everything around me was so delightful, so apparently spontaneous in its coming, that I was a complete Sybarite before I knew that I was in a position at all unusual, and in which a power beyond myself had placed me. I did not reason on the matter at all, but resigned myself without difficulty to enjoyment. My mind found enough to occupy and amuse itself in alternating seasons of eager acquisition and of silent reverie. For a long time my speculative and analytic faculties confined themselves to the subjects which interested me in my books, and took little notice of the outside world; but after awhile a tendency to morbid doubt and restless scepticism developed itself within me, and rose into stronger and stronger force till it gained complete mastery over me. What I have suffered from the analysis of my dearest hopes, the morbid distrust of my truest and warmest faiths, the bitter questioning of my most generous impulses, no one, who has not suffered from the same cause, can understand. While still a child I was a victim to miserable doubts and fears which rarely assail any but mature minds, and experienced mental agony which I now look back upon with surprise, when I remember how young I then was. Unable to resist, yet always dreading and shrinking from the exercise of these demoniac faculties, I have gone from the light and glory of my new-born hopes into the utter darkness of my questionings and my doubts; have dissected and brought into naked exposure my trusts and faiths till their bare and bleeding nerves lost all life and beauty, and I threw them away as worthless; always more or less conscious that it was my own murderous process which had made them so—often weeping in the bitterness of full knowledge that they were originally full of health and beauty, and ought to have been cherished and permitted to grow into their grand spiritual proportions. I have cast away the flowers that were budding at my side, seeing in them only vile weeds,—have tortured my own heart till analysis and doubt became a part of myself. I look back upon the earliest years of my life as the time when the sunshine was not yet obscured by these clouds—I look forward with undoubting hope to a time when, beneath the sunlight of your calm, high nature, I shall throw off the last vestige of this morbid gloom and sit down free for ever from its mocking shade. You have already done so much towards restoring my heart and mind to a healthy and vigorous tone, that I willingly resign my whole nature to you, to receive from you a new impulse and a new strength. But I am wandering away from the little narrative of my external life which I mean to lay before you, not with biographical minuteness of detail, but in fragments and detached sketches of those incidents and persons which seem, to my maturer judgment, to have had the most powerful influence upon me, and to have done most towards forming my mind and heart. I must first paint the portraits of my immediate family, and set forth what I may call my inherited characteristics and peculiarities.

My father has a disposition as easy as his circumstances, his life is as equable as his serene brow betokens his spirit to be. His career has always been successful within the limits to which his calm and unambitious nature confines itself—his judgment is sound, his integrity undoubted, his sense of honor quick and keen. His imagination has always been subordinate to his slower sense, and he is rarely hurried into any impetuosity of speech or action. From him I inherit a certain quiet pertinacity, a persevering patience, which forms the groundwork of both natures. With this is, naturally enough, connected great strength of prejudice and prepossession, tenacity in regard to impressions once thoroughly established in the mind, and great unwillingness to retreat from positions once asserted. Nothing short of an irresistible conviction can effect a change of opinion in either, but, once convinced, no false pride deters from frank and open acknowledgment of the first mistake. The apparent slowness with which our opinions are made up on matters of grave import and involving decided action, arises in him, from a general moderation of temperament and impartiality of judgment, in me from the activity of the analytical and sceptical faculties, which force me into extended and intimate relations with any subject which seems to me of importance, and which admits of a variety of arguments. My father possesses a calm decision of manner and a dignity of aspect which command respect; a heart and hand "open as day to melting charity," a tenderness of feeling quite marvellous in one who has seen so clearly and so much of the falsehood of the world. Exempt by happy temperament from inward storms, by easy circumstances sheltered from outward struggle, he has yet not been unmindful of the commotion and jarring of the world about him. His observations, however, have tended to increase the natural contemplativeness of his character, and to produce a somewhat saddened acquiescence in things as they are, rather than a determination to work for changes and reformations. He is supereminently a contented man, and moves always in a quiet little atmosphere of his own, which seems quite impenetrable to the influences which make others so restless.

The resemblance I have mentioned, is the only one I bear to my father—in most other points I am singularly like my mother, though even here the similarity ceases in some particulars deeply affecting my personality. In fact, the existence of this element of patience, lying as it does in me deep down in my innermost nature, beneath the impetuous and rapid current which flows upon the surface and seems to many to embrace my whole self, necessitates very marked differences between her vivacious temperament and my own. The external resemblance I bear to my "little mamma" you yourself have often noticed, and there are other interior similarities quite as remarkable. In the tone of our minds, in the keen quest for new light, the fearless confronting of intellectual problems, as well as in the predominance of an involuntary sarcasm, and the alternations of buoyant hopes and self-created despairs, in short, in most of those movements of being which seem to be, not so much the result of our own volition as the irrepressible manifestations of the inner soul—we are strangely alike. A sympathy almost mysterious, has often revealed to each the inmost workings of the other's heart. In a certain *hauteur* of manner and an unconscious coldness of demeanor in general intercourse, we are also much alike, as well as in a weakness of physical organization and susceptibility to all nervous impressions. Our general indifference of manner is merely the outside covering which masks hearts full of passionate impulses, and alive to the most tender and delicate ministrations of love. Among our friends we become spontaneously expressional and self-forgetful, so that we appear to possess highly contrastive, if not absolutely contradictory natures, one which the world at large comes in contact with, the other that which goes forth to meet the beloved circle of our friends. And although these friends sometimes murmur at the harshness of the judgment which the outside world may pass upon us, in its ignorance of the reverse side of our natures, and feel inclined to claim for us a more general love than we obtain, we ourselves have never quarrelled with the verdict. The love of those we love best has always been sufficient for us both, and it has never failed us in our need. A more general popularity, with its insatiate demands, would be a troublesome acquisition for either of us, and a poor exchange for the loyal devotion we win from those admitted to our inner circle. The great law of compensation is in nothing more perceptible than in the rigid justice with which nature supplies the heart—demands of her different children, and equalizes the claims which different tempera- ments make upon her. I always question the strength and genuineness of those emotions of which the possessors declare themselves unable to obtain any appreciation, and to win any return. The great cause of uneasiness among these sensitive hearts, arises from their desire to obtain a different kind of appreciation or admiration from that which the circumstances admit of. Those formed to attract a general but somewhat careless approbation, sigh for the concentrated devotion of a few lofty natures; those to whom a few cling with unswerving loyalty, but to whom the general world is indifferent, too often crave a wider circle of influence.

In the absence of outward fluctuations, our family circle was kept in action by the marked contrasts existing among its members. Rarely is there a wider difference of character than existed between my father and my mother, and between my brother and myself; and the life and motion caused by the friction among ourselves were, when I was still quite a child, increased and varied by the entrance of two new and quite different elements in the persons of two orphaned cousins. My mother was all fire and impetuosity, enthusiastic in her sentiments, fluent in her expression—with a nervous organization so susceptible that it often threatened to shatter her slight frame; my father quiet, moderate, cool, and somewhat ponderous. The differences between my brother and myself were of a more subtle and delicate nature, and were often almost obliterated by the action of a few sympathetic impulses. Our intercourse, especially in my childhood, was almost always stormy, for I never could learn submission to his superior age—the difference between us being six or seven years—and it was not till we both grew older and calmer that our storms were made bearable by the halcyon

days which were sure to follow,—days when the joyous and genial
portions of our two natures came forth to greet each other, and gave
us charming intervals of communion and sympathy. The foundation of
earnest and devoted attachment was laid, when Death took him from
me just when his beauty and his strength had matured into magnificent perfection, and when my heart had found in him a protector and
a guide through the most perilous passage in my own life. His loss was
to me an irreparable one;—all the youthful differences of disposition
had died out between us or been merged into those quite compatible
with loving intercourse as man and woman;—our habits of thought
were growing daily more alike, and association had become healthful
and invigorating to us both. His personal beauty was of the highest
order. His dark grey eye was always changing as his moods changed,
the sunny and beaming glance of mirthful enjoyment was followed by
the introverted gaze of the profound thinker, the serene glow of deep
enthusiasm by the flashing glare of anger at continued resistance.
His soft dark hair clustered in heavy masses above his broad, pale
forehead, his frequent smile revealed his beautiful teeth in gleaming
whiteness, his form was tall and athletic in health, and graceful and
pliant in his long illness. It brings tears to my eyes and sorrow to my
heart that these have passed away for ever.

When I was about ten years old my cousins Louisa and Emily came
to reside with us. Louisa, the eldest, was about twenty, and possessed
of remarkable personal beauty. Even my childish admiration was
roused by her charming face and animated manner, and while she
remained in our family a degree of social gaiety much greater than
usual prevailed. She was a thorough coquette, and quite unscrupulous
in regard to the result of the admiration she delighted to awaken.
She laughed at the unsuccessful suitors whom yet she had previously
exerted herself to win, and my poor father was worried continually
with the complaints of disappointed swains. It was a joyful day for
him when she at length condescended to make a final choice, and the
rapidity with which he disposed of the business arrangements of the
marriage, which devolved on him as guardian, was so unlike his usual
moderation, that it was evident he was momently apprehensive of a
change of mood on the part of the bride elect. The wedding, however,
took place before Louisa had been with us a twelvemonth, and before
her caprices had completely worn out the patience of those whose

difficult duty it was to remedy or to excuse her inconsistencies. After her marriage she learned to control her social manifestations, and is now a very charming woman, with vivacious manners and versatile accomplishments. She petted me fondly as a child, and has always met me with kindness and frank liking as a woman. I have in my turn always felt for her a strong personal sympathy, and recognise in her the capacity for much good, which, as the years go by, is evidently developing in her life. She has never been subjected to any decided discipline, nor been forced to look at life beneath its surface by sorrow.

My cousin Emily was two years younger than her sister. She had little beauty, but was of an unusually gentle disposition—her amiability often degenerated into weakness. She has retained her soft impressibility through many sorrowful experiences that in another would have roused antagonism or developed energy. She had great musical talent—her chief gift from nature. Through this arose a certain degree of sympathy between her and myself, for, as you know, music has always been a passion with me, all the more powerful because, by a strange antagonism, I have always refused to study it technically, always reserved it as the one thing sacred from my analysing fingers. From my earliest childhood my susceptibility to musical impressions was remarked by all about me, and caused many prophetic assurances of my future career as a musician, but my repugnance to a near approach, to a practical acquaintance with its science, could never be overcome. It was yielded to at first as a childish whim, and is now one of my most confirmed idiosyncrasies. My cousin's talent was really wonderful, yet by a contradiction quite as marked as that in my own case, she was herself hardly conscious of the effects she achieved, at any rate except as scientific victories over merely scientific difficulties—the soul of music, the intangible, thrilling element, was nothing to her as it was all to me. I have seen her leave her instrument with an unmoved calmness and an unheightened color, after pouring forth strains that had electrified all who heard her, and which had brought hot tears to my eyes and stopped the very beating of my pulse. This calm immobility was her general mood; she was nearly stagnant in her daily life; the motion of the stream, if motion there were, was almost invisible. No sentiment more violent than a sort of helpless anxiety at the excessive excitement of others ever ruffled the tenor of her life while with us. I do not remember to have ever seen her angry, depressed, or exhilarated. Her only weapon in argument was silence, her only defence against wrath a sweet but not always appropriate smile. I, on the contrary, was fiery, impetuous, imperious; furious when roused, and ready to shed my heart's blood in battle for a cause I loved. Circumstances afterwards changed my manifestations, and grafted on my original nature a habit of action and a restraint of expression utterly at variance with my true self. Now that the pressure of those circumstances is lifted from my soul I am surprised to find how much of my original nature re-appears and asserts itself.

My parents lost two children in infancy, and one of my first marked reminiscences is connected with death. When I was a wee little thing of some three years, my baby brother died, and the stillness of the house, the tears of my mother and father, the hush of the darkened room where the infant lay, as I thought asleep, affected me with a vague fearfulness. The nurse took me by the hand and led me to the cradle—I started, for instead of my laughing, crowing, happy little brother, there was a cold, still image that would not open its eyes, and that chilled me when I put my hand upon the little cheek. The baby had been a source of wonder to me all its life; I thought it very odd that it could neither stand up nor speak, since it looked so wise with its large, black, mournful eyes, and was so very much bigger than my largest doll; but now that quiet form, with closed eyes and moveless hands, was a still greater mystery—one which long haunted my childish imagination and suggested a thousand unanswered questions. For years that chamber had the solemnity of death for me,—I did not understand the nature of my own feelings in regard to it, but in my wildest moods I never dared speak loudly there, and always trod softly and reverently over its floor. After this sorrow in my home, which was an incident of far more import to me than those about me supposed—for there is, after all, a wonderful degree of reserve in the childish heart in regard to its deepest feelings—there followed a long season of mingled shade and sunshine in my own individual life, and of peaceful ease and prosperity for the rest of the household. My sunshine came from what would be called a happy childhood, and reigned supreme when the childish, thoughtless element was uppermost; the shade prevailed when the graver portion of my nature awoke, filling my imagination with dreams, and bringing shadows from the untried future to imbue my heart with a vague, nameless woe. As I look back upon this period in my life, I can trace the birth and growth of nearly all the passions and opinions that have since predominated over my whole being.

But my lamp grows dim, silence and loneliness dwell throughout the house, it is long past midnight, I alone am a watcher,—so farewell for awhile; may the Everlasting Father bless and keep you with his peace till we meet again. He alone knows how much of my heart is with you, how all my hopes and all my fears, my joys and anxieties, are now bound up in your most beloved self;—once more farewell.

ETHEL SUTHERLAND

LETTER SECOND

I WRITE to you from the gloomy solitude of my own room, amid the wrathful sounds of sea and sky. A terrific storm is raging about me; the rain pours in torrents from a leaden sky; the roaring of the angry sea sounds hoarsely from the distant shore, and the winds howl like a pack of devils at my windows, clamorous to be let in, shaking and rattling my closed sashes as if to break through in spite of me. I mock at their vain attempts, secure from their attack, and with baffled rage they turn and rush among the trees, flinging the branches hither and thither in wild fury—the old elms quiver like reeds before the strong hands of the Spirits of the Storm who march forth today triumphant. It is a day for dark deeds. I would choose such a one had I a crime to accomplish. The air breathes despair through all things—something beyond depression, beyond discouragement—full of settled energy, of despairing recklessness, of longing for action;—it would supply to a vicious nature the very stimulus needed to bring evil deeds into strong and active life from the dark stillness of evil thoughts. You know how miserably atmospheric I am, how a long season of dull grey skies and drizzling rain and dense fog, so common in our climate, can sink me from one depth of depression to another, till all sunshine is forgotten, all hope crushed, all earth darkened, and all heaven shut out. But that quiet hopelessness is more tolerable than the frenzy that assails me during these wild, furious tempests. Then I grow mad, tiger-like, memory becomes as a fiend calling up the irrevocable past, with all hideous spectres to appal my shrinking sight. Distorted and exaggerated, every fault and every folly comes forth to accuse me; I seem to myself as a poor criminal amid the ghosts of his sins allowed to torture him with the rehearsal of his crimes. Ah! then I need your strong and healthful and true nature near me;—your smile only can chase away these phantoms, only in your love can I find rest and peace. Do you remember that day last autumn when you found me so utterly over-whelmed by these influences—when you wondered at finding so different a being from the one you had left so short a time before happy and hopeful? *I* shall not soon forget how you won me step by step from my depression, and brought me, first the relief of tears, and then the returning serenity of peace. The gratitude I felt was unutterable,—I knew that this experience was an assurance for the future, a seal, as it were, set upon our love to stamp it with a higher and holier mean-ing, to raise it above the earthliness of passion, and give us promise of entire union in our whole natures. The glorious fulness of your sympathy, the entering of your spirit into the innermost depths of my consciousness, the wise tenderness of your treatment of the sick soul, and the calm power with which you restored the balance of my inner forces which had scorned my own attempts at control—all this was something very marvellous to me, something for which I had pined in vain in all my friendships. It was so unlike the forced utterances and the useless consolations which had always fallen with such a cold, dead weight upon me, when in such moods. From that moment I have trusted myself wholly unto you, I have gloried in the knowledge that your strength of soul is so far above mine, while your gentle tender-ness can still sympathize in my weakness. Since that time I have felt nothing but repose in my love for you, and I offer you ever the most loyal trust, I bring you tribute of all that is most worthy in myself.

It is singular in what different ways different persons are affected by these atmospheric changes, which are such palpable realities to persons of my temperament. To some a beautiful day, when the beneficent sun shines lovingly into the heart, is suggestive of nothing grander than a boisterous pic-nic in the woods, with its accompa-niments of cold chicken and warm flirtations. The riotous winds of March are only rude enemies of their delicate complexions to most women: they hear nothing of the pouring forth of long pent-up glee among the trees, as the breeze comes shouting aloud to them of the returning Spring, and then flies off to carry, with wild mirth, the same glad tidings to the still frozen streams. To some the violent storm suggests ideas of their own comforts within-doors, heightened by the contrast from without, causes a more complacent survey of the bright fire, the thick carpets, the heavy curtains closed to exclude the night air,—induces a lazier stretch into the luxurious depths of the comfortable arm-chair,—sometimes the undefined impression that all these luxuries must, in some way, be the reward of their own merits, a conclusion adapted to render them still more valuable. But to me there comes a fierceness with the storm; the winds claim kindred with me as they hoarsely shout; magnetic influences sway me; I become, as it were, a portion of the storm, feeling its wild unrest, responding to its unearthly voices, obeying its weird suggestions; my sympathies, my heart, my very life, are mysteriously absorbed into it. Every rushing of the blast, every sobbing of the rain, echoes and vibrates through my inmost consciousness, as the harp-string quivers and gives forth its tones when the breeze sweeps across it.

The storm to-day has brought before me one remembrance of the past with peculiar force. I will endeavor to relate it to you as one more link in the history of my life. You see that, for one like me, a steady and continuous narrative of incidents is quite out of the question, nor would such a one, however minute in external details, help you to a full understanding of myself. I must be fragmentary and irregular in my story, for my life has been episodical and violently contrasted. My inner struggles, my various psychological phases, my soul-life, are what you wish, for they are myself: the external frame-work with which they have been built up into visible existence is valuable chiefly as a means for arranging them in some degree of definiteness, and of displaying the connection they have with one another. External changes and external sounds and sights have often passed before me as a panorama, tame and spiritless compared to the turmoil and excitement which filled my inner world, that world to which so few have been admitted, but wherein those few have ever been welcomed as right royal guests.

But to return to the remembrance suggested by the storm. You once asked me why I always shuddered and grew pale at the mention of Sidney Clarkson's name. I did not tell you then, but promised that, at some future time, I would tell you a long story about him and myself, and you should cease to wonder at a repugnance I am wholly unable to conceal. You know him only as a plausible, agreeable, handsome man of the world, full of outward courtesy and grace, and apparently careless and thoughtless of all grave and deep matters. Yet I remember you once said, that you could hardly understand how such a man as Clarkson *seemed* to be, could have such an eagle eye and such sharp-cut, firmly-closed lips; and that there was something in his smile that made you shiver. The truth is, that Sidney Clarkson is not what he seems to the world to be: he is a deep, unscrupulous, daring man, utterly devoid of principle, who hides his real nature behind a conventional mask, only that he may pursue, unmolested and unsuspected, the dark and tortuous paths of his own plans. He won the hand of Eleanor Walsingham in spite of herself; he conquered her, and she quailed before him, fearing even while she seemed to love him; her feeling for him was not love—it was a fascination, a subduing. Their courtship was a trial of strength between them; he won the victory, and led her like a slave—the beautiful trophy for the crowd to gaze at. How it happened that he thought it worth his while to struggle so hard for a prize which, with his cold worldly views and boundless ambition, could have been of little worth to him, must, I suppose, be explained by his liking for the struggle itself, and by the impossibility of gaining any victory without first establishing a closer intimacy than could exist with so proud and haughty a woman as Eleanor, without an open suitorship, an acknowledged engagement. Natures like his seem often to be, in their turn, dominated over by an irresistible necessity—they *must* give battle whenever they meet those possessing a certain degree of antagonism to themselves. To him the meeting with Eleanor was a direct challenge, which he had no power to resist; the contest must be fought, the victory must be decided. To a nobler mind than his the prize might have seemed a glorious one; but he was incapable of appreciating the great capabilities of her nature, and he passed like a blighting wind over her youth, and changed her fresh vigorous promise into dying helplessness. I used to wonder what had become of her overweening pride, her haughty coldness, her superb self-assertion, when I saw her bow down like a timid child before his cold, courteous requests. I did not then know the iron will which she saw beneath those few, well-chosen words.

It was during a visit I made at their charming country residence about a year after their marriage, that I learned myself to know what Clarkson really was. It was the attainment of this knowledge, involving as it did a severe struggle between us, that caused the cessation of all intercourse. It was on just such a day as this that the crisis came, and the different stages of the battle are associated in my memory with the rising or the lulling of the storm, the howling of the wind, or the hushed piteousness of the weary rain. He had frequently annoyed me by too personal an interest in my affairs, too keen a scenting into my modes and habits of life. He delighted in asking leading questions in regard to myself, boasted quietly of having wrung from Eleanor various particulars of my past life, which it was positively painful to me that he should know, and declared himself magnetically able to read in my countenance the most subtle changes of my emotional nature. He was fond of planning conversational surprises, commencing with harmless topics and by abrupt transition reverting to something touching myself, looking sharply at me all the while, to note any change of countenance or any unguarded remark—determined to break down in some way what he termed my unaccountable reserve. Eleanor's knowledge of me was itself imperfect, and, certain that his could be no greater, I thanked the constitutional reserve that had always prevented me from any but slight confidences and unimportant revelations of myself. What he knew had only awakened what I considered at first an idle curiosity particularly unbecoming an intellectual man. But his appetite for mental conflict was aroused, his enjoyment of struggling was at work, he knew enough of my individuality to see that it was one even more difficult of conquest than that of his wife; his spirits rose and his strength developed at each repulse he received, and he was confident that by putting forth all his reserved power, he must, eventually, bear down my bravest opposition; so he was disposed to prolong the stratagems and the skirmishes preliminary to marching into possession of the conquered country. He skilfully attempted to win my willing confidence by delicate expression of his sympathy for what I had suffered, and for aught he knew was still suffering; referred with tears in his eyes to his first meetings with me, declaring to my infinite astonishment that there had arisen from the first, a wonderful degree of sympathy between us, and, with suggestions so impalpable that at times they seemed never to have been really uttered, hinted touching regrets that we had not met before the existence of ties on both sides necessitated a conclusion which he expressed only by a deep-drawn sigh. But this Werterian aspect was too transient and too intangible for any action on my part, and while maintaining the existence of mutual affinity and his thorough understanding of my nature, he explained, with eloquent fervor, that his excess of reverence had always prevented him from entering into the inner sanctuary of my feelings, though knowing that he held in his hand its master-key. When I laughed at his rhapsodies he grew angry and sarcastic; when I was silent he became penitent and reverential again. At intervals he would lay aside all these personalities and be for days what he knew so well how to be—the most agreeable of companions, the most courteous of hosts; would captivate all who were within his home-circle by the charm of his manner, the brilliancy of his wit, and the variety of his accomplishments. So contrastive an organization I have never met in any one else, or one so completely under the control of its owner. His peculiarities extended into every aspect of life. Princely in his expenditure, magnificent in all his tastes, shrewd in acquisition though daring in speculation, and reckless of all established rules, he gloried in living upon the very crater of a volcano, and was exhilarated by the constant watchfulness and innumerable stratagems which his pecuniary affairs required. Even when the crash came he showed a fierce enjoyment of the new form which his excitement took, and held his poverty with the same iron grasp with which for a time he had held his wealth.

On the day to which I refer, he had roused me beyond myself, by his ever-changing yet pertinacious attacks, and I was chafing with an inward rage which it required all my efforts to conceal. The hours passed on, the storm with its powerful influences was oppressing my very soul, and I longed for the solitude of my own room, yet knew that he would regard my retreat as an acknowledgment of cowardice, which I did not really feel; as dread of a battle which, as I was now sure it must come some time, might as well come then. So I kept my storm-susceptibilities as quiet as possible, and my manner as serene as usual, while I inwardly prepared my forces for desperate conflict. What result he looked for in case of my ultimate surrender I did not ask myself—I doubt if he exactly knew himself. He fought for the sake of the battle, and would wait for the inspiration of the victory to suggest the disposition of the spoils. I fought for my soul's life, and with every energy I possessed, and yet through it all I never felt one pang of fear or one doubt of myself. I even enjoyed a sort of pleasurable excitement such as a spectator may feel in watching the movements of a champion on whom he feels an immutable reliance. I hardly knew what I was struggling against, yet with the unquestioning obedience I always offer to my instinctive perceptions, which warn me when I am in the presence of dark and bad natures, I buckled on my armor and kept my sword in my hand. My questions I put aside till, the battle over, I should be able to examine and answer them in fuller knowledge and more serene certainty. Our spirits rose as the warfare continued, till it was hand to hand and life for life. I kept guard over myself with all my power, my old discipline standing me in good stead; neither by taunt nor by entreaty, by question nor assumption of acquiescence in his proposed conclusions, would I reveal one glimpse of my heart, either in its past or its present, or allow that I had ever perceived any affinity of nature, of intellect, or of heart, between him and myself. What had at first involved only my intrusting him with my personal confidence grew to include the revelation and surrender of my consciousness and free will. For hours the wordy conflict lasted; I did not waver and he did not fall back. But he lost, to some extent, his power over himself, and as his excitement increased and his self-revelations became more decided, I grew, by very reaction, colder and calmer and better able to comprehend and fathom him. As he grew eloquent I grew impassive, as he lost self-command I grew serene, as passion made him weak just in proportion as it made him sincere, so all fear, all excitement died away within me, and I smiled to think how much I had really dreaded the encounter. Now I knew that there was no affinity between us; that the mere similarity of tastes, the outside likings of the intellect which by their resemblance had sometimes troubled me, were not incompatible with an actual separation of the two natures, as wide, as deep as, in this moment, I was proud to assert it. He had not followed my change of mood as closely as I had his; absorbed in his own feelings he was no longer cool enough for observation, and his astonishment was excessive when, interrupting him in the middle of a most romantic, and under other circumstances, a really touching appeal, I rose, and standing before him, gazed so steadily at him that his eyes fell beneath mine, and, slowly, calmly, scornfully I defied him and his wrath. I told him what I saw in him of serpent-cunning and of vilest wickedness; that he moved my will no more than the idle prattle of a child could do; and that, though at first I bore with him, as only half-understanding his crooked nature, he now stood revealed to me as only worthy of my scorn. I must have spoken strongly and daringly, for the change in him was instantaneous, and he attempted no remonstrance. Only he rose from the low seat on which he had been sitting, and bending his face to mine, he looked into my eyes as if to read my very soul. How I bore that intense gaze I do not know, but a power within me seemed to give me strength, and I did not quail or move—till, sinking once more upon the little seat, he covered his face with both his hands, murmuring as he did so, "Always yourself! I might have known you *could* not be as others!"

I turned away from him, and, without another word, left the room. He made no attempt to detain me, and I gained my own room unmolested. It was long past midnight, as the striking of the old hall clock told me as I went up the staircase. I remember only that I found my chamber door open, and that I mechanically closed and bolted it. I must have fainted immediately after, for, before the early summer morning broke, I found myself lying in the middle of the floor and suffering from such exhaustion that I could not at first recall any of the occurrences of the previous day, or comprehend how I came to be in such a condition. The shock to my nervous system had been so great, the tension of all my faculties so violent, that the reaction was fearful. I undressed myself, however, and went to bed and lay for a long while planning an immediate escape from the trying circumstances about me. It was impossible for me to risk seeing Mr. Clarkson again: yet I loved Eleanor too well to do anything which should cause her pain, and I had always reverenced the womanly reserve that had surrounded her every mention of her husband's name, so that I did not know how little or how much she understood him, or how much trust she might feel in my own loyalty to herself. Her health, even then very delicate, obliged her to keep early hours, so that she had retired the evening previous some time before the conversation between Mr. Clarkson and myself had passed beyond the bounds of courteous argument; but I knew that she would, as usual, come to my room in the morning and chat with me as, in my indolent way, I made my very gradual toilette. I soon heard her knock at my door, and her "Good morning, Ethel; are you up yet?" in which I could detect little change from her usual tone. I replied, through the closed door, that I was not very well, but would be down stairs soon after breakfast. She admitted the excuse, but added that her husband had left home at daybreak to visit a farm he owned some miles distant, and would be absent two days. Before those two days were past I had bidden farewell to poor Eleanor, who clung to me with most expressive fondness, and was on my way to my own home. It was long before I was able to recover my usual tone, and the complete exhaustion I experienced was proof that the struggle had been greater than I had imagined: the demand upon my strength more stringent than I had any idea of at the time. I have never been able to resist the paleness and the shudder which you noticed, when I am reminded of it, and I feel even now a sensation of exhaustion stealing over me at the memory. I have never referred to it, save in my own heart, and have kept the seal of secresy upon it all, even in my correspondence with Eleanor, which continued as friendly as ever for some time after my return. I never saw her or Mr. Clarkson again; they quarrelled soon after, and her friends insisted upon a separation. His affairs were in hopeless disorder, and her little fortune was swallowed up in the general ruin, while his character suffered severely in the investigations which followed his bankruptcy. He wore the same cold and haughty mien through all, however, and, after a year of separation, he, by his strange magic, brought his wife once more to his feet. Her naturally delicate frame had received terrible injury from the mental suffering she had endured, her proud spirit was broken by shame and misfortune, and she died very soon after her return to her husband. He has never crossed my path since, and the scenes which, in the passing, were so full of interest and action, have now faded into the past,—but they will never quite lose their painful power over me, or be for me an utterly dead remembrance. Poor Eleanor! her love and trust in me were very precious to me; and by a loving message sent to me from her death-bed I knew that she had understood all, and that she held me high in honor through an experience on which her wifely dignity imposed silence between us.

ETHEL

LETTER THIRD

I HAVE been ill, my beloved, ill in soul and body—I have needed you, and you were not nigh—but the thought of you has never left me. Your picture hangs by my bedside, and I have lain, hushed and still, gazing upon it, till the soul I knew so well has seemed to speak through those calm eyes, and I have held communion with you through that mute image of yourself. And now I am able to read your letters, which mistaken friends kept from me for awhile,—ah! they have done me more good in both my maladies, than all the draughts I swallowed, all the slumber I could grasp. I am growing stronger every day, and my mind is recovering its tone; before you are able to reach me I shall be quite well, and we will spend the summer-time, which waits but for your coming to make it completely beautiful, in delicious wanderings by the seashore and amid our grand old woods. I look with longing for you, my beloved; my heart is hungry and my spirit is athirst for you,—only in your presence am I entirely myself. The fulness and freedom with which the magnetic current flows through my veins when you are near me, is wonderful even to me, who am so subject to its influences, so responsive to its changes. The subtle element is always at work within me; always demanding some outlet of expression, some positive direction for its action. When poured forth too freely it produces an exhaustion so entire, a prostration so universal as to be fearful. Only once or twice in my life have I thus lost command of myself, thus abandoned my individuality, and then it seemed as if recovery were impossible, as if the physical frame so shared the suffering of the spirit that its weary weakness could never more become strength and health. When pent up within myself too closely, and denied utterance, as it has been in several arid seasons in my life, this magnetic force accumulates and flows back upon myself, chafing and wearing at the very fountain of my life. Never has it found such harmonious and healthful outlet as through my love for you, never have I felt such delicious and invigorating movement through my inner life as when it mingles with your own equally strong but far better directed forces.

I remember once talking with a very dear friend upon this very subject; a friend made such with a rapidity which the pressure of outward circumstances added to inward attraction, could alone explain. We were placed in circumstances of peculiar isolation, thrown into each other's hearts for shelter from the weary conventionalism of all around us, and our love grew, as it were, in a hot-house atmosphere with all the cold winds shut out. We lived within our own little love-dwelling, with none to even ask for entrance. In one of the many long and confidential conversations which we held together, after perfect freedom had been established between us, I said, "Do you believe that any person has power really to infuse his own vitality into another, really to supply fresh impulse to another's exhaustion, and to feed and refresh with renewing force those who have ceased for a time to supply their own needs?"

"How should I *not* believe it," was the reply, "when I have myself experienced it? Have not you 'infused vitality' into me? When we first met, was not I in a state of deplorable and utter stagnation and depression—and have not you lifted and restored me to myself? Have you not poured the warm current of life into my cold, faint pulses, and made my blood throb full and strong again? The shadows that encompassed me are fled, and I stand in the clear sunlight. The chilling atmosphere of indifference is dispelled, and I revel in the more than tropic warmth of living love. How or why it is that you have done all this, or why, with your brave strong nature, you have stooped to love so poor and weak a thing as I am, I ask not—I care not—it is enough for me to acknowledge and to feel grateful for it. But I tremble to think that the time is coming when our parting must throw me into a sadder state than ever; sadder it must be, for I have known such joy and peace of late that the darkness must seem still deeper by force of contrast. Therefore do not leave me utterly, but in some way let me feel, from time to time, that you are not all lost to me. You will not need me, but I shall need you, oh, so much!"

And so I am ever conscious of this strange, incomprehensible spiritual influence within myself. Only rarely do I exercise it outwardly, only rarely do I give it position and new direction with my will. Usually I satisfy its needs by letting it flow along through the old channels of my established friendships; but when, as in the case I have just told you of, I meet with such a temptation to do good, I rejoice to give of my abundance to one who is perishing from want. There is need, of course, of some stimulus through the affections; I feel attracted by the individual or my will remains dormant;—I know not even that I *could* give of my own vitality unto one I did not love, or if it could be received into a nature antagonistic to my own. But when there exists a sympathy between the emotional natures, my will can send a living flood through the heart, and I thrill with an answering joy and rise to a higher delight as I see the renewing of the life of my friend. In this instance the process was peculiarly apparent and full of interest to me. The physical sympathies were very ready in the organism of my friend, my own sensational powers were at that time in full strength, and the attraction which drew our spiritual natures together was followed by a mingling of some of my superfluous inner energies with her prostrate and enervated susceptibilities.

It is quite extraordinary how great a difference there is, not only in the proportion of active, outgoing, magnetic power in different individuals, but also in the simply receptive element. Some who can give seem absolutely incapable of receiving—the most delicate and subtle returning fluid fails to win entrance at the door which opens but for egress to those within. Those persons strike us as hard and cold of nature, and even in subduing others, they chill and mortify the grateful and generous impulses which would come forth to meet and pay them homage. Others seem to have so large a capacity of reception and are so open to all floating magnetic forces, that it is matter of continual wonder that the accumulation does not of itself become active and pour forth of its abundance upon the other lives which stand about it in bitter need. But the two powers in persons of each class remain always distinct; the first cannot receive, the second cannot give; the want of wholeness of nature, of harmony of development, from time to time reveals itself, and disappoints those who had hoped for higher and grander manifestation. There are, however, exceptional natures capable of both giving largely and receiving fully, in which the flux and reflux of the magnetic element is as the mighty tide of ocean, not like the tributary flowing of the river, bound on its unreturning errand to the sea. These natures move grandly on through their own orbits, rejoicing in their own fulness and planetary serenity of steady force, and render a large obedience to the great laws which regulate the universe—an obedience as full of grandeur and of power as their own sovereignty over lesser things is complete. These spherical natures are very rare, and have almost infinite influence over the inferior ones brought in contact with them; and it is fortunate that their very greatness necessitates a loyal and noble truthfulness to great principles, and that they would scorn to use their strength for any but the noblest and most elevated objects. I do not hesitate to write to you, beloved Ernest, all my thoughts about this magnetic element, so little understood, so little even guessed at by careless natures. To me it seems one of the grandest and most effective of all psychological forces, the master-key of our human nature, the manifestation of our sympathy with the divine mind, the power by which all spiritual attainment both for the individual and for the mass is to be harmoniously and profitably directed and carried on. In its grandest development it is the propelling power of the universe, in its lesser expression it warms the heart and modifies the life. It is great enough for the first, and it does not disdain to render beautiful the last. Its diversity and inequality make its social movement; its possessors are lords and peers among men, and none are degraded by paying them reverence, for their dignity comes from no accidental circumstance, but is of divine ordaining. Its possession brings a responsibility quite commensurate with its value, and weighs down to sadness even the strongest and most hopeful. I know that you regard it as I do; that you share as largely as myself, in the possession of this wonderful intangibility; and that although we rejoice in our gift, yet we can never lightly use it and never dare to desecrate it. Neither can we sit down contented with ourselves and leave it in inaction. Those who possess it, and in whom it moves, as the Spirit of God once moved over the face of the waters, are ever looking earnestly for the light, and striving to create order out of the chaos about them.

Susceptibility of this kind is almost always accompanied by a high degree of susceptibility through the imaginative and even through the sensational nature. All impressions are readily received, whether they come in the tangible form of daily variety, or in the subtle and invisible essence of mental phenomena. In delicate physical organizations this vibration of impressions becomes more visible than in stronger and more robust natures. In me it is constantly perceptible, at least to myself. It is an ever present influence, which throbs within me as the waves of the ocean surge and swell; it continues even during my sleep. The character of my slumber is as that of my waking hours to those who know me beneath my external seeming, and see the movement under the apparent stillness. My repose is physically quiet, to a remarkable degree; not a finger moves, not a breath is quickened, as I have been told by those who have watched my sleep till they have wakened me, out of very fear that it was sleep no longer. But in my heart and brain a storm may even then be raging, or a delirium of enjoyment swaying me hither and thither. I hear the muttering of thunder and the hoarse murmur of the threatening winds, or I melt in deepest ecstasy over Elysian fancies, and glow beneath the fiery excitement of my dream-creations.

It was but yester-night that I was visited by fair and beautiful and joy-giving dreams. Whether they arose from your loving letter, which lay near my heart, and were obeying the impulses which distort conclusions a great way from their legitimate premises, as often happens in dream phenomena, I do not know. But with such a garb of glory did they invest the night, that I mourned when the rude touch of morning rent in pieces the delicate rainbow-tinted fabric. Past my rapt senses swept a train of visionary joys; through the charmed atmosphere swelled the Æolian dream-music, and through my tranced soul thrilled passions and emotions and sensations, glowing, tremulous, intense, as the most subtle inspiration of Hasheesh. I caught such glimpses of the olden days as they lay far away in the faint dawnings of the Eastern sky—such scintillations of the future, as it gleamed in the golden glory of the Western clouds, that the brazen hardness of the garish noon-tide, which is really above my head, and beneath which I pant so wearily, passed into happy forgetfulness.

Sometimes these dreams were vague but delicious, unreasoning and without order or regularity. At other times they took tangible forms, and I lived through them a life-like experience; my heart throbbed quick and strong, as in seasons of actual and concentrated emotion. You will smile, when I retrace the most vivid of these, to

see what form its presiding spirit chose to take. I seem to find in the
circumstance one more confirmation of the theory, which, though I
shrink from it, I cannot but believe in—that however free we may be
in forming and beginning our heart-ties, and creating our friendships,
our freedom cannot extend to their destruction after they have really
obtained an existence. We may make the image if we will, but, if it
prove hideous, we cannot rid ourselves of it when we weary of it or
discover its enormity—it clings to us as the monster to Frankenstein,
and appears from time to time to prove to us that it is ours. So, if a
friendship is once formed, once incorporated into our being, we can
never utterly destroy it, nor be as if it had never been. The subtle
life-spirit, once evoked, will not die; its influence will not entirely fade
away. This restraint upon our volition, I remember, you once indignantly denied, but afterwards acknowledged with a sigh. Well, my
dream seems a confirmation of this matter,—an assertion that, when
the conscious and directing powers are in abeyance, when spontaneous and unrestrained impulses are at work within, the images and
the heart-realities we thought laid asleep for ever can rise up in their
old strength and declare to us their continued dominion. This dream
will long linger in my memory: I was, as I thought, lying on my couch
in a delicious reverie; summer perfumes were about me; the breath
of roses entered at the open window; the hum of bees made the air
musical, and their soft droning sound wove itself into my musings with
a sweet and soothing power. As I lay thus in a trance of quiet bliss, the
door opened quickly, and Leonora entered, with that peculiar rushing
step, which, with her, is always an indication of intense excitement,
and produces such effect from its contrast with her usual quiet movements and almost passionless manner—that manner with which she
strives to hide that stormy, fiery, tempestuous nature of hers. Turning
her eyes upon me with all that intense expression of passionate love
with which she used to greet me after an absence from me, and which
I never saw in any mortal eyes but hers, set forth with such glowing,
almost painful, intensity, she threw herself upon my neck, and clasping me with the fierce fondness of a lioness to her heart, till I felt its
throbbings against my own, she bent over me with that longing, burning look, as if to read my very soul. In a moment, however, that look
changed to one of dewy softness and timid supplication, and sinking on
her knees, with her arms still around my neck, she smothered me with

hot kisses, and murmured in my ear, "Is it not all forgotten, my beloved Ethel? say it is all forgotten!" And as those sweet tones of entreaty fell upon the air, a magic spell came over all things, and it *was* all forgotten, and I pressed her once more to my heart and soothed her with words of endearment, till I hushed those tremulous beatings into stillness, and she rested in my arms as a little child. And, as we lay there side by side for uncounted hours, as it seemed, the charm of the old days came back upon us; the thrill of old loving returned; we felt that there was no longer any need of asking or of giving pardon for the old offences, but that they might pass into a deep, unbroken slumber. And then ensued such passionate outpourings of her long pent-up love, such eloquent prayers from her sweet lips, such tears from her wonderful eyes, that all the past rose up in new strength, and I knew that a strange and irrevocable tie still bound us two together, and we could never really part.

I gave myself up with delirious joy to this impression; for a time I lived but for her and her love, and grew proud and happy as I saw the light in her eyes become once more the soft, sweet trustfulness of the old time. She seemed to resign herself once more utterly to me, to have no consciousness but mine, to live through my life, and even while leaving off all her own strong individuality, to thrill me with a sense of renewed and increased vitality, to throw her own rapid pulses into the calmer current of my veins, and make me, in spite of myself, share in her own superabundant passion. And when, at last, I woke and found myself alone, I could not believe that the cloud which is between us was not dispelled, the coldness was not gone, the wrongs were not lying in slumber, and our hearts were not beating in unison. A sensation of sickness came over my heart, an irrepressible longing weighed me down; I yearned, for a moment, with an overpowering desire for one more hour with her I had loved so well. But I looked up at your picture, my beloved Ernest, and in that one instant I regained my calmness,—I was once more myself, and dream-fancies fled away before the magical influence of your serene gaze. I bless the artist every day of my life for the faithfulness with which he has portrayed your worshipped image. There is in the picture the same marvellous strength and calm earnestness, which is so predominant in yourself— how should I live without it when you are far from me? The image of Leonora faded away, her strange fascination was at an end, her moral image seemed to emerge from her bewilderingly beautiful physical one, and to stand forth for my condemnation as a traitorous and unworthy nature. But was it not strange she should come to resume her influence over me and acknowledge the supremacy of mine over her, in moments when all voluntary disguises are laid aside and the heart seems able to assert itself without restraint or direction from the will? Does it not prove that I am right when I say that spite of the coldness which I myself have maintained in my relations with her, spite of the contempt I feel for her, and which she knows I feel, spite of absence, of silence, of estrangement, we are, after all, not utterly separated? Strange, wayward, beautiful serpent that she was, that same invisible bond united us on the higher ground on which she walked erect so long, that it seemed she could never fall. The faithful reproduction of so many of the old elements of our connexion, made my dream most vivid; and the peculiarity which these dreams of mine often possess of allowing a sort of double consciousness in myself, through which I am able to pause and examine, as it were, each subtle change in emotion, quite impossible when waking hours are swayed by any strong impulse, imparts a strange power to these dream-episodes. They seem, in the retrospect, quite as real as any true and actual experience of the past—they exhilarate or they depress, excite or subdue my whole spirit. My dreams of you are always thus vivid; they are so free from any distorted exaggerations, you come to me with words and looks so like your own, that I sometimes think that absence is cheated of half its sadness, and that you really do visit me on the wings of the night-wind. It would gladden your very heart within you, sometimes, and bring your most loving smile to your lips, to be really present at one of these intangible interviews. I will not tell you all their sweetness till you come yourself to fill out the grand proportions of this ideal being who comes through barred windows and bolted doors, in spite of storm and darkness, and heedless of distance and time and space, to cheer the heart which the long day has made dreary and desolate. Come still unto my dreams, true heart!—the inmost recesses of my own stand open with a welcome—no door is closed, no corner hidden from your eyes. I am all yours, and sleeping or waking I am ever ready for the entrance of my king.

ETHEL

LETTER FOURTH

EITHER my last letter to you, dear Ernest, or the dream which I related to you in it, has brought up the remembrance of Leonora to my mind so forcibly, that I have not been able to banish her from my waking or my sleeping thoughts, without going over step by step and memory by memory, that portion of my past which is so closely connected with her. I always find this the best way to get rid of fancies which haunt and annoy me—allow them full sway for awhile, let them carry me whither they will, and as long as they will, by their own impulse,—neither hurry nor retard them in their progress, and after a time, their force is spent and the whole matter subsides into its true place. The evil spirit is exorcised, and I am at peace without the wearisome struggle by which alone I could have combated and conquered them. I have, therefore, been dwelling much upon the past since I last wrote you, have been recalling the incidents in which Leonora bore so prominent a part, living over again the vehement emotions which then tore my heart; and in connexion with this, have once more indulged the habit of analysis so natural to me, and against which you so lovingly caution me. It is my first transgression, dearest, and I believe that, in this instance, you would sanction my course as the one best adapted to restore to me a degree of contentment and acquiescence in the circumstances which took her from me. I am steadfast in my nature, as you know, and strong attachments once rooted in my heart are not readily eradicated; and it is only through repeated proof of the poisonous nature of the plant I have cherished, that I find power to tear it out from my life.

The more I think of Leonora, the more extraordinary contradiction does she appear to me; the more do I wonder how I had strength to carry me through the struggle that ended in my putting her from me for ever. You must not think from this that I regret the course I felt obliged to follow, or that I would swerve from it, were it to be done again—but, oh, Ernest, I *do* wish that it had never been necessary, or that at least I might have broken the bond more tenderly—for I know she loved me in spite of all; and even in what she did, those strange, contradictory attributes of hers enabled her to separate the friend whom she was loving from the woman whom she was injuring. Her duplicity seems to me an unfortunate gift of nature, by which she was compelled to live a dual life, and in each aspect of it to be acting a lie. Her whole existence was vibratory; she swung hither and thither almost at random, traversing all extremes of loving sweetness and pathetic tenderness, as well as of revengeful bitterness and stormy passion. Her intercourse with me was one unbroken manifestation of the better and more beautiful part of her nature, and I had seen so many glorious capabilities that I felt within myself a tender sorrow at her sin rather than an anger at being the one injured by it.

Yet we both know, Ernest, do we not? that anything less than the stern words spoken, the entireness and severity of my condemnation of her, would have been worse than useless. How I did it all is now a mystery to me, and my brain reels to think of it. She had been so much to me, and had so carefully guarded, as she thought, against all possibility of my discovering aught in her save the loving, sunny side of her nature which she turned towards me, that I sometimes think she might have learned to really love and feel the purity and truthfulness she was striving to make me see in her, and that her words were true when she said, "I am better when with you, Ethel, than I am at any other time, therefore keep me with you, and do not leave me to myself." But when I grieve myself with thinking that I may have thrown away the only opportunity for raising and ennobling her, and charge myself with selfish disregard of her better aspirations, the recollection of what I know of her in other relations of her life, proves to me that her apparently noble moments were but episodes in a life full of dark and degrading impulse and unworthy action. It needed no other proof of her extraordinary mental power and strong discipline than to see, as I did, how she could keep out of sight during our long seasons of intimate intercourse, every one of those, at other apparently uncontrollable evil impulses of hers, which broke out in such savage and peculiar directions. The serpent slept while the flowers blossomed about him, and the gleaming of his glossy skin seemed only the sunshine lying on their fresh sweet leaves.

It pleased her so much to think I only knew her in her relations to myself, only in the present that existed for us both, and which was, from a combination of peculiar circumstances, entirely disjoined from her own actual past—that I had not the heart to tell her how thoroughly her antecedents were known to me, how vividly the picture of her whole past had been painted for me by that quaint colorist and far-seeing Everard Stanley. He used to delight himself and annoy me with revelations of every possible kind in regard to Leonora, and urged his sister to say what he dared not utter; and though I could not but regret that there was so much for them to tell, I kept their secret to the last, and she has never known how I became possessed of her history, as I felt it my duty, when we separated, to let her know that I was. I knew that Everard and Alice were true as truth itself; I knew that he regretted nearly as much as I the crooked falseness of Leonora, even while my apparent incredulity tempted him into more and more graphic details, and piqued him to a greater accumulation of facts; but I clung to a secret hope that the present might be a turning-point in Leonora's life, and I wished her to know that I would stand her friend, in spite of her past, if she would but remain loyal to me, against whom she had then never sinned, not so much for the effect it might have upon myself, as because an unswerving loyalty to me would imply a promise of and a longing for something higher and truer in her whole future. I did not feel myself to be compromised in this, for I felt that my complete knowledge was itself a sufficient protection, and I ever held certain portions of myself aloof from her touch, keeping sacred much of my dearest and most interior soul-life. It was chiefly in my intellectual nature that she came closest to me; and although there were, as I have said, certain other strong affinities between us, making daily intercourse full of charm   yet I should never have depended entirely upon her or felt willing to lift for her the curtain of my innermost reserves. I had no need of her, however, in this way; I was already rich in true friends, and my nature does not require to pour itself forth in unreserved expression to each new claimant of my heart's hospitality. The deepest love of my heart, the richest gift of my soul, the offering of my past sorrow and the trembling hope of coming peace, had been laid at your feet, and I could crown but one king within my heart—to him and to him alone, could I reveal myself completely—yet though I wish not to worship but one, I could have loved her and enjoyed much with her on a different level. I would not and could not have made of her a planet in my heaven, on which to depend for the regulation of my inner forces, nor yet have placed her among those few fixed stars from whose clearness and calmness I learn lessons of spiritual serenity—but she might at least have been something better than a meteor shooting with brilliant flash across my sky, to fall at last a dark and useless heap of stones.

The study and analysis of such an organism as hers are full of interest to one who possesses the key to its contradictions. The inconsistencies of women are generally more subtle than those of men, and affect their actions with a more delicate and intangible power. Women often love each other with as much fervor and excitement as they do men. When this is the case, there is generally rare beauty both in the feeling and in its manifestations, great generosity in its intuitions, and the mutual intercourse is marked by charming undulations of feeling and expression. The emotions awakened heave and swell through the whole being as the tides swell the ocean. Freed from all the grosser elements of passion, as it exists between the sexes, it retains its energy, its abandonment, its flush, its eagerness, its palpitation, and its rapture—but all so refined, so glorified, and made delicious and continuous by an ever-recurring giving and receiving from each to each. The electricity of the one flashes and gleams through the other, to be returned not only in *degree* as between man and woman, but in *kind* as between precisely similar organizations. And these passions are of much more frequent occurrence than the world is aware of—generally they are unknown to all but the parties concerned, and are jealously guarded by them from intrusive comment. "There is a gloom in deep love as in deep water," and silence and mystery help to guard the sacred spot where we go to meet our best-beloved friends. The world sees only the ordinary appearances of an intimate acquaintanceship, and satisfies itself with a few common-place comments thereon—but the joy and beauty of the tie remain in sweet concealment—silent and inexpressive when careless eyes are upon it, but leaping into the sunlight when free from cold and repelling influences.

I have had my passionate attachments among women, which swept like whirlwinds over me, sometimes scorching me with a furnace-blast, but generally only changing and renewing the atmosphere of my life. I have loved so intensely that the daily and nightly communion I have held with my beloved ones has not sufficed to slake my thirst for them, nor the lavishness of their love for me been able to satisfy the demands of my exacting nature. I would "have drunk their soul as 'twere a ray from heaven"—have lost myself and lived in them—and this too in spite of that trait of non-absorption which you so often tell me I possess. I absorb others, yet am never absorbed by them; but I have longed to be so, have yearned to leave off for a little while this burden of individuality which cuts into the very soul of me as sackcloth grates upon the shrinking flesh. Oh, how I have at times wished to lie down and fall asleep in another's consciousness, and give my panting, quivering vitality a little rest. There have been seasons when this unattainable desire to leave off my own separate existence with its too intense experience, and merge my own heart-life in the less fluctuating and less extensive alternations of another, has exhausted every energy of my soul, and made my inner self rise up before me in gigantic and frightful proportions, seeming like some fearful phantom ever walking by my side and holding me bound fast in strong but invisible bonds.

I loved Claudia thus—loved?—nay, I worshipped her, I poured out at her feet all the wealth of my young girlish heart; and what a glorious life I led with her strong high soul, which took me into such lofty companionship—so far above me as she was—and yet the greatness of my love lifted me to her. My soul sought and found in her every emotion which passed over it, and my confidence flowed forth in one unswerving, unfaltering trust to her. The proof of the grandeur and truth of this love of mine was not only in the length of time it continued, but still more in the fact that it grew up side by side with another grand passion which devastated my nature, and destroyed for a while in me the very fountain of my inner life. Had not Claudia been the truest and most loving of friends, my heart would have withered and died out in the struggles of that time.

Leonora could never have been to me what Claudia has been—the serene loftiness, the entire truthfulness, the unselfish devotion, which made Claudia so perfect in all the relations of friendship, were all wanting in Leonora. But there was a great deal in the feminine beauty, the bewitching grace, the delightful piquancy, and the brilliant intellect of Leonora to fascinate and to subdue. She disarmed judgment by her charming ways, she overpowered coldness by her magnetic attraction. Our intercourse was delightful—there was no repose in it, but the action was of that delicious, self-sustaining sort that never wearied or exhausted either. When I think of the hours we have spent together, a smile, as at the recollection of an intense pleasure, rises to my lips. She acted as a continual spur to my intellectual activity, and was always ready to join me in the race after an intellectual prize. The demands she made upon me, she made also upon herself; and the amount of brain-work which she exacted from herself to remedy the insufficiency of her early education, was really astonishing. You knew her only as a handsome coquette, a somewhat daring inquirer into men and things, a not over-scrupulous searcher after experience; you could never see her as I have seen her, when all the higher and better parts of her contradictory nature were in full force. You never saw the gay and vain ball-room belle of the evening transformed into the serious student of the morning; or heard the lips that seemed formed for repartee and gay nonsense grow eloquent upon great themes. If her heart had been as true as her mind was comprehensive, she would have been a rarely-gifted woman, but her flight into the heavens was impeded by sordid chains and mean obstacles. She had not even truth enough to be really sincere in deploring her own deficiencies, or to make any hearty efforts towards a higher plane. Her aspirations were strong, and lifted her at times to an apparent height; but they were not true, and did not really raise her above herself, and after the momentary effort was over, she returned to her earthliness and was contented in that as before. Each mood was an episode, each impulse valuable to her as supplying new sensations, and all in turn lost their value and their meaning when they lost their freshness and ceased to bring her exciting experiences. She seemed not under her own control in these matters, and in spite of her unusually powerful will, which bent to her purposes nearly all those with whom she came in contact, she was often swayed herself by influences to which she scorned to acknowledge her susceptibility. To be sure, these influences seemed always to have their birth within herself, they rose as vapors from the soil, and she was marble to all external forces, impenetrable to persuasion, untouched by entreaty, unmoved even by open scorn in her daily intercourse with others. It was something to be proud of, after all, to be able to bend her iron will to my own, to force my own volition through her thoughts and acts as I have often done. And the proud humility with which she could submit, the loving glance with which she gave her obedience, were full of an indescribable charm to one with a temperament like my own, full of its own strong contrasts and antagonisms.

You know all the circumstances which revealed her whole nature to me and brought our intimate communion to a sudden stop. I rejoice that you were near me to sanction all my words, to sustain me through the pain I suffered at first, and to encourage me in the despondency which followed. You forgave my many evidences of weakness, had patience with my complaints over my loss, and soothed the regrets I could not help but feel. It was my first quarrel—it was the first time I had been called upon to express contempt for any one for whom I had felt love—pray Heaven it be the last!—and but that indignation supplied the necessary impetus to my expression, I might have kept silence. I have sometimes, on minor matters, had seasons of quite refreshing indignation, but they have almost always been in behalf of others or for matters not really interwoven with my own consciousness. To those who have crossed my orbit at those rare intervals when Mars has been in the ascendant, I have sometimes spoken or written harsh things with a momentary enjoyment. When I speak them, it is always in a low voice and with apparent calmness, the result, I suppose, of the concentration of my emotions upon a given point; when I write them I always write boldly, freely and rapidly, dash on the ink and spread open my pen that the venom may flow forth with the black fluid. My page assumes a hardness and sharpness of outline in consonance with my feelings, and it affects the motion of my hand to such a degree, that I cannot immediately divest myself of it, but continue for days to write in a large, bold hand. The very contrast which this affords to my usually unexpressional nature supplies a kind of fiery enjoyment for the moment. There is a charm in honest anger, a pleasure in its outburst, when there is no motive for its concealment. Such seasons of tempest are very exhausting to me, however, and it is well that they come but seldom. Anger is not a common feeling with me, and when it comes, it implies a long, or at least an intense previous experience. I am so generally indifferent to those matters which rouse anger in others, that I often seem amiably self-possessed when I am merely unconscious. But the effect of this is an accumulation within of a concentrated power of expression when the real occasion comes. When I am roused I rush fiercely and warmly into the conflict, I feel completely awake, my brain grows active, my words come fluently and with more point and pithiness than at other times, I fancy my perceptions are keener, my mental faculties are all on the alert, I like the conflict while it is fresh and new, and until I am *tired of it*, I can do battle with vigor and effect. But almost always I get weary of the whole matter, and am the first to smile at my vehemence—very, very rarely have I felt long-continued anger—only once or twice in my whole life has positive passion pervaded me with its white heat of power. Then it has burned even my own nature, after scorching those on whom its first blaze lighted, and eaten into my own energies like a subtle poison which destroys even while it exhilarates.

Leonora has passed out of my daily and active life—I shut her out also from my heart, yet she does and she will meet me sometimes in my inner consciousness, when I abandon myself to reverie, or when night brings me dreams. I shall probably never see her face again, I would not if I could; if we meet it will be as strangers, and yet the niche in my heart and life which she filled remains unoccupied; and I know, though my name may never cross her lips, that I visit her in the night hours as she visits me—that a wailing cry for the love she has lost sometimes escapes her—that there is an invisible bond which still unites each to the other. If repentance and regret could have availed aught in such a case, there was no lack of either on her part, I am sure. Our subtle essences mingled and assimilated too thoroughly ever to be entirely disunited. I do not miss her in my daily walk in the world, for in the world we were little associated together; but in my dreamy hours, or in my intellectual labor, I turn involuntarily for her assistance, her sympathy, her quick appreciation. I would like at some time to discuss more at length with you this peculiar relationship of one individuality to another, with its apparent indestructibility, and in connexion with it to know what you think of the influence of character upon affection, as it shows itself in our likes and dislikes, and enters or remains on the outside of our deepest heart experiences. It is a subject full of contradictions, and, as it seems to me, involving many spiritual phenomena and concealing great spiritual truths.

And now, dear Ernest, that I have exorcised this haunting demon Leonora, have laid her to sleep again, we will turn from her and the traitorous air she breathes to our own warm and pure atmosphere of life and love and truth. How the remembrance of those sunny summer days we spent together comes over me now with life-giving beauty! And how those pictures of the woods and streams by which we wandered, come up in this dark, sad, winter-time,—when I am doubly widowed of you and of beautiful Nature—to gladden and encourage me. Your letters are like the summer flowers to me, your love is as the great ocean by which we sat so often and whispered our whole souls unto each other. Summer is coming again, my Ernest, and with her comes my summer's crown of life and light—yourself. Oh, how my heart expands beneath the blue and open sky, how it fills itself with glory and with bliss, as the summer breeze brings me your words of love mingling with the soft wooing air! Oh, come, sweet summer, and, oh, come my sweeter love! Your own

ETHEL

LETTER FIFTH

My own dear Ernest,

As the snows of winter wear away, as the stern coldness yields little by little to the wooing sun, as the bits of grass show themselves with a whispered promise that they will ere long be green and bright once more—the thought of you comes with more of welcome, more of renewal, more of promise to my heart than even summer can offer to weary Nature. It is a source of joy to me that your image is so interwoven with my summer dreams, that our interviews, our mutual associations are so completely removed from the sphere of ordinary conventionalisms and all "social fictions," and lifted into the purer and more serene atmosphere of external nature. Our hearts have learned to love and trust each other—not in the midst of gaiety and fashion, not in the ball-room, nor even by the fireside with its pleasant and genial but also varied and broken inner life—but in the clear air of heaven, and amid the sweet influences of the glorious summer. We have worshipped in a hypæthral temple, and the sun has beamed upon us with warm and loving glances as we have grown to love each other, or the moon has smiled on us as we have acknowledged that love, while the sea has chanted its sweetest, grandest, fullest anthem, as we have hushed our hearts into awe-struck but happy silence. We have joined in its great Te Deum, though our lips have not moved, and in our devotion to each other we have not forgotten the Great Father from whom our love and our joy have come. I should have loved you, doubtless, had all environments been otherwise; my hand would have thrilled in yours had it been clasped in the gayest dance, my heart would have gone forth to meet you had we been hedged in by the most formal courtesy, and my whole soul would have melted beneath the fire of your glance had it fallen on me only as I stood amid the crowd. But it is beautiful not to struggle with these adverse influences,— beautiful to have been spared all these drawbacks, all these chilling and dwarfing environments. It has been the more delightful to me because my heart was already so weary with those outside shows; that it longed so for relief from what had weighed it down till it seemed there was never more to be any freedom for it.

And, more than all, dear Ernest, there has been the sense of contrast to me in all our intercourse: the contrast with that first feverish dream of mine. How can I be thankful enough that I dare speak of the past to you as to my own soul; that you know even as I know, just what that experience was; that you understand just how much of my heart and life were absorbed by it, and just how much remained untouched! Above all, that you recognise as I do, how powerful that experience has been in developing, in strengthening, and in bringing out all of myself which is best worth knowing and being. A less generous man than yourself would have reproached me when I have sometimes trembled at my recollections; a less loving one would not have forgiven my first wayward struggles against your growing influence over me; a less noble, a less wise, a less far-seeing man, would never have understood, have sympathized with, assisted and trusted me, as you have done. You can never know how full of grandeur your position towards me has been, for a portion of its beauty has consisted in the very unconsciousness and simplicity with which you have acted out your own self. And the reward is yours in all its fulness. The dream is passed and powerless; more than all, it is known to have been a dream, and the reality of my whole life has been almost untouched; the strength of my whole soul has been unimpaired; the fire and earnestness of my whole being have been unexhausted, that I might stand forth in full knowledge of myself, and give myself to you for ever. How every feverish emotion, every childish impulse, every extravagant outburst, fade away into fantastic shadows, and pale before the clear and glowing sunlight of my great love for you. Now I *know* what it is to love. I smile to think what I once imagined it to be.

I was so young when all that I now call "the past" happened to me! It seems so far away, so mist-like and vague, compared to the sharp-cut and real emotions of the present. I was but sixteen when I first met Percy Hamilton. Was he not a fitting hero for a young girl's romance? I look at him now from a simply æsthetic point of view, and I cannot wonder that, upon an impressible, enthusiastic girl like me, he produced the effect of a god-like apparition. I wonder at this no more than I do at my perfect calmness in looking back upon it, or at the utter powerlessness for influence which such a person would have upon me now. How magnificently handsome he was! The very absence of manly energy was an additional charm to that delicate, spiritual, poetic face of his; to my inexperienced judgment it told, not of weakness and inaptitude for a world of reality, but only of refined ideality and poetry. The dreamy languor of those large soft eyes seemed so in keeping with the sweet low voice, the slight and fragile figure, and even those small white hands which many a woman envied. But I think, after all, the great fascination he exercised over me, apart from the charm of his long-continued wooing, lay in the fact that with me he was so utterly unlike what he was in the world at large. His calm and high-bred indifference and languor were exchanged for a timid eagerness, an excitement almost uncontrollable; his voice would tremble when he spoke to me, even in the presence of others. I have seen him turn pale when I entered the room, even though it seemed impossible that he could, from his position, have observed my entrance; and have seen his countenance vary in apparent response to what I have said to others, at so great a distance as to preclude all possibility of his having heard the words I uttered. Whenever I was in the crowd I knew that he saw me, though he never attracted the attention of those about him by appearing to follow my movements; his languid and somewhat careless general manner never varied so as to be perceptible to a stranger. I never saw him really look at any other woman, or appear to be aware of the gaze of others upon him; though he was a decided favorite in general society, he seemed only sufficiently conscious of the presence of others to go through the external forms of politeness in his own graceful way, remaining, so far as their individuality was concerned, in the complete solitude of his own soul. But when his eye met mine it was as if his whole heart longed to pour itself forth in one glance. I used to tremble at his look, spite of my delight at calling it forth; the intensity of that mournful longing, the depth of that sad bitterness which dwelt there when he thought me cold to him, or the triumphant gleam, the fiery exultation, which flashed like lightning over me if he won any expression of love from me,—oh, it was all so strange from him, and so different from what the world saw in him, that there was all the charm of mystery, all the piquancy of exclusiveness to heighten it for me.

I never had time for thought, he wrapped me up in the whirlwind of his own passion, and swept me along so rapidly that I lost breath as it were in the flight. I had little opportunity for self-questioning or examination, for sensation followed sensation and action succeeded action—I had no time to study him dispassionately, for his phases changed with every interview, and he varied in everything but in his love for me; he used to say that his love was really himself, and that all his other feelings, actions, words, were but as the garments which he put on for a day or for an occasion. Yet I could always soothe his wildest excitement even as I roused it, and a storm of reproaches about some trifle, or the intensest outpouring of passion which would follow some fancied injustice towards him, would yield to the sweetest and most confiding trust, the most entire and unquestioning self-surrender. He was of a most jealous temper too—I was continually in fear of a scene—perhaps needlessly so, since the conventional self-control he had acquired through so much intercourse with society, never really deserted him, and his pride also stood him in good stead;—but when we were alone together, the paroxysms of his jealous rage were frightful—and yet I never loved him half so well as when I needed all my own energy to withstand him, and when he was lifted up from the position of a suppliant lover into that of an imperious tyrant. You may imagine what a strange and changeable intercourse we had—I was in a kind of delirium of excitement all the time, there was no lack of romance, no deficiency of sentiment; I thought there was in the world no grander and no truer love. I sometimes think there was incipient madness in his veins, for storm followed calm and calm followed storm faster than the clouds pass over the face of heaven. I have dreaded sometimes that in his fear of losing me he would kill both himself and me—he often threatened to do this; for he declared, in moments of despondency, that he knew that Fate would separate us unless he put it out of the power of Fate to do so. Do you not think he meant to do it at the last? I think so, though I have never breathed the thought to any but yourself.

And when Fate, or, as I am glad to think, the good God—took up this thread of my life and lifted it far out of his reach or of my own, when human words and human deeds were alike powerless—when Heaven seemed to point its finger with a gesture not to be mistaken or disobeyed, and when with streaming eyes and yearning heart I turned away from him, to follow in the Heaven-directed path—a strange calmness came over him—from which, fool that I was, I augured well. I left him with a heart full of hope for him, I fancied that I had in some way over-estimated the strength and violence of his passion, and in the satisfaction which this thought gave me came the first gleam of consciousness that my own love was not my life as I had always imagined it to be.

Six hours afterwards I stood beside his corpse, feeling myself a murderess as I gazed on that pale brow and kissed those closed eyes which had never looked on me in aught but love. I had never dreamed of this horrible termination of our love, even though he had often sworn to part from me only with his life, for I had become so accustomed to his fiery expressions that I looked upon them as a part of himself, harmonious with his general intensity of tone, and not indicating any settled purpose of action. But the letter which he wrote after leaving me in the morning, the careful arrangement of all the minor details of the fearful deed, and the journal which was sent me with all his other papers in accordance with his will—all revealed his long-formed determination. Can you wonder that the thought of doubt with which I had parted from him, the faint suspicion that entered into my mind as to the entireness of my devotion to him, should have seemed the blackest treason to my dead lover, and that remorse and reaction should have brought back all my tenderness? It seemed but a poor return for his own great love. The horror of the circumstances, the shock and mystery of such a sudden "death in life," the bitter anguish of knowing that he died by his own hand and went, stained with blood, to meet his God,—and then the thought that but for me all this would not have been—came upon me with such mighty power that I sank under it. For months I lay hovering between life and death—the first violence of delirium changed into a settled and silent melancholy, in which I prayed only for death, and it seemed to those who loved and watched over me, during that long and dreary time, that my sun of life was setting, even before the noon had come. But in these long hours of silence, self-questioning arose within me; I lived many years of thought, I began to learn the secret of my life, and very gradually and very sadly to prepare myself, not for the death for which at first I had so vehemently prayed, but for a joyless, though not aimless life. I learned to know, as a truth personal to myself, that God had ordered all things well, that I was but an instrument for some great purpose, and that out of seeming evil, I could hope to bring actual and great good. I learned to look at my own love for Hamilton in its true light, and to accept its ministration to my heart. And although I found that it had not destroyed in me the deepest energies of my nature, it did not lose its dignity and truth, but remained, as it must always remain, an honest but an insufficient reality. In its birth it was the quick enthusiasm of my own heart, responsive to the demands of another, in its death it retained its beauty, though it lost its active influence.

As my physical strength returned to me, my mental balance was completely restored. I felt as if awaking from a long and vivid dream, a night-mare of the consciousness. Very slowly I returned to active life, very gently was I led from the seclusion of my chamber and the silence of its darkness to the fair scenes of the nature I loved so well. I cannot describe my emotion when I first breathed the external air, first lifted my eyes to the blue sky, first felt the delicious warmth of the sun. It was an unmingled delight, though I was exhausted and silent from my extreme weakness, which made even this an excitement greater than I could bear. But I was soon able to drink in large draughts of the renovating air, to enjoy to the utmost the sunshine and the breeze. In the scenes of nature there was nothing to jar upon me, nothing to awaken sudden and startling images of the past. My intercourse with Hamilton had always been in the midst of society and city life. My remembrances of him were associated with lighted halls and gay music; my most quiet recollections of him were connected with my own city home, and mingled with a thousand gay and changing externalities. Our nearest approach to solitude had been amid books and pictures, our isolation had been self-created and never wholly dissociated from companionship. My mother now took me to the seashore, and I spent all the hours of that long and thoughtful summer with the sound of the eternal sea mingling in my dreams by night and in my thoughts by day. From that sound itself there seemed at last to come forth a promise that I should emerge from the stagnation of my sorrow and sometime arise to renewed life and effort, and when I grew stronger and could sit by the shore itself, I drew in with each breath renewed vitality and hope through sight and sound of the wonderful ocean. And the summer sun warmed the cold pulses of my blood, and I grew in that sweet solitude once more myself, or not myself alone, but a new power had been added to me. I was myself, but with new, and better, and higher principles of life; the gay and thoughtless exuberance of my old spirit had grown up to a more settled and earnest purpose, the keen susceptibility to all emotions, though saddened, was not subdued; the intellectual power, though chastened, was not weakened. All that the sea and sky said to my sick heart during those months of communion I may never hope to tell; but you know now why I love the sea and the summer-time so well—I owe my life to them.

The following winter I spent in my home again, but in the strictest seclusion. My friends all acquiesced in my desire for repose, and I am grateful still for the gentle consideration, the kindly neglect (sympathy I could not then have borne) of those about me. When the spring opened once more, another fearful blow fell upon me—my brother Eustace died. He was the only one from whom sympathy and pity had been tolerable to me at the time of Hamilton's death; the only one to whom my heart had gone forth in my hour of desolation, as he was the only one who had dared to come to me with all the cruel but necessary details of that tragedy. From him I had first learned that another drop of bitterness was added to my cup—that the death of my lover had made me wealthy to excess. Hamilton, who loved and trusted him before I had learned to do so, had implored him to keep secrecy upon the tenor of his will, made some six months before his death, when the severe illness which had threatened to terminate fatally, suggested to him the absence of all legal claim which the woman he loved had upon aught that he possessed. He seems even then to have had a presentiment that I should never be his wife, and in the impulsive generosity of his nature, made a will by which he settled all his great wealth unconditionally upon me. I could not keep that wealth; it was impossible for me to regard it as any thing but a sacred trust. With my brother's aid I therefore executed all the legal instruments for conveying the property into those channels which I thought most in unison with the tastes and habits of poor Hamilton. I would have given it all to his few and distant relatives, had I not known that they did not need it, and that he neither loved nor had reason to love them. For the honor of his name, however, I gave them a portion of the family estate, but after that claim was satisfied I felt that I might guide myself entirely by my knowledge of his sentiments on all subjects of charity and objects of liberality. I reserved for myself only his choice library, a few of his favorite paintings, and several trifles especially associated with my own intercourse with him. To my brother I gave the beautiful horse which was Percy's pride, and his huge dog, who is savage to all the world but me, still remains the companion of all my rambles, the guard of my slumbers, and the terror of all my more timid friends. I receive a richer income from my own heart, and a more lavish pleasure from looking at those who have thriven under the bounty which has thus passed through my hands, than from all which that wealth might have purchased of selfish enjoyment. I even dare to feel certain that he has looked on approvingly at all that I have done in his name. It was in the intimate communion which these arrangements brought about between Eustace and myself that I first learned to appreciate the true nobility of his nature, to look beneath his cold reserve of manner to his strong manly heart, and to love him with a more intense and individual devotion than the blind affection common between brother and sister. His sympathy was so unexpected, his understanding of and reverence for my feelings so complete, his consolations so delicate, and his counsels so manly and straightforward, that I trusted him implicitly, and learned to love him with intense fondness. We would gladly have left the will a secret, but circumstances rendered it utterly impossible; and you may imagine how hard an ordeal it was for me to come a second time before the world in the character of a heroine, while my heart was so sad and my spirit so weak within me. But Eustace was always near to shield or to cheer and support me.

When he became ill I knew that he must die; from the first moment I had seen the shadow of death upon him. He, too, felt the warning, and to me, but to none else, could he speak of it; the atmosphere of sorrow and death in which I had so long dwelt made our conversation less jarring and less unnatural than it could be with those to whom gloom and darkness are new experiences; there were already so many sources of sympathy established between us, too, that we felt no reserve in speaking with each other. It seemed to me my heart must break as I watched him, day by day, releasing more of his hold on life, breaking link by link the chain which bound him to earth, and serenely adjusting all his personal affairs, as if glad to be able to relieve others of any charge in regard to them. He arranged with scrupulous care all his private papers, closed up all his business connections with the outside world, with the same calm and even cheerful countenance with which he came to talk with me of his hopes and his faith in the future. How much he taught me during that sad season God alone, to whom he led me, can ever know. How his weak and failing nature, wrung by torturing pains, imparted strength and courage to her who should have been strong enough to give to him, in that dark hour, the Power from whom he drew his strength can alone tell. So well did I learn my lesson that I was able to lay him in the dust with a calmness that surprised all who knew how dearly I had loved him, yet did not know the sources of my inward strength.

I wrestled with my two great griefs in silence and alone, but my health did not again sink under my sorrow. I seemed lifted by it above physical ills or susceptibilities, to live my outer life only as subordinate to the inner, and as removed from it by a barrier impassable to my own consciousness. I asked no friendly sympathy as yet, I wished only for solitude and freedom, to solve, if possible, the still perplexed problem of my own experience—to regain the balance within myself, and to look steadfastly at the past and the future. My twenty years of life must be spread fairly out before me as a chart for study; and the apparent incongruities and contradictions of feeling which marked it must be reconciled and explained to myself, or the future would have no guiding knowledge, no assured path. Again I sought the sea-shore—again I met the calm, serene summer-time. And, more than all, oh! Ernest, I met you. For a long time I did not heed those calm dark eyes, nor hear that deep-toned voice, nor in the selfish seclusion of my sorrow recognise the presence of a spirit that was, ere long, to obtain so powerful an influence over me. But as the summer weeks went by, and you were still near me, offering the unobtrusive courtesies of daily life, and quietly respecting my evident desire for solitude, when my heart renewed its sad memories, I gradually emerged from my isolation, and recognising your truth of character and your superiority of intellect, learned, as I said to myself, to esteem you highly as a friend—to prize the occasional hours which you bestowed upon me as rich gifts of intellectual treasure. Oh, Ernest, how blind I was, and how patient you were through all those summer days and all those sweet autumn scenes! How you bore with me when, at last, I would have scorned you as a friend, because you prayed to be my lover—when I indignantly denied your laughing assertion that I did not know my own heart, as I told you that the future would be for me only the grave of the past. And when we sat together upon those sea-shore rocks, beneath that calm blue sky, and I told you that my heart was utterly dead within me, and related with my own lips the history you had before only learned from others, and revealed even more than I was aware existed within me, of life which that past had not exhausted, you did not alarm me by showing that you discerned the germ and possible promise of a new love in my heart, but controlling your own pardonable exultation, you kept to the strictest office of a friend and spoke no word of the passion I had bidden you to check. (It must be confessed, Ernest, that you made yourself most bounteous amends afterwards!) And I went on in my proud unconsciousness, thinking I could do without you when the near hour of your departure should come, and yet strangely contented that that hour should so mysteriously postpone itself. And when we parted I would not own, even to myself, how bitterly lonely I felt, or acknowledge how much you had been to me, but returned to my old home-routine, thinking to find among old friends even more than I had found in you. But that winter unveiled me more and more unto myself, and as my heart grew hopeful and my griefs faded into a holy slumber, I could visit the graves in which the beloved ones slept, and feel that it was well with them, and that they would that it might be well with me. And so gradually did your image weave itself into my life, so much did I associate you with my beloved dead, that there was no shock to me when the full knowledge came that you were something more to me than even they could ever have been. There was no conflict in my thought as I was able to discern the relation of myself to the past in a true and less exaggerated aspect than the first bewilderment of affliction would allow. They stood as near as ever to my heart, those two noble spirits, but their companionship was peace and strength now, not hopeless sorrow or blind dismay. I think I was almost happy that long cold winter, for summer was coming to my heart, and the warmth of renewed vitality quickened in my veins.

Again you followed me to the sea-shore, though you had religiously obeyed my request not to come to me in my own home. I shall never forget the intense eagerness of your first glance at me, nor the trembling of your strong hand as it grasped mine. The winter had been a sad trial-time for you, my beloved; you knew not of my rapidly growing love for you, saw not the hopes and the aspirations which arose within me, had no assurance of the result for which you prayed. Forgive me that I still delayed for a little while that full assurance for which you longed so feverishly. The pleasant hours wore away, the sunshine and the sea grew even more dear to me, and at length I told you of my winter-life, and once more seeking the memories of the past to reveal their new significance to me, I stood forth in the presence of my dead lover and my dead brother, with no disloyalty to them in my heart, as I confessed my love for you; I felt in my inmost soul a sweet assurance that they sanctioned and approved. That conviction has never left me; my young, passionate, girlish love, and my trusting, reverent, sisterly affection have led the way and prepared my heart for the reception of the great love which is to be the master-principle of my true being, the crown and beauty of my mature life. I had found out, too, that it was yourself, more than sea or shore, that had brought back my life to me; but I did not love my ocean or my summer less—they combined themselves with your own image, mingled with my thoughts of you and with my recollections of your words and looks—and now, at least, you will not quarrel with me for loving them so well. Were they not by when you told me that you must speak again, and that your words must be of love? Did they not whisper to you, before I dared do so, that you might speak with no fear of a second repulse? Did they not listen as intently as I did to every word that fell from your lips, did they not hear the throbbing of my heart, and did not the sea give to the shore the same exulting kiss as that which burned upon my cheek? Did not the sun smile upon us as we sat side by side, and the summer breeze whisper its knowledge of our happiness? Oh, yes! and you too love the summer and the sea even as I love them.

And we shall have our first home by the sea, as you say, and our first unbroken communion shall be, as our first, young, timid utterances were—witnessed and hallowed by those loving influences. I have learned to trust myself so entirely to you, to live so in your being, that, in some sense, summer and winter, seashore and city, are now alike to me; but I confess that another joy seems added to the picture of my future, when I think that we can leave the world behind us for awhile, and that you, like myself, find pleasure in the thought that the first months of that united love that shall so soon commence, to be ended neither on earth nor in heaven, will be passed with only Nature as companion unto us.

How can I be glad enough, dearest, that I have learned to know myself before I really give myself away? Above all, how can I be glad enough that you, to whom I give myself, know what you are taking, without disguise, without reserve, without one shadow which might else rise up to dim our future as it has that of many another life. I am glad that you will have me thus go over and study out my past; I rejoice to reveal all that it contains to your searching but loving gaze. I lay it all, with my heart, at your feet—take of it as it shall please you—it has all tended to ennoble, as it is all included in, my devotion to yourself. Your own

ETHEL

LETTER SIXTH

You tell me, dear Ernest, that you are not yet weary of my chaotic reminiscences, that you can even make order and sequence out of them, and seem to arrive, little by little, at a more thorough understanding of my inner soul as I reveal more and more the past history of my inward consciousness. I am glad that it is so with you, and that you ask from me, not so much a recital of events, as of states of feeling and contrasted moods of mind, which, in one constituted as I am, are of infinitely greater value in forming a true estimate of my individual attitude in regard even to the externalities by which I am surrounded. I would have you know me thus deeply, thus thoroughly; I would spread out before you those isolated but strongly painted pictures of my past, which represent me when the accumulation of influences from without and from within have brought about a crisis of my heart, have concentrated into visibility the usually unseen emotions which sway the inner pulses. These pictures I place before you just as they come up to my own memory, without arrangement and almost without date; it matters little when an incident took place so long as the results of that incident upon the character are clearly perceived and fairly allowed. I must only regulate myself by those sympathetic influences which arise within me as I look back upon "the days that are no more," and which, at different times, cause different recollections to come with more power and demand more minute description. Therefore you have in my letters, not only the relation of the past, but, running parallel with that, a transcript of the present state of my mind, through the selection which I involuntarily make from the many different scenes through which I take you. We learn little of an individual nature from seeing, even with a great degree of intimate intercourse, only the daily, external life one leads; we learn much, if even for a moment he lifts the veil which covers and conceals the working of his motives, the springs of his feelings, the sources of his inspiration and the result for which he labors. Just in proportion as our friends reveal unto us their inner mechanism, just in proportion as they can impart and we attain to a true knowledge of the interior nature which lies behind all their visible life, just so much are they really *ours*. If the capability of this understanding be mutual and spontaneous, we see the most holy and beautiful friendship that can exist—its very rarity makes it seem more fair—its superiority to all low obstacles and clogging earthliness, makes us recognise its inherent immortality. It seems to me, beloved Ernest, that between us two it may exist in perfection, that we can each infuse into the other, in a wonderful degree, those influences which modify or control each of our minds, that we, to an unusual extent, find ourselves swayed by similar emotions at the same moment, that the natural current of our psychological forces flows without effort in the same direction, governed by the same impulses, and responding to the same magnetic vibrations. Oh, do you know what peace I find in this thought—what a beautiful future it opens before us? That there should be no need of struggle between us, no yielding upon one side because there shall be no conquering upon the other,—how serenely joyful it will be to us who have already had enough of struggle and enough of victory. Sometimes I wonder at your almost feminine intuitions, your exquisite appreciation of the most delicate shades of feeling—since your life has been no idle summer dream, no mere poetic fancy; but a hard fought battle with the stern reality of things. How can I be glad enough that through all you have kept this truth of heart, this quick spiritual insight, this warm and ready sympathy, and that now it is all for me! What am I, oh, Ernest, that Heaven should grant me such a boon? I almost tremble at the richness of my treasure, when I remember the poorness of my own desert; but I glory in the possession of a heart so strong and high, a nature so full and great as yours. None less than thine could give repose to mine, none less responsive supply the feverish haste of my own longings in the dark hours of my soul's life. Thou must be to me a perennial fountain, else I shall perforce drain thy heart. A fate is on me hitherto that I should draw so relentlessly upon my loves that I have learned shame of myself at finding how soon there was nothing left to slake my thirst, and have questioned if they were really "shallow cisterns holding no water," or if I were a guilty spendthrift of their precious gifts. But with you, Ernest, I am at last at peace—I seem to have turned away from the streams which bubbled in the careless sunshine long ago, to have outrun the rivers that flowed noisily on their way, only to find myself upon the glorious ocean, to rest in the unfathomable depth of your noble nature. What can even the mighty torrent of my own free, mountain-born stream add to the grandeur of your swelling tides? I lose myself in you with joy!

But I look in vain for reasons why you should be all mine—I find but one most selfish one, and that is, the greatness of my need of you, the deep unsatisfied longing, the bitter loneliness that must have been mine had you not been sent unto me. You tell me very sweetly that the readiness, the absolute eagerness of response I meet in you, is owing to your having never loved before, that all your better nature, rigidly locked up within itself, needed but the master-key to open the gateway to the pent-up flood; you laughingly caution me against my danger of drowning from the accumulations which, in others, have been gradually disposed of in minor loves and more various passions, but in you have never had but this one outlet. Pour forth the swelling floods without measure and without stint, oh, rarest heart—I ride upon the mounting waves, I revel in the rushing waters, the noise of the surging billows is music in my ears and strength unto my heart.

How amid the self-seclusion of your heart-life, the self-imposed silence of your emotional nature, you have kept your susceptibilities so keen, your sympathies so ready, and your expressional power so full and rich—how you have avoided doubt and distrust and sceptical analysis, I, with my tendency to morbid weakness, can hardly comprehend. With so much to contend against, so many obstacles to conquer, and so much hard work to be done, why have not you, like other men, grown hard and cold and scornful and bitter? With a man's strength you have kept a woman's tenderness, with the voice which can speak the sternest words I ever heard, when there needs to be a stern word spoken,—you can whisper the sweetest and most gentle message of encouragement and help. I have never, for a moment, seen the tenderness tinged with the sternness, and never known the sternness weakened by a misplaced tenderness. Yes, you are indeed like my own ocean, Ernest;—no petty breezes ruffle your serenity, but the sunshine finds its own calmness reflected in you, and only the mightiest winds and the solemn murmur of the waves are like your wrath when the storm is really awakened. I should love your tenderness less and rejoice in your gentleness with more of doubt, did I not also know this other side of your strong manly nature. I should nestle in the sunshine less securely, did I not know the power of the storms that have raged, for in both your aspects I find equal sympathy for my own wayward and contrastive moods. You have my contrasts without my waywardness, you have greater power of direction than I, and you shall guide me as you guide yourself, not by repressing and condemning even the power of anger and of contempt, but by giving it honest work to do and lofty sweep of action. May I but fill the loving part of your nature with genial tenderness, as you fill my weak heart with strength, and thus make up to you in your future for all the isolation of your past!

Such an external barrenness as surrounded your early life in reality, I used, in my morbid seasons, to fancy was about myself. I have told you of my tendency to reverie, and of my long-continued day-dreams, but I have not told you how bitterly I suffered for a long while from the hopelessly gloomy coloring which they finally acquired. I suppose the delicate state of my health must have had something to do with this morbid sensibility, and at any rate it increased my inability to struggle against it. It however became so much a part of myself, it interwove itself so thoroughly into the very texture of my heart's life, as to enslave every perception I possessed, and to dominate over every impression I received. Nothing but the living actuality of abundant and most patient love, poured on me with no niggard hand, conquered this misanthropic bitterness and drove away this moral gloom. You have seen me only since this tendency has been dead within me, and can hardly understand how it once tyrannized over me and what danger I was in. It was even worse than my habit of analysis, and for a time seemed less likely to be subdued. It reigned paramount in my days of earliest womanhood, and perhaps nothing short of my somewhat stormy experiences would have sufficed to drive out the demon. I sometimes indulged these fancies with a kind of desperate enjoyment, but generally I struggled heartily against them, though in vain. Unlike other spiritual and intellectual difficulties, the power to conquer came from without. The wayward imaginations which filled me with bitterness, the conviction that weighed me down in those days of presumptuous ignorance, haunted me with the belief that I was born for misery and loneliness, and must go through life unknowing and unknown to the sweet influences of a noble friendship or a true love. I know that it is very common for the young to have passing fancies similar to this, and to imagine it a proof of greatness to be unhappy; to find a strange charm in unsatisfied longings, and to turn from happiness as too common-place; but there was none of this affectation of sentiment in my misery; it was a dark reality, at which I often rebelled with all my strength, which crushed my soul within me, in spite of all my efforts to escape from its galling bondage. It assumed every variety of form, and tinged every emotion I experienced. Sometimes it seemed to me that there was really no heart within me; no warm and kindly blood in my pulseless, passionless frame; no out-going energy, and no capacity for reception of it from without. I seemed to myself a completely exceptional organization, outside of the laws which governed those about me; impenetrable to the influences which swayed their existence. I had no feeling save that of stupid and cold indifference. These seasons of torpor were so heavy that there was no power in imagination to paint pictures fair enough to awaken one emotion of interest or rouse one thrill of expectation; nor could the most vivid image of suffering or prophecy of woe cause any shrinking or any dread. All was vague and shadowy; happiness was an insane fancy, sorrow only a disagreeable sound. I could never enjoy the one, and I need never fear the other. The strongest passions and the truest attachments were only dreamy speculations, varied involuntarily by the temperament and position of the individual nature in which they arose. I lost all heart and hope and faith in others and myself. I doubted all capacity in my own heart, and all existence in others, of any active, spontaneous, ennobling emotion. I finally sat down, contented, as I thought, in my miserable delusion, trying to persuade myself, not only, that all was hollow and unreal, but that I was satisfied that it should be so: and that I asked for nothing else. I reasoned myself into a state of negation so thorough that I neither loved nor hated, desired nor dreaded. I was a sort of moral somnambulist, walking through the world with my eyes open, but my perceptions closed. The daily life around me, the home-circle in which I dwelt, were all shadows; people belonging to it came and went before me as a pageant on which I looked with passive indifference. It seemed to me that I possessed complete control over my own organism; that I could do anything within my consciousness except be happy, and that being an impossibility for any one whose spiritual eyes had been opened, I had no reason to complain over an inevitable necessity. I fancied there was no misfortune that would call forth a tear; no loss which would be worth a sigh; no hope which could make my leaden heart beat quicker than its wont, but that I could maintain the same immovable indifference, the same unshaken pulse, through any possible experience. Had this condition been produced by any actual disappointment, any acute suffering, or any really discouraging circumstances, it would have been followed at some time by a natural revulsion of feeling; it would, like a fever, have had its crisis and its limit, beyond which its violence could not go, and after which, in one so young, it would have retraced its steps and brought me to a more healthful and buoyant condition. But in my case it came on without apparent cause, and so gradually, that it seemed merely the development of some inborn quality; it raged with no violence, roused little antagonism, was content without manifestation, and asked for no relief in sympathy; in short, it was a subtle poison breathing through my whole being. There was danger that this would always remain the prevailing tone of my mind. Still there was behind all a timid hope, not quite dead, though mainly silent, and only at rarest intervals appearing even to my own heart, of something better. I dared not quite believe that there was no blue sky high up above the darkening clouds that closed in over my head. I would have welcomed any storm that would have broken those dark rifts; but I would not acknowledge or believe this till I felt the glad rebound of my heart when the clear sunshine at last burst forth upon me.

Sometimes this morbid disposition took another form, and induced seasons of intense suffering. It was no longer indifference that I felt—I was no longer in a state of stagnant unconsciousness, but in a felt darkness and desolation. My heart was not senseless, but only too keenly alive. The least jar gave me exquisite pain; a careless word stung me to the quick, and a loving one brought unbidden tears to my eyes—the tension of my whole nature was frightful. I lost the balance of my faculties, and sought the completest solitude and the strictest silence to conceal my wanderings from the knowledge of others. My dreams grew fanciful with horror or radiant with intangible delight. I revelled in imaginings of the bliss I was capable of, only to turn with loathing from their impossible suggestions. I shrank with affright from the fearful agony that visited me at other times and thrilled through every fibre of my being. And though in the movement of my daily life I emerged from these paroxysms into the more real experiences from which I could not quite seclude myself, it was only to complain within my own heart of the common-placeness of my every-day comfort. The happiness which satisfied others, and which seemed to be equally within my own reach, was too prosaic to be worth grasping,—I would have none of it—I would prefer the brilliant lies of my dreams, and pay the penalty of their alternating terrors. I grew very wretched, as I thought that I must wander through a world externally so beautiful, and never find in it the nourishment I craved—never obtain the bliss I knew myself capable of feeling, never meet with hearts that could really answer unto mine. I scorned what the rest of the world seemed to find well enough. I asked for friendship higher and purer, sympathy more vast and elevated than any one seemed able to give me—I demanded love far more passionate and far more holy than the ignorant admiration of those of my social circle, who approached me with their homage, appeared capable of experiencing.

How dark the heavens were above me—how the summer air chilled me—how coldly the sun smiled at me, and how far-off the stars seemed! I met no glance of pity for the intense, unsatisfied longings of my young heart, and I wept bitter tears of anguish. But this state was more hopeful than the first, because it was more active and more extravagant—it bore within itself the seeds of a revulsion—the promise of a change.

I was indeed destined to awake from this abnormal condition of mind and heart, through a personal experience which I could not deny or put aside, as I had always done the less obtrusive suggestions of my calm daily life. I had doubted the existence of everything beautiful and true in the human life—I was destined to see that which I had despised rise up in grandeur before me. I had doubted the possibility of friendship, and Claudia was to come to me and prove my doubt a treason against truth. I had persuaded myself that the natural affections of family and kindred were merely the result of monotonous habit, in which we acquiesce, partly from indolence and partly from fear of finding nothing better if we gave it up,—I was destined to behold the very heart-beats of a mother's love—the strong pulsation of a father's devotion. I had questioned my own susceptibility and my own dependence—I was to find myself a helpless infant in the strong arms of love, a thing of nerves and sensibilities that every wind of heaven could awaken. And this new life was given me, not through the sharp and stern lessons of sorrow and affliction, not through lacerated or crushed affections, not even through severe mental conflict—but amid physical suffering and utter helplessness which, though hard to endure in the passing, seem to my remembrance but as the throes which were necessary to usher into existence my new-born soul.

I was about sixteen when this terrible illness attacked me. Perhaps my mental condition aggravated the violence of the disorder; however that may be, the fever assumed a contagious and most malignant form. For a long time my delirium was frightful, my agony intolerable, no words can express what I endured of torture and of horror. Visions of all fearful things, dreams of darkness and phantoms of dread hung over my couch as I lay there helpless for long weeks. It was on emerging from my delirious state that I was able to realize how much I was beloved by those to whom, in my distrust, I had done so much injustice. Long before I could utter the simplest words of gratitude I had read whole volumes of love and prayed long prayers of true repentance. The time of my delirium had been no blank in my consciousness. I could, to be sure, recall only in a confused way my own sensations and expressions, but what others had done remained before my eyes as a freshly painted picture, at which I was now able to gaze with understanding interest. The faces that had clustered around my bed with all their variety of anxious and awe-struck expression—my mother's pale face and tearful eyes, my father's prostrate grief, my brother's vain attempts at self-control, and my cousin Emily's quiet but evident distress, were indelibly impressed upon my memory at the moment when they supposed me beyond all sensation and passing into the silent unconsciousness of death. I knew that all this anxiety and grief were for me, and yet I hardly understood why it was, at that moment, brought to such culmination of expression. All I was conscious of was a sudden thrill passing over me, a delicious sense of joy in the possession of so much love. I think it saved my life, for it infused such new energy into my heart, that against all prophecy, against all precedent, I turned away from death's open gate, to re-enter on the path of life. In the long interval which elapsed before I recovered my strength, I had leisure to review and analyse more truly my past, and to make fresh resolutions for my future. How could I ever repay so much love, which, now that the veil had been lifted from my eyes, in that hour of revelation, had continually renewed its manifestations? What was there in me that could merit such lavishness of affection, such fulness of love as that on which I fed from day to day, as a plant feeds on the air in which it grows? How beautiful it was to be so watched over, so cared for, every moment of the day and of the night. How transfigured in the light and glory of their unselfish love stood all those who bent over me with their unwearied devotion to the helpless sufferer! How my heart throbbed when I was told that not one of all those around me had been afraid of risking life in remaining near me—that danger had lurked in every breath in that sick chamber, yet that its close and heavy atmosphere had been dearer to them than the air of heaven. How I wondered that I had never before detected the clear love-light which beamed in my mother's soft, hazel eyes every time she looked at me, never discovered how much her beauty was enhanced by the depth of affection which beamed from every look, now that I sought for it instead of turning from it. How I trembled with pleasure to notice the softening of my father's voice when he spoke to me, the tenderness of his glance when he thought me asleep and dared to look at me without the assumed cheerfulness he put on whenever he saw that I observed him. How I longed to be well again that I might do something more than receive all this love so bounteously bestowed. I bless God that He has enabled me, since then, to prove my gratitude and repay a portion of my pleasant debt.

Until this illness, Claudia had been only an acquaintance, whom I regarded as somewhat more noble and true than the world in general, because circumstances had made me acquainted with several instances of her magnanimity and generous self-denial. I had seen too that she was not only attractive of more love and reverence from others than she was inclined to give them in return, but that she treated me, in our not very frequent meetings with each other, in a manner totally unlike that which she manifested towards any one else. I had even noticed with a faint surprise, that she seemed strangely conversant with my tastes and habits of mind, that her mood was often in unexpected unison with my own, and that she not unfrequently gave utterance to the very thoughts which I supposed shut up in my own heart. But I was so weighed down with my morbid fancies, so utterly inert in my misanthropy, that I permitted her image to pass by in the dream-procession which moved before my mind with little more perception of her than of the rest.

I remember that I thought it very singular when I looked round on the sorrowful group awaiting my last breath, to see Claudia among them, and to discover in her face a depth of agony quite as intense as that which revealed itself upon the features of my relatives. But I was too weak for anything but the most transient emotion of surprise, and I fell into the habit of depending upon her without asking how it happened that she had ever begun to nurse me, or whether there need be any termination to her attention. Of much greater physical strength than my mother and clearer mental judgment than my cousin, she soon became the chief companion of my convalescence. She was the very sunshine of my day before I knew that she was aught but the kindest and most patient of nurses. It was not till a month after the fever had left me, that I learned that she had come to my mother, upon the first intelligence of my illness, and besought her with tears to let her be with me. For ten weeks she hardly left my bedside. And as I grew better she would talk to me for hours in her sweet, low, soothing voice, as I lay quietly happy on my bed, of how she grew to love and know me in spite of myself, drawn by what she playfully called my irresistible magnetic attraction,—how she had suffered at my unfeigned indifference and yet never lost faith that her great love must meet with ultimate recognition and return, and finally that my illness had seemed to her the appointed way for our friendship.

That convalescence was a pleasant time in my life, dear Ernest,—the whole earth seemed new to me, and fair as new. Such a wealth of love was awakened within me, that my whole life seemed too short for its expression, my whole heart too small for its dwelling-place. But above this general beneficence of mood, aside from this universal kindness which clothed my every-day life, there rose up within me a passionate love for Claudia, which seemed to take root in the very depths of my being. Every day revealed her noble nature to me more clearly, every day I looked deeper into her loving and true heart, and learned better to appreciate her high intellectual gifts. The reserve she maintained towards others melted utterly away for me, and nothing could be more charming than the transition from her usual manner in society to the

delicious *abandon* and merry carelessness that accompanied her every
word and motion in the seclusion of our mutual intercourse. I found
that she had been a busy student among the books I loved the best, a
thinker upon subjects that had interested my whole soul, and that, in
spite of the many points of difference in our characters, we were in
matters of intellectual liking wonderfully agreed. She read aloud finely,
and many of my favorite books have the pleasant echo of her flexible
and musical voice still lingering among their pages. Certain passages
of poetry are inseparably associated in my memory with the soft rich
tones with which she repeated them to me, while I was lying, languid
but not suffering, during my convalescence. Her talent for drawing, too,
she brought into requisition for the amusement of my invalid hours,
and it was like a sweet breath of country air to look at one of her sunny
landscapes, and hear her description of the scene where she sketched
it. It was in her drawings that the peculiar characteristics of her ideal
nature showed themselves most decidedly, and her portfolio was full
of strange and almost supernatural pictures, which seemed doubly
wild and fearful by the side of the sweet and serene scenes which she
always selected when she sketched directly from nature. She grew
very eloquent when explaining to me the meaning of her imaginary
pictures,—they always had some deep meaning hidden in them, and
the key to this once supplied, they became full of interest and fascination. They furnished the undercurrent of my dreams very often, at the
time, and even now recur to me occasionally with vivid power. Claudia
was in every respect a most delightful companion, full of delicate tact
and simple kindliness, rich in resources, but never exhausting one's
patience by the display of her accomplishments. She never wearied
me even in my hours of greatest prostration; whether she spoke or
whether she remained silent, she was always a pleasant and positive
adjunct to the scene. This wonderful gift of fitness at all times, to the
necessities of the moment, might have been partly an acquirement in
her, for she had seen much of the world, but it seemed to be all nature,
and made her the most delightful person imaginable when she was
in a situation in consonance with her own tastes. The days flew by on
wings of light while she devoted herself to me, and played by turns the
careful and gentle nurse, and the brilliant and intellectual companion.
Her tastes were somewhat too decided and peculiar to allow of her

being a very general favorite among her casual acquaintances, but her very exclusiveness was an additional charm to me.

It was about this time, too, that I first met Hamilton. My brother brought him to the house as an old college friend of his own, the first evening that my physician allowed me to join the family circle for a little while. I imagined that it was merely my excessive paleness and extreme languor that made him turn his eyes so often upon me, and the involuntary pity of a healthy organization for one so weak and shattered, that made him, from the first, assume an apparently unconscious tenderness of manner towards me. From that first visit he was an established friend of the whole house. My brother already loved and esteemed him, and had told me often of his accomplished and poetical mind, and his fastidious tastes, sometimes laughingly asserting that his fastidiousness reached nearly to the extreme which my own was supposed to attain unto—for this charge against me was a common jest in the family. My mother was charmed by Percy's graceful deference to herself, my cousin Emily was won by his ready appreciation of her musical gifts, and even my father would lay down his newspaper to hear what Mr. Hamilton had to say on any subject, emphatically pronouncing him "a very sensible fellow in spite of his handsome face." I withstood the general fascination longer than anyone, for even Claudia caught the infection and became enthusiastic in his behalf. I used to smile as she built up sumptuous castles in the air and described their splendors to me, for they were always to be inhabited by Percy and me, whom she had placed together from the hour of his advent among us. She saw, sooner than any one, how he turned to me even while speaking to others, how uneasy he became when I left the room, and how his face lighted up when he found me growing better and stronger in health. His constant and delicate devotion to me, and his passionate utterance of it, completed the cure of every symptom of my old misanthropy and doubt. There was absolutely no room for questions in my happy life, no excuse for scepticism; the love and trust of those about me taught me to judge the whole world more kindly, and to see in the whole human nature more of truth, of grandeur, and of beauty, than I had ever guessed at in the old days. I have never retraced my steps—have never felt the chill of doubt returning upon me; and now I can sit down without fear in the serene sunlight of my love for you—a love which is the crowning point of all my efforts, for which all my other loves seem to have educated and prepared me—a love which is, as it were, only the development and accomplishment of myself. Look back kindly with me, dear Ernest, on all which has served to prove and try me, rejoice with me that I have been so taught, rejoice with me still more that I have been so richly rewarded. I would that heart and life were worthier, for both are yours.

ETHEL

LETTER SEVENTH

I come again and again unto you, true heart, as the bird flies back to its mate, and in writing to you of myself, I seem not so much a selfish egotist as a willing recorder of that which you please me by setting so high a value upon. You tell me what you find in me now; you recount my "capabilities for greatness," as you call them; you describe my many peculiarities quite as minutely and faithfully as I could do, only you always throw a beautiful rosy veil over these last, while I should often drag them pitilessly out into the sunshine and make them show themselves anything but charming. But, though you know me so well in the present and can prognosticate wisely for the future, the past does not thereby become unmeaning for you, nor its incidents fail to increase the light thrown upon my character and habits. So I have gone on from one reminiscence to another, pleasing myself, and, I trust, not wearying you. It has indeed been pleasant to me to revisit the old scenes of my life; and though my letters have jotted down so many of my recollections, yet my thoughts have by no means stopped short where my pen has. A thousand little things, too small and unimportant in themselves to be worth the labor of my writing or of your reading, but which nevertheless have retained enough vitality and individuality to prevent them from falling into oblivion, have taken occasion to present themselves before me, just as the rabble follow at the heels of the great man and manage to obtain footing when the doors are opened to allow his entrance. Words and deeds have returned to me since I commenced my little history, that would seem to have been of no value or meaning except at the very moment of utterance; and persons who flitted in the most transient manner across my life, when that life was most various and full of external changes, come smiling and bowing or frowning upon me as they present themselves under shelter of some reference to the past.

I should probably never have really unearthed the past but for your expressed wish, but now that I have been busy in the process I find it strangely charming. The incidents of each life may be trivial and common-place enough, viewed simply as incidents, but set in the stronger light of their interior meaning to the soul of the individual, they grow into something of more importance and become worthy of the study of the person to whom they belong. It is by looking back that we learn to look forward, for, having studied ourselves in the past, we are able, upon the knowledge thus acquired, to give definiteness to our ideas of the future; becoming familiar with our own aspect in the events which have filled up the by-gone days, we can, by simple transposition, in time, determine how we may be affected in the future. And, although we may find much to help us forward, by seeing how much we have already advanced, still self-study in the past is, in the main, a somewhat saddening occupation. We see so many instances wherein we might have acted more wisely, or more kindly, or more truly. We see how small the groundwork of our most violent prejudices and prepossessions really was, and wonder how they could have hurried us into such extravagance of action. You must often have noticed how impossible it is, after a night of sound sleep, to retain the same degree of violence and excitement upon a matter, which seemed, the night before, to be perfectly legitimate, and only proportionate to the demand of the occasion. And this becomes ten-fold more manifest when not only a night, but years, have passed since the occurrence of that which, when new and fresh, moved us in the very depths of our being. It is fortunate that this is the case, for we could never bear the fearful strain upon our natures which would ensue upon a greater steadfastness of emotion. If the recollection of an excitement restored the excitement itself in its pristine force, we should be for ever swaying in the blasts of passion.

It is amusing, in looking back over a young girl's life, to see what a large proportion of its movement comes from the presence of love in its various manifestations. It seems actually to be the very Master of Ceremonies, and to determine all the social etiquette and all the machinery by which the connection with the world at large is maintained. The homage of those to whom a woman remains personally indifferent has some positive influence upon her development; the love which, though she does not respond to it, yet which wins her respect and esteem, has still more; and when the crowning sentiment of her life, the absorbing and delicious reality of love, comes, then she is placed beneath a formative influence indeed. Much of a woman's character may be learned only from knowledge of the men she attracts about her, and from the manner in which she comports herself towards them. It is by the active antagonisms or attractions which enter into her sphere from this source that she obtains some little amount of knowledge of the world and some insight into character, which, from the sheltered position assigned to her sex, she has lamentably small opportunities for acquiring in other ways. While a boy is thrown at once into the arena, and allowed to look about him and prepare himself for the conflict of his life by the contemplation of his battle-field, and the study of warfare by seeing it before his very eyes, girls are still shut up in the secluded unconsciousness of their homes, and see human life and human passion only as its manifestation bears upon their own personal existence. The opportunities for studying character come in isolated instances, and it is only when they embrace strongly contrastive natures that her opportunities are at all commensurate with her needs.

In the less serious aspect of her life, in the merely social career which she pursues as her young ladyhood progresses, this love-element is also of prominent importance and it needs not that she be very sentimental or that she be coquettishly inclined, for it to produce very positive and inevitable results upon her. Her manner unconsciously moulds itself into greater self-possession, her energies come forth to sustain her, and she walks with a step quite as maidenly but more assured as she finds out her inherent power as a woman to influence men who are deeply engaged in the work of their own lives, and who, at a first glance, would seem to be altogether too much absorbed in that work to be turned aside by any but the most powerful influences. It is only in shallow natures that much devotion from men produces silly vanity; when the tone of character is pure and high, the effect is elevating, and women become more and more worthy of the sentiments they call forth, and it is no shame to the most true-hearted man to yield to the charm which such women exercise. No woman of a strong, true nature can listen to the earnest and honest utterance of a manly love, without rising higher than all womanly vanity, and finding within herself the power to console and to encourage even while she steadfastly denies; and such a woman may almost always, in time, exchange the impassioned and disappointed lover for a firm and admiring friend. Women almost invariably regard their discarded lovers with a degree of kindly liking, and are keen to discern and remark upon any noble traits of character in them: and even if this comes from no loftier motive than a reversionary self-admiration, it is good so far as it extends, and often helps to heal the wounds of the past. The fact that most of the supposed eternal attachments of young hearts have really a singularly brief existence, does not necessarily divest them of all their dignity while they are still alive. It is only a merciful arrangement for the relief of the general wear and tear of the human heart. This is generally well enough understood by women, and they are frankly glad to see a man they cannot love meet with a heartier recognition from some other woman. I have known the greatest friendliness arise among the three concerned in one of these little dramas.

Much of this long chapter upon love has been suggested to me, dear Ernest, by the pleasant tidings I have received from Grahame Elliott, of his rapturous happiness in his newly wedded life. I have never told you what a frantic little lover of my own he once was, but now that he is in a position to smile as freely at his past extravagances as I myself am, I will give you a little outline of the episode. It was not a very long, but a most violent and extraordinary one. It is only a year ago that the poor fellow actually thought himself dying of love for me, and felt himself bitterly aggrieved when I refused to believe in his approaching end. Our acquaintance commenced during my visit at L., which you remember. He was a student in the office of my host, and being the orphan son of an old friend, was received as a resident in the house, so that, although my visit there lasted but a month, we were thrown very much together. As I, intrenched in the majesty of my one-and-twenty years, first looked upon the pale and delicate youth of twenty, I felt an almost motherly impulse of kindness steal over my heart, for I knew that he was alone in the world. As our acquaintance progressed, and I found his intellect was that of a full-grown man, I learned a little more deferential feeling for him, but still felt myself to be in a very safe degree of seniority to him. We studied German together, a language of which we were both extremely fond, and really our progress in it was marvellous for the length of time we devoted to it. He read aloud the impassioned verses of our favorite authors, till he caught the infection, and fell to making poems for himself—which, at first, I supposed from simple courtesy to his fellow-student, he addressed to me. I hardly noticed that his strains grew more and more intense as they grew more and more personal to their object. I did not even apply to myself a charming little poem he one day brought me, which contained the most exquisite history of an intimacy like our own, and of which the denouement, though left in uncertainty, was suggested with delicate and timid entreaty for my indulgence. I frankly admired the poem, and even praised the poetic skill with which he had rescued himself and his hero from the ordinary and stereotyped conclusions of such romances. I saw him change color and look at me with a very peculiar expression; but so much had I deceived myself in the beginning, by the simple misunderstanding of a remark of his own, prophetic of an unsuccessful love he declared himself doomed to suffer from, that I believed the love to have been in existence before my coming, and interpreted every subsequent reference to it in accordance with my self-created theory of the matter. So I continued my pleasant intercourse with him, never dreaming of the result which followed, and believing that, although the world was ignorant of the tie which united me to you, yet that my manner and my indifference to society were sufficient indications that my heart had already found satisfaction for its needs. I must do myself the justice to say, that even in the moment of Grahame's most uncontrollable excitement, he acknowledged that my manner had always warned him of this, but that he had refused to heed its warning, and had remained wilfully blind to many things that he knew were sufficient to prove the impossibility of success in his suit. At last, a short time before the day appointed for my leaving L., as we sat upon the piazza one charming moonlight evening, and I was vainly endeavoring to keep my thoughts which would wander off after you, wondering what your own occupation might just then be—upon the subject of conversation between us, so as to pay him a proper degree of attention when he spoke,—he suddenly broke off in the middle of a poem he was reciting and commenced a most impassioned declaration of love to myself. His words came so impetuously that I could not stop their utterance, and when at last he actually threw himself upon his knees before me, and seized my hand in the

manner of the knights in the German stories we had been reading, my
first idea was that the scene was superlatively ludicrous.

But as he went on, and his first passionate outburst subsided into
a more simple though hardly less violent language, I saw that it was
no high-flown romance, but a most unfortunate fact. When he would
let me speak, I strove, first of all, to calm his agitation and to lessen
his excitement. But it was a long while before I could soothe him into
a condition to hear reason. He swore that he would win me or die,
and threw out violent menaces against some imaginary individual
whom he called his rival. He was sure of winning me by his faithful
and great love, he said, if only I would not send him away for ever,
and would say that I was not bound irrevocably to any other. He would
go away at once, if I said that he must; would gain fame and wealth
somewhere and somehow,—he should be sure of doing so if only he
might seek them for my sake,—and he would come back to lay them
and himself at my feet, even though years must pass in absence and
solitary effort. All this was poured forth with the vehemence and
poetry natural to an intellectual and impetuous boy, and when I strove
to bear with him as such, and waited patiently for the violence of the
storm to wear itself out, he reproached me for looking upon him as
a boy, when he was, as I ought well to know, a man in all but years
and hardness of nature. My patience, however, at length received its
reward, and he sat down upon the low step on which he had been
kneeling, and with a somewhat subdued manner, begged me to tell
him what his fate must be, but to be very gentle in the telling, if there
was to be no hope for him even in the remote future. So I told him
that there was no hope, and tried to make him see the absurdity of his
wish, dwelling upon my superior age, and exaggerating it as much as
possible, by asserting that though but a twelvemonth in point of fact, it
was, as existing between him and me, ten-fold greater, since he knew
nothing of the world, and I had lived for years in its experiences. All
this, however, had no effect, nor could I paint the hopelessness of any
practical result to his devotion, before the lapse of years should place
him fairly among men, and give him a right to woo a woman as his
wife, with sufficient power to chill the ardor of his hopes and subdue
his ambitious fancies to any degree of possible accomplishment. At
last, despairing of success in any other way, I told him that I loved and
was betrothed to another, long before I had seen him; and that if he

had not been absorbed in his own romantic fancies, he must have seen innumerable indications of the fact in my speech and manner—for though I sought no publicity, yet I shrank from no simple and honest acknowledgment, in my domestic and friendly relations. As I went on he grew calmer and more reasonable, though he trembled visibly, and looked so very wretched that my heart was full of pity for him, even while my experience told me that his suffering would be more transient than he could then believe possible. I spoke very kindly, even affectionately to him, and in one or two subsequent interviews, did my best to console him, and reconcile him to the life which he declared intolerable to him. My efforts were not very successful, however, and I left him in a state of apparent despair. He wrote me several impassioned letters, afterwards, and even came to see me two or three months later;—I treated him as I would have done a sick child who needed only to be kindly cared for, to get well of himself. Some four months ago I had a letter from him, written in a much more cheerful strain, in which he gave me most eloquent thanks for my long forbearance with him, declared himself more than ever persuaded that the world did not contain another woman comparable to myself, but avowing that he was doing his best to conquer a passion that he knew to be hopeless. I replied to this letter—I had left all his others unanswered—and told him that the conclusion of his letter gave me the most heartfelt pleasure, and that I hazarded a prophecy that the future had in store for him, greater happiness than any he had yet dreamed of. My prophecy has already proved a true one, for I received yesterday, a half dozen sheets from him, filled with the story of his new love, its successful wooing and rapid consummation. He had been married three days to "a woman, or rather a child, of sixteen, not as yet like the peerless Ethel, but in time I trust to grow somewhat like her, if I read the promise in her charming face aright." This last act of homage to myself was very gracefully done, was it not? and were I less willing than I am, to abdicate the throne of such a sovereignty, it might help to reconcile me to my fate. He is an honest-hearted fellow with all his rash impulsiveness, and I doubt not will remain loyal to his new love, for, from all I can learn, it is likely to be the real love of his life. He will bring her to see me in a few days, having, as he tells me, honestly laid before her the story of his first love and all its extravagant manifestations. I fancy that in addition to his wish, that two women whom he values should meet, he is not averse to the opportunity it will afford him, of proving to his pretty little wife, that the old love was really "off," before he was "on with the new," and in that belief I shall do my utmost to assist him in dispelling every suspicion of jealousy which may arise in his wife's mind, and which the shortness of her own acquaintance with him would render quite natural in her. And thus ends, as all such romances should end, the episode of Grahame Elliott and Ethel Sutherland, which I relate for your edification and amusement. It shall not lead me any longer ramble into the tangled wild-wood of romance, or entail upon you just now, any more of the minor "affaires du cœur," which have sprung up into mushroom existence along my path, as they do in that of most women who move much in society, and are not positively incapacitated from influencing those who are brought into relationship with them. These experiences, transient as they are, and without any very marked results, have yet some effect upon the character of both parties, and may be made of service in self-study. Our intercourse with others becomes, of necessity, of some importance to us, the moment it passes beyond the bounds of ordinary conventionality; and it is for this reason that even the most transitory connection between persons who are brought into intimate personal relations which reveal the real nature clearly, often assumes proportions grander than our ordinary acquaintanceships ever attain to. We all know how fast friendship developes out of acquaintance under the influence of isolation from the outside world, how readily the heart reveals itself to any one who has gained our confidence ever so recently, if the times and seasons of communion are undisturbed by jarring interruptions. Even the external environments aid or restrain the growth of friendship, and that which strengthens and expands in summer rambles and twilight loneliness might never have found expression,—if hedged in by the formalities of social etiquette. The true man who stands before a woman with an honest love for her in his heart, seldom fails to utter words worthy of a manly nature. If there be any latent strength or beauty in him, it is transfigured in the light of his sentiment; he is lifted by it above the ordinary restraint of personality, and lays aside the rigid rules which regulate his expressional nature before the world. He has a right to speak and to be heard—he assumes, for the time, an entirely different position in regard to the object of his love from that which prevails in the daily atmosphere of social intercourse.

You see, dear Ernest, that in these days of quiet which surround me now, my mind wanders about in all directions, swayed only by the caprice of the moment. There is a certain fascination for me in following out any train of thought which suggests itself, no matter whether or not it appear very well worth attention in the beginning. I rest my mind in this way, after a season of close study and concentrated thought, just as I rest my body by a walk, after a long seclusion within-doors. In these rambles I pick up at random whatever catches my eye at the instant, it may be nothing better than a blade of grass, or it may be a fair flower worth examination,—a pebble from the wayside, or a gem hidden beneath a rough exterior. I return home laden with my spoils, and in my letters I spread them all out before you, recalling, by their aid, all the little incidents of my walks, all the thoughts that have been suggested by them. You will not scorn them because they are so often of little worth, but find some value in them all as expressions of myself. It is a delight to me to find in myself such freedom of utterance towards you, to feel no hesitation in expressing the most passing thought, no fear as to your sympathy and interest. To you as to my own heart I come, and always find you ready to listen and to respond. More than all, you give to me the same full confidence in return, and when I find such deep enjoyment in the smallest fragment of your daily thought, I am sure that you are also glad to know of mine. How fast we learn to know each other in our heart of hearts! How full of pleasure does the future seem in the light of this knowledge! Every day brings new confirmation and new increase to our love. We shall grow stronger and stronger in this atmosphere of serene trust, and learn to fear nothing in the future, for we are one for time and for eternity. Your own

ETHEL

LETTER EIGHTH

My own beloved, I am still dizzy with the excitement and hurry of your visit, and the confused sorrow at your departure. I ask myself, again and again, if you have really been with me, if I have seen you, and, above all, if I have in truth had strength to bid you farewell for such a long and weary time. I could doubt it all with pleasure, and bring myself to a half-persuasion of its falsehood, did not an ever-present loneliness oppress me with its leaden weight. I cannot shake it off even in my sleep, it makes my slumber feverish and my waking like the rousing from some distressing dream. I have striven, from the first, against the depression that assails me, sure that you wish me to be strong and hopeful in this trial-time of our love. I say over to myself all the precious words of strength that you whispered to my dull ears in those last hours that we spent together. I wear that tiny note of farewell that reached me after you yourself were gone, as an amulet, next my heart till it seems to hush its throbbings and grow more and more calm. I see, whenever I close my eyes, the picture of a steamer parting from the land while eager hands stretch out to it in vain. I watch the crowd upon its deck, and single out one form that towers high above the rest, one face that looks steadily upon the shore, and seems to know that the poor shrinking, weeping woman standing there, is murmuring blessings on him as he goes. The sunshine gleams upon the gladsome waters, the vessel rides proudly over the waves, the people who came to gaze idly upon her departure go away one by one, till none are left but her who sends forth her heart in one long last look, as the huge steamer melts away to a mere speck in the distance. Where shall she find strength and patience for the coming days? Alas, she sees no brightness in the sunshine, no beauty in the sea. Forgive her for a little while; though she faint in the outset she will prove herself, by-and-by, not all a coward.

I have retraced, step by step, that last walk we took together, and lived over again all that we said and did in that last day. Sometimes I close my eyes that I may fancy you still sitting in the arm-chair, or standing by the western window, where you and I have stood so often. I almost hear your last words, through the hush of twilight, as I sit alone and think of you. I thought, when you were indeed with me, and we looked forward into the desolate waste of absence, that I realized all that was involved in that sad farewell; but now that you are gone, I seem to have just learned its meaning. Now that I think of the lengthening miles between us, I see all the threatening possibilities that may arise in our separation. Were it not for the deep and fervent faith I have in our love, as a reality for all eternity, and in its immortal essence raised above the reach of time, I should be bowed to the dust at thought of these months that must grow up between us. You were absent from me before, to be sure, but then you were not far away; when the length of the journey between us could be reckoned by hours, you seemed not hopelessly removed, but now that hours have expanded into days, and miles are counted by thousands, I do indeed feel bitterly alone. There was so little time for preparation after your decision was made, that I lost all power of making allowance for the length of time so generously given you before action was necessary. While a matter remains vibrating in uncertainty it is nearly impossible to regard it as it will appear when it is settled in permanency, or to pursue the trains of thought which will follow inevitably upon its conclusion. So, although the prophecy of your going was in my mind, and the dread of it in my heart, I did not really grasp the idea of absence, of distance, and of withdrawal, until the words were spoken which rendered it at last an indisputable fact. Your letter, therefore, announcing your decision, came upon me with almost the suddenness it would have possessed, had I never heard of the plan: yet I had known and written and thought so much of it that I fancied myself familiar with its every aspect. All the while, however, I had left out the living soul which should give vitality to the dry and senseless form, had never dared to place your own actual self in the midst of all this array of circumstances that I was contemplating with such attention. Every little detail was carefully enough planned in my imagination, all the movements of some unnamed individual were mapped out; but it was not you, not my own beloved Ernest, that was to go forth alone and leave me. Therefore all my elaborate imaginings were useless, my preparations of no avail; I was found shelterless and bewildered when the storm fell on me. To have but one week together was a very niggard gift of fortune, and yet I fear that the courage I had nerved myself to show would have broken down utterly if I had been obliged to stand longer face to face with a sorrow ever close at hand. I was spared the shame of distressing you by unworthy weakness, I spoke no retaining word which might have made you hesitate to go forward; thank Heaven, I was even able to say a worthier and less selfish utterance at the last. How should I now take shame upon myself had I weakly yielded to my fears, and urged you to leave undone a work so noble, and for which so few are fitted! I stand erect in the knowledge of my love for you, and it is tested more by this trial of my strength than most loves are in a long and equable lifetime. The privilege, though a sad one, is a glorious one, and through all my first prostration and all my subsequent depression, I have felt a secret pride at being able to prove to you that even in the power of endurance and forgetfulness of self, I may stand by your side, my noble lover.

If good wishes may have any genial power on the elements, or any ameliorating effect upon obstacles, your path over the deep must have been unbroken sunshine, your progress in your errand will be one unmingled triumph. You won many hearts in that little week here, and from them all you have a kindly Godspeed on your journey. I find on all sides of my daily life a quicker, readier sympathy than ever, since you have been amongst us, and have become for others a reality instead of a faith. You are one of those who, almost at first sight, individualize the impressions that they make upon others; you never merge yourself in the crowd, but, once seen, once heard, you are known and remembered. After this first moment, everything you do helps to deepen and confirm the impression, and I am surprised to see how clearly you define yourself in social intercourse, without appearing too self-conscious, without seeming to put others aside in the least. It is an inherent quality in some persons, and is quite unattainable by those who do not possess it by nature; it is as distinct from vanity and forwardness, as it is from diffidence and self-distrust. In a man, especially, it is a gift for which he may be very grateful, and to one called out to take an active part in the world's work, needed to influence others and to go straight to their hearts, it is most invaluable. Your serenity in yourself, and the quiet certainty of your speech and manner, carry conviction to many minds to whom any self-originated certainty is unattainable, and who require that, as each separate subject comes before them, it should be decided for them by some other and stronger mind. The self-reliance that you have is a glorious gift; your intuitions never fail, and the time that so many need to spend upon the preliminaries of any great work, is at your disposal for the work itself. You seem to others strangely at ease when they are discomposed and undecided beneath the influence of contradictory demands, simply because, from the first, you are prepared to act upon a decision which comes to you simultaneously with the question itself. There are a great many matters upon which it is customary for a man to deliberate, and take credit to himself for his deliberation, upon which quick decision and prompt action would be far higher and nobler. The true and keen insight of an uncompromising spirit cuts the Gordian knot of circumstances and doubts and uncertainties, and sees but two clear and distinct aspects—the right and the wrong. This world needs a score or two of such clear-headed men as yourself, in each hemisphere, to cut short the long discussions of the time, and substitute for them the simple principles which they cover up and obscure, till the crowd forgets that there is any principle at all involved, and looks eagerly upon some issue quite aside from the original question. The man who has the gift from Heaven to speak from his own heart straight to the hearts of others, is responsible for every word he utters, and needs not only quickness of intuition, that no time may be lost, but also an interior calmness which shall balance and direct his promptest action.

I fully participate in all the hopes that brighten your path, and share the satisfaction you cannot but feel in the greatness of the work to which you are called. Help me, henceforth, to lay aside all the selfish egotism of my love, and to rise to a higher plane, from which I may see all connected with you in the light of your duty and in the greatness of your power of accomplishment. Help me to put off all personal fear and all distrust that may arise in my woman's weakness. I would that my love should be ever your solace and delight, never your weakness or your restraint. The strength that you impart to me I would, in some small measure, give to you, through other avenues and in other seasons of need,—the sympathy with which you ever gladden my heart I would make a perennial fountain, at which you may always find wherewith to slake your thirst.

I long for your first letter, Ernest,—it will put the seal upon my certainty of your absence. I trace over the letters of your foreign address with a kind of dreamy wonder, until it becomes a sort of hieroglyphic inscription to me. Alas! the meaning of it always returns to me and speaks of distance and of peril. Thanks to the magic of the pen, we can still approach each other, and count the beatings of each other's hearts. When I sit in my little room with all sights and sounds shut out, I am with you, from the moment that I take my pen; my thoughts flow forth fast and without reserve, and I seem to catch the response of yours, as if no distance intervened between. I can utter on paper, too, many words of love that rush to my heart, that my lips might refuse to form if your passionate look were on me, and your eager ear were bent to listen. I cannot always speak the thoughts of which my heart is full, nor put into clear utterance the emotions that thrill me with their power. You know that you sometimes see me apparently cold, just when you are sure that I am, in reality, most moved, and that I seek to shelter myself from the violence of my emotions by silent repression of their utterance. I rejoice that you are keener of sight than most of those who surround me,—that you know that I do this as a protection against my own self, not as a guard against others, and that often my only safety against the most passionate outbreak of feeling, is in the impassible manner with which I cover up the first movement of the inner flood. I would not have you think me really cold, as others do, and it is well that between us there have been peculiar influences, strong enough to break down every barrier of heart-reserve, and to reveal me, almost in spite of myself, as the organization of fire and flame that I really am. You do not regret that to the world outside I seem but ice beneath a powerless sun. It is strange how easily the world is deceived in such matters, and how readily it accepts any representation of yourself that you may voluntarily or involuntarily present to it, and how faithfully it adheres to the first picture, even when you are continually contradicting it by subsequent ones. Once establish yourself before the little circle which for you represents the world, either as cold or sympathetic, frank or reserved, and you may stand upon that ground and win praise or blame accordingly, with little actual confirmation from yourself of the awarded judgment. Even in our deeper experiences, the semblance often exists long after the insufficient reality is gone, and habit has power to retain us in observance of much that has ceased to possess any inner power of its own over us. How many act upon the supposition of continued love, long after a positive indifference has usurped its place! How many tremble at imagined coldness when that coldness has changed gradually into ever-growing love; how many continue to entrust confidences long after the first faith, which prompted and inspired them, has grown weak and useless! A part of this is doubtless owing to the shame one feels at acknowledging the fickleness implied in change; it is like giving the lie to one's own heart to confess that what was once of priceless worth to us, has ceased to have any value for us, or that what we once cast aside as valueless, has insinuated itself into our inmost hearts. To question the reality of the past seems to attack the possibilities of the future; to give up our hold on the old feeling is to cast a doubt upon the duration of all future emotions; to acknowledge present vibration implies the chance of never-ending vacillation. We go on, therefore, striving to seem the same even to ourselves, when everything in us has changed—we play at summer when there is winter in our hearts, or shiver and pretend that we are chilled, when every leaf and bud in our being is longing to burst into full life. Sometimes this process is no impeachment to our honesty, for it is mainly involuntary and inevitable—the change comes on so gradually that we do not perceive what we are doing, and are not aware that a new feeling has crossed our threshold until we discover it enthroned in the highest place within. This is especially true in regard to a growing love, which sometimes has birth amid a crowd of preju- dices and antagonistic circumstances, so adverse to it that its advent seems impossible. But love scorns antagonisms, it delights in contra- dictions and inconsistencies, it has a sweet logic of its own, by which it makes all things which happen quite reasonable, and persuades us that those attachments which nobody could have expected, are, after all, the most simply natural things in the world.

I cheat myself into transient forgetfulness of the present by these unconnected thoughts, dear Ernest, and bring you nearer to me by indulgence of their expression to you. I seem to wait for your reply after each new sentence, and I know you now so well that I can proph- esy your answer with such certainty, that I am continually incited to new questionings, if only that I may have the delight of replying to them in your name. The external life flows on for me just now so noiselessly, that it does not take me out of myself, but leaves me ample time for undisturbed communion with you, in the poor insufficient way possible through letters, which are, by turns, the most charming or the most provoking things in the world; the most charming when they offer themselves as messengers of burning thoughts which are debarred all other mode of expression, the most provoking when, their first fresh glory faded, they bring the after thought of their insufficiency as conveyances for the ever-changing moods and fancies of the heart that longs to lay its whole self before another.

The short, dull days of Winter are upon us, the long nights close around us with a tightening grasp. I do not love winter, for it shuts up the bounteous hand of Nature, and chills my heart till it grows sick and weary with longing for the flowers and the sunshine. I wish for the freedom and expansiveness of summer, and pine for the sweet influences of warmth and freshness. This winter I shall, however, lead a life comparatively independent of the season. I set apart a certain portion of each day for exercise,—not a large portion, for I am still indolent in that respect, spite of all your good advice. The rest of the time I abandon myself altogether to the sway of inner influences, and surround myself with a magic circle, within whose precincts few practicabilities dare enter. This arrangement is not only in accordance with my inclination, but is, to some extent, a necessity, for although I find my health slowly and surely reëstablishing itself, I am not yet strong enough for long-continued exertion, and do not forget your oft-repeated cautions against imprudence. I learn to be very docile beneath the loving restraints of those about me in this matter, for I think of the terrible suffering and anxiety I should subject you to, were I to be ill while you are away. Therefore I lay aside the more active duties of society, and content myself with more quiet occupations. I resign to Claudia the discharge of all my outside charities, and with so faithful an almoner, am willing to devote myself for awhile to more selfish enjoyment. You shall see with how much profit to myself I shall spend these winter months in study and in thought. My life, which was so long swayed by changing impulses from without and from within, has learned, ere this, to steady itself into greater concentration. I, who once wandered hither and thither as the mood suggested, have learned to make each successive mood help on the general movement. My external life, once so full of change and excitement, has, since I have known you, calmed itself into repose and afforded me the opportunity I needed for ascertaining my own powers and for giving them some assured direction. I am still busy at the work, still striving to attain, and therefore quiet hours are needful for me. While waiting for you I must not be idle, but as you have for a time left far behind your native land and home and friends, so would I also leave all past restraint and press on to a new land of effort and of labor.

I would there were new words in which to clothe my love and trust in you, beloved—the old are all I have to utter. They strive in vain to say all that is in my heart, and to convey my soul's longings to you. Were it not that love transfigures them into greatness, it were useless to speak them; were it not that time hallows and intensifies them, they were indeed worn out; were it not that you know all that they fail to say, silence were better than words, but now each syllable is rich with meaning from my heart to yours—

ETHEL

LETTER NINTH

My heart yearns after you, my own beloved wanderer, and follows step by step the path you are taking over such wide earth-spaces. With one effort of my thought, and in one moment of time, I come where it has taken you weeks to arrive by the slower methods of ordinary travelling, so much faster and less encumbered is the movement of the heart when it is impelled to go forth upon long journeys. But my return is as rapid as my going, and just as I am settling myself fairly into the belief that I am with you and that you are about to speak to me, something, pertaining to the immediate present, starts up to assure me that I am still at home and you are still away, and that the distance between us is really none the less because I have spanned it, for a moment, with a pretty dream-bridge strong enough to transport a host of pleasant fancies over, but not sufficient for any more substantial purpose. Then I revert to your delicious letters, which come to me all breathing with love, all palpitating with strong, fresh life. I read them so many times over, that not only does every word in them become familiar, but I am able to enjoy them in a great variety of ways, and after having fed my heart with their loving meaning, I find another satisfaction in their intrinsic beauty, and delight my intellectual fastidiousness with their brilliant style and their clear-cut excellence. Your foreign sketches and picturesque descriptions charm me not only as a lover but as an artiste. So far as they extend over ground familiar to me, they bear the additional charm of association, and suggest a thousand lively reminiscences of my own European experiences; and now that you are moving on far out of the range of my personal knowledge, I am quite as happy in having all my information come through the freshness and piquancy of your description. In fact, so well do I see the pictures which you paint for me, that the actual limit of my own travelled line is becoming dangerously dim, and I fear that in some unguarded moment I shall actually proclaim myself to have been a traveller over many lands, whereon I have as yet never set my foot. It pleases me to find how very often, in going where I have been, you have been attracted by those things which interested me the most, and impressed with those aspects of the old-world life which roused me to the most observing attention, but which many travellers either do not see at all, or notice only with a careless indifference. I seemed once more to walk the crowded streets of Paris, when I read your letter written thence—once more to study the meaning of those many faces which passed by, unconscious of my gaze, and to see in the magnificent incarnation of physical and sensational existence which Paris, above all cities, presents, a problem as unanswerable as it is fascinating. Again the ponderous gloom of London weighed me down to depression, and the gaunt spectres of its midnight beggary and vice affrighted me. Again I floated dreamily over the Rhine, and peopled the ruins on its banks with mailed knights, and its laughing vineyards with blushing peasant girls. Again I stood hushed beneath the awful grandeur of Mont Blanc, as the sun came forth to do it reverence after its lonely converse with the majesty of darkness; or gazed enraptured, as the same sun, grown bolder by his long beholding, dared at parting to cast a burning glance upon its snowy beauty, that brought a divine and rosy blush upon the white brow of the mountain. Pictures, and statues, and people, have all passed again before me, as your letters call up, one after another, the different episodes of my own pleasant travelling experience. The separate incidents of travel have each a distinct meaning and a different beauty to him to whom they belong as personal remembrances, and are apt to break up one's memory of past journeys into fragmentary and inharmonious reminiscences, so that the narration of them becomes tedious to a listener, long before they lose their zest to those to whom they have been living realities. But the true use and meaning of extensive travel to the individual is, not that by it he shall have beheld so many more cities and people, and dwelt in so many more climates than others have done, but that, by these experiences, he shall have infinitely widened his views of life, cultivated his tastes, and increased and made wiser his sympathy with humanity at large. The elements of the variety he has met should be absorbed into his mental and spiritual circulation, to cause a freer and heartier and ruddier glow. The different modes of his life should be fused into one grand whole, and he should develope into a larger-hearted, a more wise, more genial, more harmonious, and more serene man; not merely into one rich in anecdote and gifted with a variety of tongues. The rough points of character and disposition should be rounded off into graceful proportions by attrition with the world, and a wider charity be learned through observation of the innumerable aspects which this human life presents to a thoughtful person, the endless involutions of circumstance and temperament, of races and of climates. I sometimes think a travelled man should be a somewhat saddened one, for truly this world of ours is no easily-read riddle, no childish play-ground, no summer dream. The questions, which intercourse with it rouse in the mind, are apt to press heavily in hours of thoughtfulness; the scenes of vice and misery, and even the pictures of enjoyment and happiness, through which it takes us, seem to have a hidden meaning, unto which, with all our study, we cannot be quite sure we attain. We cannot always resolve the clouds into angel-faces, though sure that the Great Artist is true to his work. If there be any groundwork of true thoughtfulness in a man's nature, a life of movement must (unless utterly without seasons of quiet and repose) serve to eliminate it into positive manifest existence.

And you, dear Ernest, are having such glorious opportunity for all this cultivation, all this harmonizing of your own inner and outer life. Your years of study have so prepared you to understand the meaning of what you see, that you need fear no over accumulation of facts, which, when heaped up in a less cultivated and less philosophic mind, might produce a complete and hopeless chaos. Your knowledge of your own country enables you to institute comparisons, and to make deductions, which will prevent all one-sidedness of result; and your magnetic force of character and wonderful discriminative powers will open before you a thousand paths, which to the mere external traveller would never be suspected. I see in your letters the working of all these forces, and you lead me with you through all your wanderings, whether they take your external sense through palpable scenes of life, or entice your imagination into labyrinths of speculation. With you to guide me, I am superior to all fatigue; with you to teach me the meaning of what I see, I grow wiser than myself, and find unceasing interest in each new glimpse of the active life in which you mingle, and each new revelation of the thoughts which visit your mind when it withdraws into itself. I hush the piteous wailings of my heart when I remember that it is only at the cost of absence and separation and distance that all this is to be won; but there are times when an inexpressible agony assails me, or when the longing to behold you rises into a horror of painfulness, and bows me to the very dust with inconsolable wretchedness. Do I not, my best beloved, see traces of a similar yearning in some of the sweet words of your last letter? You think it no shame to confess that your own great heart grows faint at thought of the time and space that intervene between us. Oh, Ernest, you are always noble, always true, always grand! For it is, indeed, grand to so embrace within the limits of one heart all the noble manliness of unflagging aspiration, and all the sweet and gentle tenderness of timid, trembling love. You never tremble for yourself, nor quail at any danger which threatens but yourself, yet you quiver with apprehension at the thought of even a rude breath upon my unworthy self. Your prayer goes up to heaven on the sweet night air, and the tears of loving weakness tremble in your eyes just as my wom-an's heart lies prostrate in its own supplications, and my courage dies away within me as I look in vain for you. Only in that prayer of utter weakness to the Help that never fails, can I find returning peace and happiness. In that I come forth into the summer region of my love and trust; I see you strong and hopeful by my side; I hear your prophecy of safe return; I glow with happy anticipation, and come forth again to resume with new energy my daily work.

Your pleasant and wise plans for occupation I am carrying out with religious faithfulness, and it is to them that I owe it that my hours of despondency have been comparatively so few. I labor at my studies as earnestly as if you saw each page that I turn over; I paint my pictures with as eager enthusiasm as if you were to see them before the colors are dry, and I walk forth every day with a stride as strong and rapid as if I were to meet you somewhere on the way. Every book that I open speaks to me of you, the perfume left by your cigar grows poetical as Araby's soft airs in the magic light of association, your pencil-marks are sweet illuminations of my text, a word of comment at the bottom of the page is a volume of new meaning to me. Every criticism, every suggestion that you have made to me in art, is, as it were, engraved upon my memory in golden letters, and glows and beams upon me as I work. And in my walks, I tread in our old footsteps, and every moment I hear your voice repeating some pleasant word, or see you smile as the sunlight comes forth and lights up some point that you have loved to look at with me. I am rich in associations, dearest, and have not wholly lost your presence.

This same power of association, how rich it is and over what endless paths of beauty it leads us! Such tiny trifles as it makes important, such charming meaning as it gives to simplest deeds! The gleam of sunlight on the grass, the breath of some common flower, the strain of simple music, are fraught with deepest significance to the heart to which they speak the mystic language of association. Some of the most ordinary articles of our daily surroundings are glorified into an upper region of sacredness by some little memory which clings lovingly to them, as if to shield them from desecration, when their more practical usefulness is passed. How we treasure up some cumbrous and unsightly piece of furniture if a beloved form has rested upon it, or find an inner beauty in something uncongenial to our natural tastes, if one we love has praised or loved it! I strive to associate with those I love, those things which have an inherent beauty however, not only from æsthetic instincts, but from loving homage to those upon whose shrines I lay my twining garlands of association. Though every hour of my day brings me some thought of you, more or less interior and pervading, yet I have so interwoven my soul with yours in one direction that it can never be dissociated therefrom—I dedicate to you the expanse of the western sky as twilight falls over the weary earth. It matters not whether that sky be glorious with crimson and gold, or gay with mists and clouds, whether it be softly luminous with summer's quivering heats or chill and clear with winter's frosts. I see it, though the close city streets shut it out from my eyes, as I behold it when there is naught between me and the horizon's utmost verge. And you stand before me then and I look down deeper and deeper into the unfathomable depths of your calm eyes, and seem to float at once into your soul and into that far-off western realm, to reach the very abode of sunset, as I feel your strong hands holding me, and learn more and more that beauty is unity, and that its mission is not to the senses, be they ever so delicate, but to the soul, which must respond and lift itself ever higher and higher unto the central source of all beauty.

The perception of beauty grows with our using of it in ourselves, and becomes more and more a medium of truth, as we listen heedfully and reverently to its utterances. As it becomes dearer to us it becomes ideal, and from ideality it gains spiritual meaning, and from spiritual it passes on to heavenly meaning. That is no love of Beauty which the vulgar feel when their admiration is called forth, nor when the earthy sense is pleased with pleasant sights and sounds—but the true sentiment is twin-sister to the religious faith, and delights to glorify and adorn its manifestations in our human life. In Heaven it may be absorbed into our worship, and become inseparable from our soul-life. Not in vain has the world built its fair temples and rung out its grand anthems and painted its glorious pictures, any more than it is in vain that God has made the whole earth beautiful with trees and flowers, with seas and mountains.

And I strive ever in dim and somewhat uncertain wise to mingle my thought of you with ever growing aspiration for myself—to surround your image with all that I can feel of loftiest beauty and truthfulness. All the other loves and friendships of my life have fallen far below the standard I strive to attain unto with you. Though some have been helpful to me, though some have been ennobling, none have reached the elevation to which I mount with you as on the wings of the morning. Apart from the deep, passionate, impulsive love in our hearts, there has been so much of spiritual effort, so much of reverent search, so much of true soul-companionship, that heart and life and soul, this world and the next, are all mingled in one indissoluble bond. No niggard response have you made to my heart, but rather outrun my eager demand—no cold forbearance have you granted to the earnest questionings of my soul, but rather, joining in the search after truth and life, have steadied my trembling steps and borne me with loving arms over the rough and stony places of my soul's pilgrimage. The sorrowful and weary paths, which others have to tread alone, have been made merciful by your companionship, and now we can never either of us be any more alone.

What shall I tell you of myself in these long days when I cannot see you? Shall I tell you more of the old past or content myself with hasty glimpses of the present? Shall I paint for you a gallery of portraits of the people by whom I am surrounded, that when you come you may already know them, or shall I still continue the heroine of my own

story, and. fill up all but the corners of the sheets I send you, with
continually repeated pictures of myself? You have had me already in
nearly every possible aspect, every variety of light and shade. Do you
never grow weary of contemplating this face that so pertinaciously
places itself before you, every lineament of which you must ere this be
familiar with, and which always looks back upon you with an unvarying glance of trusting love? You say that my moods vary, and that
although you know me to be steadfast, yet you never find me twice
exactly alike, either in look or manner; but to myself I seem, so far as
regards you, to be in one unvarying attitude, and sometimes dread lest
even my earnest love may not always be able to redeem that sameness
from weariness to you. Were it not that when with you I find myself
ever moving along with you, and that then life seems not only full of
sweetness and of love, but overflowing with rich variety and delicious
changes, I should indeed have reason to fear this constant revolution
of my heart about you as its centre. But I am glad that you find me
various enough, as you say you do, for it is your own gift to sway me
as you will, and I trust never to lose this responsiveness which makes
me so happy. To tell the truth, I do not myself like those persons
who seem unsusceptible to a change of mood, and are consequently
unsympathetic and unresponsive. The faculty of vibration by no means
implies the necessity of weakness, and because we sometimes see
the bird sitting motionless upon the nest, we do not conclude that he
cannot therefore fly out into the upper air and wing his way aloft till
the eye aches with following him. So, though I am still and hushed
when I brood over my love for you, I love to wander hither and thither,
wherever the whim takes me, in all the other aspects of my life. Even
in my most ordinary avocations I seek an impulse to move me in any
particular direction, and am full of method in a most unmethodical
way. I do with zest and pleasure—not the work which most persons
would declare appropriate to the times and seasons—but that which
there is at the moment a will within me to do. The harness of prescribed routine galls and wearies me, and the supposed necessity for
doing a particular thing at a particular moment is sometimes enough
in itself to render the doing irksome. I have known many persons
who, in consequence of putting this self-imposed yoke upon their
necks, seemed actually *never* to do what, at the time, they wished to
do, for, as the order of nature goes calmly on without regard to petty

individual plans, stupid and prosaic in-door occupations were sure to come, upon their chart, just when the loveliest days wooed to enjoyment of outside beauty, and their prescribed seasons for exercise and recreation fell upon times of storm and dulness. We are sufficiently inured to the general routine of habit to accomplish, in the long run, most of the really important matters of daily work and conventional needs, without a too slavish obedience to that routine developed into wearisome details of days and hours, and a certain degree of freedom and laissez-faire, in regard to them, makes life easier and simpler to a degree that few seem to understand. It always amuses me to see this reverence of method in trifles carried into the domain of lofty conscientiousness, as it is very apt to be by my own sex, and to hear the tone of lamentation with which positive and easily attained pleasures for themselves, and much gratification for those who love them, are put aside, because, in the regularly arranged plan of the week, the time has arrived for them to attend to something which, to put it on its highest possible ground, is a mere negative and unimportant virtue. For myself, the presence of an individual impulse carries me at once half-way over the labor that is to be accomplished, and I have never yet found that the impulse failed to appear for each successive need, in season to prevent any serious consequences from delay, even though I might appear culpably dilatory to those who follow closely upon their carefully prescribed routine. It is only in those matters, which rise into the higher and nobler portions of life, that I feel willing to yield an unquestioning obedience at any hour when they may call, and in them I recognise, without repugnance, the additional dignity and beauty they receive from being harmoniously arranged. Perhaps it is only another manifestation of my dominant spirit of exclusiveness, which leads me to draw a line between the trivial and accidental employments of life and those higher and grander duties which, in their very movement, elevate us and make us more and more free, just as I put aside, for a more careless notice, the claims of my ordinary and casual acquaintances, and think it no harm occasionally to ignore their existence, while the inner circle of my friends forms an ever-present regulating influence on my every thought and deed. Presence and absence become, in this light, less stringent, less descriptive terms, for there is always present with me a something representative of my friend, even when wide distances separate the tangible daily life. Some one says, that what we really love we really own, and I seem to myself, in this sense, to hold complete possession of my friends—the concentration of my affection upon a few seems to bring those few always within my reach; one is never crowded out by another, for where the guests are few and honored, there is room for all close by the host. I have but to stretch forth my hand to touch each member of my little household in the mansion into which my friendliness has welcomed them. And though they sometimes go away in the body, as you are now doing, yet in the spirit they are still sitting within the four walls of my little friendship-home, and meet me with a smile every morning and every evening.

I send forth a dove over the waste of waters, bearing to you all the best wishes of my heart. She is freighted with loving words, almost too sweet to be uttered save in the deepest and most private recesses of the imagination; the blushing of the dawn is not fairer than the tender glances she would bring to you, the mid-day glory is not purer than the atmosphere of love through which she flies, and the hush of twilight is not holier than the trustful impulse, half-prayer, and half-acknowledgment, which she bears from my very heart itself unto you. Her wing is strong, and she knows her errand, she flies straight and fast to you, sure of a welcome, and thrilling herself with the joy that her tidings will bring to your own loving heart. Oh, weeks and months that are to come! I could almost implore you to leap at once into the past, that I might find close at hand the coming of my absent one; but I check the wish before it is uttered; I accept the tedious unfolding of these passing days, and turn without repining to learn the lessons which they would teach. They shall not be days of stagnation, hardly days of sadness, for I will make them ministrant of all good influences to you and to myself. God is near to both of us, and in Him we are near unto each other. He will guide and guard us till we meet again; to Him I speak of you, unto Him I trust you, and through Him I bless you.

ETHEL

LETTER TENTH

THE days of absence wear slowly away, beloved Ernest, and my thought at morning, and my prayer at night, begin and end with your beloved name. Perhaps I learn to know you even better through absence than I could have done in your continued presence, for my thoughts dwell upon you now in each separate aspect of your life and being, with a more unbroken attention than they could possibly have done when you were by, to substitute one impression for another, and to change the direction of my thought, even if the object of it remained the same. In absence we call up the image of one we love, as it appears in the light of some particular quality, or as developed in one style of action; it stands before us as a statue would do, and we study it in all its proportions, make ourselves familiar with every feature, and draw from it a complete and satisfactory impression; and as time passes, we collect a series of these impressions as various as the characteristics of our friend, and finally obtain, from the accumulation of sketches, a perfect picture. But when life flows on in the presence of our dear ones, it becomes so full of action, that there is no time for steady thought; we catch a glimpse, it may be, at one moment, of something in character or heart on which we would fain dwell with fond attention, but soon the current bears us on, and we are both in new circumstances, and new qualities become prominent. It is not unusual to find members of a family much less conversant of the deeper nature of each other, than many who stand outside, for the reason that the daily life glides on too fast, and usurps, with its trivialities, the time which we give to our friends, while only those words or those deeds, which express the stronger characteristics, are brought into visibility for the world at large. Some action or some thought put in words, gives to a passing looker-on a more sharp-cut outline of a man's mind or heart, than those, who meet him every day, can form from the too numerous and contradictory impressions, which his careless daily act or word may give. The best friends are apt to lose, in constant intercourse, the perception of salient points in each other, and the influence of present love is to soften and assimilate much that in absence becomes distinct and prominent. You see that I strive hard, dear Ernest, to win some compensation from the hard present, which has put such wide and hopeless gulfs of time and distance between our daily lives. I am trying to paint your heart and soul upon the walls of my inner life, just as I am busy with painting the face which is ever before my imagination, by the help of memory alone. I have covered for a little while the portrait which hangs in my room, and I sit down each day at my easel, working earnestly, lovingly, and as I think, most successfully, upon another portrait of you, which shall be even more faithful than the one I have had so long. And as I call up your features and remember how you looked at different times when we have been together, I also summon up an image of your inner self as it has been set forth in some noble deed or generous word; I see your whole soul reveal itself in some grand enthusiasm, your heart in the sweet and tender beauty of some kindly act. I hardly know which picture I prize most, the one that daily grows beneath my fingers, or that which develops itself invisibly to all eyes but my own, and renders beautiful the inner temple of my heart. I have found more delight in these hours thus spent with your imagined presence near me, than I thought myself capable of feeling when you are really far away. The half-finished portrait greets me every morning with a look of love; the heart-picture I behold through midnight darkness as in noonday light.

The outward world goes on as ever with its routine of daily events, none of which affect especially either myself or my environments. The love of others makes each day pleasant to me, and I strive to return a grateful response to those who seek to make me happy, rather than to let the inner loneliness of my heart, without you, make me selfishly regardless of the claims of others upon me. That were but a poor and miserable love, which narrowed the nature into only one channel of expression, and for my own part, I find that in loving and working for all who should be dear to me, I seem ever to express, under some new phase, the love that finds its truest, and happiest, and fullest outlet towards yourself. What I do for others seems to me not only a pleasant duty towards them, but a loving homage to you; and even the charities, that call me out of myself to supply the needs of others, weave themselves into mystical and pleasant connexion with yourself.

Summer comes on with rapid steps, for which I listen almost as lovingly as for your own, my Ernest,—perhaps because I trust that I shall hear them both together. Your letters tell me that I may hope for this—indeed, I fancy I should do so in spite of all that might discourage my expectation. I take to my heart all the meaning of this forced absence from each other, and though it has often made me very sad, I trust it has not made me weak. It is difficult to realize that what we suffer and enjoy, what we do and what we love, are to the heart as the air and the rain, the sunshine and the dew to the plant—that their alternation is necessary to the growth of each, and that the heart can no more thrive and blossom without tears, than the flower without rain. In the deep silence of my soul I receive the sadness of my lonely hours, and seek to make of them all that they are intended to become to me. My heart loves the sunshine, and longs for its return, as it yearns for your presence, and feels but half itself when out of your companionship; but it will not, therefore, spend itself in weak complaint or idle repining. Go on, my own beloved, in your great work; let my prayers help you more than my tears restrain you; believe that the former are the expression of my higher self, the latter the necessary and unhurtful weakness of a loving woman's heart.

I think, my Ernest, that as the days go by and I dwell in the holy seclusion of my love for you, I catch some faint reflection of your own calmness,—my heart learns to regulate more and more its once spasmodic impulse, and I grow stronger and more assured within myself. I do not find my enthusiasms lessen in themselves, but I find myself less hasty in falling into new ones—though the old, established ones grow ever grander and more absorbing, as I find them true and worthy. I lay aside, as it seems to me, some of the useless and trivial excitements of the hour, to concentrate more and more upon the great work of the day. I think of you and your own grand object till I feel that I, too, can labor and press on without weariness, as you are doing. Would that I were with you in every deed; in every step forward that you take, my heart and hope are with you, and I know that you sometimes feel my presence at your side. Your letters are so hopeful, that I have long since laid aside all fear as to your ultimate success, and now have but to be patient with the necessarily slow motions of your plans. You say the *denouement* will seem sudden at the last, for much secrecy of detail has been necessary, to insure undisturbed action; it cannot be too sudden, for it will allow of your immediate return to me. I would the diplomatic clock were in my keeping for a little while, and I might make its ponderous wheels move a little faster towards the hour which shall strike forth the completion of your work. Have patience with me, Ernest; these are but the harmless ejaculations of my some-times impatient spirit—you know that my soul is strong within me, and not wholly unworthy to mate with yours. Were I with you and able to do battle at your side, you should hear nothing but triumphant strains from my lips;—it is the loneliness, the distance, that make me a little cowardly at times. When I think of the black abyss of ocean that lies between us, and then of the long waste of land—a waste to me, though full of populous and busy life—my heart indeed grows weak and dizzy, and I tremble and shed tears.

None but your own kind and thoughtful self would find time, among so many distracting occupations and harassing cares, for such long and interesting accounts of your present environments. How do you retain, amid so much that is difficult and prosaic, all your keen susceptibility to the most delicate and subtle manifestations of the Beautiful? How, in the most transient glance at the faces around you, can you read so much of the character of the individual, and in the rapid movement of your life succeed in showing forth so clearly your own warm sympathetic heart, till you win those who approach you wholly to yourself? I see that you do this, not by means of any positive narrative that you set before me, but by the frequent men-tion of kindnesses received, and the pleasant nature of every new association that you form. Your manner is such a singular mixture of personal reserve with frank cordiality, that you first attract attention and finally win unlimited confidence. It is, perhaps, because you make so few word-professions, that people rely so implicitly upon what you do say; and you seem so entirely competent to guard your own secrets from intrusive attention, that it is taken for granted that you will be quite able to protect those which others intrust to you. I watch with intense interest your present position, for utterly isolated from your own countrymen and thrown upon the hospitality of foreigners, you must, more than ever, assume and assert your own unassisted individuality—that individuality which you have always been successful in maintaining, in a marked degree, at home. Every detail, however minute, is full of interest to me, and I rejoice that you have patience to set them down for me with such loving minuteness. Yours is a love that disdains no trifle and fears no labor in the service of the one you love. The harmony of your nature is shown not only in the greatness of what you accomplish, but in the gracefulness with which you adorn the daily life with delicate and almost nameless charms. You store your memory so richly with images, that every day is a new treasure-house for you, and you are as prodigal in spending your intellectual wealth as you are indefatigable and successful in adding to it. I seem so near you when I read your letters, the incidents you relate seem to have happened but a moment before—the persons you describe seem to have just left the room, the atmosphere you breathe in your walks is sweeping at the moment past my brow.

You think then that the success of this visit will insure your return to the present scene of your labors at no distant day, and that I too must make up my mind to wander for a while over the face of the earth? The prospect has no pain in it, save the regret inseparable from the parting with family and friends, and even that is wonderfully lessened for me by the opportunity of motion, and above all, by the means it will give me of still better understanding that which must, for the present, absorb your own activity. I am, however, so absorbed in the more immediate prospect of your return, that save in the way of practical preparation for so important a movement, my thought stops short at the instant in which you set your foot once more within my dwelling. I can as yet see nothing beyond that; the sunshine of that moment blinds my dazzled eyes; I must wait till I can bear the splendor of that picture before I can turn to the examination of any other. In the mean time I trust all to you. Were it to Sahara's midmost sands that you proposed to take me, I should feel sure that you would discover there some fairy oasis, where life would be delicious, and healthful change supply itself in the midst of eternal sameness. I strive to see more and more clearly the people among whom I am to cast my lot, and for this purpose your sketches of character are invaluable. Already I have a select circle of friends in your far-off capital, and can tell in which direction my heart will quickest take root and find nourishment. I am succeeding better and better, too, in reconciling others to the impending change, and making them regard with less horror a plan which involves such a wide and long separation from them. At first the dismay was unmitigated, but as the idea grows familiar, it asserts its advantages and even brings into visibility its charms. So that now, instead of being a victim, I am a heroine, in the eyes of the home-circle. I have not the heart even to check the vastness of the preparations which my mother is making for my wardrobe conveniences, or to attempt to stem the torrent of practicabilities in which she submerges herself with such delight. One would fancy that I was going to some far-off island, only approachable by civilized man once in a score or two of years, and that the same island not only passed through every variety of climate, from the Arctic to the Torrid zone, but that, through all its vicissitudes of temperature and inaccessibility of position, the goddess of Fashion reigned with as relentless a sway as that she exercises in mid-season at the most gay watering-places. I trust the wardrobe fever will subside before the transportation of my effects becomes necessary, or that information will come, from a source my mother is more in the habit of relying upon in these particulars, than she is upon my own somewhat random remarks as to my clothes-necessities, to persuade her that it will be quite possible for me to supply all my needs in my new home. You must write her a fashion-letter, Ernest, and give her an elaborate description of the toilettes you see at Court, and then ingeniously introduce an account of the facilities your present home affords for supplying any prettinesses, which we in our transatlantic region regard as difficult of purchase. If something of this sort be not successfully accomplished, you may as well make up your mind to leave behind you a poor maiden so encumbered with merchandise as I shall be. I am not sure that my dear little mamma, in the exercise of her superabundant energies, will not wish you to send home your own measure, that she may commence the accumulation of a mountain of masculine garments, which shall be twin to that which now I behold rising before my own eyes. All this, however, serves as an admirable "escape" for her excitement in regard to my leaving her, and which might else take a form more painful for me to witness, and more sorrowful for her to experience.

My letter, though so long, has failed to utter half my heart would say to you, and were I to write twice as much, I should be as far as ever from the end of what I wish to say. Read it with your heart as I have written it with mine, and then it will not be altogether meaningless to you. Good night, and may all good angels guard you, and all skies be serene above your head. May the day bless you with its sunshine, and the night refresh you with its holy serenity. More than all, may the sweetest winds of heaven waft you on your way to me, who long for you with all the strength and all the fear, that can thrill through a loving and devoted heart.

ETHEL

LETTER ELEVENTH

OH, Ernest! can such pleasant words be true? Have I really only one week more of waiting, after all this long and weary time of absence? The letter telling me of your safe arrival reached me the same day that the papers announced the successful issue of your public mission, and I did not know how much pride was mingled in my love for you, till I felt the throb of exultation within me, as my father read aloud the words of praise with which your name was coupled. But my first, and strongest, and happiest thought is, that you are at home again, and soon to be with me. This thrills me through and through with renovated life, and fills me with a joy for which I find no fitting words. I think I should love you quite as well if no one but myself ever knew how truly great and good you are; but in my present genial and beneficent mood, I do not find it in my heart to quarrel with the world for having also found you out, and greeted you with its honors. While I knew you to be upon the way, I was miserably restless and anxious for your safety; every blast seemed to murmur of a storm at sea; every newspaper seemed to be freighted with tidings of some new disaster; every face to betray some restrained horror. All omens assailed my timorous heart, grown superstitious for your beloved sake. I was a coward in the sight of Heaven, and trembled lest the providence of God should fail me in the hour of my need. I should be ashamed to tell you all my pusillanimous imaginings, were it not that you, too, are tenderly susceptible to alarms for those you love, and know to what extremity of anguish, and blasphemy of terror, prolonged suspense will drive a loving heart. Thank God, you are safe, heart of my heart, life of my life! And yet, oh Ernest, I *was* brave, amid all my fears, for I dared to look steadily at a woe that now I tremble even to name. I gazed through the long night-hours upon that huge steamer, bearing on through darkness and storm its precious freight of human life, all concentrated for me in one beloved form. I dreamed of danger in a thousand shapes; I lived through agonies of dread; I saw all fearful sights of death, and I grew rigid in despair, for I still looked on with fascinated gaze. At one word, all these fears are dissipated, and I am as full of joy as then of misery. And now that I am at peace, and know you to be safe and well, my heart grows proud and glad at your success, and thrills and glows to know that you are also happy. I did not lack for sympathy in my nervous fears, nor do I now in my delight. The household is alive, from first to last, with your name, and the note of preparation for your advent echoes from all quarters. The general satisfaction seeks expression in the elaborations of hospitality, and were you to bring with you a whole regiment of "German mercenaries," instead of the one "slight, pale student" you describe, they would be made welcome, and all their wants amply supplied, so active is, at present, the practical element in the whole ménage. And there is pleasant meaning in all this activity, and an under-current of love and sympathy beneath this bustle, which makes it very welcome to me.

I have written to you long chapters of the past, dear Ernest, but that was when the passing moment held no immediate expectation, and was fraught with no especial meaning. While you were far off, my mind went backward without reluctance, and memory led me by the hand, a willing visitor, among the chambers of the past; but now the present fills me with occupation, and the future thrills me with anticipation. Now that you are coming, I have thoughts for nothing else; I count the hours again and again, glad at each repetition to drop off one more from the shortening chain; I become excited when I sit down to think; I catch myself smiling, when no word has been spoken; and as I passed the mirror this morning, I saw a blush rise to my cheek, so vivid that, had you been present, you must have ceased to chide me for my excessive paleness. Verily, the heart plays strange pranks with the features, Ernest, for the face which greets me from the mirror now, is far other than the woe-worn, anxious visage it has shown me of late. Happiness is a skilful physician, and the frame grows strong and the eye brilliant, when the heart is light. Your letter tells me that you are bronzed by travel, and that your stalwart form and broad shoulders will, more than ever, form a striking contrast to my own somewhat *petite* proportions. I like it thus, my giant lover. I would have you thus stalwart and thus strong; I am glad that health glows upon your cheek, and that you tremble at no wind that blows. The picture that you sent my mother, produced a great sensation. The foreign dress was pronounced wonderfully becoming, and the only comment which my regard for your modest diffidence allows me to repeat to you, was that of my cousin Emily, who said, "How extremely handsome he would be, if he would not wear such an enormous beard!" The beard, as you may remember, ranks with her among the cardinal sins.

I try to beguile the intervening days with a thousand little arrangements for your pleasure when you come, and thus give myself the pleasant task of recalling all your peculiar tastes, and bringing you continually before me in different attitudes. All the important preparations for the grand event are taken perforce from off my hands, by my busy mother, who, with half a smile and half a sigh, bids me not to lighten these her last labors for her daughter, and not to make myself weary and pale, and so win her a scolding from one who is coming. My poor Mother! happy as she really is in her child's happiness, her heart yearns for me when I am away, and she cannot but miss me sadly when I leave her. But she gives me hopeful and earnest words of counsel, and blesses me with sweet and loving tenderness. She will have two children instead of one, henceforth, for she already loves you as a son. She is very proud, too, of the distinction you have achieved, and tells your story with infinite enjoyment of its picturesque details. You will be received with all the honors of a victorious general, and must prepare yourself for a little tiresome admiration from our outside acquaintance. I shall keep the day of your arrival secret, that I may be sure of having you a little while to myself,—I cannot let others see you till I have satisfied my own eager eyes. My father looks at me so fondly in these last days, that my eyes overflow with tears; thoughts of the home I am to leave assume a tone of melancholy, as the little daily pleasantnesses are renewed to form themselves into farewell memories; those about me say many common-places about past freedom and coming cares—but, for myself, I feel no sadness, and I regret no freedom—I am lifted above the routine of my daily thought, and breathe a higher atmosphere wherein I see things in truer proportions. My true freedom commenced with my love for you, and sadness finds no place in the earnest hopefulness with which I look forward to my life with you and its wider opportunities for action. I have had enough of seclusion, enough of contemplation; my heart has learned its own secrets well, and my thoughts have dwelt long enough upon the inner aspects of my soul to be ready to commence, almost to crave for, something on which to expend its accumulated energies. In this conscious need of new expression in outward life, I rejoice that your honor and your duty call you away from study, away even from quiet. After your brief vacation, which, thank heaven, comes just in this heart of summer's warmth and beauty, and during which we will enjoy to its utmost our long-planned seashore delights, we will enter cheerfully on your new sphere, and find therein as much of mutual love and mutual sympathy, and help in the active and varied life that beckons to you, as we have already enjoyed in those quiet hours, which have given us so fully and entirely unto each other. I might have trembled at the prospect of a busy life with its intrusive urgencies, had it followed immediately upon our first avowals of love, and absorbed us before we had had time for studying each other's natures, and growing into each other's hearts. The time of waiting, which seemed then to stretch tediously far into the future, has proved of infinite value to us, for in it we have learned as well as loved each other, and now we understand all our points of sympathy and likeness, and see clearly, and without exaggeration, all the peculiarities of individual temperament, which, well understood, will serve only to create a pleasant and healthful motion in our life-current, but which, ignored or half comprehended, might have caused pain and surprise. Do you know how great cause for rejoicing we have that our tastes and habits of life are as similar as they are decided—that our minute antagonisms are so unusually few? The number is small of those, who, even in loving most fondly, and finding their happiness most completely in each other, have not to ignore their own separate tastes, and change their own personal habitudes, if they would attain to entire communion with those they love. One or the other must lay aside something of himself and assume new tastes and interest himself in new pursuits, which, save through their attraction to the other, would be utterly devoid of charm. And poor human nature, though in its moments of exaltation it welcomes and glories in opportunities for self-abnegation, and imagines that always its greatest delight must be to live only in the sensations of its beloved, yet after a little while it grows weary of flying against an unnatural atmosphere, the wings droop, the breath fails, and it turns of necessity to its old and easy course, mourning that its beloved must by the same instinct pursue a different one. I have often seen those who love each other very deeply, quite unable, from intrinsic unlikeness of nature, to enjoy much in each other's companionship, obliged to shut out all action and all movement, and to restrict themselves to the simple act of loving, or to lose the power of continuing side by side. But we, who before we met were both upon the same path, whose daily habits of thought and life were strangely similar, and whose likes and dislikes seem to be magnetically united, ah, we hardly know our blessedness and the peace and pleasure of which our daily life may be full. Now, that we not only love, but know each other, we may go out into the great world, and meet, unfaltering, all the manifold influences, which, with less of love and less of knowledge, might have been fearful antagonists for us. We shall go forward side by side, you sustaining me at your own height, and the confidence between us shall be, as it has ever been, entire and unreserved. You will not even disdain my help, for you have taught me how to be strong and helpful. I would be not merely the companion of your leisure hours, but would share your hardest labor, and be by you in your busiest and most anxious seasons. You gave me the deepest pleasure that my heart can feel, dearest, when you told me how very much you expect from me.

Claudia asks me if I do not tremble at the thought of the social ordeal through which I am to pass, and shrink from the difficult duties of the position I am to assume. I trust it is something better than a vain self-confidence which impels me to say that I feel no fear, but rather a secret joy. I confess my susceptibility to ambition for you, and I rejoice that you are to be placed where your talents will have full scope for their activity, your heart be able to carry out some of the grand schemes which it has planned. Not for worlds would I utter one word of dissuasion from such a noble career, but gladly encourage, and share in all that it implies of effort and of self-denial. I believe this to be no vulgar ambition, for your sphere of usefulness increases with its elevation, and in your plans there enter all the most glorious elements of human progress. God's blessing will be on us as we strive diligently and truly in the path to which He points us.

The hours of my maiden life are ebbing fast away, the ties of kindred lose their hold upon my outer life, as the new and more absorbing tie comes nearer and nearer to claim my obedience. I am surprised at the serenity of my own faith in our future; I feel no exaggerated emotional excitement, no nervous doubts and fears; I dream no visions of impossible, superhuman bliss, but calmly and clearly I look upon a future which stretches out before me, a future such as I would have it, full of active energy, of variety, of labor, full too, as I believe, of success and of noble rewards. I see myself leaning through all upon your faithful arm, resting in your tried love, and protected by a strong, true heart. I find in you the consummation of my being—the development of my mind in your grand intellectual nature, the fulfilment of my heart's deepest yearnings in your noble and generous manliness. I behold no sky without a cloud, no perennial summer-time of flowers and of sunshine; no fairy-land inanities woo me with their blandishments, but I see a path which, though somewhat dusty, and world-travelled, has still its charms and its promises, and on which we can walk erect, and side by side; it leads us where, as strong and willing and hopeful souls, ready to put forth our strength in all worthy effort, we would fain go. We leave the past behind us, keeping only its lessons near our hearts; henceforth every step shall be for us an onward one. The dawn is past, and we have had all that it could give of crimson clouds and golden mists; now we are strong for the midday toil, and turn our faces towards the kindling glories of the western skies. Though still young in years, we have both lived much, thought much, suffered much. We have lost no power of keen enjoyment, but rather learned to know how to enjoy; we have lost no faith, but rather won a firmer hold on all high and noble things; we have lost no strength, but have rather been disciplined to a more skilful and successful warfare; the past has been for us a prophecy and preparation, not a defeat or a disappointment. And now, each completed in the other's being, each living in the other's life, each throbbing in the other's quickened pulsation, we will give no empty thanks for our great happiness, no noisy welcome to our joy. The whole of our future shall be consecrated unto noblest uses, and our happiness be equalled by our earnest labor. Our thanksgivings shall mingle with aspirations, and in our union, we will lift our hearts above themselves. Before the world we give ourselves unto each other, before our God we give ourselves to Him. Oh, loyal heart, it is through you that I see Him, and it is He that led you unto me to fill my life with beauty and with love. My heart already hears your footsteps, and leaps to meet you and clasp you to itself.

ETHEL SUTHERLAND.

Verses

———•———

Contents

PRELUDE

THOUGH I be not Liszt or Rubinstein,
Shall I never touch my piano?
Though I be not Lind or Patti,
Shall I never hum a ballad?
Though I be not Tennyson or Browning,
Shall I never build a rhyme?
And though I be not able to shout unto the nations,
Shall I never whisper to my friend?

DEDICATION

I NAME thee not, yet ever in my heart
    Thine image may be found,
Standing from all my other loves apart,—
    Enshrined and crowned.

And though I weary oft of other minds,
    Tiring of all they teach,
My heart an ever-freshening pleasure finds
    In thy dear speech.

So, though I do not name thee to the crowd,
    Nor thy sweet titles call,
One word I whisper when thine ear is bowed
    That tells thee all!

And in these few poor words so little worth,
    I know that thou wilt see
The loving wish in which they have their birth
    To honor thee.

PROEM

AT times without my bidding
    My thoughts take shape in rhyme,
With a half-unconscious cadence
    Measure their own sweet time.

And, through some dreamy hour
    Of the soft summer day,
Like children from school escaping,
    Verses and measures play.

Or when the sad, still twilight
    Hushes my throbbing brain,
And past is the day's long toiling,
    With its weariness and pain,—

I close my burning eyelids,
    And, far from this world of sense,
I fly to delightful dreamland
    To bring pleasant fancies thence.

The sights and sounds of my vision
    Gladden my inmost heart,
And it seems as though their beauty
    Must some charm to my words impart.

So, though it is in broken
    And sadly imperfect tones
That I find I have strength to utter
    What my heart in secret owns,

Yet that which my soul is thrilling
    And deep in my heart I feel,
I am forever striving
    In some way to reveal.

Therefore these humble verses
    Have woven their web of thought,
And all these simple fancies
    Been to these pages brought.

MY FRIEND—MY FRIEND

A THOUSAND thoughts unwritten and unspoken
    Fly from my heart to find their home with thee;
And not one link of pleasantness is broken
    Which bound thee in the dear old time to me.

No day goes by with heavy step or fleeting,
    But bears its freight of loving hope and fear
With which, for thy dear sake, my heart is beating,
    As quick and fond as if thou still wert here.

No morning hour shines, or evening darkens,
    Without some question from my soul to thine,
And as for thy reply my spirit hearkens
    The winds bring answer that thou art all mine.

I know that through this dark and hopeless sorrow
    We shall love on as we have loved so long—
And though no ray of promise gild the morrow,
    Each day will prove our trust more true and strong.

What matters then for us this earthly parting?
    What though the daily life be sad and lone?
Why should such bitter tears as these be starting
    To eyes that once have looked into thine own?

No thought save one of deep and earnest gladness
    Should fill the heart which thou hast stooped to win.—
Thou art so strong, that when I yield to sadness,
    Against the greatness of thy love, I sin.

My Friend! My Friend! forgive my weak complaining,
    I shrink at thought of all these passing years!
So few are gone—so many yet remaining—
    How can I choose but count them through my tears?

But do not fear that though I now am weeping,
    No glorious lesson by thy strength is taught:
Not all in vain these vigils am I keeping—
    Not all unworthy is the work I've wrought.

LINES

SUGGESTED BY A POEM BY RALPH WALDO EMERSON, ENTITLED "BRAHMA"

THOUGH Brahma speak with voice both clear and loud,
His words are heard not by the vulgar crowd.
A god must veil his splendors from the eye,
Else mortals, blinded by the glory, die.

Though seers strive deep meanings to expound,
To fools who listen 'tis but empty sound;—
Though sacred prophets teach divinest lore,
'Tis but themselves who know what they adore.

Yet, Brahma, speak on from thy lofty throne,
Though Wisdom dwell, like Deity, alone;—
Ye seers labor, and ye prophets pray!
For in the East glimmers the coming day!

Fair gleams of promise gild the Orient sky,
And high souls watching cry that dawn is nigh;
Have patience still, ye heralds of the morn,
Say on your message till our night is gone.

TRUE BLUE

WHAT color shall my lady wear?
She's tall and delicately fair:
Her cheek is pale, her hair is brown,
And brown the eyelashes bent down
Over her eyes of Heaven's own hue,—
That's it!—of course she must wear blue!

No flaunting scarlet, pink, or green
Must on her graceful form be seen;
No yellow glare with sickly light
Upon her features calm and bright.
She's sweet and fair, she's pure and true,
And so, in sooth, she may wear blue!

The bluest wave upon the sea
Has not more pliant grace than she;
The bluest of our summer skies
Can never match her glorious eyes:
The dearest flowers that ever grew,
Forget-me-nots—and she—wear blue.

EAST AND WEST

TELL me not of Old World splendors, bid me not to keep mine eyes
Fixed forever on the picture that dream-like behind us lies;
Bright the splendors, grand the picture, let us honor well the past!
But it must not, like a glamour, o'er the future's hopes be cast.
In the East the coming morning gleams with radiant red and gold,
And, like an invading army, doth its oriflamme unfold;
So the Orient fills the fancy when we dream of those far lands,
Where the sunshine, torrid burning, lights the glowing golden sands.

Let the Eastern heavens glimmer with a glory all their own,
But the noontide will be brighter when the morn to-day has grown;
And the race once early cradled on the Orient's glowing breast,
Growing up to braver manhood marches out into the West.
India's grand barbaric splendor yields to Europe's later sway
As the crimson clouds of morning in the noontide fade away.
Like a child with toys delighted was the gorgeous East until
The great world grown older, wiser, learned to use a sterner will.

Still the day must count its hours, even noontide does not last,
And imperial Present passes into still imperial Past.
So the nations moving onward may not pause or take their rest,
But with stately step keep wending evermore into the West;
Evermore the pathway opens, evermore the Western skies
Beckon with a fairer promise, with a grander vision rise,
Till the Old World seems to dwindle, and its labor and its strife
Dwarf before the deeper meaning of the New World's fresher life.

Like some proud procession marching forward with a stately tread
All the ages, ever ripening, by the hand of God are led.
From the Egypt of its bondage every race comes forth to meet,
First a wilderness of wandering, then a Land of Promise sweet;
And the childhood of the nations, like our own sweet childish days,
Always seems, in looking backward, softened by a golden haze;
And we can no longer measure with impartial heart and eye
Thorny pathways in the distance, stony hill-sides wild and high.

In the sharp and actual present we are apt to speak as though
All the romance and the beauty of the world died long ago.
History paints in glowing colors, Fancy lends her cunning hand,
Till the Past in dazzling falsehood beams a bright, illusive land.
Dreams of beauty, tales of prowess blazon each enchanted page,
And we sigh to think we live not still in that heroic age;
Like the weary traveller faltering 'neath the burning heat of noon,
We would fain recall the morning that has passed away too soon.

Thus this Western world looks backward to the Eastern world, and
     sees
Toil that wrings our nerves and sinews, changed to Oriental ease;
And instead of daily labor earning frugal daily bread,
Pines for lordly banquets tempting, in some stately palace spread,
Dreams of young and lovely women, sparkling fountains, gardens
     fair,
Or of shining armies following eagerly the trumpet's blare.
Every thought becomes a picture, every sense by pleasure won,
When we think of those fair countries palpitating 'neath the sun.

Oh, sweet Orient! all your pictures, though they charm me as I gaze,
Cannot make me quite unmindful of these stern but earnest days;
And upon the mighty mountains of my own dear native land
I breathe deep an air that never your wide, sultry plains has fanned.
Though the East is rich in beauty, land of romance and of song,
To the West a nobler future and a worthier hope belong.
Though the Past in gorgeous glory rises fair before the mind,
We who live in the great Present need not mourn to look behind!

FROM THE GERMAN

OF HEINRICH HEINE

I WEPT erewhile, as in a sad sleep dreaming
 I saw thee lying in the cold, dark grave;
I did not cease to weep, when morning beaming
 The lie to my false vision quickly gave!

Again I wept, my dream was still of sorrow,
 Thou from my presence had with coldness gone;
And though I found thee near me on the morrow,
 My heart was heavy and my tears flowed on.

Once more I wept, although in calmly sleeping
 A dream more true revealed thee still my friend;
Alas! alas! behold, I still am weeping,
 The tears of night with morning do not end.

LOVE'S CALENDAR

IF time is measured by sensations,
  And passions make us centuries old;
If sympathy creates relations
  To which the ties of blood are cold,—
Then thou and I, though lately meeting,
  Have made the moments fly so fast,
That our two hearts together beating,
  Through years of love and life have passed.

Then do not wonder that I woo thee
  With strangely rapid words and ways,
But let me, as a lover, sue thee
  To count as years these few sweet days.
Each hour has proved a month of pleasure,
  So, dearest, I have loved thee long.
Cease then by minutes life to measure,
  Love's calendar will prove thee wrong.

MIDNIGHT VISITANTS

I

GHOSTS of the past arise
Before my closéd eyes,
When midnight's hand hath bound me in its sleep;
A pale and shadowy band
Around my couch they stand
Or glide like moonbeams thro' the stillness deep.

II

Phantoms of joys long dead,
That with my lost youth fled,
They gaze in mournful stillness on my face;
And though they speak no word,
My very soul is stirred,
For eloquence unspoken fills the place.

III

Then saddest memories
Within my heart arise,
With tears of bitterness and wild regret;
Those shadows, calm and slow,
Smile sadly as they go,
And I remember all I would forget.

IV

Must it be so for aye?
Ye sad, pale faces, say!
Is there no Lethe where my past may lie?
But must ye ever keep
Your watch above my sleep,
And with your presence haunt me till I die?

OUT IN THE COLD

I

TREMBLING I stand before
  My lady's door,—
    Yet never dare
      To enter there!

II

Each morn I pass that way,
  And every day
    I loiter near,
      Her voice to hear.

III

When she comes forth I seem
  As in a dream;
    Bound foot and hand
      Helpless I stand!

IV

I know she sees me there,
  Yet calm and fair
    She passes on,
      And soon is gone!

V

Slowly I turn away
  And sadly say:
    "Ah, foolish heart!
      "Why throb and smart

VI

"Beneath such cold disdain?"
  In vain, in vain!
    I cannot still
      The bitter thrill.

VII

And as I pass along
  Amid the throng
    And bow and smile
      To all, the while,—

VIII

The very sunshine bright
  Grows black as night,
    The summer air
      Breathes my despair.

SEA-VIEWS

NO. I

FILLING the lazy air with slumbrous sound,
    The long, low surge comes swelling up the shore;
Each crested wave in ripples falls away
    Casting upon the sands the crown it wore.

A summer mood is on the changeful deep,
    Languidly heaving 'neath a cloudless sky;
In one broad glory of fair golden light
    The gleaming sunbeams on its bosom lie.

My spirit answers to the dreamy sea,
    Till sensuous forms fade utterly away,
And bright and fair through all my musing thought
    A thousand rainbow-tinted fancies play.

Mist-like and vague grow all the woes of earth,
    Forgotten as the sea forgets its storms,—
Life is all luxury, sorrow but a dream,
    And phantoms of the brain the truest forms.

SEA-VIEWS

NO. II

WILD winds are blowing, clouds go rushing by,
  Low thunder murmurs and the sea awakes;
The lightnings flash across the murky sky,
  And on the rugged shore the strong surf breaks.

No sunshine gilds the gleaming of the waves,
  No blue empyrean arches overhead;
No tender tints upon the ocean glow,
  Its frown is dark and all its lustre fled.

Oh, lonely Heart! thy heaven, too, is dark,
  Thy hopes lie shattered by the storms of Fate;
Life's precious freight is wrecked, its promise gone,
  All helpless lies the soul once strong and great.

Oh, Sorrow, take me to thy silent breast!
  Brood on, oh storm, over the wrathful sea!
Beneath the sunshine I could dream, but thou
  To cold reality hast wakened me!

TO ⸻

LONG, oh, long have we been parted,
   Sad has been my heart the while,
And I dare not say how often
   I have sighed to meet thy smile!

In the dark and solemn midnight
   When around me all is still,
Memory of our happy meetings
   Makes my heart grow sad and chill.

Then I lie awake and listen
   Thy dear voice again to hear,—
Sad I turn upon my pillow,
   Weeping that thou art not near.

Often when amid the gayest
   I would fain be glad as they,
Till the heavy thought comes o'er me
   That thou still art far away.

Oh, that time would fly more swiftly!
   Oh, that absence would be o'er!
And at length,—oh, long beloved,
   We might meet to part no more!

YOU AND I

HOW shall we name the tie
By which both you and I
 Are bound together?
We have been fond and true
All the fair summer through,
 And winter weather.

Friendship's too cold a word,
Our hearts too deep are stirred,
 For that calm feeling!
Too full of fire are we,
Too fond and full and free
 Our heart's revealing!

Friends we can never be,
But, between you and me,
 Something much dearer!
Friends can exist apart,
We two have but one heart,
 We must be nearer!

Friendship is very well,
But we—ah, we can tell
 Of something rarer!
We know of sweeter blisses,
Clasped hands and loving kisses,
 There's nothing fairer!

Since friendship's not allowed,
And since a tiny cloud
 Our bliss still covers,—
Let us enjoy its charm,—
Let us,—and what's the harm?
 Let us be lovers!

NOW AND THEN

WHEN you and I were true
How fast the moments flew!
   Days were but hours!
We were a loving pair,
We had no thought of care,—
   Whose bliss like ours?

Each look of yours beguiled,
I worshipped when you smiled,
   Thrilled when you sighed;
And if, by chance, a frown
Brought your fine eyebrows down
   I almost died.

And you,—were not you then
Blind to all other men,—
   Deaf to their praise?
Was not your heart all mine?
Was not I quite divine
   In those fair days?

Alack! Alack! Alas!
How human passions pass
   Fleeting away!
Where once we whispered vows
We now give smiles and bows,
   Alackaday!

I find you charming still
Of course,—and you too will
   Still call me clever;
But that's another thing,
A different song to sing —
   I'm *not* your lover!

No farewells have been spoken,
No tender hearts been broken,
    And yet we've parted!
'Tis well to love awhile,
But better still to smile
    When love's departed.

THE COMING OF THE DAWN

LIKE war's proud herald comes the morning light,
     In shining vestments clad;
The trembling stars submissive take their flight;
The moon that smiled through the sweet summer night
     Hastens, all pale and sad,
To hide her modest beauty ere the day
Shall flood creation with his fiery ray.

Gorgeous and radiant through the Eastern Gate,
     From the far realms of Space,
The sun comes forth arrayed in royal state;
While every flower and bird and tree which late
     Slept in the night's embrace,
Upspringing from their slumber, joyously
Prepare to meet the Monarch of the Sky.

A low, sweet hum breathes through the summer air,
     Wooing the world to wake;
But, though responsive, Earth and Ocean wear
Rapt silence still, as if they might not dare
     The magic spell to break,
Until the Day-god with resistless might
From her last covert drives the vanquished Night!

THE SABBATH BELLS

RING out your call to praise and prayer,
  Oh, holy Sabbath bells!
Sweet on the calm and listening air
  Your solemn music swells!

Like angel accents float along
  Those tones serene and clear,—
As if a mighty seraph throng
  To Earth were drawing near.

Oh, fairest day of all the seven
  Be ever set apart!
Bring to our souls sweet thoughts of Heaven,
  Oh, Sabbath of the heart!

On thy sweet breezes waft away
  Each low-born thought of care;
Let Heaven bend down in peace to-day
  To hear Earth's whispered prayer.

Ring out again your solemn tones,
  Oh, holy Sabbath bells!
Till every heart your message owns
  As your grand anthem swells!

BUDS AND FLOWERS

YES, youth is as fair as the bud on the rose,
But there's many a secret that youth never knows!
And not till the bud shall have burst into bloom
Can the bee taste its sweets or the world its perfume.

MY DREAMS

WITH every night's returning season
  I dream the sweetest dreams of thee,
Not filled with fancies passing reason
  But glowing with reality.

Thou comest with a kiss of greeting,
  And sittest down as friend with friend;
And with the rapturous joy of meeting
  The nameless charms of Dreamland blend.

To thee I breathe each inmost feeling,
  I clasp that soft white hand of thine,
Its pulses' quickened throb revealing
  How true thy thought responds to mine.

And thus these fairy visions woo me
  When with the night and thee alone,
Till thy dear presence thrilling through me
  Makes the hushed midnight all thine own.

I wake unwillingly each morning,
  Yet know that though, through the long day,
I cannot meet thee,—night returning
  Will my poor waiting heart repay.

Nor deem I that the gracious vision
  I must with morning all unlearn;
For, spite of all these hours Elysian,
  I keep the truth my heart has sworn

Nor seek I till the word is spoken
  To break the spell thyself hath cast,
I patient wait until the token
  Shall tell me thou art mine at last.

SADDEST IS SAFEST

SERENE beneath the lowering skies we stand,
    No tempest frights us, for no storm can harm;
Guided by Sorrow's chill but fearless hand,
    We walk unscathed by horror or alarm.

Saddest is safest, yes, we know it well,
    Our hearts are shielded now from joy or woe;
Alike the merry peal, the mournful knell,
    Alike indifferent the friend and foe.

Thou knowest, dear, that when our life was gay,
    When sunshine smiled and flowers were everywhere,
That shadows hovered in the cloudless day,
    That dark forebodings shivered in the air.

While we were happy we were not at rest,
    We trembled as the slightest breeze went by,
Did we not know bliss was a transient guest,
    That every smile would have an answering sigh?

The darkness gathered and the clouds came fast,
    The sun was hidden at our highest noon;
Still our weak hearts hoped on until the last,
    And pleaded wistfully, "Oh, not so soon!"

Our fears were answered and our hopes were slain,
    Our sunny day was changed to dreary night;
Returning dawns now break for us in vain,
    We dread no darkness and we prize no light.

Saddest is safest,—now we are at rest,—
    Our tremblings and our terrors all are fled;
Sorrow's strong armor panoplies the breast
    Whose hopes and fears lie buried with the dead!

MY LOVE

My Love is like the Day!
Beneath the sunshine of her calm, blue eyes,
Serene and still my spirit ever lies,—
At peace alway!

My Love is like the Night!
Her presence soothes away the sordid cares
That fret my soul amid a world of snares,
And brings delight!

My Love is like a Flower!
That blossoms in the garden of my heart,
And joys perennial sweetness to impart
Through sun and shower!

My Love is like a Bird!
Filling my home with sweetest melody,
And fraught with music that is all for me
Her voice is heard.

Like all fair things is She!
The richest crown of all my life's delight;
Dearer than flower or bird, fairer than day or night,
Is she to me!

"THE ELMS"

TALL elms around my dwelling
   A stately watching keep,
A dreamy stillness hovers
   Within their shadows deep.

Like guardian spirits ever
   They look down upon me;
Through all the changing seasons
   Dear friends they seem to be.

In summer mid their branches
   The glittering sunbeams play,
And happy birds flit through them
   Throughout the livelong day.

In winter dark and threatening
   Against the cold, gray sky,
Their mighty limbs wave sternly
   As the storm-wind passes by.

Sometimes in the dim twilight
   I watch their moving lines
Tracing strange hieroglyphics
   As their branching intertwines,

Till I fancy I can read there
   On that strangely written page,
A message of lost wisdom
   From some forgotten sage.

A child, I gazed upon them
   Half charmed and half afraid;
A maiden, dreamed sweet dreaming
   In their soft, soothing shade.

And as time brought slowly, surely,
 Its sorrow and its care,
Still more friendly seemed their shadows,
 Still more sweet the summer air.

Oft to my troubled spirit
 They have whispered words of cheer,
They have hushed my wild complaining
 Or calmed my foolish fear.

In Memory's light I see them
 A mystic glory wear;
Like dear friends they stand before me,
 Those Elms so tall and fair.

RENAISSANCE

IN the old years we were loving,—shall the new years be less dear?
We were very near each other, can we not now be as near?—
If as old friends we were true friends, shall we not as new friends
　find
That our power of truthful loving has not yet been left behind?

Many a dream we dreamed together,—can we never dream again?—
Hours of sunshine made us happy, hours of darkness saddened
　then;—
Sunshine cheers me, shadows chill me still as in those golden days,
And methinks I see the brightness and the sadness in your gaze.

Then your hand was warm and ready, clasping mine with firmest
　hold,
Then your lips were overflowing,—telling all that could be told:—
And to-day your hand you proffer in the same frank, loyal way,
And your lips find quick expression for the tender words you say.

Naught is changed in outward seeming, and, believe me, naught
　within
But can shine with brighter glory, and a sweeter bliss can win.
Hands as warm and hearts as loving are our own to plight anew,
You shall give me yours, my darling, I will give my own to you.

Lift your eyes to mine with glances which your inmost soul reveal,
Trust me with your lightest fancies nor your deepest thoughts
　conceal;
Love me with your fondest fervor, cover me with kisses sweet;
Hold me to your heart and listen,—hear how true our pulses beat!

"SWEETS TO THE SWEET"

WHEN blue eyes melt in liquid light,
   My bosom swells with languid pleasure;
When black eyes gleam like stars at night,
   My pulses throb with quickened measure;
And then when gray ones flash and glow
   And shed their radiant beams upon me,
Upon my word, I scarcely know
   Which of these lovely orbs have won me.

Redundant locks of raven hair
   Befit a heroine of story;—
While auburn tresses floating fair
   Bewilder with their golden glory;
And simple bands of shining brown
   Suggest a Raffaelle's Madonna;—
Which of these heads should wear the crown
   I cannot tell, upon my honor!

That sylph-like girl with fragile form
   Seems like an artist's fairest dreaming;
This tropic beauty takes by storm,
   And charms by being, not by seeming.
Ethereal saints to rapture wake me
   And lift me to the upper regions,—
But earthly houris quickly take me
   Back to their own unholy legions.

One day I kneel before a shrine
   And offer up a reverent duty;—
The next, if all the world were mine,
   I'd give it to some naughty beauty.
So till one woman shall combine
   The varied charms of all the others,
This changing fate must still be mine,
   To be first yours and then another's.

"SO NEAR AND YET SO FAR"

WHY comest thou in dreams to paint anew
    Thine image on my heart,—
To gild afresh each worn and faded hue
    With thine own magic art?—

Why give the glory of old days to Night,
    When, at the touch of Morn,
My prayers are powerless to delay thy flight?—
    In vain I curse the dawn!

Why bless the hours when I am wrapped in sleep,
    To make the day more lone,—
Why seem such tears of penitence to weep
    To turn again to stone?—

Could'st thou but know the welcome my heart gives
    In spite of all my wrongs,—
And see the yearning love that in me lives
    And still to thee belongs!

One word of tender pleading from thy lips
    Would rend these clouds away,—
Would clear the heavens, break the long eclipse,—
    And give us back the day.

If I must shut thee from my heart and life,
    O haunt my dreams no more!
Why seek forever to renew the strife
    For a reward so poor!

If thou still lovest as in days of old,
    Come in the noon's broad light,—
Let all the treason of thy past be told,
    Nor stoop again to flight.

Come not thus stealthily to mock my rest
With promise sweet and fair,—
Or be once more my heart's most honored guest
And thine old lustre wear.

Such nights of joy, such bitter days as this,
Would make a hell of heaven;—
Bring me no tempting prophecy of bliss,—
Or,—stay,—and be forgiven!

THE CHILDREN'S TABLE

Written for the great National Fair held in New York, March 25, 1864, for
the Sanitary Commission; and printed copies sold at a table taken care of
by little children.

WHILE the wise men are all seeking
    Ways to save our native land,
And the brave men are all fighting
    Heart to heart and hand to hand,
While the grown-up women labor
    For the soldiers night and day,
Would you have us children idle
    Minding nothing but our play?

Little hands we have, but willing,
    Little hearts, but loving well
Those who languish sorely wounded,
    Those who fill the prisoner's cell;
And we know the names of heroes
    Who have fallen on the field,
Gleam with never-dying brightness
    Blazoned on our country's shield.

We have toiled with busy fingers
    Many days to gather here
Little treasures that may tempt you
    With full purses to draw near:—
For they tell us that with money
    Many great things may be done;
Never had it nobler uses
    Since this big world was begun.

Let the great and glorious impulse
    Now astir throughout the land
Make us welcome as we greet you
    Coming with this new demand.
Give us then, oh, generous people,
    Ready purchase of our wares,—
And we'll give you children's blessings
    Won from Heaven by children's prayers.

THE BEAUTIFUL GATE

OH, beautiful Gate! oh, Gate of Love!
    Open thy portals fair,—
For love is all things else above,
    And we would enter there!
Through thee we see the Eden we have lost,
The rest most welcome to the tempest-tost.

Oh, beautiful Gate! though fair thou art
    And eager though we be,—
'Tis only the true and trusting heart
    That entrance wins through thee.
Weakness and coldness must stand without,
No room in thy realm for distrust or doubt.

Oh, beautiful Gate! through thee we glide,
    We neither pause nor fear;—
The world without is far too wide,
    The world within too dear.
Here in the careless crowd we are alone,
In thee we find a kingdom all our own.

Oh, beautiful Gate! to us so clear,
    Glowing in rosy light,
Many and many stand watching near
    Who never catch the sight.
Cold in the darkness wondering they stand,
While we are entering the Promised Land.

DUSK AND DAWN

UNTO my love I go
    When the sun is in the west,
When beneath the sunset glow
    Earth and heaven sink to rest.
Long before I reach her side
    Darkness closes round
And no more can be descried
    My shadow on the ground!

Forth from my love I go
    When the sun is in the east,—
As the morning wakens slow
    Ere the hush of night has ceased.
When I reach my home again
    The sun is shining high,
And adown the grassy lane
    I see my shadow lie.

So to me the night
    Wears the hues of morn,—
Darkness is my light,
    Sunset is my dawn!
Promise gilds the west
    With its brightest ray,—
The world goes to rest
    When begins my day!

RENEWAL

LAST time I walked abroad the silent earth
Bereft of all that had made summer fair,
Or Autumn glorious with fruitage rare,—
Stood mid the Winter's cold all bleak and bare.

But now fresh life is throbbing in her veins,
She hath put on new sunshine and new flowers;
She recks not of her last year's faded bowers,
But blithely dreams of this year's dawning hours.

With charméd ear she listens as the Spring
With false but wooing voice breathes forth again
The very sweetness that made the pain
Of last year's broken vows and promise vain.

The earth and I were sad and lone erewhile;
I loved her when her mourning robes she bore,
For hues like hers my own dark spirit wore;
Now she is gay with lovers by the score.

Alas! I cannot thus like her renew
My withered hopes, and new-born raptures feel;
Each day but serves more clearly to reveal
Wounds that no coming bliss can ever heal.

Unto her mother-heart I could draw near
And weep upon her breast when both were sad;
But now that she forgets the grief she had
No tie unites the wretched and the glad!

SWEET WORDS

THOUGH you cannot hear me speaking,
    Let me say sweet words to you;
For my heart is ever seeking
    To express itself anew;—

To say over the old feeling
    In some new and fresher guise;
To find new ways of revealing
    The deep love that in me lies.

Though a distance long and dreary
    Still between us stretches far,
Yet my spirit never weary
    Turns unto you as my star.

In my heaven you are glowing
    With a light serene and still,
And sweet influence from you flowing,
    All my nature seems to fill.

Absence cannot change you, dearest;
    Distance cannot make me cold;
Presence does not bring friends nearest,
    Time does not make all things old.

And though loving words should never
    Find their way from me to you,
I should trust your love forever,—
    You would know me to be true.

Yet I find delight in telling
    To the unresponsive air,
Thoughts that in my heart are swelling
    And some breeze to you may bear.

And I fancy that you hear me
    When I breathe your cherished name,
And that sometimes, as if near me,
    You, too, fondly do the same!

SELF-DECEPTION

MY heart was sad, I went unto my friend
    To tell my secret grief:—
Sure that his loving sympathy would lend
    Solace and sweet relief.

I found him in the merriest of moods,
    His face one broadening smile;
His hands were heaped up high with this world's goods
    Garnered by this world's guile.

There was no room for sorrow in his heart,
    I could not check his mirth;
We were dear friends, but now we stood apart
    Far as the heavens from earth.

Then to the queenly maiden I adored
    I bent my thoughtful way;
There all the passion of my heart was stored,
    There all my treasure lay.

I found her brow serene with peaceful thought,
    Her spirit free from care;
I could not offer her the gift I brought,—
    What right had sorrow there?

So to my home I turned again and sighed
    To think how oft in vain
Each restless heart so eagerly has tried
    To share its inward pain

Cheating itself with ever new belief,
    And ever deeming near
That twin-born soul to whom its joy and grief
    Shall as its own appear.

BY AND BY

LITTLE Bertha sitting by me
   Tells me all the hopes and fears
That with mingled shade and sunshine
   Fill her childhood's tender years;—
Then with burst of eager loving
   Her soft arms are round me thrown,—
"By and by I'll be just like you
   "When I am a woman grown!"

Harry plays beneath my window
   Riotous with hoop and ball,—
He is somewhere near eleven
   And is growing strong and tall.
Says, in confidential converse,
   "By and by, when I'm a man,
"Which will be in a few summers,
   "I shall marry cousin Fan."

Walking in the deepening shadows
   Watching sunset's dying gleams,
I drew near a youth and maiden
   Lost in love's delicious dreams.
She was hushed in happy silence,
   But he spoke his thought aloud:
"By and by I shall win honors,
   "Of your love you shall be proud."

Entering at the open doorway
   Of the artist's quiet room
I beheld him sitting sadly
   In the twilight's gathering gloom.
As I paused in reverent silence
   Hope returned to cheer his heart,
And I heard him murmur proudly,
   "By and by, beloved art!"

Toiling through uncounted hours,
   Never resting day or night,
Sits the scholar, pale with watching,
   In his eyes the fever-light.
Youth and health and strength are flying
   From his grasp with footstep fleet,—
"By and by I'll stop and rest me,
   "When my great work is complete."

In the chamber of the sick man
   Hear his faint, low whisper tell
"Though I now am weak and suffering,
   "By and by I shall be well."
And as hope revives within him,
   Promise lights his weary eye,
And he smiles as we are going,
   "I will join you by and by."

Tread more softly,—we are coming
   Into holy precincts now,—
See the glow on those wan features,
   Watch the light on that pale brow!
List the words that break the stillness,
   Hark the mourner's stifled sigh,—
"I go first, my own beloved,—
   "You shall follow by and by!"

Thus forever and forever
   Does this poor, fond human heart
Paint the image of its future
   Bright with too delusive art
Youth and hope are ever singing,
   "By and by we shall be blest";
Age and sorrow ever sighing,
   "By and by we shall find rest."

SILENCE

SHOULD the deep and sacred feeling,
When sweet thoughts are o'er us stealing,
Every sad remembrance healing,
    Seek for utterance in speech?—
No! let silence make still deeper,
Like the deep dream of a sleeper,
Or the mourning of the weeper,
    Thoughts no human words can reach,—
      Lying even "too deep for tears."

In those rarely given hours,
Which in after life, like flowers
Such as grew in childhood's bowers,
    Gladden the way-weary soul,
We forget the chains that bind us,
Seeing only those behind us,
Which most pleasantly entwined us
    In a willing, sweet control,—
      The dear ties of early years.

Words would break the fond illusion
With a bold, unwished intrusion,
Waking into wild confusion
    Fatal memories in the breast;—
Then no more can peace returning
Calm the ever-restless yearning
That within the heart is burning,
    Or give back that blessed rest;
      Then let silence keep us dreaming.

Would the dream might ne'er be broken,
Or the bitter words be spoken,
Which must be to us a token
   That our dearest hopes have flown.
Ah! it would be sweet forever
To sleep on in bliss, and never
Wake to feel our heart-strings sever,
   Wake to find ourselves alone,—
      Find our bliss was but a seeming.

THE VOICE OF THE SEA

I LAY me down on the wild sea-shore,
  And heard, as in a sleep,
The ceaseless moaning, the sullen roar
  Of the dark and restless deep.

I listened long to the muffled tones
  Of that solemn, heaving sea;
For it seemed to strive with those dreary moans
  To utter some mystery.

And every wave, as it neared the land,
  To die upon the shore,
Seemed to whisper brokenly to the sand
  The secret that it bore.

And the land gave back a soft, low sigh
  Of pity to the sea;
While the wave's hoarse murmur, the shore's reply,
  Re-echoed ceaselessly.

Wildly and sadly those tones of woe
  Thrilled through the summer air,
And the Voice of the Sea in its surging flow
  Breathed ever the same despair.

THE PILGRIM'S PLAINT

AS if across Sahara's sands,
Dear love, to thee I stretch my hands!
Between our hearts the desert lies
Barren beneath the burning skies.

Each morn to cross the arid waste
I start and strive with eager haste;
Each night I see at set of sun
My journey is but just begun.

Sometimes beneath the noontide glare
The mirage gleams before me fair;
Only to lure my weary feet
Still farther with its fond deceit.

Long trains of travellers pass me by,
Careless of all the crowd am I;—
Uncharmed by all that they most prize,
Untrammelled by their strongest ties.

But as alone I wander on,
Seeking the way thou may'st have gone,
Methinks the desert sweet might be,
Could I but keep clasped hands with thee.

Could I but lift my eyes to thine,—
Light heart and lighter step were mine;
Apart from thee, the lengthening way
Grows darker, drearier, day by day.

Open thy passionate soul to me,
Clasp me again so close to thee,
That dreams of desert sands may fly,
And safe on thine my heart may lie.

THE CITY STUDENT

MY little study window looks out on a crowded street,
And I hear from morn till midnight the sound of passing feet;
But I rarely lift my eyelids as in my book I read,
To mark which step moves heavily or which with joyful speed.
The ceaseless hum of human life to my rapt fancy seems
Like a faint and wordless echo from some far-off land of dreams.

Sometimes it rises louder, like the deep and sounding roar
Of the mighty ocean billows as they dash upon the shore;—
And then it dies away awhile, to soon come back again,
With a softer, quicker motion, like the pattering of rain;—
But still I bend above my book and let the world go by,
It cares not for my loneliness, nor for its crowds care I!

I never wish for other sounds such as the poet loves,
The music of the south wind, the cooing of the doves,
The humming of the honey-bees, the murmuring of the streams,
Where the soft shadows slowly creep or the fair sunlight gleams.
I care not for the sweetest song of all the summer birds,
The breeze among the sighing pines, the lowing of the herds.

I was not born mid rural scenes or reared in country air,
My only childish play-ground was the dusty city square;
The only trees I ever see are gray with dust and age,
The only birds I ever hear sing from a gilded cage;
But with my books and with my pen and with my crowded street,
I would not change my lot for that of any one I meet.

WATCHING

FAR out into the twilight
　　I gaze with throbbing heart;—
At every sound I tremble,
　　At every footstep start.

Faster the darkness deepens,
　　Faster the night comes on,
And through the long, long hours
　　I sit and weep alone.

The neighbors' lamps are lighted,
　　And from each window shine
Bright beams of friendly welcome,—
　　There is no light in mine!

Their households are assembled,
　　Their homes are full of glee,—
Their shadows flitting swiftly
　　Across the light I see.

And there is one whose coming
　　Would make my home more light
Than those which glow the brightest
　　This dark and dreary night.

And though my heart grows heavy,
　　I still must watch and wait;
For surely he will enter
　　Some night within my gate!

THE SEA

HEAR me, old ocean, as I kneel by thee,
   And watch thy mighty billows' ceaseless roll,
Teach me thy strength, thy silent energy,
   And breathe thy calmness through my restless soul!

Bearing the burden of unuttered woe,
   I lie down wearied on thy lonely shore;—
The pulse of life is beating faint and slow,
   And weakness whispers, "Wherefore struggle more?

"What do thy strivings bring but weariness,—
   "What thy fond loving win for thee but pain?
"What poor rewards thy mightiest efforts bless!
   "Alas, poor tired one, they are all in vain!"

From my weak heart I turn to thee, O Sea!
   Thy deep tides fail not though the day be past,
My coward spirit shall learn strength from thee,
   And I will labor bravely to the last!

THE "LAST SUPPER"

of Leonardo Da Vinci

This painting, at a first glance, appears hopelessly dilapidated, but as you look long and well upon it, the injuries of time seem to disappear and the picture to come forth anew, so marvellous is the power of those defaced outlines. The face of Christ, less injured than the rest, retains its heavenly beauty and godlike serenity, and as you gaze upon the group, the figures become more distinct, the colors glow afresh, and the whole picture asserts itself to the imagination, till we wonder how we dared deem it a ruin.— [Journal of 1855].

THERE are fair palace chambers high and vast,
    Glowing with golden sheen;—
Adorned with costly relics of the past,
    Fit dwellings for a queen.

There are proud halls where kings may sit in state
    And, robed in all their pride,
See thronging multitudes, who cringe and wait,
    Surge through the portals wide;

And spacious galleries where gems of art
    In rich profusion meet,—
That charm us, till unwilling to depart,
    We turn reluctant feet.

Mansions there are whose solemn atmosphere
    Bids every true heart swell,
Where the pale ghosts of those who suffered here
    Seem evermore to dwell.

Yet pillared hall, or palace chamber high,
    Or lofty, gilded dome,
Bring not such tears as fill the gazer's eye
    In this neglected room!

For on the walls so ruthlessly defaced,
    A vision, far more grand
Than aught of these, was in the old days placed
    By a great artist's hand.

The colors long have faded and grown dim,
    Yet still Time fain would spare,
As if through reverence, the face of Him
    So calmly seated there.

And as with loving awe we stand before
    The picture,—we behold
Those faded tints their first fresh glow restore,—
    No longer dim and cold!

Not with brief glance its wondrous power we learn;
    But long and earnest gaze,
To those scarred walls will make again return
    The glory of old days!

And that poor hall, so naked and forlorn,
    Will with a splendor shine,
Such as no royal dwelling may adorn,—
    Shed from that face divine!

APRIL

THE year's young bride brings royal dower
Of bursting leaf and budding flower,
Of smiling sun and blessing shower.

The earth awakes to life and bloom,
Emerging from the icy tomb
That held her in the winter's gloom.

The skies bend down with loving looks,
The sunshine woos the long-sealed brooks,
And violets bloom in sheltered nooks.

The willow-stems are all aglow,
And through their veins the juices flow,
As if they felt it bliss to grow.

The buds upon the elms begin
To quiver with the life within,
That long has hushed and dormant been.

The grass is peeping from the ground,
The sheep upon the hills have found
Fresh herbage on each sunny mound.

The air with melody is stirred,
At morning through the woods is heard
The carol of the happy bird.

At eve across the stillness float
The croakings of the bull-frog's note,
The winter's cold still in his throat.

Wherever now we turn our eyes
Upon the earth, or to the skies,
The sweet spring visions seem to rise.

All the dark thoughts of gloom and cold,
That like a wintry shroud enfold
Our hearts, fade like a legend old.

Earth fears no more the freezing blast
That rudely o'er her bosom passed,
And in her lap the snow-drifts cast.

But field and forest now are rife
For summer's growth of gentle strife,
Eager with newly quickened life.

The sunshine sheds prophetic rays,—
This blossoming time of joy repays
For winter's dull and dreary days.

We too would learn, oh kindly Spring,
Our wintry thoughts aside to fling
Fresh life to our dead souls to bring.

Teach us our hearts to open wide,—
Let hopes that with the past year died
Be now forever laid aside!—

Or, better still, like ripened grain,
That last year smiled upon the plain,
And since has, safely garnered, lain;

To bring them forth and plant anew
For Spring's soft rain and Summer's dew,—
And give them culture long and true.

So when the harvest time draws near
And brings the homage of the year,
We too with full hands may appear.

THE LAUGHING SEA

HEAR what the sea,
The laughing, leaping sea,
The riotous, plunging sea,
Hear what it says to me!
I am in a merry vein,
Drinking in the summer rain,
As you mortals drink rich wine;
Drops that in the sunlight shine,
Mingle with my yeasty brine,
And the winds that bring the showers
Murmur of the trees and flowers,
Whispering of the pleasant land
Which, with light touch, they have fanned;
And the pretty tales they tell,
Please old Neptune's fancy well.
See, while I my nectar quaff,
How I lightly leap and laugh!

Hear what the sea,
The dark and moaning sea,
The melancholy sea,
Hear what it says to me!
I am tossed with deep unrest,
Ever lonely and oppressed;
Clouds from Heaven looking down
Harshly on my sorrow frown.
Vainly with white crests I crown
My fair waves, and woo the shore,
Vainly my libations pour;
Earth disdains my homage still;
Even the tiny mountain rill
Brings me gifts, but will not take
One salt droplet for my sake.
Think you that I'll always mourn?
Laughing scornfully I turn.

Hear what the sea,
The fierce and angry sea,
The wild and stormy sea,
Hear what it says to me!
I hate the dull old earth;
Her soft airs are not worth
One breath of the strong blasts that sweep
Across the breast of the great deep,
Waking the echoes from their sleep.
Hark! how they shout aloud to me,
Those northern gales so fierce and free!
See how the lately scornful shore
Trembles beneath their mighty roar.
My waves are quivering with delight,
I laugh to see the earth's affright;
My storms are out, and she shall know
The sea can be a fearful foe!

Hear what the sea,
The cruel, deadly sea,
The cold, remorseless sea,
Hear what it says to me!
All my work I've grandly wrought,
Winds and waters well have fought;
Now,—the noise of battle o'er,—
Count the wrecks along the shore,
And, upon my ocean-floor
See the wealth of treasure spread,
And unnumbered mortals dead.
The proud ships that yester-e'en
Floated on my silver sheen,
Earth's fond hearts in vain await,
I have captured crews and freight;
Nevermore will favoring gales
Fill their torn and useless sails.
How the poor souls strove to save

Their weak lives from my wide grave!
Far enough below they lie,
And I laughed to see them die.
Now I'll sleep a little while,
And to-morrow on you smile;
Yes, while I my nectar quaff,
You shall see me leap and laugh!

OUR COUNTRY'S CAUSE

Written for the Sanitary Commission Fair, held in Philadelphia during the
Civil War.

WAR'S cruel ploughshare cleaves the land
　　With furrows wide and deep;
Each furrow is a hallowed grave
　　Where our loved heroes sleep.
But costly seed we're planting now
　　In weariness and pain,
Shall, at the harvest-time, bring forth
　　Fair fields of priceless grain.

Our hearts are saddened by the sight
　　Of sick and wounded men:—
It seems as if God's summer air
　　Could ne'er be pure again.
But, side by side with War's dark sins,
　　Man's noblest virtues shine,
And woman's sweet compassion beams
　　With lustre half divine.

Sweet Mother Earth with tender care
　　Covers her wounds with flowers,—
And we would learn her loving art
　　For these deep wounds of ours.
For, though our tears fall sadly now,
　　They, like the summer rain,
May bring rich blessings for the time
　　When sunshine comes again.

Only for thee, dear native Land,
　　Could we thus bear our woe:
Only for thee, see day by day
　　Our brave men thus laid low.
But though our griefs must inly bleed
　　Through many a coming year,
Each sorrow makes our Country's Cause
　　To patriot hearts more dear.

CHAFF

WHY search in the fair fields of wheat
    For growing tares?—
When joy is here why go to meet
    Approaching cares?—
Why watch the sunshine with distrust
    Foretelling rain?—
Or weep because the morrow must
    Bring tears and pain?—

Let the wheat ripen in the sun
    To golden grain,—
Bask in each sunny moment won
    Ere the day wane.
The Summer needs not Autumn's thrift,
    Youth needs not tears,—
There's time enough the chaff to sift
    From the ripe ears!

ALAS!

ALAS, that life should fly so fast!
That love's bright dreams should never last;—
That even when love and life are true
Sorrows are many and blisses few!

There's many an unsaid care and fear,
And many a bitter unshed tear;
And many dreary doubts that wait
To mock us at the hands of Fate.

And ofttimes darkness deep enfolds
All that our inmost being holds
Most sweet in life, most dear in death,
Chilling our souls with icy breath.

We seem with tearful eyes to stand
And gaze on Love's own Promised Land;
Nay! dwelling in it side by side,
Yet of its sweetness half-denied.

Yet we, whose hearts are strong and true,
Can surely string our harps anew,
And from the chords attuned to pain
Bring forth sweet melody again.

Come! let us cross this dark abyss
And climb once more our heights of bliss,
And thrill again with passion's power
Our hearts, now deadening hour by hour.

What though for thee life's dreams have fled,
Love's deeper fires are not yet dead,—
And I still feel when near to thee
That earth holds precious things for me.

STANZAS

WHEN at the early dawn I wake
    From sweetest dreams of thee,
Which fill my heart with bliss, and make
    The night a heaven for me;—
I turn in sadness back,—in vain
    I woo those dreams to me,—
Alas! they will not come again,
    I wake to sigh for thee!

Through the day's long and weary hours
    I muse on those gone by
When Time so "softly trod on flowers,"
    For, dearest, thou wert nigh.
But now that thou art far away,
    No sunshine smiles for me,
I sit in sorrow all the day,
    I sit and sigh for thee!

When the sweet hours of twilight bring
    Their stillness to my breast,—
And darkness, shrouding everything,
    Brings its own transient rest;
Then hope comes whispering to my heart
    And breathes its spell on me;
But naught avails its flattering art,
    For still I sigh for thee!

There is no music to my ear
    So sweet as thy dear voice,
Its lightest cadence soft and clear
    Makes my fond heart rejoice.
And when I sit and strive in vain
    To catch its melody,—
With saddest heart I turn again
    And ever sigh for thee!

NIGHT AND MORNING

MORNING dawns,—the blessed sunbeams
    Drive the night's cold gloom away:
Shadows fly and spectres vanish
    In the clear, calm light of day.

While the night in thraldom held me,
    While the darkness closed around,
Frightful visions filled my fancy
    Till I trembled at each sound.

Troops of elfish forms went tramping
    Through my chamber's dreary gloom;
Wizard shapes of goblin phantoms
    Glided round my silent room.

Soon a mocking semblance offered
    Of the long since loved and lost;
But no loving glances gave me
    As upon my couch I tossed.

But their eyes, with scorn dilated,
    Burned into my very brain,—
For I felt they knew my secret,
    And I writhed 'neath their disdain.

How I wept and prayed for pity,
    How I turned and sought for rest,
Still the weary hours lingered,
    Still remained each hateful guest.

So at night I am a coward,
    And alone I dread to be;
But by daylight I grow bolder,
    With the world to shelter me.

Then I bear my secret boldly,
　　And I look around as though,
Heart serene and conscience stainless,
　　I had never dreamed of woe.

But I know that in my chamber
　　Lurk those dreaded foes of mine;
Waiting for their time of power,
　　Waiting for the midnight chime.

A GREETING

IF friendship only comes with years,
　　We two are strangers still,—
The hours we've together spent
　　But little space would fill.

I have not watched you day by day,
　　Seeking with eager eye
To see the gradual growth of love,
　　As weeks and months went by.

I have not sought you first of all
　　In times of joy or woe,
Finding an impulse in my heart,
　　That bade me to you go.

I never wept a single tear
　　Upon your faithful breast;
Nor whispered of a single hope
　　That grew a welcome guest.

And you have never pined for me
　　When you were lone and sad,—
Nor longed to bring me joyful words
　　When your own heart was glad.

Yet spite of all the carelessness
　　Between us in the past,—
A chain there is, though slight 'tis sweet,
　　Which holds us close and fast.

And fragments of most pleasant speech
　　The missing links renew,
As, touched by memory's magic wand,
　　I pause to think of you.

Bright smiles and gentle words there were
　　That linger with me yet,—
And rapid interchange of thought
　　That I shall ne'er forget.

We watched the summer glory fall
　　Upon the calm blue sea,—
We talked beneath the sunset sky
　　Of Nature's mystery.

And even when Autumn's winds were chill
　　And wintry skies grew drear,
There still was much we loved to see
　　And much for each to hear.

For then we thought of graver themes,
　　And sadder words were ours;
And deeper confidence we gave
　　Each other in those hours.

And so we met, and met again,
　　Perchance with little thought
Of how it was that, more and more,
　　We were together brought.

An hour here, an hour there,
　　At morning or at eve,—
They were but few, and yet how clear
　　The memory they leave!

And I still feel that kiss you gave,
　　When twilight's dusky veil
Falling around us as we stood,
　　Half hid your face so pale.

It seemed a prophecy of love,
    A yearning at your heart,
Which said that, though we lightly met,
    We could not lightly part.

And the strong pressure of your hand
    Which I held clasped in mine,
Told me that without spoken words
    You could my thought divine.

But now life's current sweeps along
    With motion strong and fleet,
And, borne upon our different ways,
    Again we shall not meet:—

Yet we *are friends!* what matter now
    The parting and the pain!
They cannot rob us of the past
    Nor make its promise vain.

I breathe "God bless you!" on the air
    Wherever you may be,
And know your inmost heart will thrill
    Whene'er you think of me.

THE TWO PRISONERS

MY little bird sits in his cage,
 And thro' the bars he looks
Upon me as I sit in thought
 Or busy at my books.
And when I pause awhile to rest,
 Sweet wood-notes wild and free
Come gushing from his tiny throat
 In bursts of melody.

And when I pace my narrow cell
 With steps of wild unrest,
And think that I, like him, am caged
 In durance I detest;—
He bends his sparkling eyes on me
 As if my thoughts he knew,
And then he sings those notes again,
 With cadence sweet and true.

His song breathes courage through dismay
 And solace in despair,—
He fills my prison with the breath
 Of Heaven's summer air.
We both are prisoners, 'tis true,
 Yet, though we are not free,
We'll keep stout hearts within our breasts,
 And sing of liberty.

If e'er in freedom's blessed air
 I may once more rejoice,
Then thou in thine own native woods
 Shalt lift an uncaged voice.
Dear bird, since thou dost teach me how
 My prison life to bear,
The hour that shall set me free
 Thou shalt my freedom share.

THE LADY OF MY DREAMS

THROUGH the hush of stillest midnight comes the Lady of my
 Dreams;
Very fair and very stately in her loveliness she seems:
Like a queen she smiles upon me, like a vassal I bow down;
Never yet did mortal woman grace with wearing fairer crown!

But though proudly she doth bear her, and though regal is her mien,
Yet within her blue eyes' heaven, depths of sweetness may be seen;
And her smile is very gentle as she turns her face to mine,
And a woman's loving softness mingles with her grace divine.

Like a vassal I adore her when as Queen she passes by;
And my heart stands still within me when she pauses proud and
 high;—
But when bending down upon me all the glory of her eyes,
Then my pulses throb with fire, and from off my knees I rise.

Rise with all my manhood in me, to pour forth my passion's might:—
All my wise-made resolutions in a moment taking flight;—
All the distance,—all the danger, that between us ever lies,
Fades away in sweet oblivion 'neath the magic of her eyes!

And my dream grows fairer, fairer, till I seem to see her smile
As she listens to my wooing, growing bolder all the while;
Till, at length, with blushes glowing, all the Queen she lays aside,
And a simple, loving maiden, she is standing by my side.

I forget that I am dreaming, but my waking comes at last,
And I rouse to day's stern labor, when the heavenly night is past;—
But that queenly lady knows not that in dreams she visits me,
Nor that in those dreams Elysian I her lover dare to be!

THE LONG-DELAYED

THE wintry night
With stars is bright,
And on the ground the snow lies white;
While, loud and cold,
The night-winds hold
Revel around this house so old.

Now loud, now low,
The breezes blow
Above earth's winding-sheet of snow;
And through the street
Pass still and fleet
The hurrying steps of homeward feet.

They all pass by,
Nor know that I
Here in the darkness sit and sigh;—
My straining ear
Seeming to hear
A footstep ever drawing near!

Sweet summer crowned
All things around,
When his "farewell" breathed its stern sound;—
I did not start,—
I hushed my heart,
I never dreamed he could depart!

And now these tears
And cruel fears
Will vanish when his face appears!
Alas! my pride
His prayer denied,
No more he cometh to my side.

Day after day
Of long delay
Is wearing heart and hope away;
And yet—and yet—
Can I forget,
Or say, "Would we had never met"?

THE CHRIST

WITHIN the sculptor's room there stands,
  Mid statues finished fair,
All molded by his skilful hands
  And carved with patient care,
A single block of marble white,
  Untouched by chisel-stroke,
Still shapeless, as when first to sight
  It from the quarry broke.

From pure Carrara's hills it came,
  Long months and years ago;—
Must it forever be the same
  Unshapen mass of snow?
The artist-hand has given form
  To many an artist-thought,
And shall no statue, breathing warm,
  Be from this marble wrought?

Even now before it, hushed and still,
  The artist stands in vain;
The subtle thought evades his will,
  He turns away again.
Within the silent stone he knows
  Some shape of life resides,
Which yet in stern and cold repose,
  Relentlessly abides.

Then Fancy paints upon his mind,
  With outlines bold and free,
The dreams of beauty long enshrined
  Within his memory.
A thousand images arise,
  And one by one they pass
Before his keen and searching eyes,
  As figures in a glass.

Lonely and sad, a maiden young
    Stands on a rocky shore,—
With hair dishevelled, harp unstrung,
    That harp so sweet before!
He sees her gaze upon the sea
    Immortal in despair;
But Sappho's sorrow cannot be
    The thought imprisoned there!

And now on Naxos' yellow sands,
    Where summer sunshine lies,
A woman, stretching forth her hands,
    Rends the soft air with cries.
She weeps, and calls, and prays, in vain,
    For, with still swifter flight,
Her lover's sail speeds o'er the main
    And vanishes from sight.

Another, and still fairer face,
    Lights up the charméd air,
Undraped save with most queenly grace,
    She claims to be "most fair."
On Ida's mount she stoops to charm
    The king-born shepherd boy,
And bears from Pallas' self the palm
    All radiant with joy.

The admiring sculptor bends his knee
    Before that vision bright,
Then, slowly and reluctantly,
    He waves it from his sight;
He dares not from that spotless stone
    Fair Aphrodite bring,—
A moment, and her form has flown
    On swift and viewless wing.

He lifts once more his eager eyes,
    For, through the sunlight clear,
A form whose grand proportions rise,
    In godlike grace, draws near.
The peerless brow,—the glorious face,
    That won with magic art
The maiden to its cold embrace,
    To sigh away her heart.

So gods and goddesses of old
    Glide through the artist's dream,—
The heroes of the age of gold,
    The ancient poet's theme.
He scans each bright historic age,
    And gazes eagerly
On martyr, poet, saint, and sage,
    As slowly they pass by.

Sweet, loving, women and brave men,
    Whose very names are dear,
From out their ashes rise again,
    In graceful groups appear.
Fantastic figures gleam beyond,
    From legends old and strange,
And mailéd knights and maidens fond
    Through the long vista range.

Yet still the artist turns away
    Dissatisfied with all,—
Till from the heavens dim and gray
    The evening shadows fall.
Then, forth into the crowded street,
    He bends his way, and still
Those phantom-shapes, with footsteps fleet,
    The pathway seem to fill.

He wanders on till far behind
    He leaves the city's roar,—
How sweet the stillness thus to find,
    How fair the shining shore!
The solemn ocean swells and shines
    Beneath the moon's pale light,
The breath that murmurs in the pines
    Gives greeting to the night.

Farewell the daylight's feverish thought,
    Farewell its toil and care;
Its rush and turmoil fade to naught
    In the night's holier air.
Deeper the shadows fall around,—
    The wearied artist lies
Prostrate upon the perfumed ground,
    Beneath the midnight skies.

No sound the Sabbath stillness breaks,
    Save the low night-wind's sigh
And the sad moan the ocean makes,
    As the waves ripple by.
A spell from out the Land of Sleep
    Falls on the artist's brow,
And, through his slumber sweet and deep,
    New visions wander now.

Up through the skies, so still and bright,
    He seems to swiftly glide,
While angels clothed in shining white
    Stand, hushed, on every side.
Amid their glittering ranks he sees
    All forms of beauty rare,
And lowly on his bended knees
    He breathes the rapturous air.

Awhile amid the angel host
　　He kneels in dumb delight,
Nor deems that even Heaven can boast
　　A form more dazzling bright.
But soon through the assembled throng
　　One impulse deeply thrills,
One burst of universal song
　　All Heaven's archway fills.

As the loud Hallelujah rings,
　　The glittering hosts divide,
And veil their faces with their wings,
　　For, opening high and wide,
The portals of the upper skies
　　Reveal a light so fair,
That not the purest angel eyes
　　That inner glory bear.

Out from the dazzling golden gates,
　　With solemn step and slow,
Comes one upon whose movement waits
　　The reverent throng below.
The heavenly sweetness of his face,
　　The glory of his mien,
Transcend the highest angel grace
　　That Heaven has ever seen.

It is the Master drawing near
　　The adoring hosts to greet,—
He gently bends, as if to hear
　　Their strains of worship sweet.
The Hallelujah dies away,
　　The chorus sinks at last,—
The heavenly vision will not stay,
　　The artist's dream has passed.

The morning sunbeams flash and blaze,
    As, starting from his sleep,
A moment more he seems to gaze
    On Heaven's refulgent deep.
Then rising from the grassy ground,
    With thoughtful step he turns
Homeward his way,—a bliss profound
    Within his bosom burns.

Once more within his studio stands
    The sculptor,—but no more,
With aimless eye and idle hands,
    That untouched stone before.
Stroke upon stroke his chisel gives,
    No model now needs he,
Within his inmost soul there lives
    A single memory.

With hand unwearied, nerve unspent,
    The summer days go by;
Strange power to his frame is lent,
    Strange lustre to his eye.
The help that with a throbbing heart
    He asks each night in prayer
Is surely granted, mortal art
    Ne'er fashioned aught so fair.

At last the marble can no more,
    And art has done its best,—
His task of love and prayer is o'er,—
    His artist heart at rest
Yet though to all the crowd it seem
    A Christ from stone unsealed,
He sees still fairer in that dream
    The Master's self revealed.

SELF-POISED

WHO reads one heart well can read all, they say;—
Who sees by night can better see by day;
Who walks unswerving may point out the way
For weaker souls to walk in as they may.

He who is earnest in his own behoof,
Needs not to ask that others stand aloof;
He who is doing battle for the right,
Cares not how many watch him through the fight.

Nor does he care though no one cheer him on,
Or rush to praise him when his victory's won.
Calm in his conscious power he remains;
He recks not losses and he counts not gains.

SWEET HEART

SWEET Heart! Sweet Heart! keep me anear thee now!
  Dear Love! Dear Love! leave me no more alone!
Enshrine me in thy breast and teach me how
  To build for thee in mine a fitting throne.

Once loving, ne'er forgetting, we will fear
  No ills that timid souls with terror fill;
Tho' oft apart we will be always near,—
  Near in the trusting thought the single will.

Count we not time, for days and years no more
  Our blessèd certainty of love can harm;
Dread we no change, for chance and change are o'er
  When earthly faith has caught from Heaven its charm!

Then love me, Love, and keep me in thy heart!
  Sweet Heart! Sweet Heart! beat only now for me!
Once having met, henceforth we cannot part,—
  Near or remote, together we must be!

THE TIMID LOVER

THERE is a lady fair
　　Who holds my spirit fast,
While she goes free as air
　　And scatters smiles broadcast,—
　　　　Till high and low
The blessing of her bounteous greeting know.

With timid step and slow
　　I follow where she leads,—
And in my face I know
　　My passionate love she reads;—
　　　　But with a smile
She gently bars my utterance the while.

One glance from her bright eyes
　　Hushes my very heart;—
My word gives place to sighs,
　　Breathed to myself apart.
　　　　All I would say
Fades from my memory utterly away.

A kindly fate allots
　　My life near hers a place;—
No stain my lineage blots,
　　My name knows no disgrace,—
　　　　High in the world
I bear the banner of my race unfurled.

I trust my soul is free
　　From all but honest thought,
That friendship may with me
　　By all true men be sought;
　　　　And that my hand
Has strength to compass what my brain has planned.

I never quailed through fear
 In battle's fiercest strife;
I've smiled when peril near
 Has menaced my poor life;
  What man may dare
Methinks my heart would bid me do and bear.

And so the days go by,
 The precious hours pass,
So dull with her am I
 That she must think, alas!
  That I am blind
In heart and sense, in body and in mind.

And yet, did I not dream
 That, as we met last night,
A rosy blush did seem
 To flush her brow so white?
  And once her look
So gentle grew that I her glance could brook.

If, when we meet to-day,
 She will but blush again,—
Or turn her face away
 As timidly as then,—
  I feel as though
Before *her* fears myself would bolder grow!

And yet no coward base
 E'er knew a deeper dread
Than, when I see her face,
 Is through my being spread,
  A trembling fool,
I bow in speechless terror 'neath her rule!

No tyrant seemeth she,
   And yet no monarch bold
More absolute could be,
   More ruthless sway could hold!
     My love is true,
And yet that lady fair I dare not woo.

Out of her sight I weave
   A thousand phrases rare,
By which she shall perceive
   What form my wishes wear;—
     But when we meet
Away fly honeyed words and fair conceit.

Hope the bright vision paints,—
   I hasten to her side,
Before my courage faints,
   To woo her for my bride.
     Ye gods attend
My rapid way and my true cause befriend!

GIVE ME THE NIGHT

GIVE me the night, let others take the day,
　I grudge them not the sunshine's garish light;—
The light is fair, the sunshine for the gay,
　The world may have it, but give me the night!

Give me thy Heart, let others take thy smile,
　I grudge them not the unessential part
Of kindliness and courtesy the while
　Thou walkest with them,—but give me thy Heart!

The day was made for toil, the night for bliss,
　Thy smile was made for all, thy heart for me,
Both day and smile may shine, I know but this,—
　When the night comes it brings me bliss and thee.

THE BRIDE OF THE SEA

DEAR, beautiful Venice! Fair Bride of the Sea!
In this cold northern clime I am pining for thee;
My heart turning ever with fondest regret
To the home I have lost, but can never forget;
  Where my childhood flew by,
  'Neath thy warm glowing sky,
And life seemed all sunshine so happy was I!

I shall never again hear the soft plash of oars,
As my gondola floats by thy fairy-like shores,—
Or gaze on the waves of the silent Lagoon,
As they gleam in the silvery light of the moon,—
  While she sheds her soft ray
  Till the night dies away
In visions that fade in the cold light of day.

I sigh for thee ever, my own native land;
Though fond hearts are near me, though friends clasp my hand;—
I thank them, I bless them with tears in my eyes,
But still long for one glimpse of dear Italy's skies;
  And my thoughts fly in vain
  O'er the blue rolling main,
For, alas! I shall never behold them again.

SEPARATION

THOUGH seas divide us and though months pass by,
Uncheered by touch of hand or glance of eye,—
Though thoughts which long for interchange in vain
Lie folded back upon the weary brain,
While every precious memory of the past
Deepens the shadow on the present cast!

Still there are moments when my throbbing heart
Dares to believe that we are not apart,—
When deep within a secret pulse is stirred,
As at the magic of some mighty word,
Which, sweeping far away Love's sad eclipse,
Brings your sweet kisses to my waiting lips.

MY LADYE LOVE

I HAVE a little ladye love,—
    I shall not tell her name,
Nor yet how it has chanced that she
    My ladye love became;
For if one half the pleasant things
    About her I should tell,
I'm sure you'd try to find her out
    And want her, too,—as well.

I'll only whisper that she's small,
    Just big enough for me:
And she has tiny hands and feet,
    Almost too small to see.
Then, like most little folks, she knows
    All sorts of winning ways,
And gives a very piquant turn
    To everything she says.

Besides, she is a sprightly elf,
    She's foremost in the dance,—
And if it's fun you want,—just see
    The mischief in her glance!
And list! the music in her heart
    Steals to her finger-ends,
And to the melodies she makes
    A subtle magic lends.

My little lady has her faults,
    Thank Fortune for them all!
I should not like your perfect folks,
    Their sweetness soon would pall.
She has a thousand wayward whims,
    She flashes up like fire,—
And if you think she's meek and mild,
    I only say,—just try her!

Her nature on the surface shows
    Each fresh impression made,
And every moment gleams or glooms
    Bright sunshine or deep shade.
She's never anything by halves,
    And when she laughs,—she laughs,
And when she's sad, the cup of woe
    Down to the dregs she quaffs.

Now she and I know very well
    She's just the one that I
Can love with all my heart and soul,
    'Tis no one's business why.
Good people! don't you trouble us,
    And we'll not trouble you,—
But wish you each may find a love
    As fond and strong and true.

THE USELESS QUEST

POOR, tired seeker, cease thy useless quest:
Rest in the axiom that what is, is best.
All thy far-reaching fancies come to naught:—
Thy thought pursues what is beyond all thought!

Thy deep philosophies still end in dreams;
Thy keenest vision only sees what seems;
The vast unknown outreaches man's conceit;—
Why boast of wings when thou hast only feet!

HOME

I long for home!
My feet are weary wandering away,
Farther and farther, with each passing day.
    I would go home!

    How fair it looks!
In the sweet distance of the long ago,
Ere I knew aught of misery and woe,
    Save from my books.

    By night and day
A thousand pictures busy memory brings
Of all the dear and once familiar things
    Now passed away.

    The humble cot
Beneath whose sheltering roof tree I was born,
Glows in the brightness of the summer morn,
    A fairy spot.

    The little stream
Beside whose rippling waters oft I played,
The dim old forest in whose shade I strayed,
    Lost in some dream.

    The very skies
Seem in my memory far more softly bright
Than this gay, shameless, foreign noonday light,
    Which meets my eyes.

    My mother stands
In the low doorway waiting for her child,
Who wandered long ago through pathways wild
    To distant lands.

My father prays
To see once more the darling of his age,
To hear her read the well-worn sacred page,
    As in old days.

Oh, let me go!
I am not ill, I yet have strength enough
To bear me home, e'en were the way more rough,
    Each step I know!

I cannot die
So far from all that I have loved so well;
Were I at home I might bid earth farewell
    Without a sigh.

I must depart,—
All words are powerless to detain me here.
Away each doubt, away each timid fear,—
    Courage,—my heart!

At home once more,
I may cast off this burden that I bear,
I may forget my sorrow and my care,—
    But not before!

Alas! Alas!
I have no longer youth, or home, or friends,
No matter where or how this poor life ends,
    So let it pass!

SEEMINGS

THE rosy curtains of the opening dawn
    Seem to disclose a glimpse of that lost Heaven
From which each earth-born soul must journey on,
    And sin—yet hope to have its sins forgiven!

The golden glory of the setting sun
    Seems like a gateway to the realms of space,
Through which the soul, its earthly labor done,
    Might seek, at last, a quiet resting-place.

The starry dome of the deep midnight sky
    Seems like a temple vast, within whose gloom
The soul might lay its earthly vesture by,
    And rise to bliss, untrammeled by the tomb.

The ceaseless murmur of the surging sea
    Seems the deep whisper of some sacred word,
Which, but for grossness of mortality,
    Might by each soul that it would save be heard.

Each human heart, with other hearts entwined,
    Seems to have foretaste of undying love;
As if Earth's faith, by Heaven's own signet signed,
    Were pledged below to be fulfilled above.

So the long hours of solitary thought
    Oft lead the way to seeming Heaven-sent dreams;
Like messages by shining angels brought,
    They thrill the spirit with divinest themes.

Thus all the sweet analogies of life,
    The fair procession of our days and nights,—
Seem with such promise of the future rife,
    That man, impetuous, claims Eternal life.

And could it be that prophecies like this
    Were but the product of an o'erwrought brain,—
And were our only goal that dark abyss,
    Where Death would end our pleasure and our pain;—

Then, were it not that my poor human heart
    Clings, with fierce strength that will not be denied,
Unto the few it loves, I would depart,—
    And, with my life, cast hopes and fears aside!

SONG

GIVE me no kiss at meeting,
 When our meeting is by day,
And a careless crowd around us
 May hear each word you say;—
But with one of your keenest glances
 Look deep in my faithful eyes,—
And let yours with a glad assurance
 Tell of trust that never dies.

Give me no kiss at parting,
 When the same rude world is by,—
Though our hearts are heavy with aching,
 And each breath comes with a sigh;
But speak your words of farewell
 In a low and half-veiled tone,
That shall hide your tender sorrow
 From all hearts but my own.

Then let your welcome kisses
 Come like the stars at night,
Or the sunbeams that gently enter
 My room with the morning light;—
Let them seek my lips as in silence
 We sit by the solemn sea,—
Or safe in some home seclusion,
 Where feeling and thought are free.

Your kisses are too precious,
 Your words of love too dear,
For other eyes to see them,
 Or other ears to hear.
So keep them for sacred seasons,
 When you and I are alone,
To seal your love with their sweetness,
 And your trust in my love to own.

THE HEAVENLY GUEST

*That they should seek after the Lord if haply they might feel after Him and
find Him, though He be not far from any one of us.—St. Paul.*

OH, happy heart, make ready with thy best,
    Bring forth thy treasures, spread thy choicest cheer,
Prepare thy dwelling for the Heavenly Guest,
    Peal forth loud welcomes as He draweth near!

The King is coming,—let thy voice be heard,
    Shouting the tidings of our wondrous bliss:
Let every heart with wildest joy be stirred,
    The Lord of heavenly worlds descends to this.

Rejoice my Soul to see thy Lord at last,
    Count every moment that He gives to thee;
Drink in His presence,—hold His image fast,
    That it may light thee through Eternity.

Perchance the mighty Lord of Life may see
    How long thou hast been pining for His grace,
Thy fervent prayers may find acceptancy,
    And mid His hosts He may grant thee a place!

Ah, foolish Soul, what idle words are these!
    Knowest thou not the Lord is always near!
The inmost throbbing of thy heart He sees,—
    And while thou goest to meet Him, He is here!

"Not far from every one of us" He stands,
    No royal progress through His world He makes,
He "dwelleth not in temples made with hands,"
    In one embrace the universe He takes.

No world so great, no heart so small, but He
    With love beholdeth and with bliss can fill;
His loving-kindness stoops to comfort thee,
    Though worlds on worlds hang breathless on His will.

THE INVALID

IN the hushed stillness of a darkened room,
　Through the long days I lie,—
Buried and hidden, in a living tomb,
　Shut out from earth and sky.

Lonely and sorrowful, and weak and faint,
　Stretched on my couch of pain,
The oft-repeated utterance of complaint
　Comes sadly forth again.

And in the depths of this poor aching breast
　So dark a sorrow lies,
That I cease not to inly crave for rest,
　My only language sighs!

Thus the sad hours have slowly passed away
　Through all the weary years,
These silent walls have witnessed day by day
　My anguish and my tears.

Oh, Heavenly Father! unto thee I turn,
　And with humility
Strive evermore the lesson sweet to learn
　Of perfect trust in Thee!

I know that through this weight of pain and woe,
　Thou, in thine own good time,
Wilt raise my spirit, now so crushed and low,
　Up to that height sublime, —

Where in thy presence, 'neath the golden light
　That streams from thy "white throne,"—
My earthly faith changed into heavenly sight,
　I shall feel peace alone!

HEAVEN'S GATE

OH, sunset glow, oh radiance fair,
That floods the sky, that fills the air,
Bathe my rapt soul with flashing light,
Before you die in coming night!

Oh, golden clouds, oh, western sky,
Open your portals wide and high,
Mine eyes from earthly dimness clear,
And show me Heaven,—it must be near!

On your soft wings, oh, sunset hours!
Ye waft the fragrance of fresh flowers,
And song of birds with tenderest notes
In at my open casement floats.

But ye must waft a fairer freight
Than song of birds to Heaven's gate;—
And sweeter than the breath of flowers
Is what I give ye, sunset hours!

As fleet thy moments, dying day,
So fleets my earthly life away,
With thy last beams my soul, set free,
Springs to a glad eternity.

More glorious than thy purpling gleams
The light from Heaven upon me beams;
Rapt in prophetic bliss I wait
My entrance in at Heaven's Gate.

"LET NOT HIM THAT GIRDETH ON HIS HARNESS BOAST HIMSELF AS HE THAT PUTTETH IT OFF"

O THOU, who standest in the morning dawn,
  Whose pulses quicken and whose heart beats high,
Longing to gird the untried harness on,
  Flushing with ardor,—sure of victory;—
Thou little know'st how long the day may be,—
  Nor how its heat and toil may waste thy strength,
Youth's buoyant confidence can only see
  The conflict's opening,—not its weary length.

The blood and dust may stain thy snowy plume,
  The tired hand may fail to strike the blow;
The morn that smiled may prove a day of gloom,
  And hopes, that rose in joy, may set in woe.
Traitors within and foes without may wound,—
  Friends that are dear fall prostrate by thy side;
Through the long day upon the battle-ground
  Thou must remain till the full even-tide.

Then hush the boastings of a thoughtless pride,
  Put on thine armor, draw thy flashing blade,
God for thy strength, and Jesus for thy guide,
  In naught exulting,—yet in naught dismayed;
Fight bravely for the cause of Truth and Right
  Through the long day,—and when the setting sun
Shall bid thee hail the welcome shades of night,
  All heaven and earth shall own thy victory won.

BE STRONG

If thou hast run with the footmen and they have wearied thee, how shalt thou contend with horses? And if in the land of peace wherein thou trustedst they have wearied thee, how wilt thou do in the swelling of the Jordan?—Jeremiah XII.5

IF midst life's little cares
    Thy heart grows faint,—
And, like a coward, dares
    To make complaint,—
What hope can e'er be thine
    That thou wilt win
The nobler life divine,
    And conquer sin?

If in thy days of youth
    Thy love grows cold,
How wilt thou fight for Truth
    When thou art old?
If now thy faith is dim
    In morning's light,
How wilt thou trust in Him
    Through the dark night?

If, while thy pulses thrill
    With glowing life,
Thou bring'st no earnest will
    For patient strife,—
How,—when the shades of death
    Are drawing nigh,—
When fails thy last poor breath,
    How wilt thou die?

"FEAR THOU NOT FOR I AM WITH THEE"

FEAR not, poor trembling, faltering heart,
    As through life's weary day,
Encompassed by bewildering mists,
    Thou goest on thy way.
Though danger in its myriad forms
    About thy path may be,
Trust in the promise of thy God,
    Fear not, He is with thee!

Fear not the world, though bright and fair
    Its tempting lures are spread,
Though flattering thousands join to place
    The laurel on thy head;—
Fear not, although thou knowest well
    Thy hardest task may be,
Amid the plaudits of the world
    To keep thy spirit free.

Fear not thy joys, though trembling still
    To see their long array,
Knowing how little thou canst do
    Their giver to repay;—
But in their sunshine calmly walk
    In deep humility,
And for them all, with grateful heart,
    Thank Him who is with thee.

Fear not the sorrows that may dim
    Thy life with gathering gloom,
Nor thine own lonely journey through
    The darkness of the tomb.
In joy and woe, in life and death,
    These words thy strength shall be,
"Be not dismayed, I am thy God,
    "Fear not, I am with thee."

HEAVENLY VOICES

VOICES from the distant Heaven
  Float around us everywhere;
Angel-warnings to the spirit
  Murmur through the dreamy air.

Feebly borne upon the breezes,
  Sighing mournfully along,
Come those voices,—oft unheeded
  Falls the cadence of their song.

In the midst of love and gladness,
  In the hour of deepest woe,—
Darkest night or brightest noonday,
  Sound those voices soft and low.

Vainly do we strive to gather
  The full meaning of the strain;
Earthly noises jar and mingle
  With their sweet and pure refrain.

Yet some few and broken fragments
  Reach us when the world is still,
When with holy thoughts and prayerful
  We our listening spirits fill.

Words of warning if we wander
  From the narrow path away;—
Words of sweetest consolation
  If we labor, love, and pray.

FOR MAN WALKETH IN A VAIN SHADOW

BRIGHT in thy path a thousand pleasures smile,
  The sky is blue above, the earth is fair;
Hope's brilliant dreams the passing hours beguile,
  As yet have frowned no sorrow and no care.
Thou wonderest at the Psalmist's mournful words,
  The fleeting world seems real and true to thee,
Thy harp of life sounds only joyous chords,
  No harsh ones yet have marred the melody.

Yet there are moments when the heart stands still,
  Thrilled with a strange, inexplicable fear,—
When half-formed dreads the youthful bosom fill,
  And vague yet hateful phantoms hover near;—
When through the brightness of the sunniest day,
  And in the darkness of the deepest night,
A voice—as of a spirit—seems to say,
  "Sorrow must follow joy, and darkness, light."

And thou must live to find the promise true,—
  To see thy cherished pleasures vanish fast,
And the bright morning lose its roseate hue,
  Its sunshine clouded, and its splendor past.
Yet as the shadows fall and night draws on,
  If thou hast upward looked while all was gay,
A light more dear than that so quickly gone
  Shall glad thy spirit with prophetic ray.

WAITING ON THE LORD

AH! what have I wherewith to serve my God?
 I do not stand among the world's encrowned,
With menials waiting to obey my nod,
 And eager servants on my errands bound.

I have no stores of concentrated wealth
 To feed the hungry and to clothe the poor;
I have no skill to bring the sick to health,
 I am untutored in all helpful lore.

Nor have I word of eloquence to thrill
 The hearts that hear me, with a power divine;
I cannot guide a single human will,
 Or make one weak soul strong with strength of mine.

My labors do not help the harvest-time,
 I bring no solace to the suffering soul,—
My tears atone not for another's crime,
 I run no race while others reach the goal.

There seems no place in the broad world for me,
 I faint and tremble 'neath the noonday sun;
Yet though I weary and would fain be free,
 I must be patient till the day is done.

I do not murmur at my pain and woe,
 I only ask this gift from my dear Lord,
That he would let me serve Him ere I go,
 And draw some music from the stricken chord!

But with no brain to think great thoughts of God,—
 No hand with strength to strike a blow for Heaven,—
No force to mark the pathway I have trod;
 Will work be asked for, when no tools were given?

No tools, poor weary one, at life's noon spent?
  Look once again within thee and behold
How to thy heart thy heavenly Master lent
  Graces and virtues rich and manifold.

For, though so fruitless seem the hours of pain
  Which keep thee from the work that thou wouldst do,
Thou hast not borne a single pang in vain;
  Thy suffering has been thy working, too.

Patient, tho' sad, through all thy weary life,
  Thy martyr-lesson has been nobly learned;
Thy battle field has seen a goodly strife;
  Thy Heaven-lit torch through deadly mists has burned!

Thou hast endured with never-failing love
  The bitter burden of thine adverse fate;
Look up, sad soul! and see thy crown above,—
  "They also serve who only stand and wait."

L'ENVOI

GO, little Book! my greeting take
To every friend, who, for my sake,
Will see your faults in softened light,
And all your virtues doubly bright.

ESSAYS

A Chapter on Novels

1. *Zaidee; a Romance.* Boston: John P. Jewett & Co. 1856.

2. *Tolla; a Tale of Modern Rome.* By Edmond About. Boston: Whittemore, Niles, & Hall. 1856.

3. *Rachel Gray; a Tale founded on Fact.* By Julia Kavanagh. New York: D. Appleton & Co. 1856.

The works of popular novel-writers follow one another in such quick succession, that an immense amount of reading is forced upon those who would keep up with the times in this branch of literature. It becomes therefore necessary, as a safeguard for the future, to examine with sharp scrutiny the claims put forth by every *débutant.* A word of praise given to a new author may be the means of unlocking innumerable writing-desks, which, but for that word, might have remained closed for ever. It is indeed, if we may judge from the heaps of novels on our table, only *"le premier pas qui coûte."* In accepting the first novel, we, as it were, grant a ticket of admission to the very field of battle; it behooves us, therefore, to look well at every candidate, and to be sure that he will prove a stanch warrior. The time for "men of straw" is past. It having been once proved that a novel may, without losing its hold on the imagination, be something far higher than a sentimental love-tale, we feel that we have a right to insist upon receiving it in its best form.

With the romance which stands at the head of our list, we have a new claimant upon public favor. It is not difficult to trace a little youngness throughout the book. It shows itself sometimes pleasantly in freshness and keenness of perception, and a happy abandonment in description. In other instances it betrays itself in rawness and want of artistic skill in the development both of plot and character. With much that is pretty in the way of episode, many really admirable bits of scene-painting and a genial kindliness of atmosphere, there is a want of definite aim and of force in the book as a whole. If we allow the beauty of disinterested affection to be its leading thought, we must quarrel with the exaggerated, school-girlish form it is suffered to take, and also with the perfect squareness with which the tangible reward of the sacrifice is arranged, or rather by which the whole effort is defeated and made useless, as well as senseless. The history of Zaidee's struggles to be a victim teach either no lesson at all, or else one which nobody ought to follow. A good degree of power is visible in the first cast of the characters, and several piquant touches induced us to form expectations which we were sorry to find disappointed. Some of the descriptions of nature are remarkably vivid and picturesque. The *dénouement* is decidedly hackneyed, and unworthy of the beginning. The author who cannot dispose of his own *dramatis personæ* satisfactorily, fails in the very point where the public will least forgive the failure. Miss Oliphant needs to study mechanical details more carefully to make her story move freely; and must take her lovable but foolish little heroine down from her lofty stilts, if she would make her walk the earth a graceful woman. We allude the more freely to these defects, because there is, in spite of them, so much of promise in "Zaidee," that we look for something by and by from its authoress, far beyond her actual accomplishment in this first work.

In "Tolla" we have a story quite in contrast with "Zaidee." It has produced a sensation, in some circles, far greater than its merit demands. It seems to have derived its fame chiefly from its being founded on facts, thereby possessing that mysterious interest which appertains to scandal and gossip. The characters are all commonplace, most of them disagreeable. A faint halo of pitying interest surrounds Tolla herself, partly, perhaps, because she is kept somewhat out of sight. Still, if we get provoked with Zaidee for her pertinacious endeavors to continue a victim, we are quite incensed with Tolla for not seeing through the vapid weakness and indolent selfishness of the stupid lover for whom she dies. The absurd helplessness of everybody who ought to do anything, is absolutely ludicrous. If the book be, as it pretends, "a picture of Roman society," Roman society is not worth painting. The flippant style of the author has a taking *nonchalance* about it which beguiles the reader over the pages, but which sober second-thought condemns, and which palls before we get to the end. The book belongs to a class which we feel sorry to see increased or perpetuated. It can be of no possible service to any one, and is hardly more of an addition to one's library than a pretty well got up report of an ordinary breach-of-promise suit.

"Rachel Gray" is another proof of the fatal facility with which some of our modern authors write. The success of "Nathalie" brought out in a surprisingly short time "Daisy Burns" and "Grace Lee," neither of them approaching their predecessor in merit. Now we have, from the same pen, "Rachel Gray," inferior to either. It may be considered all the more a failure, since Miss Kavanagh has not succeeded in making an attractive fiction out of a fact, which, in its naked simplicity, is not without interest. It is simply not enough for a romance. Inasmuch as Rachel is not a victim of her own making, she is entitled to our sympathy; inasmuch too as she bears her discipline bravely, we ought to feel interested in her struggle; but we fear many who have commenced her story have never finished it, or have forgotten how it ended. It could have been told as well in two pages as in two hundred. Miss Kavanagh would do well to follow the example of Miss Bronte, one of the few authors who have had the good sense to refrain from writing until, as she so forcibly expressed it, they had "accumulated."* It required some heroism, and showed much true wisdom, in the author of "Villette," to hold her peace when all the world clamored for her to write. Quantity is no test of power, and diffuseness has grown to be a disease in the literary world. The inordinate desire of the public for new books has produced a fever among authors. The novelist, knowing his book will be pushed aside immediately by some newer one, and determining not to retire from the lists, sits down, too often, himself to write the later romance, which shall supersede, if it cannot rival, the earlier one. But in so doing, he strikes a blow at his own breast, and separates himself from those earnest and self-forgetful minds who labor for something higher than to gorge the pampered appetite of an undiscriminating public. There are still some who know it to be better

---

* Our own estimate of "Rachel Gray," as may have been inferred from a brief notice of it in our April number (p. 579), is much higher than that of our present contributor. We have not, however, deemed it expedient to mutilate an article, with every other opinion in which we fully accord.—ED.

to write one book, the concentration of ten years of thought and life, than to fill shelves with undigested and unworthy matter.

We have selected these three novels from the multitude about us, not because they individually call for an extended notice, but because they are types of prevalent fiction, and as such they serve well as a text on which we would enlarge. In speaking of them, we include all which bear a family likeness to them,—their name is Legion. In regarding them as *insufficiencies*, we would make them suggest more perfect works. In examining their claims to stand among the novels of the age, we must not shrink from comparing them with the best which the age produces. If they fall by this standard, it may as well be early as late. In none of them do we discern the elements of greatness, the indications of immortality. In none is found the glowing, passionate life of Currer Bell's creations, the wonderful world-knowledge of Thackeray, the intense psychological insight of Hawthorne, or the healthful moral energy of Dickens. Our age is rich in novelists; we have a constellation in the zenith, and now, as in all time, the rush-lights must go out while the stars shine on. We propose to trace in brief the history of novels; for they, like men, have had a childhood and a youth preceding their present maturity.

In no branch of literature has a more radical change taken place, during the last seventy or eighty years, than in that which embraces the fictions which have satisfied the public taste at the time of their appearance, have wrought the work for which they were created, and claim to be ranked among the important utterances of each age. The contrast between the novels of our day and those which thrilled the hearts of our sentimental grandmothers and drew tears to the eyes of our heroic grandfathers, is as strongly marked as that between the plain black suits of the gentlemen in our ball-rooms, and the peach-bloom coats and silken breeches of those same ancestors of ours. Who weeps now over the harrowing griefs of Amanda Malvina, as set forth in "The Children of the Abbey," or can study the perplexities and delicate distresses of Sir Charles Grandison and his charming Harriet, without roars of laughter that would grate harshly upon the ears of the author?

The modern novel differs from the old-fashioned one in so many points, that hardly any similarity remains, save that which is implied and necessitated by the realm to which they appertain, and the allegiance which both owe to the imaginative faculty of their creators. They differ, not only in choice and arrangement of materials and agencies, but their motive powers are totally unlike. The successful novel of the present day is strictly a work of art, amenable to all the laws of art. When tried by the rules of criticism, and tested by severe analysis, it must be able to prove that its conclusions follow fairly from its premises, to show that its effects proceed from sufficient causes. Too many liberties with probability are inadmissible for the purpose of bringing about the catastrophe. Artistic beauty of style must accompany the creation, development, and completion of the plot. Harmonious and dignified expression must follow powerful conception in the romance that would win and retain a strong hold upon the public taste. In this category are not included the popular ephemera of the day, which have a brilliant but short existence from causes independent of their intrinsic merit; but only those works of genius, which make the novel a medium for the promulgation of some great truth, involve some high teaching, or picture forth human nature with a master-hand. Neither would we degrade the public taste by confounding it with the ignorant admiration of the masses for that which dazzles with a meretricious glare, or feeds an appetite for sentimental horrors.

In the days when Richardson, Mrs. Radcliffe, and Miss Burney wrote romances which set the literary coteries of England in a blaze, there entered into the composition of a novel certain conventional ingredients which were made use of in each fiction. The genius of the author might display itself in the more or less skilful arrangement and management of these, but the most daring writer did not venture to disregard them. Incidents were his "main stock in trade"; it was only by a succession of startling events, by accidents and surprises, by secrets and discoveries,—by a series of *tableaux-vivans,* as it were,—that he could hope to keep alive the interest of the reader. The element of conversation was not made use of, as it now is, to light up and enliven the story, and to allow the characters to unfold their individuality through the medium of their own expression. In the old novels, the conversation was merely the narrative put into the mouth of a different person from time to time. Each individual told his own story for the edification of the rest, and thus relieved the author from the task of unfolding it for himself. The narrator appears generally to be heard with more interest by his audience, than the life and spirit of his tale would warrant. No one can fail to perceive this great deficiency in the old-fashioned novel. The highest conversational effort rarely gets beyond a rhapsodical love-declaration, or a succession of stilted reflections and trite observations. Incident, as before said, was the pith of the whole matter,—development became, in consequence, merely a mechanical sequence of events.

The first ingredient in the old novel is a faultless heroine,—one whose transcendent loveliness and angelic perfections of body and mind, while they place her in some degree out of the pale of our sympathies, and far beyond the reach of our emulation, are to win for her the envy of all the other women in the book, and the loving persecution of every man who crosses her path. The author pours down on the head of this charming innocent all his vials of wrath, through the conventional three volumes, with the trifling exception of the last two pages, wherein she is, by some utterly unexpected turn in the tide of her affairs, to be made supremely happy. From the motley crowd of besieging admirers, one is selected to play the part of the hero, and is forthwith invested with the masculine accomplishments corresponding best with her feminine perfections, and adorned with a high-sounding name and a gorgeous wardrobe to make him more completely worthy the attention of the painted wonder at whose shrine he kneels. At most, a few peccadillos, such as the polite world agrees to pass over as "wild oats," are allowed to vary his otherwise monotonous perfection. He may gamble away his fortune, and put a pistol to his brainless head, as his only means of getting out of his difficulties; but the pistol must be snatched away at the right moment by a rich uncle from India, whose pockets are full of rupees at the young man's service. If a still more startling tableau is desirable, the heroine herself strikes the pistol from her lover's hand, and then falls fainting in his arms, taking care to remain in her swoon till he forgets all about his project of suicide, while the money necessary to relieve him from his financial embarrassments makes its appearance as suddenly as if it dropped from the sky.

Of course, but little variety of incident can arise in the mutual relations of two such persons, unassisted by external influences. So a monstrous villain "enters," by whose wonderful cunning and malicious plotting, misunderstandings, separations, and evils of all descriptions are brought about. He continues, with the help of occasional hot-headedness in the lover and opportune fits of dignity and coyness in the lady, to harass them through the necessary number of chapters. He himself is, of course, consigned to condign punishment when his "mission" is ended, that is, when the public are supposed to be tired of reading. The hero and heroine are permitted to become the dupes of this villain to an extent which would for ever disgrace their reputation for common sense in any actual community. If the tragic is particularly the *forte* of the author, he indulges in killing off his strong-minded villain under all the circumstances of baffled revenge, or with the agonies of a late remorse.

In all this we see that outward agencies produce the results. We have before us the machinery of plots and counter-plots, assaults and accidents, showers of misfortune followed by equally heavy showers of fortune,—all busily and visibly at work to bring about the simple *dénouement* of a marriage. Meanwhile, the hero and heroine, although apparently most concerned in the issue, are least useful in bringing it about. They sit like spectators idly looking at a show, or, at most, they are but the puppets which move at the will of others, smiling when the wires pull one way, weeping when they are drawn the other. Designed as they are to appear perfect at the beginning, no progress, no interior development, is possible. With no faults to expiate, and no necessity for cultivating their already full-blown virtues, they remain, inevitably, types of immovable absurdity. They originate nothing from the depths of their own nature, evolve nothing from the mutual action of mind or sympathy, and are wanted but for one purpose,—to love each other in a blind enough way, through thick and thin. Their characteristics, if they possess any, are the same at the conclusion of the book as at its beginning, and the reader, having finally moored them safely in the wide harbor of matrimony, may lay down the volumes with the pleasant conviction that no after-experience can disturb the placid current of their united lives. The heroine, in order that she may win our sympathy and excite a greater degree of pitying interest, is subjected to a course of misfortunes, and kept upon a regimen of afflictions which would crush any ordinary mortal beyond recovery. She, however, has the gift of endurance and wonderful recuperative faculties, so that, though her cheek grows so pale that we fear the roses will never bloom again upon it, and her form becomes emaciated to such a degree that we are sure her constitution is seriously impaired, at the first moment that the pressure is removed she rebounds like an

India-rubber ball to the place she started from. Friends and fortune are taken from this "victim" in the most merciless manner; her virtuous actions are misinterpreted into proofs of shocking calumnies; destitute and bowed down with contumely, she becomes so pitiable an object, that only to those who consider marriage as the *summum bonum* of happy fortune does the compensation which the catastrophe offers seem sufficient to repay her for her sufferings, or to place her in a position to enjoy herself very thoroughly. It was, to be sure, in the management of the misfortunes that the skill of the artist was most decidedly shown over the tyro, and it is wonderful that success so often crowned efforts necessarily so restricted.

The region of the supernatural was also open to the old novelist. When he required some wonderful performance manifestly impossible to human capacity, and consequently beyond the accomplishment of his villain, the author could stalk at once into the nether world and call out some restive ghost who wished for a little excitement, or some wide-awake supple devil ready for any work. This supernatural element tells with great effect upon youthful minds, even in this nineteenth century of ours; though the intercourse which is at present supposed by many to exist between the embodied and the disembodied bids fair to do away with the awe that has so long encircled the ghostly realm with a protecting cloud, and to make even little children regard their buried ancestors merely as gossiping intermeddlers with this world's trivialities. But in our own young days, tables remained securely on their four legs, so long as their legs lasted, and we remember with perfect distinctness the nervous qualms consequent upon our perusal of "The Three Spaniards" and "The Mysteries of Udolpho," at the mature age of eleven, while "The Five Nights of St. Albans" unsettled us still further, at a slightly subsequent period.

In the novels of Fielding and Smollett, which rank among the old-fashioned, both by date of utterance and style of composition, though still read by all who wish to be well read in English literature, a different type of hero is at once adopted. Whether the change from the impossible perfections and sublimated refinements of the Lord Frederic Augustus Fitz-Mortimers, to the coarse and vulgar mental and physical qualities of Tom Jones and Peregrine Pickle, is really an improvement, must be decided by the taste of the reader. In human elements, in actual naturalness and vitality, they stand far above the pasteboard excellence they replace. In a certain kind of manliness which clings to them throughout, they win our interest, even while they excite our disgust. The product of a sensual age, they exaggerated the tone and painted in stronger colors the worst weaknesses of the social life they were intended to represent. As works of art, however, the novels of this class occupy, without doubt, a higher position than those which they succeed. Something resembling conversation begins to show itself, brilliant though coarse humor lights up the page, and, what still more insures present interest and future attention for a work of fiction, actual specimens of character appear,—varieties of the human being, lifelike, well defined, and skilfully diversified. Much greater advance is made in the delineation of men than of women. The women have still only two modes of action,—one to fascinate through the senses, the other to suffer through the affections. The power and beauty of woman's spiritual influence seem to have been little understood by the authors of the old romances. Possibly in their own lives they felt this influence, but without analyzing it or understanding its worth and force in the machinery of fiction. Not one among them could shadow it forth with the delicate yet powerful touches of a Dickens, a Thackeray, or a Currer Bell.

The historical novel has always kept strong hold upon the taste of the public. It seems a pleasant way of cheating one's self into the notion that one is reading "for improvement," and acquiring useful information, if a thin sprinkling of fact is sifted over a mass of fictitious matter; though, in the hands of the unscrupulous, subjects, themselves matters of history, are so tortured and disarranged, as sadly to disturb the previous historical acquisitions of amateur readers. Scott, of course, stands first among historical romance-writers, and has seldom departed from the truth in any particulars wherein accuracy is of great importance. He has adorned and softened, or strengthened and deepened, the known characteristics of the age or of the individual, made the bald pages of early chronicles warm and vivid with vitality, and clothed our vague and shadowy impressions of the persons and things of bygone years with flesh and blood. In his hands we are comparatively safe; yet still, any degree of tampering with the historic element is dangerous. To the young and enthusiastic it is often absolutely injurious, by leading them far away from the real facts and merits of the case, and gaining their belief by first enlisting their sympathy. The cold facts of history, afterwards ascertained, fail to eradicate the glowing impression made by a favorite author. Scott may create sympathies which Hume and Smollett shall never be able to destroy. At all times a little fogginess will be the result of the historical novel. It is probable that many others, like ourselves, have received a more vivid image of Mary, Queen of Scots, from "The Abbot," than from any history of her time; and that the mention of her name calls up in their imagination the beautiful and sarcastic woman at Lochleven Castle, more readily than any veritable appearance of hers as queen of her Scottish subjects. The fiction that pleases us best is that in which the characters are nobody and nowhere out of the book,—types of a general humanity, which we recognize as men and women from their fidelity to nature,—which appeal to our sympathies and enlist our approbation by their intrinsic excellence and interior beauty, unassisted by the halo of a great name, undisturbed by doubts derived from previous knowledge.

It is in this absolute creation of character that our modern novelists so far exceed all that their predecessors were able to accomplish. In variety of individuality, in successful delineation of the action of one character upon another, or of internal will upon external circumstance, or the struggle of earnest natures against adverse influences,—in these, the themes of the modern novel, Nature herself is almost rivalled. And here, again, comes up the contrast with the old romance. It is now *the struggle itself* which interests, the development of character which commands attention, as it does in the real life about us. It is not the mere fact that the hero and heroine are in love, that makes us wish them success; it is the effect of that love upon the inner nature, that makes us hope or tremble for the result. It is the growth and beauty of the sentiment that we study; not the simple, yet universal fact of its existence. Heroes and heroines are not now born into the full blossom of perfection, nor does their discipline come only from the stereotyped misfortunes of loss of gold and plottings of enemies. The sorrows and sufferings endured are intended not merely to delay the happy moment, but to develop strength and excellence, and to discipline impetuous carelessness into earnest endeavor. They arise from the internal organism of those who suffer, as often as from a pressure of outward difficulty; and even when they originate in the external, they strike home to the inner heart, and become something more than mere incidents,—else we are dissatisfied with the conception of the author.

The high requirements which criticism has lately made, have placed the novel on an elevated grade, not only as a composition, but as an assistant in mental and moral culture. He who does not read the good novels of the present day is not only but half acquainted with the tone which literary labor has assumed,—he loses one very important source of improvement for his own intellectual and spiritual nature. We owe much to those who have opened this new avenue for the transmission of healthy social influences, and a more and more general appreciation of their efforts will reward their continuance.

Most of the great novels of the present age are written to set forth some leading idea in the author's mind, to call the attention of the public to some great evil or to some great want, or to encourage the struggles of some class of human beings by showing them that their feelings are understood and sympathized with. Because the moral of a book is not written out in a few pithy words on the last page, it does not follow that the book has no moral. No faithful transcript of human life and human passion can be clearly and powerfully exhibited, without, of necessity, containing a deep and searching moral, all the more forcible to the thinking man because it is subtile and beneath the surface. Is not Thackeray's "Vanity Fair" a sermon of the most stringent application? Its author holds a mirror to our hearts, which reveals to each of us many a spring of action that we blush for, many a littleness and weakness, with much of worldliness and vanity, which we have never before been forced fairly to acknowledge, even to ourselves. We lay down the book, confessing, in spite of ourselves, that it is a faithful likeness of a large part of our human nature, and this confession is followed by a pang that is not always useless. The study of human nature in all its manifestations is of benefit to him who thinks deeply, furnishing in itself a spur to the attainment of those qualities which command admiration and respect, and to the dropping of those which call forth contempt and condemnation. Much self-knowledge may be attained, much healthful humility promoted, by having, as it were, the picture of our own hearts set forth before our astonished eyes, touched by the hand of a skilful and fearless master.

To persons who read books as they ought to be read, who abandon themselves entirely to the study of what is before them, who enter, *con amore*, into the story, and become themselves actors and participators therein, a good novel is more like an episode in their own lives, than a tale which serves to while away a few hours of leisure. Friendships are made in the world of fiction, as real and as true as many a visible connection in the world of fact. Who, that thus reads "Villette" and "Jane Eyre," does not recognize Lucy Snow and little Jane as living and suffering intellectual organisms? Who sees not the heart of fire beneath the quiet daily aspect, and longs not that they should know how earnestly their progress has been watched? Who does not feel better acquainted with Becky Sharp and Major Pendennis than with his next-door neighbor, whom, perchance, he meets every day in the street? Does not a smile of recognition pass from face to face at mention of Aunt Betsy Trotwood? Have we not all heard her call "Little Blossom," and seen her drive the donkeys from her garden? Characters which call forth our sympathy, in books, exercise, in some degree, the same magnetic influence upon us that they do when we meet them in real life. These impressions are more or less deep and prolonged, as the sympathy established is more or less complete. Some never wholly die away, but take their places in the halls of memory, as old friends who have, merely for a time, passed out from our sphere of action.

The novel of the present day has a noble mission to perform,—one which should not be lightly undertaken. It has become the most popular of all instruments for producing great effects in the literary world, and for the successful employment of great talents. It is becoming a happy medium for the spreading of truths, which, clothed in this guise, shall win a patient hearing among many that would have turned impatiently or scornfully away, had they met these same truths in a less attractive form. Politics, metaphysics, theology, have all found utterance through the novel. It has ceased to be the plaything of an idle hour, and we look to it for greater depth of thought, a higher range of ideas, closer fidelity to abstract truth, and a more manly grappling with error and falsehood, than ordinary minds are capable of supplying. Therefore let ordinary minds cease to flood the world with idle tales and powerless absurdities, arrogating to themselves a title made honorable by the genius of others. Let ordinary minds, we say, fall back and leave the field to stouter soldiers, who shall do more valiant battle for the cause. We have had patience long enough with vapid story-tellers and self-styled novelists. Let them fill the pages of ephemeral magazines or the columns of country newspapers, if they must write at all, and rest content with the fame consequent upon such efforts. But let the novel be the lofty and enthusiastic utterance of noble minds, the earnest protest of true hearts, the brilliant offspring of intellect and imagination, and we shall have high thoughts arrayed in fitting garb, truth poured forth in "words that burn," and elevating influences at work in fields often closed to all other effort. Many who, from force of habit, rush to a novel for mere amusement, shall be awakened, as from a lethargy, by the stirring truths which lie in wait among the pages. Many a literary voluptuary shall be recalled to strength and action by the very work in which he sought only the gratification of a fastidious taste; sure of beauty and of elegance, because of the promise in its author's name. All of us shall read these books with deep and true enjoyment and real profit, shall place them among our best-loved authors, to return to them again and again with ever new delight. All honor to those who bear within themselves the magic power. May the immortality which is their due be their reward.

Charlotte Brontë and the Brontë Novels

1. *The Life of Charlotte Brontë.* By E. C. Gaskell, Author of "Mary Barton," "Ruth," etc. In two volumes. New York: D. Appleton and Company. 1857. 12mo. pp. 285, 269.

2. *The Brontë Novels.—Jane Eyre. An Autobiography.* Edited by Currer Bell (Charlotte Brontë).—*Shirley. A Tale.* By the Author of "Jane Eyre."—*Villette.* By the Author of "Jane Eyre" and "Shirley."—*Wuthering Heights.* By Ellis Bell (Emily Brontë).—*The Tenant of Wildfell Hall.* By Acton Bell (Anne Brontë). New York: Harper and Brothers. 1857.

3. *Agnes Grey.* By Acton Bell (Anne Brontë).

4. *The Professor. A Tale.* By Currer Bell. New York: Harper and Brothers. 1857. 12mo. pp. 330.

The first thrill of regret which passes over the community on the death of a favorite author, in the prime of his power, is tinged with a very decided selfishness. We count the years which we thought would bring us new volumes from the same pen, and feel ourselves defrauded of a promised treasure. Our expectations have been raised by what has been achieved, and our appreciative welcome prepared for what the future might bring. This feeling is independent of any personal interest in the dead, and when that has already existed, or is subsequently awakened by circumstances, is soon merged in a less selfish sorrow for the broken life. The genius which wrought for our delight assumes the proportions of a friend, over whom we claim the right to mourn, and upon whose memory we dwell with loving interest. Thus we take up our pen for the task we have now set ourselves, not as a cold and distant criticism would suggest, but with reverent friendliness and warmth of interest, which we believe fully warranted by the circumstances of the case. The author of "Jane Eyre" is no longer a mere abstraction to the reader's mind, but instinct with vitality and clear in individuality. We know her henceforth even better as a woman than as a writer. When we reflect that the impression made by Currer Bell was produced by only three works, we feel all the more deeply that the powers so carefully and conscientiously used could never, had she lived, have been desecrated by any hasty or incomplete publication, that no outside pressure would have induced hurried utterance, that the reticence which marked the past would have characterized the future, and that the high ideal before her mind would never have been lowered at the instigation of popularity or by the temptation of gain. The works already published would have been followed by others worthy of their predecessors, and if they came more slowly than our eagerness desired them, their merit would have constrained us to acknowledge that time was necessary to ripen into full maturity the fruit which boasted such rare flavor. This hope blasted, this future denied, we cling the more closely to the treasures we already possess, and turn eagerly towards every avenue for gaining knowledge of the nature which originated them, rejoicing when our cool judgment allows us to approve what our tenderness for the dead induces us to value.

The world does not need to be told that the works of an author are not always counterparts of his actual experience; we have long known that the merriest quips often come from the saddest hearts, and the most lachrymose sentimentalities from the jolliest natures; yet we feel, nevertheless, that in the life of an author we are to search for the secret of his power, the clew to his imaginings, the explanation of his literary position. When we criticise a work with no personal knowledge of the writer, we obtain an impartiality of judgment in some respects, at the expense of thorough and sympathetic understanding of his point of view, his qualifying circumstances and his personal enthusiasms and prejudices. The blunders of inference which follow upon letting loose the astuteness of professed critics over an unknown country, are often ludicrous, sometimes disastrous. The knowledge of an author's life, by increasing our power of throwing ourselves into his position, sheds light on many a dark passage, explains many a seeming paradox, and more than compensates for the loss of entire impartiality of judgment, with its accompanying indifference of criticism. Indeed, a perfectly impartial criticism is almost impossible, since the desire to criticise at any length implies that the heart is interested in favor of, or the feelings excited against, the work in question. In the absence of this motive power we can furnish only a tame and spiritless statement, little better than a table of contents. The critic who throws himself *con amore* into his subject is not necessarily warped out of his critical perpendicular, and a genial appreciation of the merits of his author or a quick perception of his defects need not degenerate into fulsome flattery or bitter invective.

In the search for information concerning an author, we are fortunate when we come upon a biography like that which Mrs. Gaskell gives us of Miss Brontë. We find in it, not only the satisfaction of an urgent curiosity upon many points of personal history, but a key to Currer Bell's fictions, which sends us to their reperusal with a new and more tender interest. And in the glimpses given of the sisters Emily and Anne,—those strange mental organizations in which peculiarities were carried almost into deformities,—we learn to account for the strange elements present in their works. We find the atmosphere of the novels predominating in the "Life,"—the "counterfeit presentment" of persons and incidents known personally or by tradition, placed before us in the romances. This is especially true in Charlotte's case; for her mind was less narrow by nature, and her life more varied in feeling and in action, than that of either of her sisters. The most repulsive and the most contradictory of her fictitious characters prove to be but the careful elaboration of outlines sketched from her own circle of experience. In the vivid description which Mrs. Gaskell gives of Charlotte Brontë's life, we are surprised to find how little the novelist strained her privilege of coloring and intensifying the elements of character about her. Those who dwell amidst the constant friction of city life, or are subjected to steady attrition among their fellows, can with difficulty conceive how the sharp points and rough edges of character remain, and even become more prominent, in circumstances of isolation. This is as true of communities as of individuals; and however fond we may be of imagining model republics existing in isolated positions, which protect them from the enervating breath of general luxury, it is very certain that such protection must be purchased with the loss of much in the way of refinement of tone and universality of development. Hereditary traits become intensified, whether they are virtues or vices; and, alas for poor human nature! the vices too often grow more luxuriantly than the virtues; or, at best, virtues are more quiet in their development, and have less concentrated power over the imagination and hold upon the memory. Household crimes of the past are whispered fearfully by the winter fireside, long after household virtues have passed out of remembrance. All contracting influences are strengthened when they act unchanged upon generation after generation; social laws bend under the unchecked power of the hereditary rich and the exhausted energies of the hereditary poor; and public opinion sides with the strong, or contents itself with low and timid whispers of ineffectual disapprobation. To these circumstances we must look for an explanation of the state of society in that isolated portion of England in which the Brontés were born and reared, and for which we must make due allowance in reading their works.

The biographer of Currer Bell had a very delicate and a very difficult task to perform. The public naturally craved the most explicit details concerning the externals of a life of whose interior workings it had caught glimpses through the half-revealing, half-concealing medium of what we may term autobiographic novels. This explicitness would necessarily involve many persons who might object to being called before the world, and bring out in strong relief particulars of such a nature that prudence and courtesy demand silence even when indignation clamors for utterance. The temptation to speak is the greater in this instance, for the reason that the sufferings of Charlotte Bronté were precisely those portions of her life which called forth her most glowing words. The morbid delicacy of feeling which some of them induced, gave rise to her most thrilling revelations of spiritual susceptibility. The capacities for happiness, the aspirations for affection, so crushed and lacerated, sent forth the deepest cry of anguish. Fully to explain all the circumstances would be to arraign individuals connected with them; but the severity with which a tribunal of justice may ferret out evidence and pass its definitive sentence is forbidden to those who would fain probe the depths of moral torture. Yet a certain inferential condemnation ensues from those necessary revelations which the simplest and most delicate statement of incidents involves, and the occasional transcending of strict limits may be pardoned to the enthusiasm of personal friendship.

We propose, in the first place, to examine the memoirs which Mrs. Gaskell furnishes us, with special reference to those portions which tell most powerfully upon the development of Miss Brontë's mind and heart, and then to turn, with the light thus thrown upon the author, to a scrutiny of her works. We believe that this knowledge of the individual—always more necessary in judging of a woman's comparative position than of a man's, since her sphere of feeling is less rounded by external action—is in a peculiar degree necessary to a full comprehension of Currer Bell's romances. We also believe that many of the criticisms made in times past, in the total absence of such knowledge, would now, were it possible, receive very decided modification, and the general judgment in regard to her works become even more favorable than their popularity proves it to be already.

Mrs. Gaskell prefaces the memoirs themselves with some explanatory sketches of the country and the people among whom Miss Brontë was born, and the environments from which her mind received its earliest and strongest impressions. This is the more necessary, owing to the very striking peculiarities of Yorkshire and its inhabitants. Nothing less than an account of these peculiarities as they manifested themselves half a century ago, could prepare one to believe in them at a later period, or within the childhood of the Brontës, and even then it requires some effort to conceive that such relics of barbarism and such savageness of customs could exist anywhere in England in this nineteenth century. These facts, however, once established, the inevitable inferences which follow are our first help towards a complete comprehension of the reason why, when the Brontës described the men and women whom they saw, or with whose histories they were familiar through immediate tradition, the great world should have felt its delicate nerves shaken at what it regarded as exaggerated pictures of coarse and hard humanity. The persons whom the sisters met in their daily walks were quite as rough and odd as those they put upon their imaginary stage, and within the limits of their own family strange contrasts appeared, while the tales with which their old nurse nourished their childish imaginations were weird as any entwined into their fictions.

The incidents which Mrs. Gaskell relates as confirmation of the ferocity and coarse cruelty of this people, we have not room to quote; but some of them are startling and repulsive in the highest degree. And though with kindliness of intention she musters a small array of compensating virtues, which appear upon a thorough study of the nature of the people, they fail to soothe our indignant feelings, which revert again and again to the graphic but hateful narrative.

To this rude and desolate country Mr. Bronté, the father of Charlotte, brought his young wife, and amid the cheerless and forlorn scenes of lonely country life in Yorkshire the wife soon ended her days, leaving behind her six desolate little children in that dreary stone parsonage of Haworth, the mere picture of which we cannot contemplate without a shiver at its forlorn aspect. The father, an Irishman and a good but stern man, was quite as eccentric as any character which his daughter's imagination ever drew. Full of energy, but with little tenderness, charitable and laborious in his vocation as clergyman, but taciturn and solitary in his ways, he left his motherless children to nestle together and to look only to one another for sympathy and endearments. In other respects he seems to have been a good father, and to have won the esteem and reverence of his family. His hygienic theories, however, were carried out, we fear, very much to the detriment of little ones who appear to have needed precisely the opposite of his Spartan method of treatment. His naturally violent temper, though under sufficient control to prevent him from indulging in angry words or blows, found vent in the most ludicrous manner. He is described as working off "his volcanic wrath by firing pistols out of the back door in rapid succession," as burning up the hearth-rug and appearing to enjoy the stench thereof, and as sawing off the backs of the chairs during another *accés de fureur*. He did not approve of any elegance of apparel, and therefore threw into the fire some gay shoes belonging to the children, and cut into shreds a silk dress presented to his wife, which shocked his fastidiously plain taste. What his children must have thought while these oddities were before their eyes, we may well imagine, when we remember the wonderful precocity of their minds. Some of the peculiarities of the father, modified by the gentleness of the mother, may be traced in the children.

Some time after the mother's death, a sister of hers came to take charge of the motherless brood. She was an estimable but not very lovable woman, who inspired the respect rather than the affection of those about her. Her natural austerity was increased by her dislike of Yorkshire, which she never conquered, though she remained there till her death. She taught the little girls to excel in all household accomplishments, initiating them into all the mysteries of cooking and embroidery. The reader will remember many passages in the novels, where these matters find honorable mention. In the absence of all other children's society, and without any of the toys and picture-books which fairly smother the infants of more (or less?) favored regions, these little folks read the newspapers of the day, discussed the Parliamentary debates, and formed their conversation and their employment upon the models of the older persons about them. Their precocity, which would have been apparent under any circumstances, became absolutely marvellous under the strange forcing process to which they were subjected. The child-nature was lost, if indeed it ever had any existence, and the five sisters and one brother formed a community of their own, quite unlike that of any other known nursery. Even their plays, when they condescended to amuse themselves, were rather the recreations of mature minds than the frolic nonsense of childhood. In the course of time four of the sisters were sent to a school at Cowan's Bridge, of which all that need be said is, that it was the original of Lowood in "Jane Eyre"; but the two elder ones died in the course of the first year, and the two younger ones were soon after removed from the school. Mrs. Gaskell's account of the life at this school is no less painful, though less dramatic, than its counterpart in the novel. Upon the death of her older sisters, little Charlotte, though a mere child, assumed the responsibilities of chief in the diminished group, and seems to have comprehended her position immediately, and devoted herself to the duties consequent upon it with unswerving fidelity. She remained at home till she had entered her fifteenth year, exercising herself industriously in the household tasks prescribed by her aunt, or busied in the preparation of various literary compositions, which grew so numerous, that in 1830, when she was but fourteen, she made out "A Catalogue of my Books," which were twenty-two in number. These little volumes, written in a tiny hand, and containing from sixty to one hundred pages each, were devoted to a great variety of topics, and consisted both of prose and verse. In 1831 she was sent to Roe-Head, to a school very different from the Cowan's Bridge abomination, where she remained for a year, and formed some of her strongest and most valuable friendships. Taking every possible advantage of the educational opportunities here afforded her, Charlotte made great progress, and afterwards returned to the school in the capacity of teacher. During her stay at Roe-Head, her observant mind, always active, gathered in impressions of local scenery and personal character, and her memory stored itself with traditional lore, all of which were destined to form the material of her future works. Her duties as teacher were extremely arduous, and her life painfully monotonous; but she bore it with courage, though she mourned deeply over the condition of her sister Emily, at that time teaching in a school at Halifax, and worn down with "hard labor from six in the morning to eleven at night, with only one half-hour of exercise between." Charlotte's health gave way entirely, and she returned home. Emily also succumbed to the hardships of her lot. At this time the sisters appear to have made their first decided literary efforts, and letters, asking counsel, were sent to Southey and Wordsworth. Southey's reply is given at length, and, while mildly discouraging, is marked with the gentle kindness and courteousness of his nature. Baffled in this hope, Charlotte set herself resolutely to work again in a situation totally repugnant to her, and became a private governess. In this sphere she accumulated experiences and bore sufferings, which, calling out no loud or frequent complaint at the time, fermented within her, and burst forth long afterwards in her works.

It is not known that her experiences at this time were very unlike those of other women in the same social position,—or rather, to speak more correctly, in the same absence of all position. The sufferings, the mortifications, and the sorrows of private governesses have been too long a favorite theme of English novelists, to leave any possible aspect of the mournful topic untouched. Why the abuses interwoven into that system of education are not resolutely eradicated by public indignation, or, if that is impossible, why the system itself is not exchanged for something more genial and humane, can be explained only by that peculiar tenacity with which the English, as a nation, cling to their established customs, and the apathetic obstinacy with which they regard any suggestion of change. Miss Bronte, being condemned by Fate to be a governess, must meet with the same trials and annoyances under which the rest of the class have long groaned; but she being also a woman of genius equal to her susceptibility, having the gift of utterance as well as of endurance, the world has to thank her persecutors indirectly for much that glows in her writings. What persons are within themselves, influences the expression of the life far more than the incidents which make its daily tenor. Commonplace persons appear to meet with only commonplace experiences, because they have no immortal fire within to melt the ore of life into flowing metal, no creative inspiration to mould it into form and beauty. Genius makes from that same ore a bronze statue of glorious proportions, for the world to admire, and transforms into passionate utterance the incidents which in an ordinary life would come to naught, or at most cause only a transient emotion. The materials in the two cases are not unlike, but the power at work upon them is, in one case, that of a Prometheus, in the other that of an ignorant child. We find Charlotte Bronté always busy in "making out," from all that she sees and all that she feels, half-real and half-ideal creations, and moulding her acquired ideas in the crucible of her fancy. She treasures all the traditions of a country rich in startling tales of the past; she fills her mind with pictures of long-gone scenes; the mansions which she passes in her daily walks are peopled to her sight with forms unseen by common eyes; and even the ordinary incidents of the monotonous life about her reveal to her a darker tragedy and a deeper pathos. To such a nature as Currer Bell's nothing was without signification. To the plain, near-sighted, silent woman, nature found a way to reveal its secrets and reward her worship; to the introverted mind of the morbid dreamer grew mysterious insight into the phenomena of all varieties of minds; to the busy plodder amid daily drudgeries came eagle-winged thoughts of freedom and wildest soaring; and over the pent-up affections of the taciturn and diffident governess swept whirlwinds of passion, by turns the stormiest agony and the most rapturous bliss.

Discouraged and harassed by a mode of life so utterly at variance with their instincts, enfeebled in health by longing homesickness, which always hung about them when absent from their own breezy moors, the sisters determined to attempt taking a school by themselves, hoping to increase their pecuniary resources, at the same time that they secured the happiness of remaining together. This plan was never crowned with success; but the endeavor to carry it out led to a new and important change in the life of Charlotte and Emily, who, for the purpose of better fitting themselves to become teachers, went over to Brussels, and entered the *pensionnat* of Monsieur and Madame Héger. There, by unremitted application, they obtained a thorough knowledge of the French language, and increased their acquirements generally. To this sojourn in Belgium we are indebted for Currer Bell's "Villette."

They were called home, after an absence of ten months, by the sudden illness and death of their aunt. Emily never returned to Brussels; but Charlotte soon after assumed the position of English teacher in the same establishment, so that her whole residence on the Continent extended over a period of two years. Her experience during this time is set down so vividly in "Villette," that, once read, it can never be forgotten. Disagreeable as her life necessarily was in some respects, it was not without its pleasant side, if only for the reason that it afforded her in full measure those advantages she courted so much. Her mind was maturing in all ways, to an extent of which she herself was probably hardly aware; and if her solitary hours and forlorn destitution of affection and sympathy fostered the morbid susceptibility of her disposition, we can hardly quarrel with them, since the most powerful psychological portions of "Villette" could never have come into existence without them. Even her *devoirs* in French composition show the power of her mind, which breaks through the difficulties imposed by a foreign tongue.

During her whole stay at Brussels, Charlotte spared no efforts to avail herself of every opportunity of intellectual improvement, though her delicate health and sensitive temperament must often have made her tasks difficult of accomplishment. Her intellectual growth would have done credit to a far more robust physical organization. She won the especial respect of Monsieur Héger, and seems to have felt for him a great degree of reverence and grateful friendship. His peculiarities of manner and temper, his strong religious and charitable feelings, and his odd irritability, are shadowed forth in Paul Emanuel, a hero who, though he may have failed to become popular among ordinary hero-worshippers, has his select number of admirers, and was evidently intended by the author to win our esteem and our liking. The few persons outside the walls of the *pensionnat* with whom Miss Bronté became acquainted, the local scenery, the historic associations, were all analyzed and all appropriated by her, with little plan, perhaps, of future use, but simply from the inevitable and irresistible tendency of her mind thus to examine, and as it were hold in solution, those scenes and incidents which with others pass unnoticed in daily routine. Thus the lonely home of the *grandes vacances* became to her a prominent and frightful reality of experience, not to be dismissed afterwards from the memory with a shrug of the shoulders and an exclamation of disgust, but to induce nights of weary sleeplessness, to bring on fever and desperation as they dragged their slow length along, and years afterwards to recur with undiminished force, and dictate those strangely fascinating chapters on "The Long Vacation" in "Villette." The fact also of her stanch Protestantism, amid so much obtrusive Romanism, added fuel to the fire of her inner excitement, and provoked all her antagonism. She had no sympathy with, no admiration for, the ceremonies of that Church; the *messe* was to her always "idolatrous," and "the uncompromising truth" of her character would not allow her to shrink from the maintenance of opinions, which could hardly be received with complaisance by those among whom she dwelt. Her position at Madame Héger's became less and less tolerable to her, and the increasing troubles at home, resulting in part from the misconduct of her brother Branwell, and in part from the threatened blindness of her father, combined with her own homesick yearnings to induce her return to Haworth.

And now ensued a long stay upon the moors, a quiet resumption of home habits and daily-recurring duties, her literary labors still pursued, silently but with undaunted courage. The story of the publication of a volume of poems by the three sisters is well known. Then followed the acceptance by a London publisher of "Agnes Grey" and "Wuthering Heights," by Anne and Emily, and the rejection of "The Professor," Charlotte's first fiction. Undismayed even by this, she commenced "Jane Eyre," and its opening chapters were written while she was in close attendance upon her blind father. Her life was at this time as monotonous as Haworth life must necessarily be. The walk upon the moors was the most agreeable event of the day; the evening talk, when the sisters were together and the rest of the family asleep, was the charm of the night. When a naturally active and energetic intellect is placed in circumstances devoid of variety and interest, other influences, which in seasons of social excitement remain dormant, rise into importance and wield a dominating power. The phenomena of external nature, with their daily variety,—the inevitable and seemingly spontaneous changes of thought in long seasons of uninterrupted meditation, united with a sense of thraldom under a condition at variance with the impulses of the heart,—these are the influences which are set at work, and which produce in weak minds a deadness or mental paralysis, and in strong ones a feverish restlessness. Traces of this restlessness are occasionally apparent in Charlotte Bronté; but the steadfast courage with which she combated both this and the miserable ill-health aggravated by it call forth our esteem and admiration. Indeed, a quiet, undemonstrative energy was one of "Currer Bell's" most marked characteristics, and the unshaken firmness with which she bore a life-long monotony, to a temperament like hers a constant martyrdom, continually displays itself upon the pages of her biography. Some of her fictitious characters are endowed with similar organizations, and possess the same power of endurance, the same reluctance to accept means of escape which in the least jar the moral sense, the same force to bear without uttering one cry till the crisis of agony is past and words can be spoken calmly. Something of her singularly self-contained spirit is revealed in the characters of Jane Eyre and Lucy Snowe. It would seem that neither of these was intended as a likeness of her nature, as she herself understood it; but most readers will discover remarkable resemblance as to the workings of the inner heart and the endurance of interior conflict and suffering. Not the least of Currer Bell's artistic talents is that which she possessed of emerging from the intense introversion which marks the conception of some of her characters, and plunging at once and vigorously into the stormiest action and the most demonstrative passion, vividness and vitality accompanying every change in the movement.

The power of passive endurance in Miss Bronté, united with the strength of active perseverance, which she possessed in an equal degree, can alone explain the fact that this fragile and delicate woman, whose health was enfeebled by frequent illness, whose nerves were wrung by all depressing influences, and whose heart was smitten by repeated afflictions, was able to turn from the darkness about her, to rise from the exhausting minutiæ of household cares and the physical fatigue of laborious attention upon others more ill than herself, to make for herself an atmosphere, full of change and of charm, in the fair land of romance, and, after a night spent in the passionate vehemence of Jane Eyre's personality, to renew the same faithful performance of daily prosaic duty. Tenderly attached to her sisters and her father, forbearing to the brother whose recklessness made his home wretched, we find her always forgetful of herself and devoted to others. The faithfulness of her devotion through those long and weary years of dismal Haworth life, varied only by rare visits made and received among her very small circle of friends, is set forth with simple pathos by her biographer, and forms one of the most touching chapters of womanly experience. Those who have been accustomed to regard Currer Bell only as an author who has dared to speak on certain topics with a plainness somewhat unusual among fashionable lady-writers, and have consequently assailed her for coarseness and immorality, will stand abashed before this record of womanly virtue and tender affection. Miss Brontë never lost her keen perception of the desolate monotony of her home-life, through familiarity with its routine. She writes to a friend: "I can hardly tell you how time gets on at Haworth. There is no event to mark its progress. One day resembles another; and all have heavy, lifeless physiognomies. . . . . . I feel as if we were all buried here. I long to travel; to work; to live a life of action."

To add to her depression, her eyes, which she had injured by her minute style of drawing and by her miniature handwriting,—a fac-simile of which Mrs. Gaskell introduces,—became very troublesome, so that the fear of blindness tormented her, and her amusements, already so limited, were still further curtailed. Her father's eyes were much relieved by a surgical operation undertaken in compliance with Charlotte's earnest entreaties. Her own eyes never entirely recovered, and she was often unable to use them for reading or for writing,—a deprivation keenly felt by her, and doubly distressing as an aggrava-tion of her loneliness. Her brother's sad and disgraceful history was another bitter ingredient in her cup of sorrow. The story is simply and plainly told by Mrs. Gaskell, and clearly explains how the author of "Wildfell Hall" should have known so well the details of a vicious life. The suffering and mortification which he inflicted upon his innocent sisters were no slight addition to his offences against virtue.

In the mean time the novels of the two younger sisters had been accepted, as we have seen, and Charlotte's returned upon her hands. As "The Professor" is now before the public, an opportunity is afforded for judging of the critical acumen of the six London publishers who declined to usher it into the world. An indication of character quite in keeping with Currer Bell's other peculiarities is apparent in the cir-cumstance of her using the same wrapper for her manuscript during all its pilgrimages, so that each publisher was able to see the names of his brethren who had refused it before him. "Jane Eyre," however, was doomed to a better fate, and we rejoice as we remember that the strong heart, so long unable to find acceptable utterance, at last received a worthy welcome. The graphic account by Mrs. Gaskell of Charlotte's method of composition, and of her patient fulfilment of household drudgery when her brain was on fire with the creative impulse, proves that it is by no means necessary that literary women cease to be bound by domestic laws. In the private correspondence of Miss Bronté we trace a resemblance to Jane Eyre's own style, playfulness when her heart is sore within her, resolute courage in the struggle of life, and a smile because she will not weep.

With the publication and immediate popularity of "Jane Eyre," Currer Bell entered upon an active literary career, which, however, never prevented her from giving her wonted attention to her home duties. We find her easily assuming the dignity of a successful author, neither disdainful of praise nor elated by its novelty. Her letters at this time become doubly interesting. Her reading was extended through the kindness of her publishers, who supplied her with books otherwise inaccessible to one in her isolated position, and her mind seized with avidity, yet with discrimination, the food placed within its reach. Her criticisms are keen and pithy, and show a ready grasp of whatever subject she took up. "Jane Eyre" was published in October, 1847, at which time Miss Bronté was thirty-one years of age.

Owing to the confounding of the pseudonymes of Currer, Ellis, and Acton Bell, and the consequent mistakes of the publishers, Charlotte and Anne determined to go to London to establish beyond a doubt their separate existence. They remained but three days in the great city, and every circumstance of their stay is harmonious with the individuality which they have already asserted so strongly before the mind of the reader. The next year Branwell died, and Charlotte writes to a friend: "All his vices were and are nothing now. We remember only his woes." This was in October, and the following December Emily also was taken. The story of her last days is unsurpassed in tragic pathos; we read almost with horror of her struggle against her inevitable doom. "Stronger than a man, simpler than a child, her nature stood alone. The awful point was, that, while full of truth for others, on herself she had no pity; the spirit was inexorable to the flesh; from the trembling hands, the unnerved limbs, the fading eyes, the same service was exacted as they had rendered in health." In truth the strength of her will and the power of her resolve, joined to the peculiar tastes and tendencies of her nature, made of Emily Bronté a very extraordinary woman, and we find in her the germs of much, which, placed under more favorable circumstances, must have developed into nobility and grandeur. Sorrow followed fast on sorrow, and poor little Anne, after bravely endeavoring to resist her insidious foe, consumption, died in May, 1849, during a visit to the sea-shore, made with Charlotte, in the vain hope of benefiting her health. Charlotte returned to her desolate home, to take up again the battle of her life, now utterly alone. She writes to her dearest friend:—

I tried to be glad that I was come home. I have always been glad before,—except once;—even then I was cheered. But this time joy was not to be the sensation. I felt that the house was all silent,—the rooms were all empty. I remembered where the three were laid,—in what narrow, dark dwellings,—never more to reappear on earth. So the sense of desolation and bitterness took possession of me. The agony that *was to be undergone* and *was not* to be avoided, came on.

And again, some little time after:—

Sometimes when I wake in the morning, and know that Solitude, Remembrance, and Longing are to be almost my sole companions all day through, that at night I shall go to bed with them, that they will long keep me sleepless,—that next morning I shall wake to them again,—sometimes, Nell, I have a heavy heart of it.

She was at the end of the second volume of "Shirley," when all these home afflictions came upon her. As soon as she had recovered from the first prostration of her grief, she resumed her work, and the first chapter of the third volume bears for a title, "The Valley of the Shadow of Death." This work was soon finished, and was published just two years after "Jane Eyre." It excited almost as much interest, but not quite so much severe criticism, as its predecessor. And now it began to be known who Currer Bell was, and a visit which she made at the house of her publisher, in December, brought her in personal contact with as much of the literary society of the metropolis as her shy manners and feeble health would permit. The meeting with strangers was an ordeal to which she could never accustom herself, and the excitement of a dinner-party, or even of a call, would bring on that enemy of all woman-kind,—nervous headache. She met Thackeray several times, and exchanged the strong but distant intellectual admiration she felt for him for a personal esteem and friendliness, though she still retained her power of criticism upon his works, and clearly perceived his faults. Always kindly in her own judgments, and genial in her criticisms, she felt keenly the philippics launched from some quarters at "Jane Eyre," and even wept on reading a severe review of "Shirley" in the "Times," though she uttered no remonstrances, and insisted on perusing all adverse criticisms, heroically maintaining that they "did her good."

Her history henceforth alternates between lively intellectual experiences set forth in pleasant letters to and from critics and authors, and the old routine, seldom broken, of household avocations. "All knew the place of residence of Currer Bell," says her biographer. "She compared herself to the ostrich hiding its head in the sand; and says that she still buries hers in the heath of Haworth moors; but 'the concealment is but self-delusion.'" She succeeded in accomplishing a large amount of reading, in spite of the weakness of her eyes. Solitude and sad memories made her heart often heavy; and the bleak and desolate storms so frequent in that country told fearfully upon a nature so susceptible as hers to every variation of temperature, and brought about a constant recurrence of those symptoms of consumption which were always hovering near her. The long and melancholy days and the still longer and more dreary nights dragged slowly on, exhausting mind and body in the effort to bear up against them, so bravely but so vainly made. Her imagination grew morbid, her nerves lost their vigor, her fancies conquered her reason in those lonely night-seasons, and few can imagine what she endured as she paced up and down her solitary room after all else were sleeping. The gloomy situation of the parsonage, in the midst of a churchyard "literally paved with rain-blackened tombstones," and never a healthy residence, any more than it was a cheerful one, became in the damp weather of spring fearfully unwholesome, and the family suffered constantly in health. Miss Brontë's friends were affectionately urgent for her to make them frequent visits; but her father's dependence upon her, and her own lofty sense of duty to him, prevented her from indulging in long absence from home. She was not one to leave the simplest duties unfulfilled for her own pleasure; so she clung to her old father, and plodded on in the pestilential air and among the sorrowful associations of Haworth. The shadowy forms of her dead sisters were ever by her side, and in the lone, sad night-hours her yearning for them grew so intense as to win almost audible response to her excited mind. Every little taste of theirs was remembered, and everything about her was connected with them. The moors reminded her of Emily, whose love for them was a passionate vehemence, and she says: "Not a knoll of heather, not a branch of fern, not a young bilberry-leaf, not a fluttering lark or linnet, but reminds me of her. The distant prospects were Anne's delight, and when I look round, she is in the blue tints, the pale mists, the waves and shadows of the horizon." What wonder that her own cheek grew pale and her imagination morbid, left thus alone with these sorrowful memories! The wonder is that such a delicate organism kept any healthful action, that the harp swept by such rude gusts retained any tone of music responsive to lighter breaths. When her rarely occurring pleasures did come, when a short visit to a friend checkered the monotony of her life, we are astonished at the receptive faculty she exhibits for all the pleasure that presents itself. Her feeble frame shivers and trembles at the social ordeal; she grows nervous at meeting strangers; but her inner nature is a bold one, after all, and she is able to seize the intellectual enjoyment, and to exercise her critical and analytic powers, even when apparently overpowered by her *mauvaise honte*. After a brief sip from the cup of pleasure, the return to her gloomy home calls forth no harsher expression of the inevitable reaction of her spirits than a rare utterance like this: "I would not write to you immediately on my arrival at home, because each return to this old house brings with it a phase of feeling which it is better to pass through quietly before beginning to indite letters." Two days which she spent in Scotland were like a glimpse of fairyland to her, and each moment of them made its own deep and distinct impression upon her fancy. Her anxiety for her father's health was constant, and openly expressed, and was reciprocated by him with the strongest solicitude on his part, when he believed her to be ill. She felt that this anxiety was injurious to them both, in leading them to think too much upon symptoms which they could not remove, and she did her best to lay aside her dread both for him and for herself. But she always spoke and wrote with unfailing interest in her father's health, and Mrs. Gaskell says, "There is not one letter of hers which I have read, which does not contain some mention of her father's state in this respect."

Charlotte Bronté is described by her biographer as she appeared at their first meeting, as "a little lady in a black silk gown. She came up and shook hands with me at once. I went up to unbonnet, &c., came down to tea; the little lady worked away and hardly spoke, but I had time for a good look at her. She is (as she calls herself) *undeveloped*, thin, and more than half a head shorter than I am; soft brown hair, not very dark; eyes (very good and expressive, looking straight and open at you) of the same color as her hair; a large mouth; the forehead square, broad, and rather overhanging. She has a very sweet voice." And as they walk or drive in the open air she gives a "careful examination of the shape of the clouds and the signs of the heavens, in which she read, as from a book, what the coming weather would be"; and tells her new friend that she can have "no idea what a companion the sky becomes to any one living in solitude,—more than any inanimate object on earth,—more than the moors themselves." The readers of the novels cannot fail to have been struck with the many marvellous sky-pictures therein painted, and the powerful description of all weather phenomena.

During the composition of "Villette," Miss Bronté suffered more than ever from illness and consequent depression of spirits, so that, with the most willing heart in the world, she was unable to prepare it for the press until after long and vexatious delays. She felt conscientiously unwilling to write when her mind was below its proper tone, and she replies to the importunities of her publishers:—

If my health is spared, I shall get on with it as fast as is consistent with its being done, if not *well*, yet as well as I can do it. *Not one whit faster.* When the mood leaves me, (it has left me now without vouchsafing so much as a word or a message when it will return,) I put by the MS. and wait till it comes back again. God knows, I sometimes have to wait long,—*very* long it seems to me.

The vigorous activity and persevering industry with which she wrote when "the mood" did come back, prove this inability to have been no weak affectation, no silly desire to be flattered into the resumption of her work. "Villette" had to be written, too, with no friend near to whom she could go for sympathy and criticism, as she had before resorted to her sisters; and in a letter written at this time she says: "I can hardly tell you how I hunger to hear some opinion besides my own, and how I have sometimes desponded, and almost despaired, because there was no one to whom to read a line, or of whom to ask a counsel." Her knowledge of her own mind, and of the kind of power she possessed as differing from that of other popular novelists, is shown in a few remarks relative to "Villette":—

> You will see that "Villette" touches on no matter of public interest. I cannot write books handling the topics of the day: it is of no use trying. Nor can I write a book for its moral. Nor can I take up a philanthropic scheme, though I honor philanthropy; and voluntarily and sincerely veil my face before such a mighty subject as that handled in Mrs. Beecher Stowe's work, "Uncle Tom's Cabin."

"Villette" appeared in 1852, and with this work, which more than sustains the author's previous reputation, closes Currer Bell's literary career, and we are called upon to lay aside our sympathies with her as an author, only to take them up again—if her biographer has succeeded with others as well as with ourselves, in awakening a very strong personal interest—the more decidedly with her womanly sorrows and deferred hopes. The sunshine of married life which eventually warmed the bereaved heart, and made even the old parsonage a cheerful home, did not rise unobstructed by clouds and portents. When the long-silent and patient-waiting, but much-loving Mr. Nichols, found words to speak his own heart and to waken a response in Miss Brontë's, the old Titan, her father, had so long survived his own tender feelings, that the lovers found no encouragement for their hopes from his astonished perceptions, and so decided was he in the expression of his disapproval, that Charlotte bowed her head before the storm, and the poor curate was obliged to leave both the lady of his love and the field of his labors. After a year of dutiful submission, the details of which may be imagined by all who have been witnesses of similar domestic circumstances, the stern old father yielded, and we find Charlotte busied, with quiet trust and hope, in preparations for the modest wedding. It took place in the little church at eight o'clock in the morning,—precisely the hour (and under not altogether dissimilar circumstances of loneliness) at which little Jane Eyre was to have become Mrs. Fairfax Rochester. During the nine months of her married life, Mrs. Nichols enjoyed a serene contentment, a quiet satisfaction, quite unlike any of her previous experiences, and the sympathetic reader rejoices at every word which tells that the stout, but storm-weary heart has found a resting-place at last. We have only occasional glimpses of her home now; for the public has no right to enter. The authoress is "not at home," even though the matron remain as hospitable as before. But the shadow was never to be fairly lifted from this life; the picture was to receive only a few faint tints of cheerful coloring upon its sombre canvas; and soon after we congratulate the husband upon the possession of his wife, we are called to mourn with him over her loss. The sympathy of the world can do nothing to lighten such a bereavement; it cannot cheer the desolate home, or break the spell of bitter memories; but after the hush of reverent silence is over, it urges its claim to offer a word of respectful and earnest sympathy.

We close this sketch of the Memoirs with Mrs. Gaskell's own words:—

> If my readers find that I have not said enough, I have said too much. I cannot measure or judge of such a character as hers. I cannot map out vices, and virtues, and debatable land. . . . . I turn from the critical, unsympathetic public,— inclined to judge harshly because they have only seen superficially and not thought deeply. I appeal to that larger and more solemn public, who know how to look with tender humility at faults and errors; how to admire generously extraordinary genius, and how to reverence with warm, full hearts all noble virtue. To that Public I commit the memory of Charlotte Brontë.

Mrs. Gaskell has not only given us a graphic delineation of the incidents in the life of her friend, and a clear and delicately outlined portrait of her personality, but in the very doing of this she has nobly fulfilled her own desire to vindicate and to honor the memory of Currer Bell. Without flattery, or violent declamation, she has eulogized her friend in the most fitting and effectual manner, by simply permitting facts to speak for themselves. The best vindication of a true life is to tell the plain, unadorned history of that life. The world has a shrewd, and after all a pretty fair judgment, when it is in possession of a sufficient number of facts. The unavoidable distortion which the circumstances attending a prominent position before the public receive, from the great amount of handling they are subjected to, is best remedied by a straightforward statement from some responsible quarter. The final judgment of the community is almost always in accordance with the dictates of generosity and truth. Character, like water, finds its own level, if it have but time to settle, and we soon discover that the frothing and turmoil which lifted certain waves into apparent height, or opened caverns whose depth we could not fathom, subside when the gale is over, and allow us to estimate the true depth of the stream. Great natures never fear this subsiding process; serene as the ocean in grandeur and in depth, the sounding-line may be cast down and the plummet allowed to tell its reckoning fairly. Therefore in this Life of Miss Brontë the truest service has been rendered to her memory, and the best panegyric uttered over her tomb, by a simple and candid recital of the environments of a nature so peculiar, yet so noble, the endurances of a heart so tender, yet so strong, the struggles of an intellect so powerful, yet so susceptible. The literary history is a rare one, in this age when intellectual strength of all kinds rushes eagerly to the arena, when even mediocrity is unwilling to sit silent in the chimney-corner. The inner record is as strange, in its picture of steady self-denial and struggle, when the heart, sensible of its own weakness and of the strength of its adversary, the imagination, still waged battle against morbid fancies and nervous depression, and, though sometimes conquered, refused to yield. Few persons would have felt the pressure of filial duty so strong as to prevail against such an array of hostile circumstances. With every temptation to leave a desolate and sickly home, and go where honor and the hope of renewed health brightened the prospect, the courage and devotion which could sustain Charlotte Brontë through those long years upon the Yorkshire moors was no small virtue. We learn from her works, even better than from the occasional outbreaks in her private correspondence, how varied and how eager were her longings and her capabilities. The thirst for action, the yearning for change, the power of emotional enjoyment, the intelligent desire to travel, are all revealed to us in her fictions, though jealously guarded and conscientiously repressed in her daily life.

Few who read the Brontë novels when they first appeared could have suspected, in ever so faint a degree, the strangeness of the private history which lay concealed behind the friendly shelter of those oracular names. It is questionable whether the criticism which attacked them from some quarters so ferociously and so blindly did not, in the end, prove a benefit to them. It drew the more attention to the defects indisputably existing, in the works of the younger sisters especially, but with that attention has come a more impartial judgment and a higher award of praise; for the knowledge that the authors painted life as it lay around them in their daily path is sufficient refutation of the charge, that they revelled in coarseness for coarseness' sake, and drew pictures of vice in accordance with their own inherent depravity. The materials were not selected by them, but thrust upon them by circumstances clamorous for utterance. The narrowness of their general world-knowledge could hardly be suspected by themselves. They probably did not regard their sphere as an exceptional one, but supposed that in their circle they saw, in little, what the world was in large, and when their imaginations pictured fairer scenes and softer natures and gentler emotions, then they fancied that they were straying into realms of impossibility. And looking at these novels in the strong daylight cast upon them by our study of the hearts and brains in which they had their birth,—no longer mere creations of an imagination which leaves a cheery social circle at its will, to retire to the study and indulge its untrammelled powers, able to return at any moment to healthful and happy influences from without,—they come to us as the very outpouring of pent-up passion, the cry of fettered hearts, the panting of hungry intellects, restrained by the iron despotism of adverse and unconquerable circumstance.

Few novels have called forth, even in these days of violent literary sensations, such decided opinions and such contradictory criticisms as "Jane Eyre." Upon its first reading no one seemed able to pronounce a moderate judgment. Some were enthusiastic in admiration, others rabid in detestation. All possible merits and all conceivable defects were discovered in it. Immorality, coarseness, and unnaturalness were seen by some, while others beheld only a brilliantly colored picture of the human heart. Critics fell upon it, for it challenged criticism; sagacity speculated upon it, for it defied surmise; explanations were hazarded without contradiction, for the author remained silent, and apparently undisturbed by the commotion awakened. Some readers traced only the bold, broad strokes of a masculine hand; others discerned the touch of a woman's delicate fingers; and the wise ones declared it the production of a brother and a sister, not the effort of any single mind. Like a meteor, it swept across the literary heavens, drawing towards it the gaze of thousands.

The public judgment still remains somewhat undecided as to the tendency of "Jane Eyre," viewed simply in its moral aspect, and this is, perhaps, so long as the majority is on the side of a favorable judgment, no small testimonial to the general truthfulness and power of the story. For the same result ensues upon actual occurrences about us, when the circumstances are peculiar and in any way tinctured with romance. Parties are formed for and against, champions are full of enthusiasm and faith, adversaries of bitterness and condemnation, and the judgment of those who wish to be impartial remains long suspended. The situations in "Jane Eyre" are powerfully drawn and brilliantly contrasted; but there is nothing impossible in the circumstances, and we are able to follow every change of scene, and to trace the working of each heart with understanding interest. To those who track "little Jane" over the stony road of her temptation, and go forth with her as she goes into the desolate world, impelled by the unerring instinct of her conscience, no further search for moral power will be necessary.

The book has been too universally read and too fully criticised to need more than a passing notice from us in regard to its literary merit. But there are several points wherein our present knowledge of the author decidedly modifies, and others in which it totally changes, opinions passed upon it in the absence of such knowledge. Not long after the publication of the work, the world outside concluded that it was in great measure autobiographic; but this, so far from uniting the different opinions, only placed the battle upon a new ground, and the writer became as fruitful a topic for discussion as the work itself, while the point where truth blended with fiction was decided at the pleasure of the critic. We now know it to have been autobiographic chiefly in that sense in which true genius throws its very self into its work, pours its lifeblood through its creation, making it throb with vitality, and then, by right of kingship, calls its conquered territory by its own name. The first part of "Jane Eyre," the child-life of the heroine, deserves a more special notice than it is apt to receive; for the more rapid and tumultuous play of passion that succeeds obliterates the impression made by it. It is, however, artistic in the highest degree, and, viewed as a prelude to the main plot, is almost unequalled in its preparatory movement. Every stroke of the pencil which paints the heroine as formed by nature and influenced by circumstance, is of value in sketching the precise outline which is afterwards filled up. There are no waste lines or uncertain etchings, and the fidelity with which the first conception of character is clung to is quite marvellous. The childhood of Jane, with its embryo qualities, its nascent strength, its nervous imaginings, and its strong antagonisms, develops in steady preparation for the fervid passion-life of the woman. The strong but long-repressed impulse, the passionate heart, the conscience and right principle dominant over both by virtue of native vigor alone, take us into regions of struggle, and unveil to us a conflict which romance-writers have usually left untouched, or but weakly portrayed. It is somewhat singular that this new and fascinating field of romance should have been selected by one living far from all literary competition, and with only her own judgment to decide upon its fitness. It was a kind of literary clairvoyance which enabled Currer Bell to see that the time was ripe for such utterances. Novel-readers now-a-days are not satisfied with pictures of external and social life, however brilliantly colored they may be, or however various in style. The demand—to speak in mercantile parlance—is for a better article. We ask for deeper insight into character, for the features of the mind and heart rather than of the face and figure. Heroines cease to be miracles of beauty, yet prove themselves still powerful to charm; heroes are no longer of necessity stalwart and Herculean, yet they are still victors in the life-arena. The author plays the part of anatomist, and dissects heart, brain, and nerve, to lay them before the reader for examination and analysis. Perhaps Thackeray may be regarded as the most skilful in this dissection, though he enjoys the work more as if he were pulling an enemy to pieces with malice aforethought, than as a surgeon regarding the result only in a scientific light. Currer Bell is more genial than Thackeray, and never loses her faith in the heroic element of humanity. She delights and interests us in persons who are neither magnificently handsome nor superlatively magnanimous, but who have warm human hearts and active minds, and the battle of whose life is no ignoble struggle, though it may be a silent and single-handed one. It is this single-handed conflict, indeed, that she delights in, and depicts with greatest power, believing, as she says herself, that "Men and women never struggle so hard as when they struggle alone, without witness, counsellor, or confidant; unencouraged, unadvised, and unpitied." The reader of Miss Brontë's life may judge whether or not she knew what such a lonely life-battle really was.

In "Jane Eyre," as the first positive outburst of long-repressed vitality, we might excuse much more violent demonstrations than we find. The reticence so evident in Currer Bell's personal character often asserts itself in her writings, and although at times the volcano bursts forth, and hot lava-streams scorch the air, yet we feel that but a small portion of the internal fire finds its way to the surface. We hardly need to be told that a large part of "Jane Eyre" was written in a wonder-fully short time. The whole movement of the Thornfield life betokens an irrepressible impulse in the author, and establishes in the mind of the reader a confidence similar to that we acquire in a great musician, whom we have heard successfully surmounting difficult passages of his art; breathing freely once more, we lay aside all anxiety for the future, certain that the power will be equal to the strain made upon it. The characters in "Jane Eyre" are stronger than most of the surrounding circumstances, to which, with consummate skill, they are made to seem to yield. It is in the accumulation of circumstances tending in one direction, and the indomitable will of the heroine which breaks this linked chain when the crisis comes, that we find the moral of the tale. Her moral strength and her unswerving instinct are out of the range of ordinary minds, as the sphere of her conflict is removed from com-monplace environments. Isolated alike from restraint and from assis-tance, from praise and from blame, she is clothed in a God-given armor of proof, and wins the victory in the very strength of her woman's weakness. Natures like hers present extremes and approach paradox; strength and vigor of action in a crisis are balanced by impres-sionableness and superior receptivity for the magnetic force in others, producing a sort of fascinated submission to a certain point, at which the tremendous revulsive power is awakened. In Rochester a study of another kind is placed before us, as successfully managed, though less admirable in itself. Indeed, he makes no attempt to win our admiration, but he gains from us the somewhat surly liking which would suit him best were he aware of it. We can even understand how he managed to "suit little Jane" "to the inmost fibre of her being." Knowing the difficulties of his position, and the original and acquired faults of his character, we judge his short-comings rather as we do those of our own prodigal sons, for whom our hearts yearn and our lips frame excuses, than as judges on the bench do those of criminals whose antecedents are nothing to them. This may be wrong, but it is true to human nature, which never can divest itself of these warpings of judgment, or fail to discover the under-tone in the Rochester nature, and believe in its nobility while it condemns its errors. The predominant feeling is, that the nature is bent out of its true course by adverse influences, not that it loves best of itself a distorted growth, and we keep hoping for calmer airs to allow it to rise erect once more. In St. John, the third type of character, self-denial soars (paradoxical as it may seem) into an intense selfishness; and in laying aside all the humanizing and pleasurable influences within and around him, he immolates others at the shrine of self as remorselessly as Rochester's eager and impulsive selfishness would do. Jane in both instances enjoys the struggle with their iron wills; ultimate victory we are sure must be with her, and we watch the contest with faith in our chosen champion. Like David with the Philistine, she takes no sword too large for her handling, nor tries to wield a lance too heavy for her strength, but with the small stone in the sling she slays her adversary, she herself hardly knows how. There is no bravado in her onset, no panoply of war, and her nerves tremble though her heart is strong, when the Goliath of her battle shakes the ground with his terrible tread. Like David also, she can return to the tending of her sheep, no whit puffed up by the great deed she has done. She has mounted no stilts upon which she cannot remain, yet from which it is mortifying to descend, and ordinary mortals are not afraid of her, though she has fought with and slain giants.

The most prominent artistic defects in the work are, in our opinion, the too highly colored pictures of the physical distress endured by Jane after leaving Thornfield, and the somewhat hackneyed melodrama of the discovery of her cousins in the persons of her chance benefactors, and her subsequent acquisition of a fortune. The former removes our interest to a new range of antagonistic experiences without relieving the tension, for the introduction of starvation and physical exposure as additional suffering for the lacerated nature does not harmonize with the general effect, or add force to the *dénouement*; and the latter detracts from the generally unique management of the characters and the plot.

Miss Brontë was always keenly alive to the attacks made upon "Jane Eyre," and it is certain that any trenching upon the limits of delicacy or of morality was far from her thought, and that, in telling her story as it arose in her imagination, her obedience to the truth of her perceptions of humanity is as complete when she paints its sins as when she dwells upon its virtues. If the alternative is to be true to the life-picture she tries to paint, even by confounding our perceptions with our sympathies, as she sees them constantly confounded in those around her and in her own self, or to sacrifice the fidelity of her coloring in order to throw into stronger relief the line between wrong and right, her decision as an artist may be different from that of a political economist. The public voice has declared in favor of retaining the faithful picture, and there are those who do not despair of finding in it profitable study. It is not always in those works which make the loudest claims as moral utterances, that the most searching truth and the keenest strength are to be found.

The general tone of "Shirley" is somewhat unlike that of its predecessor; the characters are more numerous, the scenes more varied, the interest less concentrated. It lacks the impetuous impulse, the passionate glow, the lava-rush towards a single point, and gives us instead, more changing tableaux, more general friction, wider varieties of emotion. It retains the spiciness of seasoning however; the viands are still of racy flavor and delicate concoction, but we detect more common and familiar ingredients in them. We still have vivacious conversations sparkling with repartee, descriptions quite Turner-like in their brilliancy of painting, and touches of deep pathos side by side with sunny and gleeful scenes. In the opening chapters we have a rough "charcoal sketch" of characters, a bold outline of coarseness quite unlike the usual efforts of the feminine pen in such directions. We are glad to learn from the "Life" that the curates did not originate in the imagination of Miss Brontë, or derive their absurdities from any desire on her part to cast a slur upon the profession to which they belong. The characters in "Shirley" are nearly all of them drawn from life, and their behavior under the circumstances created for them by the author is in perfect keeping with the tendencies which her analysis of their characteristics enabled her to discover and set in motion.

It is pleasant to trace the delicate revelations of Miss Brontë's own tastes and habits in her writings. We find her love of nature, her keen perception of the changing moods of earth and sky, and all her atmospheric susceptibilities, continually peeping out. She sets it down against one of her characters in "Shirley," that he "was not a man given to close observation of nature, he could walk miles on the most varying April day, and never see the beautiful dallying of earth and heaven, never mark when a sunbeam kissed the hill-tops, making them smile clear in green light, or when a shower wept over them, hiding their crests with the low-hanging, dishevelled tresses of a cloud"; and we feel directly that Currer Bell neither likes, nor means that her readers shall like, that man. The heroine in "Shirley" was intended as an impersonation of Emily Brontë, as her sister fancied she would have shown herself under more genial circumstances than those which surrounded her in reality. We detect the touch of a loving finger in the arrangement of the drapery around this peculiar figure. That incident in the romance which has been condemned as too melodramatic,—the bite of the mad dog,—is an exact transcript of a similar experience on the part of Emily Brontë. Caroline Helstone represents a much-loved friend of Charlotte, and is evidently a favorite with the author, though a stronger contrast than that between such a disposition and her own Jane Eyre-ish nature cannot well be imagined. She gives us in the two Moores men nearly as selfish as Rochester and St. John, and endowed with the power which selfish men almost always possess when they are shrewd and energetic. They obtain that which they really set their hearts upon having. It is undeniable that Currer Bell's heroes love themselves very much even in loving their mistresses. Having acknowledged this, or any other element of character in her creations, she never avoids for them any legitimate consequence of its existence, never shrinks from any situation into which it brings them, from fear of jarring upon the prepossessions of the reader. Inexorable as Nemesis, she forces upon them the mortifications and the disasters which are their due. Few writers would have dared the strain upon our liking given in the mercenary love-making of Robert Moore to Shirley, since Robert is intended to win our respect on the whole; but this was the natural consequence of the premises established in Robert himself, and we have to go through it as we may, and get over it as he did. In the delicately painful descriptions of illness we trace the experience of Charlotte Brontë by the bedside of her dying sisters; and there is a frequent tone of sadness in "Shirley," which tells us that the author is by no means sitting in unclouded sunshine. The characters arrive at conclusions which we feel that the writer herself has reached, and in passages like the following, we feel that she speaks her own carefully wrought-out philosophy.

> I believe—I daily find it proved—that we can get nothing in this world worth keeping, not so much as a principle or a conviction, except out of purifying flame, or through strengthening peril. We err; we fall; we are humbled,—then we walk more carefully. We greedily eat and drink poison out of the gilded cup of vice, or from the beggar's wallet of avarice; we are sickened, degraded; everything good in us rebels against us; our souls rise bitterly indignant against our bodies; there is a period of civil war; *if the soul has strength, it conquers and rules thereafter.*

In this conflict of life within itself in which Currer Bell finds the secret of progression, the labor of the soul upon itself and the fulfilment of its appointed work, she is very skilful to interest us and powerful to reveal its movement. We feel that the hard discipline of her men and women is like that which we make for ourselves, and that the process by which they struggle into greater freedom is that by which we must ourselves emerge from bondage. "Shirley" excited nearly as much attention as "Jane Eyre," and its admirable portraiture of Yorkshire people and scenery led to the detection of its author's identity.

In 1852 "Villette," Currer Bell's last work, was published. In this novel the scene of action is removed from England to the Continent, it being, as we have seen, a transcript of her own residence in Belgium. In some respects "Villette" is her most remarkable work. It possesses a more classic elegance of outline and a more delicate finish of detail than either "Jane Eyre" or "Shirley." In its analysis of character it is absolutely clairvoyant. The heart of Lucy Snowe,—that name so rightly chosen,—a volcano white with drifts without, glowing with molten heat within,—is laid bare before us, and we may watch every flicker of the flame, every surging of the fiery billows. No anatomist could more clearly describe the physical vitality, than she has sketched this weird and wild, yet hushed and still nature. She plays in the romance a part similar to that of Charlotte Bronté herself in the world,—that of a silent, unsuspected analyzer of others. Miss Bronté says of her: "I was not leniently disposed towards Lucy Snowe; from the beginning, I never meant to appoint her lines in pleasant places";—and we feel that ordinary sources of happiness were necessarily closed to such a one. In eloquence of language, also, "Villette" bears the palm, rich as the others were in choice diction and fitting phrases. Certain passages in "Villette" rise to a height of sublimity or reach a depth of pathos which moves the very soul. Sadness is its prevailing tone, the hand of Fate casts its shadow from the beginning, and we know that it will fall upon us at the last.

There are, however, certain defects in "Villette" which Miss Bronté herself acknowledged, though she felt powerless to remedy them. She writes to her publisher: "I must pronounce you right again, in your complaint of the transfer of interest, in the third volume, from one set of characters to another. It is not pleasant, and it will probably be found as unwelcome to the reader, as it was, in a sense, compulsory upon the writer." The childhood of Paulina, also, promises more than it performs. She is much more of a woman when she is a child in years, than when she is fairly grown up. The queer little girl impresses us as "quite a character," and we are disappointed when she degenerates into a mere pretty woman. The giddy, shrewd-witted Ginevra is decidedly more entertaining; her whimsicalities amuse and her absurdities provoke us as they did Lucy, while she manages to keep the same place in our liking. Paul Emanuel is a personage apparently after Miss Bronté's own heart, and she evidently enjoys dwelling upon the dark-complexioned, irascible little man. He is strangely effective in the pages of "Villette," and our admiration for him grows with the progressive development of the story, till our affections twine about him whether we will or no. In regard to his fate as set forth in the last paragraph, the meaning of which has been often disputed, we have now the confirmation of its tragic import from Miss Bronté's own lips.

Indeed, the romance would have been imperfect without it, every stroke of the pen prepared us for it, and the author would have been false to "all the unities" had she forced a different *dénouement*. The oracular style of its announcement was merely out of deference to her father's request, that she would "make them happy at last."

From these three works we must make up our estimate of Currer Bell's genius; for "The Professor," written first, but not published till the halo of an assured reputation surrounded the name of its author, hardly influences our judgment either way. Its faults, which are many, were redeemed in her subsequent works; its crudeness, which is great, gave place to exquisite finish both of plot and of character; and its choice of material, which reminds us of her sisters rather than of herself as we now know her, was replaced by more genial and more natural specimens of humanity. Its best portions are developed in "Villette" with more power and richer charm, and, so far as Currer Bell is concerned, the publication of "The Professor" might still have been omitted; but viewed by itself, and compared with most of the romances issuing from the prolific and not over-fastidious press of the day, we confess some surprise that the occasional flashes of talent in its details, and the unquestionable strength of its conception, should not have won the attention of some one of the publishers to whose inspection it was submitted. One inference we may certainly draw from its perusal now; if "The Professor" was destined to be followed by such works as "Jane Eyre," "Shirley," and "Villette," we might fairly have expected a rich harvest from the minds that in their first efforts could originate "Wuthering Heights" and "The Tenant of Wildfell Hall." Had the two sisters been spared, "the Brontë novels" might have become a long and illustrious list of noble fictions.

In one respect Currer Bell is not altogether unlike her favorite, Thackeray; for she selects for her *dramatis personæ* no impossible abstractions, but warm human hearts with a fair share of imperfections, and presents us with characters which neither awe nor astonish, but which we make welcome in our family circle. But she does not, like Thackeray, become jocosely bitter over the natures she evokes, nor abuse them till the reader is roused in their defence. Sarcasm with her does not dip its arrow in poison. There is more of good than of evil in her characters; and we feel confidence in their latent heroism, draw strength from the contemplation of their struggles, and rise from the perusal of her works without bitterness. The charge of coarseness has occasionally reappeared; but, after the vindication of Mrs. Gaskell, we think it must take rank with those suggestions which recommend a "Shakespeare for the use of private families" and a mantilla for the Venus de' Medici.

We have room for but a brief notice of Emily and Anne and their works, but the public is familiar with their history. Emily seems to have been a very Titaness with her imperious will and her uncompromising ways, though Charlotte declares, in her delineation of her as Shirley, her faith in her capacity for more genial development. The best criticism of her novel, "Wuthering Heights," is by Charlotte, and that is an explanation rather than a criticism; for it is only in the author that the key to such an extraordinary story can be found. She described human nature as it appeared to her distorted fancy, and it bore the same resemblance to healthful humanity, that a faithful description of an eclipse of the sun, as seen through smoked glass, would bear to the usual appearance of that luminary. Charlotte says:—

> What her mind gathered of the real, was too exclusively confined to those tragic and terrible traits, of which, in listening to the secret annals of every rude vicinage, the memory is sometimes compelled to receive the impress. Her imagination, which was a spirit more sombre than sunny, more powerful than sportive, found in such traits materials whence it wrought creations like Heathcliffe, like Earnshaw, like Catharine. Having formed these beings, she did not know what she had done. If the auditor of her work, when read in manuscript, shuddered under the grinding influences of natures so relentless and implacable, of spirits so lost and fallen,—if it was complained that the mere hearing of certain vivid and fearful scenes banished sleep by night, and disturbed mental peace by day,—Ellis Bell would wonder what was meant, and suspect the complainant of affectation.

This would naturally be the case with a mind capable of creating such monsters, and marshalling them coolly through all the movements of a romance; the shrinking from them must have been on their first appearance to the imagination, or not at all. The power of the creations is as great as it is grotesque, and there is, after all, a fearful fascination in turning over the pages of "Wuthering Heights." It calls for no harsh judgment as a moral utterance; for its monstrosity removes it from the range of moralities altogether, and can no more be reduced to any practical application than the fancies which perplex a brain in a paroxysm of nightmare.

Anne, the younger and more gentle sister, was of a different mould; yet some passages of her "Tenant of Wildfell Hall" would lead us to suppose that she was gentle chiefly through contrast with her Spartan sister, and that the savage elements about her found an occasional echo from within. "Agnes Grey," which appeared with "Wuthering Heights," made little impression; her reputation rests upon her second and last work, "The Tenant of Wildfell Hall." For a criticism of this, we turn again to Charlotte; for though different in scope and style from "Wuthering Heights," it is nearly as inexplicable at a first glance.

"She had," says her sister, "in the course of her life, been called on to contemplate near at hand, and for a long time, the terrible effects of talents misused and faculties abused; what she saw sunk very deeply into her mind. She brooded over it till she believed it to be a duty to reproduce every detail (of course with fictitious characters, incidents, and situations), as a warning to others. She hated her work, but would pursue it. She must be honest; she must not varnish, soften, or conceal."

It must be owned that she did not "varnish" the horrors which she painted, and which her first readers did not suspect of causing the artist so much suffering. We can now trace the quiverings of a sister's heart through the hateful details of a vicious manhood; and if the book fail somewhat in its attempt to become a warning, it may at least claim the merit of a well-meant effort.

The history of the Brontë family is a tragedy throughout. Seldom have we been allowed to unveil such peculiar natures acting upon each other in one home-circle, and emerging from profound isolation into brief but dazzling publicity. With the death of Charlotte ends the sad history, and we have now only the memory of what they were. The world will not soon forget them, and would gladly offer them a more kindly tribute than it could conscientiously have given while ignorant of so much which now reveals the virtues, the struggles, and the sufferings of the sisters in that desolate Haworth parsonage.

We once more thank Mrs. Gaskell for her labor of love, so gracefully executed, and echo to the letter the indignant language with which she condemns the too hastily uttered comments of ignorant criticism.

It is well that the thoughtless critics, who spoke of the sad and gloomy views of life presented by the Brontés in their tales, should know how such words were wrung out of them by the living recollection of the long agony they suffered. It is well, too, that they who have objected to the representation of coarseness, and shrank from it with repugnance, as if such conceptions arose out of the writers, should learn, that not from the imagination, not from internal conception, but from the hard, cruel facts, pressed down, by external life, upon their very senses, for long months and years together, did they write out what they saw, obeying the stern dictates of their consciences. They might be mistaken. They might err in writing at all, when their afflictions were so great that they could not write otherwise than they did of life. It is possible that it would have been better to have described only good and pleasant people, doing only good and pleasant things (in which case they could hardly have written at any time). All I say is, that never, I believe, did women, possessed of such wonderful gifts, exercise them with a fuller feeling of responsibility for their use. As to mistakes, they stand now—as authors as well as women—before the judgment-seat of God.

THE FRIENDSHIPS OF WOMEN

———•———

The Friendships of Women. By William Rounseville
Alger. Boston: Roberts Brothers. 1868.

The perusal of this very interesting book leaves us with a pleasant
sense of having been in the company of most agreeable, high-
minded, thorough-bred people; and also with a clear perception of the
skill of the author in so bringing this company together and arranging
the manner of their presentation, that along with the conviction of their
nobleness comes a pardonable self-complacency at the warmth of our
appreciation of and the extent of our sympathy with them. They appear
before us, not only in their strength, but their tenderness; reveal themselves in the light of that friendship which illumines the faces of our
own personal friends, giving us a more intimate community of feeling
with them than is usually imparted by historic characters. The subject
of the work is full of attraction; its treatment graceful and vigorous;
the argument well sustained by facts accumulated with evident care.
As a tribute to woman it has the rare merit of not placing her under
a meretricious glare of apparent adoration, but calmly assigns her an
equality with man, through virtue of the humanity common to both
and dominant over the distinctions between them. The unity of the
subject, though not disturbed, is diversified by a variety of anecdote, by
the piquancy of its digressions, and the tact with which side facts are
subsidized for the benefit of the main proposition. A strong sympathy
is established with the reader by the enthusiasm of the writer, and also
by the occasional glimpses allowed us of his own personality; as when,
by the loving, lingering way in which he dwells on some especial portrait, he reveals, perhaps unconsciously, the sensitive temperament and

magnetic insight by which alone he attains to full comprehension of the natures he describes. It would seem that he grew fonder of his work as the pages multiplied beneath his fingers, gaining more and more of that warmth of enthusiasm without which such work is valueless; and with which it becomes vitalized for the reader, as well as rewardful for the writer. All love-labor brings thus its own recompense.

The friendships of women become more interesting and of greater importance as the biographies and correspondences of women win a larger space in our literature. Certain feminine qualifications, as shown in running commentaries on current events, have long been recognized as especially valuable to the historian in obtaining vivid pictures of men and manners. When light is needed on the character of the women themselves, their correspondence is of course the richest source of information. History becomes every day more analytical, more psychological, and the fact is acknowledged that much of the worth of a recital of historic events lies in the same direction in which its fascination is found—just where the advance of humanity in general is most perceptibly connected with the growth of the individual soul. The moral and social position of an epoch may be traced not only in the rush of external events taking place in it, but in the faithful portraits of the great actors and thinkers of the age. The emotional incitements of those who participate in a crisis are as worthy of study as the crisis itself.

Mr. Alger's book is an admirable plea for the greater freedom of woman in all directions, as well as a proof of her right to high rank in one usually appropriated by man—that of friendship. In proving her to be as well fitted for the highest offices of friendship as a masculine nature can be, he claims for her a place side by side with man in everything which contains opportunity for the improvement of a humanity common to both. That both men and women are human beings more than they are men and women,—that sex is intrinsically subordinate to humanity, is ample ground on which to rest this claim.

The examples given of the friendships of women comprise nearly if not quite all the instances which have come down on the records of time. The patient labor of such an accumulation of illustrations must have been immense. The classifications are skilfully made and the original matter in which they are enshrined renders them doubly interesting. Friendship itself, as set forth here, is full of the greatest and best elements which the heart needs in a sentiment, which should be a life long joy in this world and have place among the grand formative forces for another. It is exhaustively treated by Mr. Alger, and each variety of it is allowed its full weight. Even the much ridiculed school-girl sentiment is touched with the tender kindliness which it deserves for it is after all, puerile in appearance only, as the unfledged effort of that which may afterwards wing a lofty flight. The difficult topic of Platonic love receives long and careful attention, and contains many choice sentiments and eloquent illustrations. The chapter on Friendship in Marriage is perhaps the most impressive from its simple concentration and the pure height to which it ascends. Also the friendships between women give opportunity for some charming discussions and delicate analysis of character. In this connection we are struck by the contrast between the demand made by the simply historic idea of friendship and that which grows up in the mind which contemplates it as one of the steady and permanent influences in life. The historic idea of great characteristics seems to be fully satisfied by some grand instantaneous culmination, some single efflorescence in the sight of men. Damon and Pythias could die for each other, therefore they become types of what friendship can attain. Just so, the intensified enthusiasm, often the result chiefly of moral contagion and transient exaltation—which led many to the stake, sufficed to win a martyr's crown to be worn through eternity. A thoughtful judgment discovers that it is easier to mount, at some moment of excitement, to heroism than to resist the wear and tear of long-continued prosaic influences and still keep alive that beautiful enthusiasm of which novelty is too often a necessary part. It is really easier for some persons to walk bravely into the flames, than to keep heart, soul and body in long unwavering subjection to the Christian rule. The true demand of friendship is that it shall resist not only the wrenching of a violent attack, but the insidious rusting of prosperous ease; shall not only come to the rescue like a god in time of trial, but be the daily rest and comfort, or spur and stimulant which our every day needs require. And thus the simple dignity of an unflawed relationship for sixty years makes the friendship of Eleanor Butler and Sarah Ponsonby dwarf all the achievements of young and fervid enthusiasm.

We cannot refrain from quoting a few of the laconics of Mr. Alger which especially remain in our memory. "The gist of a noble friendship is the cultivation in common of the personal inner lives of those who partake in it." "If you choose a crow for your guide, you must expect your goal to be carrion." "Ever so correct a perception of what we despise and detest leaves our moral rank undetermined." "Poor and feeble souls exact most from the world."

This compact little volume contains an immense amount of reading and represents a degree of labor and thought hardly realized by the general reader—but to those accustomed to measure the literary results of intellectual effort it will be acknowledged as a rich accession to their stores. As a book of reference for the subjects it comprises, it is almost encyclopedic in its grasp. As a component part of the "History of Friendship," promised by its author, it ensures a thorough welcome for the completed work.

THE NOVELS OF GEORGE SAND

A study of the literature of languages other than our own is daily
becoming more necessary to the completion of an even mod-
erately good education. To those who aim at culture, an extensive
acquaintance with foreign works is imperative. The limits in this
direction widen rapidly; and everything which makes this source of
knowledge accessible is of value to the public, and demands acknowledgment. The announcement of a translation of the novels of George
Sand is an event of importance in the history of American literature,
and renders appropriate a somewhat elaborate examination of the
claims to our attention possessed by this writer, who is almost without
dispute allowed to be the greatest of French romance-writers. A brief
analysis of some of her numerous works will serve to indicate, in some
measure, the rich fund of entertainment and the vast stores of thought
contained in the romances of George Sand. We hope that most of them
will be given to the public in the promised series. No single author
could better serve the purpose of exemplifying the most prominent
and contrastive qualities of modern French genius, or enable us to
obtain a more complete idea of its development under the forms of
philosophy, politics, religion, and all other social problems.

Aside from the intrinsic differences which exist between the idioms
of the two languages, there are other strongly marked dissimilarities
in French and English literature which seem to be inherent in the
nature of each. If the idioms present what may be called mechanical difficulties in the translator's path, since it is certain a precise

equivalent cannot always be given in one language for an expression in another, so that the translator is not infrequently obliged to choose between a literal verbal accuracy which fails to render the subtlety of the author's thought, and a free translation which opens the way to a diversity of style; so, also, what we should call the national differences tend to preserve the foreign tone and aspect of the book in its new tongue. It requires not only skill and quickness of perception to translate successfully, but also the power of taking on the very garb and fashion of another's mind, in order to give those delicate shades of meaning which help to make up that impalpable but positive thing which we call an author's style. Of this we have more than usual promise in the translations before us.

French novels have shared with their English contemporaries in the great impulse which has carried them to a high position among the social forces of the time. They have become a favorite medium for the dissemination of new theories, the discussion of difficult social questions, and the promulgation of new remedies for human ills. "Telemachus" and "Paul and Virginia" have yielded to romances which elucidate the mysteries of Mesmerism and Fourierism; of Communism and Agrarianism; or set forth in Protean forms the conclusions of aristocratic Atheism or fashionable Pantheism. Some are devoted to the building up of political constitutions, others to the tearing down of religious creeds. Others, again, content themselves with the narrower field of observation contained in a single human heart; but even then they bring to the analysis of their subject the aid of previous metaphysical practice, and assemble together the rarest psychological phenomena. In the painting of exceptional character, in the skill with which the inner springs of action are laid open to the reader, George Sand has no rival but Balzac, while in the choice of her subjects there is more geniality and more faith in human nature.

It is useless for the warmest admirers of French novels to deny that there is very generally prevalent in them an atmosphere of immorality, a disregard of many restraints dear to most English hearts. This element is more or less prominent, more or less offensive to the taste, according to the breadth or delicacy of handling it receives. It is judged dangerous or culpable by each reader for himself, according to the degree of closeness in his own moral reasoning; for the term immorality, when applied to novels, is remarkably elastic, and there are few subjects in regard to which a wider diversity of judgment exists. When the objectionable quality is in coarse and conspicuous relief,—when it is made the mainspring of action in the characters and the plot,—when, in short, it is the grand intention of the book,—it generally assumes a repulsive form, and becomes so uninviting as to prove comparatively harmless. There is much less mischief to be apprehended from such productions than from those in which an evil meaning is veiled beneath a skilful drapery of sentiment, and adorned by the elegant refinement of a poetical taste. This finds an insidious way into the mind, like those poisons, which, administered by imperceptibly increasing quantities, penetrate through the whole system with but little visible sign. Those works, on the contrary, which bear their mark unblushingly upon the surface, as coarse and vulgar men upon their brow, are turned away from the door at once; or if surreptitiously introduced to minister to some depraved taste, are concealed on the approach of visitors, at the impulse of a shame which is, in itself, an indication that its owner is not yet beyond hope.

Among the works of George Sand may be found some which certainly lie open to condemnation, if we judge them summarily and without regard to the circumstances under which they were written, which, in our own opinion, by furnishing ample explanation of their origin, demand from the critic, at least, a modified verdict. Indeed, even on general principles, it is not strange that she should catch a portion of the spirit of her time,—a spirit which is, as we have said, almost universal.

The reasons for the prevalence of this immoral tone in modern French literature are beyond the limits of our subject. It has been long in existence, and fostered by the protecting care of the best intellects in the nation. It has come now to be hereditary, and each new author enters upon it as upon a portion of his patrimony. His predecessors hand it over to him as they themselves received it, with such additions as circumstances have enabled them to make to it. It seems to be impossible for a French writer of the present day to entirely divest himself of a tendency to sceptical philosophizing on the gravest subjects, or to free himself from a general irreverence when he approaches the deeper mysteries of life. This is neither without explanation nor excuse, so far, at least, as the present generation is concerned; it is in the air they breathe from earliest childhood; it is in

harmony with the society of the world about them; and their choicest libraries are redolent of its subtle odor. We run the risk of great
unfairness in making up our critical judgment, if we omit this fact in
the examination of modern French literature. The time, we hope, has
forever gone by when the status of people in this life and the next can
be determined by the *ipse dixit* of a few individuals, who would apply
to all the world the inflexible rules which suit to admiration the exigencies of their own narrow natures, but which fail of all application
the moment a new variety of the human species comes forward, or the
vibrations of the human temperament obtain room for action.

Few authors have been so differently judged as George Sand; so
indiscriminately lauded, so uncharitably condemned. Those who sympathize with her have found little to censure; those who do not, have
found little to approve. A thousand idle tales about her have found
circulation and credence; wretched translations of a few of her most
ultra outbursts have done her injustice. But Time is coming to the
rescue, and a new estimate,—at least so far as all but a small circle
of readers is concerned,—is being placed upon the value and the
beauty of the creations of her genius. Something of the same change
has also passed over her works themselves; the passage of years, and
perhaps also the indulged expression of her views in her earliest writings, have cooled the ardor of her denunciations against society, and
calmed the frenzy of her resistance to established institutions. In some
of her first romances,—as in "Indiana," "Jacques," and "Lélia,"—she
earned a reputation which has clung to her like the poisoned garment of Nessus, and which some passages in her personal history did
much to confirm. "Indiana" was a flower of the tropics, blossoming in
unpruned luxuriance, and exhaling a poisonous perfume from every
petal. The other two, more carefully written and more refined in style,
culminate in a sublimated sentimentalism, and belong in a region of
impossibility as to character and plot; but in consequence of their
singularity, and the unmistakable promise of great power which they
possess, they are worthy of attention as indicative of a transient but
intense state of feeling in the author. In judging of most of the writings of George Sand, it is necessary to know more of her own life and
experience than is required for a fair criticism of most authors, for
the reason that in them she, to an unusual degree, expresses *herself.*
They have generally been considered more or less disguised episodes

in her own history, or, at least, as phases of her inner life, painted out with imaginary accessories. Though we are very far from accepting this resemblance as in any degree literal, and from believing that her characters are in any narrow sense portraits, we yet feel that her intense personality has so fused her own experiences in the crucible of her genius, so assimilated her outward influences with her inward emotions, that the result has given us rare insight into a most rich and varied life. We hear the cries of her bruised heart, the shouts of her various enthusiasms, the announcements of change and progress in her moral and intellectual position. Her first steps in the world of literature were made over the ruins of her domestic peace, and it was natural that she should endeavor to prove the intolerable weight of the social yoke, as the best plea for having herself thrown it off. The ardor of her disposition did not allow her to be calm in the battle she was fighting, or even to be over-fastidious in the choice of weapons.

The desire which the public long ago manifested for some knowledge of the woman who could pour forth such daring, passionate complaint, and who could clothe her thoughts in such a glory of eloquence, called out the most contradictory narratives concerning her. The descriptions of the life, and even of the person of George Sand, were colored to suit the supposed taste of the public, or the prejudice of the individual who furnished the information. For a long time Madame Dudevant was looked upon as a sort of mysterious vampire, about whom, however little could be proved, everything horrible might be believed. This mist of exaggeration of course disappeared after awhile, but many people felt astonished when there emerged from it a figure of most feminine proportions, a face of refined and dignified beauty, and a heart of warm and tender benevolence. The frequent indications we discover in her works of generosity, energy, grandeur, and sweetness, are all the honest outgrowth of qualities deeply rooted in her nature.

A few words are necessary to recall to the reader's mind the salient incidents of Mme. Dudevant's life, for the purpose of making manifest the intimate union which has always existed between what she has been writing for the public and what she has been living, and it may be suffering, in private. A most interesting and detailed account of her birth and early years is to be found in her "Histoire de ma Vie," which is an admirable piece of analytic retrospection. We have only space for the most meagre outlines. She claims descent from the great Marshal Saxe; and we doubt not that this ancestry, with its bar sinister, is more a matter of pride to her than if the Church had sanctified all the degrees of a humbler lineage. Born at a time when revolutions were every-day occurrences, nursed amid social convulsions, and surrounded by all the alarms of war, her earliest impressions must have taken most decided form and color from the circumstances of her infancy. Next followed a wild, untrammelled country life under her grandmother's roof, on an estate still the favorite residence of Mme. Dudevant. Then two or three years of utterly different existence in a Parisian convent, where she went through a season of religious exaltation and intense introversion,—some idea of which may be gained through the story of "Spiridion," to which it gave rise. At eighteen she married M. Dudevant, a man whom she had no reason to love, and who was utterly unsuited to her in every respect. For eight years she struggled against her fate, assailed by those perplexities and discouragements, which are all the more intolerable, because the world imposes silence on the sufferer, and is chary of sympathy towards unhappy wives. At length she left her husband to the society of his sheep and oxen,—or rather hers, for their home was her own property,—went to Paris, commenced her literary career, and Monsieur Dudevant woke up one morning to find himself famous as the husband of a woman who no longer belonged to him. Her first successful publication was "Indiana." Her choice of a *nom de plume* is said to have arisen out of a combination of the name of her friend Jules Sandeau, and the fact of the publisher's acceptance of her MSS. on St. George's Day. She is said to have written thirty vol-umes in ten years. This untiring industry shows how great must have been, to her, the relief of pouring out her long pent-up indignation and enthusiasm. Meantime a legal separation from her husband was obtained, and she was reinstated in possession of her estate of Nohant, the revenues of which had been appropriated until then by him. She suffered much from poverty in her early Paris days, and gives, in her autobiography, a very piquant account of her ingenious devices against it. One of them was the adoption, when she went out, of masculine habiliments, which proved a double advantage,—first in the way of cheapness and durability, and next as enabling her to go where she pleased unmolested. She formed innumerable friendships among art-ists, scholars, and literary men, and soon took among them a rank she has always since maintained. Her personal appearance is, as we have said, by no means that which those who regarded her and her works with horror would imagine. Her soft, abundant hair; her mild, expressive eyes,—which, as Heine pithily remarks, "recal neither Sodom nor Gomorrah"; her kindly smile, and reserved but gentle manners, are anything but Amazonian; and her tiny feet do not suggest the treading out of all the conventionalisms and most of the proprieties of life. She has sometimes been compared to the Venus of Milo; and now that age is dimming the brilliancy of her appearance, it makes more apparent the quiet dignity of her whole bearing. We see frequent paragraphs in circulation relating to her method of life, her literary and social habits, and her especial characteristics: it is well to take them without entire reliance upon them; but their number and variety are proof of the constant interest which is felt in the subject. In spite of the supposed portraits of herself, which, in the opinion of the ignorant, abound in her fictions, she has been very chary of real self-revelation; and even in the ten volumes over which her "Histoire de ma Vie" extends, she displays great skill in avoiding any disclosures or unveilings at which the most fastidious taste could revolt. But in her works of imagination her own vitality so fills her characters with life, and in her own experience so many peculiar natures have come under her observation, that it is by no means strange that her women have in some sense the stamp of her own nature, and her men the same salient characteristics as those with whom she has been in daily contact. But, as in most of the so-called portraits in fiction, for one point of resemblance we have a hundred of dissimilarity. An example of this we may quote as quite in point; it is from a letter written by a friend to George Sand, when the public were trying to establish the identity of the character of Lélia with George Sand herself: "Ça ne vous ressemble pas, à vous qui êtes gaie, qui dansez la bourrée, qui appréciez le lépidoptère, qui ne méprisez pas le calembour, qui ne cousez pas mal, et qui faites trés bien les confitures."

We make this extract with the greater pleasure, because it proves the existence of so many of the domestic, genial, and comfortable qualities side by side with the rarest gifts of genius and the creative energy of a most brilliant imagination.

It is, therefore, from a very mingled web of circumstance and temperament, from a rare union of beauty and intellect, of gentleness and defiance, from a life by turns full of activity and excitement, and absorbed in laborious and isolated study, that we must ask the meaning and seek for the key to the writings of George Sand. It is in contemplating the woman that we better understand the author, and it is in studying the author that we learn a wider charity towards the woman. We need not shrink from admitting that she has sometimes erred, both as the woman and the author, for through all we see a great heart palpitating with intense life,—swept tumultuously along at times through deep and turbid waters, but never quite submerged beneath the billows. Always grand in her anger, passionate in her love, generous in her instincts, fierce in invective, but never narrow in her judgments, there are few women formed in a mould so noble as hers. The silence with which she has met the innumerable attacks made upon her and her works; the quiet pertinacity with which she has gone on developing and enforcing and illustrating the great principles of freedom for which she strives, form, in our judgment, through its con-trast with those natures which are led only by ill-considered impulse, a strong ground from which to combat the assertion, agreed to even by many of her admirers, that in her books she has recklessly laid bare the hearts and lives that should have been sacred in conceal-ment. To an imagination so rich as hers, what need to paint too closely from life? We protest against the almost universal practice of laying rule and measure to artistic creations, which, though the germ of their conception might have arisen in the daily walk of life, remain faithful, not to the prosaic development of the persons who suggested them, but, raised into the upper air by the artist's power, live and move and act under a new heaven, or make for themselves, and the other actors on the imaginary scene, a hell of ungovernable passion. It may be a delicate task to draw the line where resemblance ceases and separa-tion begins, but it is cruel to hold George Sand responsible for broken faiths and reckless betrayals, because she first loved Chopin and Alfred de Musset, and then wrote "Lucrezia Floriani" and "Elle et Lui." Even in admitting that she had each of them in her mind, we have ourselves no question that in all the circumstances and details of her romances, she deviated very widely from those episodes which stand forth in her own life; and we firmly believe that, in spite of the way in which the virtuous world has shaken its wise old head over these sad scandals, it has really not obtained any more definite knowledge of the private life of George Sand, or the characters of her friends, from those books, than it might easily have learned from outside sources. Gossip, finding a small bone to pick, is very apt to imagine there is a great deal of meat on it, and to growl and scold over it in most dog-like fashion. If fictitious characters are not in any degree like the people about us, we declare them unnatural; if they are, we call them portraits, and denounce the indelicacy of the author. This is so common that hardly any author of genius escapes it; we hear constantly of the originals of the heroes and heroines of novels. Charlotte Brontë suffers as much in this way as George Sand, in proportion to the number of romances she wrote, and the practicability of applying the story to her own life. She was Jane Eyre, she was Lucy Snowe, everybody was somebody else; she was abused for transporting into her fictions the people and the places that she had seen and known.

We take great pleasure in quoting, in connection with this portion of our subject, some very admirable remarks published recently in the *New York Evening Post*, in regard to George Sand's last novel, "Malgrétout":

> As to the question whether that character (Mlle. d'Ortosa) is really meant for the Empress, it is one which needs no discussion for those who understand the principles on which a work of art is constructed. George Sand is an artist; and it is not an artist, but a vulgar and commonplace writer, who photographs living men and women in a novel. That the wonderful career of Eugenie de Guzman must have been in the mind of the author when she wrote "Malgrétout," and may even have suggested some of the traits in the adventuress there described, does not prove that the character she has drawn was supposed by her to be identical with any one in real life, or even to throw any light whatever upon it.

A complete enumeration of George Sand's novels is not necessary to furnish proof of her enormous industry, infinite versatility, and exhaustless imagination. We will select from among them some which may be considered typical of each class, not so much for criticism,— for they have been liberally criticised in their day and hour,—but to give to those who have not read them some faint idea of the amount of original thought, deep and varied research, rare learning, and unfailing knowledge of human nature, which meet together in one whom Mrs. Browning has so happily designated as the "large-brained woman and large-hearted man."

"Consuelo," the longest of George Sand's novels, was introduced to the American public through an admirable translation by Mr. Francis George Shaw, in 1846. It is probably the best known of her works in this country, and the character of "Consuelo" is recognized as a creation of most rare and delicate beauty. The story is highly dramatic at intervals, and in the pauses of its action there occur delightful passages about music and art, erudite discussions on philosophy and theology and mesmerism, as well as much historical information drawn from out-of-the-way sources, and made instinct with life.

"The Countess of Rudolstadt" is a sequel to "Consuelo," but inferior to it in interest. We have glimpses of the court of the great Frederick, of Voltaire, and many other celebrities. It touches upon necromancy, Freemasonry, Illuminism, and forms a most bizarre mixture of music and politics, psychology and strategy, drama and rhapsody. There are passages of great eloquence which yet linger in our memory; one, in particular, which encloses a *resumé* of the eighteenth century, which is worthy of a dozen readings.

"Mauprat," the volume with which the present series of translations commences, is the history of a nature born and brought up under the most brutalizing influences, but retaining, through all, enough of native nobleness to respond almost unhesitatingly to the demands of an unselfish love, and led with slow but certain steps,—for even when Mauprat wavers, we know he will not fall,—up to a serene height of virtue, and a sweet acceptance of a life-long sorrow.

"La petite Fadette" is quite a different kind of story, and brings before us a sweet and often pathetic picture of rural domestic life. It is like the scent of violets and the song of birds; it is one of many opportunities afforded us of discovering the intense love of nature in Mme. Dudevant, of her keen sensitiveness to its beauty, and her delicate appreciation of its most subtle secrets. Brief and simple as it is, it is most positive in tone and color, and, like a painting by Meissonier, contains a thousand delicate details on its small canvas.

"Teverino" is the history of a summer's day and night, spent upon the frontier of Italy by a lady and her lover; the motive-power of the story being found in the fact that the lover has undertaken to keep the lady well amused for the time stipulated. The condition is that she shall resign herself to his guidance entirely. They start off in a carriage, and a piquant conversation ensues, which forms the first part of the entertainment. Then follows the meeting with an odd series of companions, among them the beautiful and graceful Teverino, who produces a tremendous, but fortunately a transient, effect on the heroine. The charm of the story is in the descriptions and scenery of the book; it has the completeness of an idyl, and its repose also, except for the brief excitement of Sabina, from which no harm results.

In the charming story of "L'homme de Neige," we are transported to a climate and a society the very antipodes of Teverino. The cool, crisp air of northern Europe braces instead of enervating; the Aurora Borealis gleams with ghostly splendor, the sound of sledge-bells, and the sight of huge mountains of snow, help to heighten the effect of a romance full of interest. As a long-concealed mystery lies beneath the surface, we refrain from giving the outlines of the tale, lest it mar the zest with which our readers will enjoy its perusal.

"Le Piccinino" brings us back again to soft Sicilian skies, to the gardens, the scenery, and the sweet indolence of Southern life. In this novel, as in "Consuelo," the descriptions of out-door life in these favored regions is most exquisite. We seem to hear the sweet music of the Mediterranean waves, the singing of the nightingale, and to breathe the perfumes of enchanted gardens. One of the most remarkable peculiarities of George Sand as a writer, is the facility with which she throws herself so completely into the atmosphere of each story in succession, seeming equally at home in all. The *mise en scène* of her smallest stories, as that of "Le Mare au Diable," or "Geneviève," is as thoroughly in keeping with the occasion, as it is in the longest and most elaborate of her romances.

In "La Confession d'une Jeune Fille," a still more quiet picture of country life is painted. All the interest, and it is great, comes from the vibrations of the inner nature of the heroine; for, although the plot is skilfully managed, and the other characters present strongly marked peculiarities, yet it is for the effect which they produce upon the development of the heroine that they are of value in the story. In this romance, we have one of the few instances in which George Sand has ever crossed the English Channel for an addition to her *dramatis personæ;* her genius is continental, rather than insular, and though in this case she does not make a failure in delineation, yet she falls short of complete success.

"Leone Leoni," written in 1833, while the author was residing at Venice, is in our opinion the most objectionable of George Sand's romances. It is an attempt to describe a masculine "Manon Lescaut," and to subject to his evil dominion a feminine "Desgrieux." Painted with consummate skill, rich in all the colors of her most passionate pencil, the very lines flowing from her pen with all the honeyed sweetness of the language, which met her own ear as she was dreaming out her theme,—for we know of no other instance in which the usual staccato of the French is so interpenetrated and subdued by the soft vowels of the Tuscan,—George Sand has produced a masterpiece of psychological analysis, but one from which the heart and taste alike revolt. It may well be that such natures have existed, and done their evil work, as hideous diseases work horrible corruption on the fairest forms, but we close our eyes as we pass them, unless it is our own inevitable task to pause and labor to alleviate and console. Simply to examine curiously and voluntarily would be almost impossible, for most.

"Les maîtres Sonneurs" is a breath of fresh air after leaving the fetid odors of the lazaretto of "Leone Leoni." The change of scene brings about a change of characters; and, in returning to her own well-loved land of Berri, George Sand once more restores us to the healthful oxygen of her favorite home. She enjoys with all her heart the society of her compatriots, and whether in the close companionship of equal friendships, or in seeking to understand and to portray the idiosyncrasies of the simple but sturdy peasantry around her, she delights to give to the Berrichons the titles of comrades and of friends. In this pretty story of "Les maîtres Sonneurs," the author's love and knowledge of music come to the surface, and mingle with artistic effect in her delineation of the character of Josef; and in Brulette we have one of those gentle but fervent and self-sustained feminine natures, which wait with silent patience through the evil days, and bear without elation the vindication which time is sure to bring.

"Les maîtres Mosaïstes" is a tale of Venetian life in the time of Titian and Tintoretto. While these great painters were placing upon canvas the masterpieces that the world has ever since delighted to honor, certain other artists were busy in bringing to perfection the sister-art of mosaic painting. Among these were the two sons of

Sebastien Zuccato; and the story opens with his pathetic regrets that his sons have wandered from oil-painting, the true department of genius, into mosaic-working, which he regards as below the dignity of the artist. He mourns over the fame they might have won as painters, persists in considering them as mere artisans who can never obtain a real renown. The history of their efforts, their patient struggle against injustice from without and treachery within, their sufferings from the suspicious cruelty of the Council of Venice, the jealousy of their brother artists, and the ingratitude of one of their own pupils, are all told with a skill which reveals the intricate workings of both the better and the worse sides of the artistic nature. In Francesco we have genius and taste in connection with conscientious talent, which disciplines and steadies all his efforts; in Valério, that form of genius which works spontaneously, but spasmodically,—falling into carelessness and neglect at one time, but rising to the grandeur of inspiration at another, and with a truth and nobility of purpose beneath, which ultimately obtain complete supremacy. In the Bianchini we see the hatred and jealous envy which often found their way into the impulsive Italian artist-nature when it was not softened, and purified, and elevated by an appreciation of art for its own sake. In Bozza still another type of character is presented,—an insatiate desire for fame, with an overweening estimate of himself, prompting a reckless disregard of all restraint in seeking to make a reputation, and finally leading to crime against those who stand in his way. There are admirable pictures of the quaint devices and adornments of Venetian life; transient but vivid glimpses of the concealed but universal tyranny of the Council of Ten, and of the subtle manner in which Art, at that period of Italian history, was interwoven with the public and private affairs of all the citizens.

In strong contrast to those romances in which the love of nature or the love of art is made apparent, we may mention "Horace," in which the picture of social and artificial existence is portrayed, as clearly and successfully as if the author had spent a lifetime in its study. Of the success which crowned her efforts, perhaps the most concise evidence may be furnished from the piquant preface which accompanies the second edition of the novel. "It must be that *Horace* represents a modern type, very faithful and very wide-spread, for this book has made for me a dozen well-conditioned enemies. People whose acquaintance I do not possess have pretended to recognize themselves in it, and have called down curses upon me for having so cruelly unveiled them. I, however, repeat here what I said in my first preface, that I have made my sketch from no person whatever, but have taken it from everywhere and from nowhere." It is, in simple fact, life-like in such interior and subtle fashion, that one may well tremble at the contemplation of a personality so intense, a selfishness so deep and ingrained as to often permit of utter unconsciousness on the part of its possessor, an affectation of virtue so exquisite as to pass current even with its owner's moral sense. When enough of youthful freshness, of original talent, of cultivated taste and of fascinating grace combine to make a *Horace*, he will have admiring and devoted friends, humble worshippers, and self-sacrificing adherents. The key-note of the book is touched in its opening sentence,—"Those persons who inspire us with the greatest affection, are not always those whom we esteem the most."

"Antonia," which is the second in the series of translations, takes its name from a flower, the growth and blossoming of which enter into the plot of the romance. Suggestive, in this way, of "La Tulipe Noire" of Dumas, it is quite unlike it in having for its owner a rascal instead of a gentleman; and so far from rivalling the heroine in the affections of anybody, it falls a victim to her first expression of admiration, and by a second flowering assists amiably at her restoration to life and love. The scene of the story is in Paris, the time is in the last days of Louis XVI.; and though the Revolution is not prominently introduced, yet the disorganizing influences which preceded it help to form the social atmosphere of the book. Much of George Sand's contempt for and disbelief in the arbitrary distinctions of society are perceptible in it; and she seems to take pleasure in placing the affections of her heroine upon a man on whom the great world would look down. The character of M. Antoine is of such a peculiar cast, so made up of cruelty and kindness, of revenge and generosity, of obstinacy and flexibility, as to almost defy classification.

"Monsieur Sylvestre," which is soon to follow "Antonia," is a comparatively recent production of the author, and possesses some of the finest qualities of her genius. In it George Sand gives expression to much of the most modern form of metaphysical research into the human heart, and rehearses many of the tantalizing promises which tempt the mind into the region of abstract reasoning. The force and vigor of her style are apparent on every page,—the courage with which she meets and questions the deep mysteries of life, the eloquence with which she discourses on subjects which lie nearest to the human soul, and the calm positiveness with which she condemns delinquencies on which the world looks leniently, make of this little volume a rich mine of serious thought. Certainly the question, "What is happiness?" has seldom received such exhaustive examination under so attractive a form. The contrasts of character are admirably managed: Pierre, though dreamy and delicately constituted, is yet practical in action and patient in endurance; Philippe, whom we know, as it were, chiefly at second hand, is strong in quiet sturdiness and good sense; M. Sylvestre is genial and trustworthy through all his eccentricities; and Mlle. Vallier is wise in the wisdom which comes through discipline, and rich in qualities that develop with the demand upon them. The plot, although subordinate to the philosophy of the book, is by no means insignificant. George Sand's taste in the arrangement of details, and conscientious care in regard to all accessories, are seen in the pictures of country scenes, in the grouping of the characters, and in even the minor individualities which pass across the stage.

But it is in "Lucrezia Floriani," as it seems to us, that the genius and the poetry, the analytic power and the spiritual insight, the passion and the concentration,—in short, all the greatest of George Sand's intellectual and imaginative qualities culminate into greatest perfection. For sustained interest, for deep and subtle pathos, for psychologic truthfulness, and for artistic management of most carefully-selected material, we do not know its equal, even among her works. It would require more space than we can give to analyze and describe its marvellous power; and it has this peculiarity in common with that which accompanies the experience of those men and women who possess an exceptional temperament—they will be all or nothing to those about them. The charm of a work like "Lucrezia Floriani" is not one to receive universal recognition; but to those to whom it speaks at all it brings a message, every syllable of which is rich in meaning, and which can never be forgotten. By such it will be studied with delight, and treasured with jealous care; by others it may, perhaps, be read with only careless curiosity, from its supposed connection with the author's own experience,—a connection which, as we have endeavored to state most emphatically, is none other than that allowable to a great artist who seeks her material as the painter and the sculptor choose theirs: the sunset belongs to the one, the human frame to the other; and when they produce a picture or a statue which delights the spectator, we find in them no servile copy of narrow imitation, but the great facts of nature as seen through the idealism of art.

It will be seen that an exhaustive examination of even the surface-matter of George Sand's novels would require a volume. We pause here, not because the subject lessens in interest, or because our pen is weary, but because a proper limit has been reached, and enough, we hope, been said, to awaken renewed interest in this most remark-able and frequently misunderstood woman and artist. No one since Shakespeare has equalled her in versatility; no one ever surpassed her in the fervor of her efforts for the cause she loves; no one ever lived down such an amount of prejudice, misunderstanding, and, we may add, so many hasty and impulsive expressions of her own. If Balzac rivals her in depicting the weaknesses and unacknowledged mean-nesses of the human heart, and dissects with more sarcastic coolness nerves and fibres that quiver as much with shame as with agony, he cannot equal her in portraying those sentiments and awakening those emotions which arouse an answering thrill in our own hearts, or which send us forth into the world to act a nobler and a less self-centred part. If the lessons which she teaches do not always fit the pattern of a narrow and long-established sectarianism,—if, in the revulsion of feeling under experiences which few of us are called upon to bear, and of temptations we are not required to resist because they lie not in our path, she is sometimes irreverent of long-worshipped social idols,—they are at least rich in all the unselfish promptings of a generous heart, in the kindliness of a wide and sympathetic nature, and in the appreciation of all the great efforts ever made for the ele-vation of human nature and the freedom of the human soul.

George Sand

That "large-brained woman and large-hearted man" self-styled George Sand, of whose quiet death after threescore years of most un-quiet life the cable to-day brings us news, has left vacant an important place among the intellectual forces of our time. Her character, so kaleidoscopic while the living sunshine played upon it; her mind, so daring in its grasp of new problems; her heart, so impetuous in its search for happiness, so courageous in its endurance of disappointment; her life, so rich in thought, in feeling and in action—to-day belong to death and history.

Essentially the product of those ancestral influences which have furnished the salient characteristics of French mental and social life in the nineteenth century, Madame Sand presents one of the most interesting studies which the age supplies. If ever the action of hereditary laws had brilliant exemplification, and the doctrine that transmitted qualities play the supreme part in moral evolution ever received impressive confirmation, it has been in this long, busy and complex existence. What but a character like hers could arise from a long line of hot-headed, strong-passioned, quick-witted ancestors, half-chivalrous by nature, half-depraved by circumstance; marked examples of those strange beings who flitted across the seventeenth and eighteenth centuries, culminating in a feminine nature endowed with genius and launched among the perplexities and the exasperations of these days in which we live? How could such a one be content to dwell in decencies forever, or fail to rush into brave but ignorant struggle when oppressed by adverse personal circumstances? No more than, as time brought greater wisdom and greater skill, she could fail to prove a steady champion for the reformation of human wrongs and the advancement of human rights.

Amandine Lucile Aurore Dupin, the great grand-daughter of the bastard Marechal de Saxe, and connected by blood with three kings of France, Louis XVI., Louis XVIII., and Charles X., was born in Paris in 1804, the year of the coronation of the first Napoleon. Her grandmother, though illegitimate, was acknowledged by her father, and her name, as Marie Aurore de Saxe, was registered by act of Parliament when, at the age of fifteen, she was about to be married to Count de Horn, natural son of Louis XV. The Count was killed in a duel a few weeks after the marriage, and after fifteen years of comparatively secluded life the widow married Monsieur Dupin de Francueil, the friend and patron of Rousseau, in whose exquisite chateau of Chenonceaux the "Devin du Village" was first performed before a brilliant audience of wits and women of the world. By him she had one son, Maurice Dupin, the father of George Sand.

In contrast with this brilliant assemblage of ancestors on her father's side, she drew nourishment of the most plebeian sort from her mother. Victoire Delaborde was the daughter of a vender of canaries and linnets on the Quai des Oiseaux of Paris. Left to the mercy of the wild elements which swept over France in those years of the Revolution and the republic, poor Victoire led in her girlhood a life about which the less said the better. She was the mistress of a French General in Italy when Maurice Dupin, then a young soldier, four years her junior, fell in love with her, and they formed a connection which ended only with his life. For three or four years they remained unmarried, partly owing to the opposition of Maurice's mother, whom he dearly loved, and partly from the indifference of Victoire herself to the marriage ceremony. One or two children were born, and a month before the birth of George Sand, Maurice insisted upon a civil marriage, in order to legitimate the coming infant. She was the only one of the children who survived the father. Maurice and his wife were both gifted with remarkable personal beauty, and George Sand tells us that her mother often frankly reproached her for not inheriting a larger share of it. Aurora's first experience of importance was a journey to Spain, made across a country torn by war. Her father was aide-de-camp to

Murat at Madrid; his wife followed him there with two children: a third was born there and died soon after. On the defeat of the French, Maurice took his family back to France, and they were glad to find a refuge with his mother at her estate of Nohant in Auvergne. Before any arrangements for the future had been made, Maurice Dupin was killed by a fall from his horse. Aurora was about eight years old. Her mother and grandmother could never live peacefully together, and between the stormy temper of the one and the exacting stateliness of the other, the sensitive, nervous child had a wretched time. After many quarrels the young widow went back to Paris upon a small pension; the grandmother took charge of Aurora's education, and made her her heir. After receiving instruction for several years from the former tutor of her father, a man of learning but violent and irascible, she went at thirteen to a convent in Paris. Here she passed three peaceful years and underwent some very deep religious experiences. At sixteen she left the convent with great reluctance and returned to the country only in time to nurse her grandmother through her last illness, which developed a strong attachment between them. She then came under her mother's authority, but not for long as at eighteen she married Casimir Dudevant, sub-lieutenant of infantry, aged twenty-seven. She had two children, Maurice and Solange. The marriage, though apparently suitable, turned out badly, and after thirteen years of varied matrimonial life, five of which had been passed in virtual separation, legal arrangements were perfected by which she became mistress of herself and of Nohant. Meanwhile her literary reputation had become established, and she had been, perforce of poverty, a most laborious worker with her pen. Her first success was "Indiana," published in 1832, and for ten years she was a steady contributor to the *Revue des Deux Mondes*, then under the editorship of Buloz, who, as she says, held the strings of her purse during that time. She won in this season of labor and privation, the love and esteem of many, but side by side with these came calumnies and exaggerated scandals, arising from her extreme opinions and the manner in which she was charged with putting them into practice. Among the closer relationships she assumed, those with Jules Sandeau, out of whose name she constructed for herself the appellation she has made immortal; Alfred de Musset and Chopin, are best known to the public and caused her the largest share of suffering and abuse. More peaceful friendships she formed with Rollinat, Michel, Liszt, Arago and a host of others; and she entered with intelligent enthusiasm into the ultra political aspirations of the day. Her winters were passed in Paris and her summers at Nohant, where she dispensed a generous but unostentatious hospitality. She devoted herself with ardor to her children, holding especially tender relations with her son. Indeed, if we may trust her own judgment on the subject, nature intended her for a nurse or a schoolmistress.

The long life of George Sand included a great variety of events in French history, and she was so warm a patriot that she continually identified herself with the political experiments of her country. Her pen was never idle when brave words were to be uttered in behalf of what she deemed the true interests of society, and in this, as in all things, she daringly generalized from the cravings of her own heart to those of universal humanity. In her writings, whether in politics or romance, there are always present the faiths she held, the enthusiasms she cherished and the hopes that animated her. Indeed, the struggles and attainments, the exaltations and the discouragements which so often convulsed her country were rendered in miniature within the bosom of George Sand herself; and as France has ever sought eagerly to evolve some political realization of its dreams of progress and final harmony, so did she strive through storm and stress to adapt her life to her ideal, and adjust her scheme of morals to her cravings for happiness. Her ardor found outlet alike in the industry and in the fervor with which she labored. Her versatility diffused itself in emotion, in experience, in study. She learned one lesson from solitary musings often verging upon morbid revery; another from contact with society; another still from art, of which she was an apt student. Above all her passionate love of nature opened to her many sweet and tender secrets. Her romances tell the story of her emotional changes and the wide range over which they extended. "Spiridion" is the analysis of pietistic exaltation; "Lélia" of impassioned scepticism; "Consuelo" of musical enthusiasm; "Jacques" of ideal stoicism. In "Monsieur Sylvestre" she philosophizes upon minor moralities; in "Lucrezia Floriani" she attacks some of the darkest problems that rack the human heart. In "Horace" she shows how thoroughly she could comprehend without in any degree sharing the mean nature of a social Sybarite, while in the passionate eagerness of "Leone Leoni" we discover her irrepressible protest against a personal tyranny from which she had just emerged. Her qualified acceptance of communistic theories prompted the story of the "Miller of Angibault"; her distrust of conventional refinements is seen in "Mauprat"; in "La Petite Fadette" she paints greatness of heart beneath a peasant's robe, and in "Cesarine Dietrich" a cold and wicked soul clothed in garments of light and beauty. In the less interior aspect of her novels we find equal variety of scenic peculiarities. "L'Homme de Neige" has the sparkle and the chill of Northern Europe; "Le Piccinino" breathes the softness of Sicilian airs; "Pierre qui Roule" is gay with adventure; "La Confession d'une Jeune Fille" is quiet with the hush of country life, and so on through the long list we have not space to name.

One looks with almost incredulous wonder at the amount of intellectual labor accomplished by this woman, whose daily life was, meanwhile, so full of emotional excitement as to suggest constant preoccupation instead of industrious literary achievement. But it was because her force of character enabled her to transmute into ever new forms the material of which her own life was made, that her outward expression grew only the more rich and full under the pressure of her personal emotions. Like the great master of all literary art, Goethe, in studying her own heart she placed no lifeless specimen beneath the lens, and even when, in passionate rebellion against restrictions she could not conquer, she poured a fierce and pitiless light upon its quivering pulsations, it revealed only a deeper sympathy with the suffering and a keener comprehension of the pain of other souls. She wrote with such enforcement of her own personality as to be accused of undue revelation of her private history; she always repelled the charge and claimed that she exercised only the artist's right to paint the characteristics she had the best opportunity to study. Her method is described in the preface to "Lettres d'un Voyageur," which she says she wrote "à la suite d'emotions dont elles ne sont pas le recit, mais le reflet." Her apparent identification with some of her characters was only partial; it was the result of her enthusiasm and ought not to be over-estimated. She says, in further explanation of alleged similarities, "Mon âme, j'en suis certain, a servi de miroir a la plupart de ceux qui y ont jeté les yeux. Je ne diffère de vous parceque je ne nie pas mon mal et ne cherche point à farder des couleurs de la jeunesse et de la sante mes traits flétris." It is quite possible that she over-estimated the degree of original resemblance between herself and her readers, for great souls are generous and do not readily admit the pettiness of those about them; certainly no one of her fictitious characters possesses the variety of traits which made her beloved as well as admired by those who knew her best. Through all the mists of exaggeration created around her there were many who recognized her as a true-hearted, tender nature, finding what bitterness or anger it felt, in the conviction that the personal suffering and injustice she endured were but the counter-part of the misery in a host of other lives. As time went by these sufferings were appeased, the rash ardor of her youth exhaled, she grew more calm in all ways, and many, many years were passed by her in a happy domestic life, of which no one had a keener appreciation than herself.

A charge frequently urged against her works has been their depreciation of marriage; but in a letter written many years ago, in reply to such an accusation, she states, with force, her ideas on the subject, and those who wish to judge her fairly should read this letter. It is, she says, because of her high ideal of what marriage ought to be that she has painted the horror of it as it too often is; it is because she would raise the standard of virtue in both sexes that she depicts the disastrous results of a different conventional code for each. It may be permitted to add that if, in following out her method of teaching, her illustrations were in consonance with confessedly corrupt conditions of Parisian society, it is a matter much less of wonder than of regret to the thoughtful reader.

Her fertility of invention is shown in the plots of nearly a hundred volumes of romance; she was especially skillful in investing her stories with atmospheric and picturesque effects and in supplying an infinitude of harmonious accessories. Her mastery of the intricacies of the French language was due to her laborious and prolonged study. Her intercourse with minds active in most of the prominent movements of the day, supplied her with the stimulant she needed to combat her native tendency to introversion and morbidness. Her extended connection with the press furnished opportunity for prompt expression of her theories and her reflections. As the public learned more and more to appreciate her sincerity and admire her genius, its demands upon her increased in authority and frequency, till it grew to be a thing of course that the chief questions which agitated the French capital should receive attention from this versatile woman, and that the public should be made partaker in the conclusions she reached.

It is not necessary now to contradict the exaggerations and misapprehensions which so long prevented her from receiving the acceptance which her mind and heart deserved. Time, the safest of all champions, has cleared her fame from many a cloud. It is difficult to realize at this day how impossible it once was to attain to any degree of truth about her. Even her personal appearance was matter of vehement controversy, and she was painted as a hideous or a beautiful monster, accordingly as prejudice or prepossession held the pen. The fact that she sometimes wore the dress of a man, a circumstance very simply explained in her autobiography, upon economic and self-protecting grounds, led to her being charged with indulging in all sorts of escapades and with a rampant coarseness of nature. She lived long enough to be seen in a truer light; to have her intrinsic womanliness assert itself, and to be recognized as respectfully in her social as in her literary aspects. Without actual beauty, she certainly possessed great personal magnetism, and she exercised a decided fascination over men of the finest and keenest natures. People raved about the splendor of her dark eyes, and the grace of her perfect hands. Shy and diffident among strangers, she was gay and gracious with her friends, and fond of all the exercises which betoken vivacity of temperament. An indefatigable walker, a fearless rider and a merry dancer, she often, in early life, presented a puzzling contrast with herself in those dark moods which at times overwhelmed her. Her long life allowed the development not only of her emotional and passional nature, but of her intellectual and moral being, and she had the happiness, not always granted to ardent souls, of outliving her first rash utterances and supplementing the feverish eagerness of ignorant zeal with the well-digested conclusions of mature conviction.

Many criticisms of George Sand's works have already been written; they judge her chiefly as a writer of romances. A fuller examination of all her literary work and of its connection with her life should now be made. Her earlier novels, exaggerated and impossible as they were in some respects, burned with the fire of genius and were glorious with the promise of power. A love of truth at all costs, a determination to pursue it at all risks, were discernible in every page. An industry which never flagged and which enabled her to complete ten volumes in three years, and a fervor of conception which accomplished—as in the case of "Leone Leoni"—a novel in eight days, were sure to bring about great results.

As a mistress of literary style her fame grew steadily with the flight of years; and foreign criticism long ago conceded to her the first place among the literary artists, not of her own country alone, but of her own times.

All this industry is over; all this genius is extinguished; all this versatility is at rest. The world will miss the author who has so long contributed to its pleasure, and a large circle of friends will mourn one who endeared herself more and more to them as the years went by. A pleasant and profitable task lies before him who, when accumulated materials shall be made fully accessible, and time has sifted wheat from chaff, shall write the history of this woman and this artist in a spirit of large sympathy and wise comprehension. Such a history will assuredly increase the admiration, we had almost said the affection, with which she will be regarded.

NOTES

INTRODUCTION

1 The phrase appears to have been appropriated from Lyle Wright's bibliography, where the notation reads: "Written in a series of letters which treat of Lesbianism" (322, entry 2413).

2 On the "Ladies of Llangollen," see Mavor.

3 Scott E. Casper tells how Laughton, when she was departing on a long European trip with her second husband, John Scott Laughton, in 1877, appointed Sweat to serve as acting regent in her absence; Sweat soon tangled with Mount Vernon's superintendent, J. McHenry Hollingsworth, over his treatment of the black employees who resided on the property (147–48).

ETHEL'S LOVE-LIFE: A NOVEL

First published New York: Rudd and Carleton, 1859.

29 "**I am a part . . . Tennyson** From Alfred, Lord Tennyson, "Ulysses" (1842), ll. 17–21 (slightly misquoted): "I am a part of all that I have met; / Yet all experience is an arch wherethrough / Gleams that untravelled world, whose margin fades / For ever and for ever when I move." In Alfred, Lord Tennyson, *The Poems of Tennyson,* ed. Christopher Ricks (London: Longman's, 1969), 563.

31 **the skeleton at an Egyptian feast** "The Dinner of the Wise Men," in Plutarch, *Moralia,* vol. II, trans. Frank Cole Babbitt, Loeb Classical Library 222 (Cambridge, Mass.: Harvard University Press, 1928), 359: "Now the skeleton which in Egypt they are wont, with fair reason, to bring in and expose at their parties, urging their guests to remember that what it is now, thy soon shall be." The phrase refers colloquially to an unwanted gloomy presence at an otherwise celebratory event. Sweat may have encountered this phrase in a poem by the popular American poet Henry Wadsworth Longfellow (like Sweat, a native of

Portland, Maine), "The Old Clock on the Stairs," first published in *The Belfry of Bruges and Other Poems* (Cambridge, Mass.: John Owen, 1845), 96–101: "In that mansion used to be / Free-hearted Hospitality; / His great fires up the chimney roared; / The stranger feasted at his board; / But, like the skeleton at the feast, / That warning timepiece never ceased,— / 'Forever,—never! / 'Never,—forever!'" (98–99).

31 **magnetic sympathy** Franz Friedrich Anton Mesmer (1734–1815), a German physician, theorized that there was an invisible energetic transference that occurred between all animate and inanimate objects, which he called "animal magnetism." His theory led to the practice of "mesmerism," a therapeutic regimen that aimed to heal illness by allowing this magnetic energy to flow freely. See Frank A. Pattie, *Mesmer and Animal Magnetism: A Chapter in the History of Medicine* (Hamilton, N.Y.: Edmonston, 1994), and Vincent Buranelli, *The Wizard from Vienna: Franz Anton Mesmer* (New York: Coward, McCann and Geoghegan, 1975). On mesmerism in the United States, see Emily Ogden, *Credulity: A Cultural History of U.S. Mesmerism* (Chicago: University of Chicago Press, 2018). References to magnetism and magnetic influences pervade *Ethel's Love-Life*. For additional instances see 41, 46, 58, 62, 63, 64, 82, 86, 122, 141, 191, 228.

31 **galvanic existence** *Galvanic* is another word for electrical.

33 **highly-wrought romances** Dorri Beam points out that reviewers in the nineteenth century often referred to the "highly-wrought" style of certain women writers, a style characterized by "ornament, profusion, and verbosity," and she counts Sweat as one of these "highly-wrought" writers. See Dorri Beam, *Style, Gender, and Fantasy in Nineteenth-Century American Women's Writing* (Cambridge: Cambridge University Press, 2010), 1, 8.

34–35 **Mentor . . . Calypso** Calypso was a nymph in Greek mythology; in Homer's *Odyssey*, Telemachus, Odysseus's son, and Mentor, Odysseus's longtime friend, go in search of Odysseus after he has been missing for twenty years. The reference here is not to Homer but to François Fénelon's 1699 novel, *Les aventures de Télémaque* (*The Adventures of Telemachus*), which fills out an episode in Homer's *Odyssey*, following Odysseus's son Telemachus as he searches for his father in the company of Odysseus's old friend Mentor. Sweat refers to this again in "The Novels of George Sand" 00, below.

35 **Gulliver** Lemuel Gulliver is the protagonist of Jonathan Swift's prose satire commonly known as *Gulliver's Travels* (1726, 1735).

35 **Church Catechism** A catechism is a summary or exposition of theological doctrine.

35 **Book of Martyrs** Probably a reference to John Foxe's *Actes and Monuments* (1563), more commonly referred to as *Foxe's Book of Martyrs*, a polemical account of the suffering of Protestants under the allegedly corrupt Catholic Church.

35 **Gentile** A person who is not a Jew.

36 **Sybarite** Historically a native of Sybaris, a town in southern Italy whose inhabitants were alleged to be characteristically self-indulgent in their pursuit of ease and pleasure.

37 **"open as day . . . charity"** William Shakespeare, *2 Henry IV*, iii, 35–36: "He hath a tear for pity, and a hand / Open as day for melting charity."

48 **Werterian** More commonly spelled *Wertherian*, the adjective means morbidly sentimental in the style of the protagonist of Johann Wolfgang von Goethe's 1774 novel, *The Sorrows of Young Werther*.

53 **subtle element** Another way of referring to the magnetic force posited by Franz Anton Mesmer as connecting all animate and inanimate objects (see note at 10, above). Elsewhere Ethel refers to the "subtle and invisible essence of mental phenomena" (65) or claims that people's "subtle essences mingled" (92).

56 **spherical natures** In Plato's *Symposium*, one of the speakers, Aristophanes, explains that humans were originally spherical creatures, with double bodies, facing in opposite directions; there were three sexes, the all-male, the all-female, and the half male, half female (androgynous). Zeus crippled humans by chopping them in half, and the separated halves therefore perpetually yearn to be reunited and made whole. Women who were separated from women yearn to be reunited with another woman; men who were separated from men long to be reunited with another man. The androgynous, men and women, wish to be reunited with the opposite sex.

57 **Elysian fancies** The Elysian fields of ancient Greek mythology, where mortals who were related to the gods would rest, if they had lived heroic or virtuous lives, in blessed happiness after death.

57 **Æolian dream-music** Named after Aeolus, the Greek god of wind, the aeolian harp is a stringed instrument that produces music when the wind passes through it.

57 **Hasheesh** More commonly spelled *hashish* today, this refers to a compressed resin derived from the flowers of the cannabis plant which may be smoked as an intoxicant or narcotic. Sweat may be alluding to the recently published autobiographical book by Fitz Hugh Ludlow, *The Hasheesh Eater* (1857), which related Ludlow's altered states of consciousness and popularized the recreational use of this drug.

58 **Frankenstein** Mary Shelley, *Frankenstein; or, The Modern Prometheus* (1818).

60 **double consciousness** Emerson, Thoreau, and other American Transcendentalists all struggled with various concepts of double consciousness or divided subjectivity. See Ralph Waldo Emerson, "The Transcendentalist" (1842), where Emerson laments the "double consciousness" that separates "the two lives of the understanding and of the soul," as well as his essay on "Fate," in which he seeks to reconcile the seemingly contradictory principles of freedom and fate by propounding "one solution . . . the double consciousness," whereby a man may manage to "ride alternately on the horses of his private and his public nature." Emerson, "The Transcendentalist," in *Essays and Lectures* (New York: Library

of America, 1983), 205–6; Emerson, "Fate," ibid., 966. See also Joel Porte, "Emerson, Thoreau, and the Double Consciousness," *New England Quarterly* 41, no. 1 (March 1968): 41–50.

64 **"There is a gloom . . . water"** Walter Savage Landor, *Imaginary Conversations*, in *The Works of Walter Savage Landor*, 2 vols. (London: Edward Moxon, 1853), II:373.

70 **hypæthral temple** A temple with no roof, that is, open to the sky.

70 **Te Deum** The Te Deum is an early Christian hymn of praise, acknowledging God's greatness, so called because of its opening line in Latin, "Te Deum lauda- mus," that is, "We praise thee, O God."

82 **"the days that are no more"** A refrain from "Tears, Idle Tears" (1847), a song within "The Princess," by Alfred, Lord Tennyson, repeated in the last line of each stanza: "Tears, idle tears, I know not what they mean, / Tears from the depth of some divine despair / Rise in the heart, and gather to the eyes, / In looking on the happy Autumn-fields, / And thinking of the days that are no more." In Alfred, Lord Tennyson, *The Poems of Tennyson*, ed. Christopher Ricks (London: Longman's, 1969), 784–86.

84 **"shallow cisterns holding no water"** Perhaps a catchphrase of Sweat's time.

102 **"affaires du cœur"** French, "affairs of the heart," that is, romantic attachments.

107 **Gordian knot** An extremely difficult or even intractable problem.

113 **Mont Blanc** French for "White Mountain," this is the highest peak in the Alps, on the border between France and Italy.

Verses

First published Portland, Me.: Lakeside Press, 1890.

137 **Liszt or Rubinstein** Franz Liszt (1811–1886), Hungarian composer and renowned virtuosic pianist; Anton Grigorevich Rubinstein (1829–1894), Rus- sian composer and pianist, also ranked among the great nineteenth-century keyboard virtuosos.

137 **Lind or Patti** Jenny Lind (1820–1887), Swedish opera singer known as the "Swedish Nightingale," renowned as one of the great sopranos of the nine- teenth century; she toured the United States in 1850; Adelina Patti (1843–1919), Italian-French coloratura soprano who performed frequently in the United States.

137 **Tennyson or Browning** Alfred, Lord Tennyson (1809–1892), poet laureate of Great Britain and Ireland during the Victorian period; Tennyson is quoted by Sweat in *Ethel's Love-Life* at 8 and 121, above. Robert Browning (1812–89), English poet and playwright.

141 **the greatness of thy love** In multiple copies of *Verses* Sweat corrected this by hand from "the greatest of thy love"; "greatness" is also the reading in a previ- ous publication of the poem in *The Galaxy, a Magazine of Entertaining Reading* 14, no. 5 (November 1872): 663, hence it is emended here.

143 **"Brahma"** Ralph Waldo Emerson, "Brahma," *Atlantic Monthly* I, no. 1 (November 1857): 48.

> If the red slayer think he slays,
> Or if the slain think he is slain,
> They know not well the subtle ways
> I keep, and pass, and turn again.
> Far or forgot to me is near;
> Shadow and sunlight are the same;
> The vanished gods to me appear;
> And one to me are shame and fame.
> They reckon ill who leave me out;
> When me they fly, I am the wings;
> I am the doubter and the doubt,
> And I the hymn the Brahmin sings.
> The strong gods pine for my abode,
> And pine in vain the sacred Seven;
> But thou, meek lover of the good!
> Find me, and turn thy back on heaven.

147 **From the German of Heinrich Heine** Heinrich Heine (1797–1856), German poet. In his *Buch der Lieder* (Hamburg: Hoffman und Campe, 1827), 159, there is an untitled poem LVI in the section of "Lyrisches Intermezzo 1822–23," of which this seems to be a freely adaptive translation:

> Ich hab' im Traum' geweinet,
> Mir träumte du lägest im Grab'.
> Ich wachte auf, und die Thräne
> Floß noch von der Wange herab.

> Ich hab' im Traum' geweinet,
> Mir träumt' du verließest mich.Ich wachte auf, und ich weinte
> Noch lange bitterlich.

> Ich hab' im Traum' geweinet,
> Mir träumte du wärft mir noch gut.
> Ich wachte auf, und noch immer
> Strömt meine Thränenfluth.

149 **my lost youth** Sweat alludes here to her fellow writer from Portland, Maine, Henry Wadsworth Longfellow, one of whose best-known poems, "My Lost Youth," expressed nostalgia for the seaside town of his boyhood. The poem first appeared in *Putnam's Monthly Magazine of Literature, Science, and Art* 6, no. 32 (August 1855): 121–22, and thereafter in Longfellow, *The Courtship of Miles Standish and Other Poems* (Boston: Ticknor and Fields, 1858), 164–69. Sweat may be implicitly importing into her own poem Longfellow's insistent masculine gendering of this nostalgia.

164 **"The Elms"** Sweat's childhood home, a mansion on the corner of High and Danforth streets in Portland, Maine, was known as "The Elms." There are photographs of it in Sweat's photograph album (Margaret Jane Mussey Sweat Collection, Maine Women Writer's Collection, University of New England, Portland, Maine, Container 040; see also 034 and 037).

167 **"Sweets to the Sweet"** William Shakespeare, *Hamlet*, 5.1: Gertrude scatters flowers on Ophelia's grave: "Sweets to the sweet. Farewell. / I hop'd thou shouldst have been my Hamlet's wife: / I thought thy bride-bed to have deck'd, sweet maid, / And not have strew'd thy grave." *The Arden Shakespeare Complete Works, Revised Edition,* ed. Richard Proudfoot, Ann Thompson, and David Scott Kastan (London: Arden Shakespeare, 2011), 327.

167 **Raffaelle's Madonna** Raffaello Sanzio da Urbino, known as Raphael (1483–1520), Italian artist, painted many celebrated images of the Madonna and Child.

170 **National Fair held in New York** Civil War "sanitary fairs" were grassroots civilian efforts held across the nation to raise funds for the United States Sanitary Commission and other charitable relief organizations that sought to ameliorate the living conditions and improve the medical care of Union soldiers. The fairs collected food, clothing, bandages, and other supplies for distribution to the troops. The Metropolitan Fair was held in New York City, opening on 4 April 1864.

177 **twin-born soul** See note to *Ethel's Love-Life* 60 above.

187 **The "Last Supper" of Leonardo da Vinci** A late fifteenth-century mural by Leonardo da Vinci (1452–1519), painted on a wall in the refectory of the Convent of Santa Maria delle Grazie in Milan. It began to deteriorate soon after it was completed due to environmental and other factors, and numerous restoration attempts over the years have not fully halted its decay.

194 **Sanitary Commission Fair, held in Philadelphia** The Great Central Fair, a Civil War "sanitary fair" (see note above) was held in Logan Square (now Circle) in Philadelphia from 7 to 28 June 1864.

208 **Carrara's hills** Carrara, a city and *comune* in central Tuscany, is the location of marble quarries that are renowned for the pure whiteness of their stone, greatly valued for use in marble statuary and architecture.

209 **Sappho's sorrow** Sappho (c. 630–570 BCE), an archaic Greek poet from the island of Lesbos, wrote many elegiac poems addressed to other women. She is often today taken as a symbol of female homosexuality, and the word *lesbian* derives from the name of her island home. Sweat seems to be alluding to a legendary account of Sappho that had her leaping to her death from the cliffs on the Greek island of Leukadia.

209 **Naxos** Naxos is a Greek island that often features in Greek mythology.

209 **A woman, stretching forth her hands** In Hesiod and elsewhere Ariadne was abandoned by her lover Theseus, who sailed away from Naxos.

209 **Another, and still fairer face ... "most fair"** The grown youth Paris awarded the title of "fairest" to Aphrodite, in preference to the other goddesses Hera and Athena.

209 **Ida's mount** Mount Ida, the highest summit on the Greek island of Crete.

209 **The king-born shepherd boy** Paris, unknown to himself, was the son of Priam, king of Troy.

209 **Pallas** Athena, sometimes called Pallas Athena,

209 **Aphrodite** Ancient Greek goddess of love, beauty, and pleasure.

224 **the axiom that what is, is best** Sweat may be thinking here of Alexander Pope's famous assertion in *An Essay on Man*, Epistle I, that "whatever is, is right" (l. 294). "An Essay on Man," in *Pope: Poetical Works*, ed. Herbert Davis (Oxford: Oxford University Press, 1966), 249. Or she may be thinking even of Voltaire's satire of this philosophy in *Candide, or Optimism* (1759), where Dr. Pangloss famously professes that in this "best of all possible worlds . . . everything is necessarily for the best purpose." Voltaire, *Candide and Other Stories*, trans. Roger Pearson (Oxford: Oxford World's Classics, 2006), 4. But most likely she had fresh in her mind Ella Wheeler Wilcox's poem "Whatever Is—Is Best," widely reprinted in the 1880s and onward, for example, in Maine's *Lewiston Evening Journal* (7 May 1887), 7: "I know there are no errors / In the great Eternal plan, / And all things work together / For the final good of man. / And I know as my soul speeds onward, / In its grand Eternal quest, / I shall say as I look back earthward, / Whatever is—is best." The poem was included in Wilcox, *Poems of Pleasure* (New York: Belford, 1888), 75–76.

230 **That they . . . St. Paul** Acts 17:27. Here and elsewhere Sweat quotes from the King James Version of the Bible.

230 **"Not far from every one of us"** Acts 17:27.

230 **"dwelleth not in temples made with hands"** Acts 17:24.

231 **"white throne"** Revelation 20:11: "And I saw a great white throne, and him that sat on it."

233 **"Let not him . . . Off"** 1 Kings 20:11.

235 **"Fear Thou Not . . . Thee"** Isaiah 41:10.

237 **For Man Walketh in a Vain Shadow** Psalms 39:6: "Surely every man walketh in a vain shew."

239 **"They also serve who only stand and wait"** The last line of John Milton, Sonnet XIX, "When I consider how my light is spent." John Milton, *The Poetical Works of John Milton*, 2 vols., ed. Helen Darbishire (Oxford: Clarendon Press, 1955), II:155.

A CHAPTER ON NOVELS

First published in North American Review *83, no. 173 (October 1856): 337–51.*

243 *débutant* French, "beginner."

243 *"le premier pas qui coûte"* French, "the first step that costs."

243 **"men of straw"** Men of weak character who lack definite beliefs.

244 *dénouement* French, "finish" or "ending."

244 *dramatis personæ* Latin, the characters of a play, novel, or narrative.

244 **Miss Oliphant** Margaret Oliphant Wilson Oliphant (1828–1897), Scottish novelist who wrote as Mrs. Oliphant. She was the author of *Zaidee* (1855), among many other novels.

244 *nonchalance* Of French origin, a state of being casually relaxed.

245 **Miss Kavanagh** Julia Kavanagh (1824–1877), Irish novelist, author of *Rachel Gray* (1855), among other novels.

245 **"accumulated"** "I have not accumulated since I published *Shirley* what makes it needful for me to speak again, and till I do, may God give me grace to be dumb." Qtd. Lyndall Gordon, *Charlotte Brontë: A Passionate Life* (New York: W. W. Norton, 1996), 204. Also, "'I have been silent lately because I have accumulated nothing since I wrote last,' is a phrase which fell from her on one occasion." Qtd. T. Wemyss Reid, *Charlotte Brontë: A Monograph* (London: Macmillan, 1877), 234.

245 **"Villette"** Charlotte Brontë, *Villette* (1853).

246 **Currer Bell** Pseudonym of Charlotte Brontë. Emily Brontë published as Ellis Bell, and Anne Brontë as Acton Bell.

246 **Thackeray** William Makepeace Thackeray (1811–1863), English novelist.

246 **Hawthorne** Nathaniel Hawthorne (1804–1864), American novelist.

246 **Dickens** Charles Dickens (1812–1870), English novelist.

246 **"The Children of the Abbey"** By Irish romantic novelist Regina Maria Roche (1764–1845), *The Children of the Abbey* (1796) was a major commercial success.

246 **Sir Charles Grandison** By English novelist Samuel Richardson (1689–1761), *The History of Sir Charles Grandison* was first published in 1753.

247 **Richardson, Mrs. Radcliffe, and Miss Burney** Samuel Richardson, see note for 246, above; Ann Radcliffe (1764–1823), English author and pioneer of the gothic novel; Frances Burney (1752–1840), also known as Fanny Burney, English satirical novelist.

247 *tableaux-vivans* French, "living pictures."

249 *forte* French, "strength."

249 *dénouement* See note for 244, above.

250 *summum bonum* Latin, "highest good."

250 **"The Three Spaniards" and "The Mysteries of Udolpho"** George Walker (1772–1847), English gothic novelist, wrote *The Three Spaniards* (1800); Ann Radcliffe (see note for 247, above) wrote *The Mysteries of Udolpho* (1794), sometimes cited as the archetypal gothic romance.

250 **"The Five Nights of St. Albans"** William Mudford (1782–1848), English writer, essayist, and translator, published *The Five Nights of St. Albans* in 1829.

250 **Fielding and Smollett** Henry Fielding (1707–1754), English novelist, author of, among others, *Tom Jones* (1749), named just below; Tobias Smollett (1721–1771), Scottish author of *The Adventures of Peregrine Pickle* (1751), mentioned below.

250 **Lord Frederic Augustus Fitz-Mortimers** This comical name alludes to the overrefined heroes of fashionable novels (sometimes called "silver-fork

fiction"), such as those ridiculed in "Recipe for a Novel," *Mirror of Literature, Amusement, and Instruction* 4, no. 91 (26 June 1824): 57: "Take a hero, and let his name be Edward Mortimer, Augustus Montgomery, Frederick St. Clair, or Charles Fitzosmond, &c. &c. &c." My thanks to Jonathan Grossman for this information.

250 **Tom Jones and Peregrine Pickle** See note for 250, above.

251 **Scott** Sir Walter Scott (1771–1832), Scottish historical novelist, author of the *Waverly* novels among many others.

252 **Hume and Smollett** David Hume (1711–1776), Scottish philosopher, usually understood to be a sentimentalist who held that ethics are grounded in feeling rather than in rational principles; Smollett, see note for 250, above.

252 **"The Abbot"** Sir Walter Scott, *The Abbot* (1820).

253 **Thackeray's "Vanity Fair"** William Makepeace Thackeray, *Vanity Fair* (1847–1848), features Becky Sharp (mentioned below), a cynical social climber, as its main character.

254 **Becky Sharp and Major Pendennis** Becky Sharp is the main character in Thackeray's *Vanity Fair* (1847–1848); Arthur Pendennis is the protagonist of Thackeray's *History of Pendennis* (1848–1850).

254 **Aunt Betsy Trotwood** Betsey Trotwood is a character in Charles Dickens's *David Copperfield* (1850); she is David's great-aunt.

255 **"words that burn"** Thomas Gray, "The Progress of Poesy: A Pindaric Ode," in *Odes by Mr. Gray* (Printed at Strawberry-Hill, for R. and J. Dodsley in Pall-Mall, 1757), III.3: "Thoughts that breathe, and words that burn" (11).

CHARLOTTE BRONTË AND THE BRONTË NOVELS

First published in North American Review *85, no. 177 (October 1857): 293–329.*

257 **Currer Bell** See note for "A Chapter on Novels" 246, above.

258 *con amore* Italian, "with love."

258 **Mrs. Gaskell** Elizabeth Cleghorn Gaskell (1810–1865), English novelist and biographer.

258 **Emily and Anne** Emily Brontë (1818–1848), known for her only novel, *Wuthering Heights* (1847), published under the pseudonym Ellis Bell; Anne Brontë (1820–1849) published two novels, *Agnes Grey* (1847) and *The Tenant of Wildfell Hall* (1848), under the pen name Acton Bell.

261 **Mr. Brontë** Patrick Brontë (1777–1861), Irish priest and author who spent most of his adult life in England; father of a family of writers including Charlotte, Emily, and Anne Brontë.

261 *accés de fureur* French, "outburst of fury."

263 **Southey and Wordsworth** Robert Southey (1774–1843), English poet of the romantic school; William Wordsworth (1770–1850), another English romantic poet.

264 **Prometheus** In Greek mythology, a Titan who created man from clay and defied the gods by stealing fire from heaven and giving it to humankind.

264 *pensionnat* French, "boarding school."

264 **Monsieur and Madame Héger** Constantin Georges Romain Héger (1809–1896) and his second wife, Zoë Claire Héger (1804–1887), directors of a boarding school in Brussels where Emily and Charlotte Brontë enrolled in 1842; Charlotte returned alone in 1843 to teach in the school.

265 **Paul Emanuel** A character in *Villette*.

265 *grandes vacances* French, "summer holidays."

266 *messe* French, "mass."

266 **Branwell** Patrick Branwell Brontë (1817–1848), painter and poet, and only brother of the Brontë sisters; he deteriorated in health due to drug and alcohol addiction, which led to an early death.

266 **"Agnes Grey" and "Wuthering Heights"** Anne Brontë, *Agnes Grey, A Novel* (1847); Emily Brontë, *Wuthering Heights, A Novel* (1847).

266 **"The Professor"** Charlotte Brontë, *The Professor, A Tale* (1857). This was the first novel Charlotte Brontë wrote, but it was published posthumously.

268 **brother's sad and disgraceful history** See note for 266, above.

268 **"Wildfell Hall"** Anne Brontë, *The Tenant of Wildfell Hall* (1848).

270 **Nell** Ellen Nussey (1817–1897), Charlotte Brontë's dear friend and lifelong correspondent.

270 **"Shirley"** Charlotte Brontë, *Shirley, A Tale* (1849).

271 **Thackeray** See notes for "A Chapter on Novels" 246 and 253, above.

271 **review of "Shirley" in the "Times"** *Shirley* met with a somewhat mixed critical reception. According to biographer Claire Harman, "One savage review in *The Times* appeared in December 1849 . . . [a friend] had tried to hide the paper from [Charlotte] but failed, and when he saw her later with tears streaming down her face he knew she had seen its condemnation of her book as 'at once the most highflown and the stalest of fictions.'" Claire Harman, *Charlotte Brontë: A Fiery Heart* (New York: Vintage Books, 2017), 328.

272 *mauvaise honte* French, "bad shame."

274 **Mrs. Beecher Stowe's work, "Uncle Tom's Cabin"** Harriet Beecher Stowe (1811–1896), American novelist, published *Uncle Tom's Cabin; or, Life Among the Lowly* (1852), a passionate critique of American slavery.

279 **Herculean** Requiring great strength or powerful effort, after the mythical Greek hero Hercules, renowned for performing arduous labors.

281 **St. John** St. John Rivers, a character in *Jane Eyre*.

281 **David with the Philistine** In 1 Samuel 17:49–50, David, "who had no sword in the hand," slew the Philistine giant Goliath "with a sling and with a stone."

282 *dénouement* See note for "A Chapter on Novels" 244, above.

282 **Turner-like** Joseph Mallord William Turner (1775–1851), usually known as J. M. W. Turner (or just Turner), English romantic painter known for his imaginative landscapes and sometimes turbulent marine paintings.

283 **Caroline Helstone** Character in Charlotte Brontë's *Shirley* (1849).

283 **the two Moores men** Robert Moore, a textile mill owner, and his brother Louis Moore, a tutor, both characters in Charlotte Brontë's *Shirley* (1849).

285 **Paulina** Paulina Home, who is called Polly, a character in Charlotte Brontë's *Villette* (1853).

285 **Ginevra** Ginevra Fanshawe, a character in Charlotte Brontë's *Villette* (1853).

286 *dénouement* See note for "A Chapter on Novels" 244, above.

286 *dramatis personæ* See note for "A Chapter on Novels" 244. above.

287 **"Shakespeare for the use of private families"** Thomas Bowdler (1754–1825) had in 1807 published the first iteration of his expurgated edition of Shakespeare, *The Family Shakespeare . . . In which Nothing is Added to the Original Text, But Those Words and Expressions are Omitted which Cannot with Propriety be Read Aloud in a Family*; subsequent editions appeared at intervals until 1850.

287 **mantilla for the Venus de' Medici** The Venus de' Medici is a Hellenistic marble sculpture in the Uffizi Gallery in Florence, Italy, depicting the Greek goddess of love, Aphrodite; the figure is entirely nude, thus the idea of concealing her nudity with a mantilla (a traditional Spanish lace veil or shawl), indicates for Sweat an excessive prudery.

THE FRIENDSHIPS OF WOMEN

The place of first publication of this review was probably the Boston Courier *(personal communication, Cathleen Miller, Curator, Maine Women Writers Collection, 30 January 2017); the text here derives from a clipping in Sweat's scrapbook of her own reviews. Margaret Jane Mussey Sweat Collection, Maine Women Writers Collection, University of New England, Portland, Maine, 028 "Book Notices (1867–1871)." Several corrections evidently in Sweat's hand have been incorporated into the text here: "commentaries" in place of "communications," "admirable" instead of "admissible," "formative" in place of "formation," and "god" in place of "God."*

292 **Damon and Pythias** In Greek mythology, their mutual devotion and loyalty made them epitomes of true friendship.

292 **Eleanor Butler and Sarah Ponsonby** Eleanor Charlotte Butler (1739–1829) and Sarah Ponsonby (1755–1831), both upper-class Irish women, were known as the "Ladies of Llangollen." In order to avoid marriage they chose to settle in Llangollen, a small town in North Wales, and there to undertake an unconventional life together. They lived together for more than fifty years, and their relationship attracted much curious interest during their lifetimes. They dressed in black riding habits and men's top hats, and such facts have attracted considerable scholarly attention and speculation as to their sexuality. They are buried together with their servant Mary Caryll at St. Collen's Church in Llangollen. See Elizabeth Mavor, *The Ladies of Llangollen* (Harmondsworth: Penguin Books, 1971).

THE NOVELS OF GEORGE SAND

First published in George Sand, Antonia: A Novel, *trans. Virginia Vaughan (Boston: Roberts Brothers, 1870), paginated separately after the novel, 1–23.*

295 **"Telemachus" and "Paul and Virginia"** François Fénelon, *Les aventures de Télémaque* (1699); Jacques-Henri Bernardin de Saint Pierre, *Paul et Virginie* (1788).

295 **Mesmerism and Fourierism** On Mesmerism, see note for *Ethel's Love-Life* 10, above. Fourierism refers to the teachings of Charles Fourier (1772–1837), a French philosopher and social reformer who proposed vast changes of social institutions in the interest of increasing labor productivity, erotic satisfaction, and social cooperation.

295 **Communism and Agrarianism** Communism involves a variety of schools of thought but is generally derived from the writings of Karl Marx (1818–1883), the German philosopher and revolutionary socialist who argued for a socioeconomic order premised on the common ownership of the means of production and the abolition of economic classes through social revolution. Agrarianism is a social or political philosophy that values the superiority of a simple rural life. Sweat may have had in mind the French philosophy of Physiocracy, which held that the wealth of nations derived ultimately from the value of agriculture.

295 **Atheism or fashionable Pantheism** Atheism is the disbelief in the existence of a god or gods. Pantheism identifies God with the universe as a whole or regards the universe as a divine manifestation.

295 **Balzac** Honoré de Balzac (1799–1850), French novelist and playwright whose intensely realistic novels surveyed French society with unsparing candor.

297 *ipse dixit* Latin, "he said it himself," that is, an assertion without proof or a dogmatic expression of opinion.

297 **"Indiana," "Jacques," and "Lélia"** *Indiana* (1832); *Jacques* (1833); and *Lélia* (1833).

297 **poisoned garment of Nessus** In Greek mythology, a shirt stained by the blood of the centaur Nessus, given to Heracles by his wife, Deianeira, who mistakenly believed it would ensure his faithfulness. Instead, it contained the Hydra's venom with which Heracles had poisoned the arrow he used to kill Nessus. Metaphorically, it represents a fatal misfortune, or a gift that wounds.

298 **Madame Dudevant** Sweat characteristically refers to George Sand by her married name, perhaps to mitigate subtly Sand's notorious unconventionality. See note on Sand's husband at 8 below.

298 **"Histoire de ma Vie"** *Histoire de ma vie* (1854–1855), George Sand's autobiography.

299 **Marshal Saxe** Maurice de Saxe (1696–1750), a German soldier and officer who later became a marshal (and eventually marshal in chief) in French military service.

299 **"Spiridion"** *Spiridion* (1839).

299 **M. Dudevant** François Casimir Dudevant (1795–1871), who married Amantine Lucile Aurore Dupin (later George Sand) in 1822; they had two children,

Maurice (b. 1823) and Solange (b. 1828), before she left her husband in 1831 and formally separated from him in 1835.

299 **Jules Sandeau** Léonard Sylvain Julien (Jules) Sandeau (1811–1883), French novelist who met and had a brief intimate relationship with George Sand in 1831; together they wrote *Rose et Blanche* (1831), published under the pseudonym J. Sand, from which Sand soon derived her own pseudonym. Later Sandeau wrote *Marianna* (1839), in which he portrays George Sand.

299 **St. George's Day** Also known as the Feast of St. George, celebrated by various Christian denominations on 23 April.

299 **estate of Nohant** Sand's estate, received as an inheritance from her grandmother, was in the village of Nohant in the Indre department in central France.

300 **Heine . . . "recal neither Sodom nor Gomorrah"** Heinrich Heine (1797–1856), German poet, essayist, and literary critic, wrote that "the author of *Lélia* has sweet calm eyes, which remind one neither of Sodom nor Gomorrah." Sweat was no doubt glad to find that Heine defended Sand against moral aspersions. See "Heine on George Sand," trans H. H. Foote, *Secular Review and Secularist* I, no. 11 (London, 18 August 1877): 166–67.

300 **Amazonian** In Greek mythology, the Amazons were a tribe of female warriors.

300 **Venus of Milo** Aphrodite of Milos, better known as the Venus de Milo, a marble sculpture, one of the most famous works of ancient Greek art, on display at the Louvre Museum in Paris.

300 **"Ça ne vous . . . confitures"** French, "It does not resemble you at all, you who are gay, who dance the bourree [a lively French dance], who appreciate the lepidoptere [butterfly], who do not despise the pun, who do not sew badly, and who make jams very well."

301 **Chopin and Alfred de Musset** Frédéric François Chopin (1810–49), Polish composer and virtuoso pianist, George Sand's lover in 1838–47; Alfred Louis Charles de Musset-Pathay (1810–57), French dramatist, poet, and novelist, who conducted a love affair with George Sand in 1833–35.

301 **"Lucrezia Floriani" and "Elle et Lui"** *Lucrezia Floriani* (1846); *Elle et lui* (1859).

302 **Charlotte Brontë** Charlotte Brontë (1816–1855), English novelist; see Sweat's essay "Charlotte Bronté and the Bronté Novels" in the present volume.

302 **Jane Eyre . . . Lucy Snowe** Jane Eyre is the narrator of Charlotte Brontë's novel *Jane Eyre: An Autobiography* (1847); Lucy Snowe is the protagonist of another Charlotte Brontë novel, *Villette* (1853).

302 **"Malgrétout"** *Malgrétout* (1870).

303 **Mrs. Browning** Elizabeth Barrett Browning (1806–1861), English poet.

303 **"Consuelo"** *Consuelo* (1842).

303 **"The Countess of Rudolstadt"** *La Comtesse de Rudolstadt* (1843).

303 **great Frederick** Frederick II (1712–1786), king of Prussia from 1740 to 1786, a patron of the arts and the Enlightenment.

303 **Voltaire** François-Marie Arouet (1694–1778), known by his pen name Voltaire, French Enlightenment writer and thinker, known for his wit and satirical polemics.

303 **necromancy, Freemasonry, Illuminism** Necromancy is the magical practice of communicating with the dead; Freemasonry is a fraternal organization; Illuminism denotes an Enlightenment-era secret society that opposed religious authority, superstition, and obscurantism.

303 *resumé* French, a "summary" or "rehearsal."

303 **"Mauprat"** *Mauprat* (1837).

303 **"La petite Fadette"** *La petite Fadette* (1849).

303 **Meissonier** Ernest Meissonier (1815–1891), French classical painter.

303 **"Teverino"** *Teverino* (1845).

304 **"L'homme de Neige"** *L'homme de neige* (1859).

304 **Aurora Borealis** A natural light display, sometimes known as the northern lights, featuring streamers of reddish or greenish light in the night sky.

304 **"Le Piccinino"** *Le piccinino* (1847).

304 *mise en scène* French, "staging," the arrangement of the setting or surroundings of the characters and action of a narrative.

304 **"Le Mare au Diable" or "Geneviève"** *La mare au diable* (1846); "Geneviève" may refer to Sand's novel *André* (1834), which features a heroine by that name, the long-suffering wife of the title character, André.

304 **"La Confession d'une Jeune Fille"** *La confession d'une jeune fille* (1865).

304 *dramatis personæ* See note for "A Chapter on Novels" 244, above.

305 **"Leone Leoni"** *Leone Leoni* (1833).

305 **"Manon Lescaut," . . . "Desgrieux"** Abbé Prévost, *Manon Lescaut* (1731); the Chevalier des Grieux struggles to satisfy the taste for luxury of his lover, Manon Lescaut, much in the way the narrator of Leone Leoni, Juliette, struggles to satisfy the demands of her vicious lover, Leone Leoni.

305 **"Les maîtres Sonneurs"** *Les maîtres Sonneurs* (1853).

305 **lazaretto** Italian, denoting variously a hospital for those with contagious diseases or a building or ship used for detention in quarantine.

305 **land of Berri** The French province of Berry, in central France.

305 **Berrichons** Inhabitants of the French province of Berry.

305 **"Les maîtres Mosaïstes"** *Les maîtres Mosaïstes* (1837).

305 **Titian and Tintoretto** Tiziano Vecellio (1488/90–1576), known in English as Titian, sixteenth-century Italian painter of the Venetian School; Tintoretto (1518–1594), Italian painter, also of the Venetian School.

306 **Council of Ten** From 1310 to 1797, a major governing body in the Republic of Venice.

306 **"Horace"** *Horace* (1840).

307 **"Antonia"** *Antonia* (1863).

307 **"La Tulipe Noire" of Dumas** Alexandre Dumas, père (1802–1870), *La tulipe noire* (1850).

307 **Louis XVI** The last king of France (1754–1793), before the Revolution abolished the monarchy; guillotined in 1793.

307 **Revolution** The French Revolution (1789–1799), a period of vast social and political upheaval that overthrew the monarchy, established a republic, and featured violent turmoil.

307 **"Monsieur Sylvestre"** *Monsieur Sylvestre* (1866).

308 **"Lucrezia Floriani"** *Lucrezia Floriani* (1846).

309 **Shakespeare** William Shakespeare (1564–1616), English dramatist and poet, often considered the greatest writer in the English language; the comparison of Sand to Shakespeare indicates Sweat's belief in Sand's eminence.

GEORGE SAND

First published in the World *(New York) 16, no. 5407 (9 June 1876): 4–5.*

310 **"large-brained woman and large-hearted man"** Elizabeth Barrett Browning, "To George Sand: A Desire," in *Poems*, third edition, 2 vols. (London: Chapman and Hall, 1853), I:346.

> Thou large-brained woman and large-hearted man,
> Self-called George Sand! whose soul, amid the lions
> Of thy tumultuous senses, moans defiance,
> And answers roar for roar, as spirits can!
> I would some mild miraculous thunder ran
> Above the applauded circus, in appliance
> Of thine own nobler nature's strength and science,—
> Drawing two pinions, white as wings of swan,
> From thy strong shoulders, to amaze the place
> With holier light! that thou to woman's claim
> And man's, might'st join beside the angel's grace
> Of a pure genius sanctified from blame,—
> Till child and maiden pressed to thine embrace,
> To kiss upon thy lips a stainless fame.

311 **the first Napoleon** Napoléon Bonaparte (1769–1821), French statesman and military leader, emperor of the French from 1804 to 1814.

311 **Rousseau** Jean-Jacques Rousseau (1712–1778), Genevan Enlightenment philosopher, novelist, and autobiographer mainly active in France.

311 **Quai des Oiseaux of Paris** The Marché aux Oiseaux, Place Louis Lépine, Quai de la Corse; or Quai de la Mégisserie, where another bird market is located.

311 **years of the Revolution and the republic** French Revolution, 1789–1799; the First Republic, 1792–1804, lasted until the declaration of the French Empire by Napoleon in 1804.

312 **Murat at Madrid** Joachim-Napoléon Murat (1767–1815), marshal of France and admiral of France under the reign of Napoleon; also brother-in-law of Napoleon through marriage to his younger sister, Caroline Bonaparte. Murat was in charge of the French army at Madrid when the people there rose up against French occupation on 2 May 1808.

312 *Revue des Deux Mondes* . . . **Buloz** The *Revue des deux mondes* is a French literary periodical published since 1829; François Buloz (1803–1877) was its editor after 1831, and he brought it to eminence by publishing such esteemed writers as Victor Hugo, Alfred de Musset, and George Sand.

312 **Jules Sandeau** See note for "The Novels of George Sand" (NGS) 298, above.

312 **Alfred de Musset and Chopin** See note for NGS 300, above.

313 **Rollinat, Michel, Liszt, Arago** Maurice Rollinat (1846–1903), French poet; Louis-Chrysostome Michel, known as Michel de Bourges (1797–1853), lawyer who represented George Sand in her marital separation; Emmanuel Arago (1812–1896), French politician and diplomat, or perhaps Étienne Arago (1802–1892), another French writer and politician with whom Sand shared a friendship. For Liszt see note for *Verses* 137, above.

313 **"Spiridion"** See note for NGS 298, above.

313 **"Lelia"** See note for NGS 296, above.

313 **"Consuelo"** See note for NGS 302, above.

313 **"Jacques"** See note for NGS 296, above.

313 **Monsieur "Sylvestre"** See note for NGS 306, above.

313 **"Lucrezia Floriani"** See notes for NGS 300 and NGS 307, above.

313 **"Horace"** See note for NGS 305, above.

313 **Sybarite** See note for *Ethel's Love-Life* 36, above.

313 **"Leone Leoni"** See note for NGS 304, above.

314 **"Miller of Angibault"** *Le meunier d'Angibault* (1845).

314 **"Mauprat"** See note for NGS 302, above.

314 **"La Petite Fadette"** See note for NGS 302, above.

314 **"Cesarine Dietrich"** *Césarine Dietrich* (1870).

314 **"L'Homme de Neige"** See note for NGS 303, above.

314 **"Le Piccinino"** See note for NGS 303, above.

314 **"Pierre qui Roule"** *Pierre qui roule* (1870).

314 **"La Confession d'une Jeune Fille"** See note for NGS 303, above.

314 **Goethe** Johann Wolfgang von Goethe (1749–1832), German novelist, poet, dramatist, and literary critic. Sweat alludes to his novel *The Sorrows of Young Werther* (1774) in *Ethel's Love-Life*; see note to *Ethel's Love-Life* 48, above.

314 **"Lettres d'un Voyageur"** *Lettre d'un voyageur* appeared in the *Revue des deux mondes* in fourteen parts between 1834 and 1868.

314 **"à la suite . . . reflet"** French, "as a result of emotions of which they are not the story, but the reflection."

314 **"Mon âme . . . fletris"** French, "My soul, I am sure, has served as a mirror for most who have looked at it. I do not differ from you because I do not deny my pain and do not seek to paint with the colors of youth and health my withered features."

316 **criticisms of George Sand's work** On the American reception of George Sand's works, see Howard Mumford Jones, "American Comment on George Sand, 1837–1848," *American Literature* 3, no. 4 (January 1932): 389–407; C. M. Lombard, "George Sand's Image in America (1837–1876)," *Revue de littérature comparée* 40, no. 2 (April 1966): 177–86.

Lightning Source UK Ltd.
Milton Keynes UK
UKHW012059081120
372905UK00014B/199